NO MATTER WHERE YOU GO

[THERE YOU ARE]

A LIFE TO REMEMBER

Order this book online at www.trafford.com
or email orders@trafford.com

Most Trafford titles are also available at major online book retailers.

Printed in the United States of America.

ISBN: 978-1-4269-4174-0 (sc)
ISBN: 978-1-4269-4175-7(e)

Library of Congress Control Number: 2010913054

*Our mission is to efficiently provide the world's finest, most comprehensive book publishing
service, enabling every author to experience success. To find out how to publish your
book, your way, and have it available worldwide, visit us online at www.trafford.com*

Trafford rev. 09/13/2010

 www.trafford.com

North America & international
toll-free: 1 888 232 4444 (USA & Canada)
phone: 250 383 6864 ♦ fax: 812 355 4082

TABLE OF CONTENTS

PREFACE VII
BEGINNING 1
TAKEN TO THE BEACH 18
SURFING...24
THINKING IS THE BEST WAY TO TRAVEL..........31
ROUND HOUSE 38
BURNED OUT!.. 45
MOUNTAIN MAN... 47
OFF TO WAR!...51
BACK HOME... 59
GONE SKIING 64
ONE WITH THE EAGLES 66
TAKE ME TO THE RIVER 70
LET'S GO SAILING.. 74
A TROPICAL PARADISE................................. 78
SHAKE DOWN 84
ON HIS OWN.. 88
ANGEE IS HERE.. 97
FIRST BOAT 100
THEY FOUND HER 105
THE ADVENTURE BEGINS............................ 112
SLAPPED DOWN AGAIN! 120

BACK IN THE SADDLE.................................124

THE BEGINNING OF THE END 128

LUCKY DAY 133

BLOWING HOME.......................................135

BACK TO HOME PORT..............................140

ALMOST TIME TO GO SAILING AGAIN............148

THE SHOW DOWN!...................................154

THE COOL BREEZE CLUB 158

"SMUGGLING" 169

BIG FALL!...182

ARUBA...190

COLUMBIA...199

HIJACKED 210

CUBA...220

THE DREAM..222

G-2 INTERROGATION...............................228

COMBINADO DEL ESTE............................233

RELEASED...252

THE OLD BOAT 257

BACK IN JAIL 261

PREFACE

IT ALL STARTED AS A DREAM.
WHOEVER SAID THAT "NOTHING COMES TO A SLEEPER BUT A DREAM".
THE ONLY ESCAPE THAT MILES HAD AS A YOUNG BOY WAS TO DREAM.
THE DREAMS SET A TREND FOR THE REST OF HIS LIFE. THEY OPENED THE DOORS TO ALL OF THE ADVENTURES, AND TO ALL OF THE PLACES THAT ONE COULD ONLY DREAM OF HAVING.
HE TRIED AND FAILED AT ADVENTURES OF THE MIND.
MAYBE THINKING WASN'T THE BEST WAY TO TRAVEL AFTER ALL.
HE WANTED TO SAIL, AND TO NAVIGATE, NOT UNLIKE "CHRISTOPHER COLUMBUS".
HE LOVED THE TRIALS OF THE UNKNOWN.
A LIFETIME SIMILAR TO THAT OF THE ANCIENT MARINER WAS HIS LIFELONG GOAL. HE NEEDED EXPERIENCE IN LIFE: HE THRIVED FOR IT!

HE TRIED EVERYTHING! BY THE TIME HE WAS OUT OF HIGH SCHOOL; HE HAD ALREADY HAD MORE JOBS THAN HE WAS YEARS OLD.

HE EVENTUALLY TRAVELED TO THE FLORIDA KEYS: THAT WAS THE BEGINNING TO THE REST OF HIS LIFE'S ADVENTURES.

THE STORIES THAT HE WAS HEARING AT THE LOCAL BOAT YARDS, ARE THE MAIN FODDER FOR THIS STORY,

THERE WERE MANY TRIALS AND FAILURES IN HIS LIFE ON THE OCEAN, ALSO IN AFFAIRS OF THE HEART, AND HE IS ONE HELL OF A LUCKY MAN TO HAVE EVEN SURVIVED THE TALES THAT HE LIVED TO TELL ABOUT.

THUS; ARE THE STORIES IN THIS BOOK. MOST OF THESE STORIES ARE THE EXPERIENCES THE AUTHOR GAVE TO THE MAIN CHARACTER OF THIS STORY; MILES, AND ALL OF THE STORIES ARE BASED ON TRUE STORIES. ALL OF THE NAMES HAVE BEEN CHANGED TO PROTECT THE INNOCENT.

ON THE CONTRARY THERE ARE VERY FEW INNOCENTS IN THIS STORY, BUT I HAVE CHANGED THEIR NAMES ANYWAY.

ALL OF THE TRIALS AND TRIBULATIONS IN THIS STORY CAN ONLY RE-AFFIRM ALL OF THE BELIEFS IN LIFE THAT I HAVE EVER HAD.

THEY CAN BE SUMMED UP IN THESE EIGHT WORDS.

"NO MATTER WHERE YOU GO, THERE YOU ARE".

YOU JUST CAN'T GET AWAY FROM THOSE FACTS.

01/20/2009

TODAY I OPENLY WEPT FOR THE FIRST TIME, SO SINCERELY THAT I FEEL THAT I HAVE TRULY FOUND PEACE OF MIND ONCE AGAIN.

BARRACK OBAMA HAS BECOME OUR 44TH PRESIDENT OF THE UNITED STATES OF AMERICA.
NOT SINCE 01/20/1960 HAVE I FELT SUCH RELIEF AT THE POSSIBILITIES FOR THE FUTURE OF OUR GREAT COUNTRY.

IT WAS PRESIDENT KENNEDY THAT WAS OUR RAY OF HOPE, ALONG WITH THE HELP OF OTHER GREAT AMERICANS LIKE DR. MARTIN LUTHER KING THAT FINALLY FREED US OF THE OPPRESSION OF MAN AGAINST MAN IN THIS COUNTRY.

ULTIMATELY; THEY WERE BOTH KILLED BEFORE THEY COULD FULFILL THEIR DESTINY'S.

IT HAS BEEN AN UPHILL BATTLE EVER SINCE.
WE HAVE BEEN DRAGGED TO WAR MANY TIMES OVER THE YEARS, JUST TO FATTEN THE POCKETS OF A VERY FEW AND IT ALL CAME AT THE HIGHEST PRICE! IT ALL COST US DEARLY IN AMERICAN LIVES.

THE ANTI-SEMITISM AND RACISM THAT EXISTED FOR SO LONG HAS COME TO A HEAD. I KNOW THAT IT STILL EXISTS, BUT IT IS GETTING BETTER ALL OF THE TIME.

SO I WEPT TODAY BECAUSE WE HAVE FINALLY COME FULL CIRCLE ONCE AGAIN. MAYBE NOW THE HEALING CAN BEGIN AND WE CAN SAY GOODBYE TO THE INTOLERANT ATTITUDES OF THE PAST.

IT WAS A GOOD CRY. IT WAS A CRY OF RELIEF. IT WAS A CRY OF HOPE FOR HUMANITY AND A CHANCE TO REFLECT ON THE PAST AND TO HOPE FOR THE FUTURE OF POSITIVE THINKERS OF WHICH THERE IS NOT NEARLY ENOUGH OF IN THIS WORLD.

IT HAS ALL BROUGHT ME TO THE CONCLUSION THAT
NO MATTER WHERE YOU GO. THERE YOU ARE.
EVERYBODY HAS THEIR OWN STORIES AND MEMORIES ABOUT THEIR OWN LIVES AND THIS ONE IS MINE.

" NO MATTER WHERE YOU GO "
" THERE YOU ARE "

MILES OSCAR MCGEARY WAS A CHILD OF THE 50'S AND 60'S.

HE WAS BORN TO A LOVE STARVED COUPLE OF ELIZABETH & JOHN MCGEARY. ELLIE WAS BORN IN HOLLYWOOD CALIFORNIA AROUND 1929 AND DAD WAS BORN IN PORTLAND OREGON SHORTLY BEFORE THAT.

DAD WAS AN EASY GOING SORT OF GUY. HE LOVED RIDING MOTORCYCLES AND RACING FAST CARS. HE TRULY LIVED IN THE FAST LANE OF THOSE DAYS.

HE WAS A HELL OF A MECHANIC AND WELDER. HE COULD MAKE OR BUILD ANYTHING THAT THE MIND COULD DREAM UP. MAYBE THAT IS WHERE MILES GOT HIS SENCE OF ADVENTURE.

MOM WAS A FUN LOVING YOUNG WOMAN. SHE WAS AS BEAUTIFUL AS ELISABETH TAYLOR. IN FACT; SHE WAS BORN IN THE SAME YEAR, AND WENT TO THE SAME SCHOOL.

BECAUSE SHE WAS SO BEAUTIFUL YOU COULD POSSIBLY THINK THAT THEIR RELATIONSHIP WAS A MATCH MADE IN HEAVEN BUT IT WAS ACTUALLY HELL IN THE MAKING.

FIRST THING OFF MOM GETS PREGNANT!

THE WORK SITUATION WAS IN DIRE STRAIGHTS AND DAD GOES OFF TO THE NAVY TO PAY FOR ALL OF THE PROBLEMS THAT A HARD DICK PRODUCED IN THOSE DAYS.

DAD IS HAPPY WITH THE WAY THAT UNCLE SAM IS PAYING FOR THE WHOLE THING AND MOM IS REAL HAPPY TO HAVE ALL OF THIS MONEY COMING IN FOR THE UP-COMING BABY.

MOM GETS REAL CLOSE WITH DADS BROTHERS AND STAYS REAL CLOSE WITH THEM WHILE DAD IS IN THE NAVY. YOU MITGHT SAY THAT WHEN THE CAT WAS AWAY THE MOUSE HAD A GREAT TIME.

DAD CAME HOME WHEN MILES WAS BORN AND GOT TO HOLD HIS SON FOR THE FIRST TIME AND THE LAST! ALTHOUGH HE DIDN'T KNOW IT YET!

HE STAYS A COUPLE OF WEEKS AND THEN BACK INTO THE NAVY FOR ANOTHER TOUR OF DUTY. DURING HIS VISIT MOM GOT PREGNANT AGAIN!

AFTER MOM POPS OUT A COUPLE OF KIDS. SHE MAKES SURE THAT WHENEVER SHE PLAYED WITH HIS BROTHERS IT WAS SOON AFTER DADS VISIT OR BEFORE. SHE WASN'T TAKING ANY CHANCES ON LOOSING THAT FREE MONEY.

HENCE; MILES GREW UP IN A LOVELESS HOME AND A RELATIONSHIP THAT COULD NEVER WORK.

MOM WENT ON TO MARRY FIVE MORE TIMES BEFORE THIS STORY ENDS.

FROM THE BEGINNING DAYS, MILES WAS ALWAYS A POSITIVE THINKER. HE ALWAYS LOOKED FOR THE BRIGHT SIDE OF THINGS. YOU MIGHT SAY THAT HE WAS ALWAYS ON THE SUNNY SIDE OF LIFE.

MILES LIFE REALLY BEGAN IN GARDENA CALIF IN 1960. THE THREE OF THEM LIVED AT A PLACE CALLED "SAM'S TRAILER COURT".

MILES WAS ONLY TWELVE YEARS OLD AT THE TIME.

ALL OF THE TRAILERS THERE WERE OF 1940'S, AND 1950'S STYLE MOBILE HOMES. ALL SINGLE WIDE. THE NEWEST ONES WERE OF THE LATE 50'S VINTAGE.

THE TRAILER COURT WAS ABOUT A HALF OF A MILE FROM ASCOTT RACEWAY IN GARDENA. IT WAS A PRETTY RUN DOWN DUMP!

THE TRAILER COURT WAS ALL DIRT ROADS WITH GRAVEL DOWN THE MAIN RUN TO THE STREET. EVEN THE TRAILERS THEMSELVES HAD DIRT IN FRONT OF THEM EXCEPT FOR THE LUCKY ONES WITH WOODEN BOARDWALKS IN FRONT OF THEM. EACH TRAILER HAD IT'S OWN HAND DUG CESSPOOL WITH BOARDS OVER THE TOPS OF THEM.

THE STENCH IN THE AIR WAS UNFORGETTABLE. YOU KIND OF GOT USED TO IT.

ALL OF THE KIDS IN THE NEIGHBORHOOD WOULD
GO TO THE STOCK CAR RACES EVERY FRIDAY AND
SATURDAY NIGHT.
THERE WAS NOTHING ELSE TO DO THERE.

YOU COULD HEAR THE ROAR OF THE ENGINES,
AND THE SMELL OF NITRO IN THE AIR FROM THE
TRAILER COURT.
THE KIDS WOULD ALL GO TO THE TRACK AT THE
LAST TURN, AND CLIMB THROUGH A HOLE IN THE
FENCE.
AS THEY LOOKED OVER THE HUMP AT THE LAST
TURN YOU COULD FEEL THE MUD HITTING YOU
IN THE EYES WHEN THE CARS CAME AROUND
FOR THE FINAL LAP.

IT WAS NECESSARY TO DUCK AS THE CARS WENT
BY IN ORDER TO KEEP THE DIRT AND MUD OUT
OF YOUR EYES.
IT KIND OF TOOK AWAY THE REASON FOR GOING
TO THE TRACK WHEN YOU HAVE TO CLOSE YOUR
EYES FOR THE FINISH.

WELL IT WAS FREE, AND MILES WAS BROKE. YOU
DO WHAT YOU CAN, AND WORK WITH WHAT
YOU'VE GOT. MILES HAD NOTHING, AND NEITHER
DID ANYBODY IN THAT GOD FORSAKEN PLACE!

MILES MET THIS YOUNG HOOD CALLED "PETE" BY
ALL OF HIS PEERS.
PETE WAS THE FIRST CLUB OR GANG TYPE GUY
THAT MILES HAD EVER MET.

THEY BECAME FRIENDS [SORT OF] AND STARTED RUNNING AROUND TOGETHER AFTER SCHOOL.
HE SHOWED MILES WHERE TO STEAL CHANGE SO THAT HE COULD BUY CIGARETTES. THESE BAD HABITS LIKE STEALING COULDN'T BE A GOOD THING!

THEY WENT FOR A CRUISE ONE DAY IN PETE'S MOM'S CAR.
MILES TOOK HIS ONLY TWO QUARTERS AND BOUGHT TWO PACKS OF CIGARETTES WITH THEM. TRY THAT THESE DAYS.

PETE AND ALL OF HIS FRIENDS SMOKED AND MILES WANTED TO FIT IN.
THEY WENT ALL OF THE WAY FROM GARDENA TO LONG BEACH AND BACK IN AN OLD OLDS CONVERTIBLE WITH RAGGED SEATS.
IT WAS GREAT HAVING THE WIND IN YOUR FACE AND TO BE ABLE TO THINK AND FEEL ANYTHING THAT YOU WANTED TO!
LIFE WAS GOOD!
MILES CHAIN-SMOKED THOSE CIGARETTES UNTIL THEY WERE ALL GONE. WHAT AN IDIOT!

HE GOT THE SPINS AND THREW UP FOR HOURS.

PETE AND EVERY ONE ELSE THAT WERE IN THE CAR LAUGHED AT HIM AND TOLD HIM THAT HE WAS HOOKED NOW.
THEY WERE RIGHT! HE WAS HOOKED! AFTER THAT HE STARTED STEALING HIS MOMS SMOKES.

MOM TOLD HIM THAT IF HE WANTED TO SMOKE HE WOULD HAVE TO GET A JOB TO PAY FOR THEM HIMSELF!
MOM DIDN'T LIKE PETE FROM THE BEGINNING. SHE TOLD MILES THAT HE SHOULD STAY AWAY FROM THAT HOOD.

PETE HAD A SECRET THAT HE JUST COULDN'T KEEP TO HIMSELF SO
HE TOOK MILES OVER TO HIS TRAILER AND SHOWED HIM SOMETHING THAT HE WOULD NEVER WOULD HAVE DREAMED OF, AND WOULD NEVER FORGET!

THEY WENT INTO HIS ROOM AND HE PULLED OUT A DISPLAY CASE FROM UNDER HIS BED.
HE HAD A COLLECTION OF HUMAN EARS. THEY WERE ALL DISPLAYED UNDER GLASS LIKE A BUTTERFLY DISPLAY. THERE WERE EARS FROM EVERY RACE!

HE ALSO HAD COLLECTIONS OF BUTTERFLIES, SO THAT HIS MOM WOULDN'T KNOW WHAT HE WAS UP TO.

SHE JUST KEPT BUYING HIM CASES. SHE THOUGHT THAT IT WAS GOOD FOR HIM TO BE INTERESTED IN BUTTERFLIES.
THERE MUST HAVE BEEN 30 OR 40 RIGHT HAND EARS THERE. ALL OF THE REST OF THEM WERE IN PAIRS.

HE HAD SEVERAL CASES OF THE THINGS. IT SENT SHIVERS UP MILES SPINE. THE THOUGHT OF CUTTING THEM OFF WAS EVEN MORE APPALLING.

PETE ASKED HIM IF HE WANTED TO SEE WHERE THEY CAME FROM?
PETE TOLD HIM ABOUT THE GANG WARS THAT THEY HAD EVERY WEEK.
WE HAVE ANOTHER WAR TOMORROW JUST COME AS BACK-UP.

MILES AGREED AND WENT WITH THEM THE NEXT MORNING. IT WAS QUITE A WALK DOWN TO THE RAILROAD TRACKS, WHERE ALL OF THE GANGS WOULD MEET.
IT WAS KIND OF A SWITCHING YARD FOR THE RAILROAD.

PETE GAVE MILES A LENGTH OF CHAIN TO CARRY WITH HIM.
IT KIND OF MADE HIM FEEL LIKE HE WAS PART OF SOMETHING. THEY WENT OUT BY THE RAILROAD TRACKS WHERE MOST OF THE FIGHTING TOOK PLACE.

MILES COULDN'T BELIEVE HOW MANY KIDS WERE LED ASTRAY BY ALL OF THIS GANG SHIT! BLACK'S AGAINST WHITES AND WHITES AGAINST MEXICANS AND BLACKS. IT WAS HORRIBLE!

HE STAYED UP ON THE HILL WHILE ALL OF THE OTHER KIDS WENT DOWN FOR THEIR CONFRONTATION WITH THE OTHER GANGS.

IT WAS BLOODY! PETE GOT HIMSELF ANOTHER EAR AND SHOVED THE KID DOWN A STORM DRAIN. HE KILLED THE KID! HE DIDN'T THINK A THING ABOUT IT!

MILES KNEW THAT HE DIDN'T WANT ANY MORE TO DO WITH PETE GUY!
WHEN HE GOT HOME THAT NIGHT. HE TOLD HIS MOM ABOUT THE GANG WARS AND SHE BLEW A CORK! SHE SAID: THAT'S IT!

WE ARE GOING BACK TO YOUR GRANDMA'S HOUSE. THIS IS A HORRIBLE GOD FORSAKEN PLACE AND I DON'T REALLY REMEMBER WHY WE CAME HERE ANYWAY.

GRANDMA'S: THAT WAS WHERE MILES REALLY WANTED TO BE ANYWAY.

IT WAS GOOD TO BE BACK AT GRANDMA'S AGAIN. IT FELT SO SECURE. FINALLY THERE WAS PEACE IN LIFE AGAIN.

THAT WAS THE YEAR WHEN THE DREAMS STARTED.
MILES HAD AN ACTIVE IMAGINATION ALREADY AND HIS MIND WAS ALWAYS IN MOTION EVEN AS HE SLEPT. UP TO THIS POINT HIS LIFE WAS PRETTY

SCREWED UP AND ALL HE HAD WAS NIGHTMARES. HE FELT SAFE AT GRANDMA'S HOUSE AND THE DREAMS TURNED INTO PLEASANT DREAMS.

HE WASN'T LIKE OTHER KIDS AT ALL. HE WOULD FIGHT TOOTH AND NAIL TO STAY IN BED ALL NIGHT. HE WANTED TO GO TO SLEEP EARLY AND STAY THERE AS LONG AS HE COULD!
HE CHERISHED HIS SLEEP BUT MOST OF ALL IT WAS HIS DREAMS.
HIS DREAMS WERE HIS ONLY COMFORT FROM ALL OF THE HARSHNESS OF THE REALITIES OF A POOR EXISTENCE!
HE HAD COME FROM MANY TIMES, A BROKEN HOME.
AFTER MOM LEFT DAD. HE NEVER REALLY HAD A FATHER IN HIS YOUNG YEARS. NO MORE THAN YOU COULD GATHER FROM THE START OF THIS STORY.
HE WAS FULL OF ENERGY. HIS GRANDMOTHER WOULD SAY THAT IT WAS PISS AND VINEGAR THAT HE WAS FULL OF.
SNIPS AND SNAILS AND PUPPY DOG TAILS THAT'S WHAT LITTLE BOYS ARE MADE OF.
HIS MOTHER COULDN'T HANDLE HIM. HE HAD WAY TOO MUCH ENERGY. SO HE STAYED WITH HIS GRANDMOTHER WHILE MOM TRIED TO RAISE HIS SISTER.
WHILE AT HIS GRANDMOTHERS HOUSE, HE AND HIS TWO UNCLES BUILT THE COOLEST TREE HOUSE. IT WAS VERY SIMILAR TO THE

TREE HOUSE IN THE SWISS FAMILY ROBINSON MOVIE.

THEY WOULD SCOUT AROUND THE NEIGHBORHOOD FOR SCRAP LUMBER FOR MONTHS BEFORE THE CONSTRUCTION STARTED. THEY HAD QUITE A PILE OF LUMBER ACCUMULATED BY THE TIME THEY STARTED.

THEY SPENT MANY MONTHS WORKING ON THAT CASTLE IN THE SKY. THEY HAD A LITTLE MAKESHIFT PHONE SETUP SO THAT THEY COULD STAY IN TOUCH WITH PEOPLE ON THE GROUND LEVEL.

BASICALLY IT WAS A REGULAR TELEPHONE THAT THEY HOOKED UP DIRECT WIRES BETWEEN A TELEPHONE IN THE HOUSE AND THE ONE IN THE TREE HOUSE. IT WASN'T VERY LOUD.

THE MAGNETS IN THE RECEIVER WAS ALL THEY NEEDED TO BE ABLE TO SPEAK TO THE HOUSE. JUST NO BELL. IT WAS REALLY EASIER TO YELL! THEY EVEN HAD A DUMB WAITER FOR LUNCH AND SNACKS.

THE TREE HOUSE HAD ONE FAST EASY EXIT BUT YOU HAD TO CLIMB TO THE TOP OF THE TREE TO USE IT. IT WAS ONE OF THOSE HIGH SPEED ZIP LINES WHERE THERE WAS A PULLEY WITH A LONG AXLE AND AN EYELET ON EACH SIDE. THERE WAS A ROPE STRAP CONNECTED TO EACH EYELET WHICH YOU WOULD PUT OVER EACH WRIST.

THERE WAS A ROPE THAT WENT FROM THE TOP OF THE ELM TREE TO A PALM TREE AND AN APRICOT TREE THAT WERE IN THE FRONT YARD. IT WAS A HIGH SPEED ZIP TO THE FRONT YARD.

THERE WAS AN OLD FASHIONED CLOTHES LINE THAT WAS CONNECTED TO THE ZIP TROLLEY FOR PULLING IT BACK UP TO THE TOP AND IT WOULD SECOND FOR A MAKESHIFT BRAKE IN AN EMERGENCY. MILES DIDN'T USE IT TOO OFTEN BECAUSE IT WAS PRETTY EASY TO GET HURT.
IT DID MAKE FOR A QUICK GET AWAY THOUGH. HE USUALLY JUST CLIMBED DOWN THE TREE. CLIMBING DOWN THE MAKESHIFT LATTER WAS A LITTLE SCARY.
THE ONLY TIME THAT HE CAME DOWN FROM THE FORT WAS WHEN HE HAD TO USE THE BATHROOM OR TO EAT DINNER OR TO GO TO SCHOOL.
EVERYONE THOUGHT THAT HE WAS GOING TO BE A RECLUSE WHEN HE GREW UP.
THE OTHER KIDS WOULD PLAY IN THE TREE HOUSE DURING THE WEEKENDS AND AFTER SCHOOL BUT THEY COULDN'T UNDERSTAND WHY HE SPENT SO MUCH TIME ALONE AND ESPECIALLY WHY HE HAD TO SLEEP IN THAT DAMN TREE HOUSE EVERY NIGHT!
HE HAD A WONDERFUL VIEW OF THE SAN FERNANDO VALLEY FROM HIS TREE FORT. HE COULD SEE OVER ALL OF THE ROOFTOPS EASILY WHICH WAS PROBABLY THE CAUSE FOR ALL OF THOSE WONDERFUL DREAMS.
THE DREAMS STARTED IN THE BACK YARD ON THE GRASS AND THEN TO THE TREE FORT AS SOON AS HE FINISHED IT.
THE TREE WAS A CHINESE ELM TREE AND IT WAS THE LARGEST TREE IN THE SAN FERNANDO VALLEY. YOU COULD SPOT THE TREE FROM TEN

MILES AWAY. IT WAS WELL OVER 100 FEET TALL AND ITS LIMBS REACHED FROM THE BACK YARD "WHERE IT WAS PLANTED" TO THE FRONT YARD WHERE IT'S LIMBS STRETCHED CLEAR TO THE STREET.

IT WAS A LONG AND TREACHEROUS CLIMB TO THE MAIN TREE FORT. WHEN HE WENT UP HE MEANT TO STAY FOR AWHILE.

THE MAIN TREE FORT WAS A CASTLE. LOTS OF SQUARE FOOTAGE. GOING OUT TO THE LIMBS WERE SMALLER, BUT EQUALLY AS NICE, OTHER FORTS.

DURING THE SUMMER MONTHS YOU COULD HARDLY SEE THE FORTS AT ALL, BECAUSE OF ALL OF THE LEAVES ON THE TREE.

THERE WERE PIECES OF 2X4'S THAT WERE LAG BOLTED TO THE TREE LIMBS AND THERE WAS ROPES ON BOTH SIDES OF EACH PATHWAY FOR EASIER MANEUVERING TO THE OTHER FORTS.

THERE WERE FIVE FORTS IN ALL. THEY THOUGHT ABOUT ADDING MORE, BUT NEVER GOT AROUND TO IT! ALL BUT ONE OF THE FORTS WERE OPEN TO THE SKY.

THE ONE WITH THE ROOF WAS FOR THE RAINY NIGHTS. YEAH! LIGHTENING IN A TREE. THAT WAS REAL SMART.

MILES WAS NEVER STRUCK AND NEITHER WERE ANY OF THE TREE HOUSES.

MILES DREAMED EVERY NIGHT THAT HE ONLY HAD TO STAND IN THE MIDDLE OF THE ROOM IN HIS TREE FORT AND SPREAD HIS ARMS AND

ARCH HIS BACK, TAKE A DEEP BREATH AND WILL HIS MIND TO REACH INTO THE NIGHT SKY.

HE WOULD SOAR OVER THE ROOFTOPS AND OVER THE TREES.

HE WAS GETTING TRIPS THAT TIM LEARY HIMSELF ONLY WISHED THAT HE COULD HAVE. AS HE DEEPLY INHALED. HE WOULD SOAR STRAIGHT UP IN TO THE NIGHT SKY. HE WOULD TAKE DEEPER AND DEEPER BREATHS TO GAIN ELEVATION UNTIL HE WAS HIGH OVER THE ROOFTOPS. SOMETIMES THOUSANDS OF FEET OVER THEM.

HE ESPECIALLY LOVED THE WINDY NIGHTS. THE SOARING WAS WONDERFUL THEN. HE ONLY HAD TO LEAN INTO THE WIND AND SPREAD HIS ARMS, AND HE WOULD TAKE OFF LIKE A ROCKET.

HE WOULD CATCH UPDRAFTS IN HIS DREAMS THAT WOULD TAKE HIM THOUSANDS OF FEET ABOVE THE BUILDINGS.

WHAT A SUPREME RUSH! HE THOUGHT ABOUT SUPERMAN AND THE ABILITY THAT HE HAD FOR SOARING INTO THE SKY. HE TOO FELT THE SAME WAY. NOT THAT HE WAS SUPERMAN BUT THAT HE COULD FLY JUST LIKE HIM.

HIS DREAMS EVOLVED TO JUST THINKING THAT YOU ARE THERE, AND YOU ARE THERE! I THINK I AM, THEREFORE I AM. I THINK.

JONATHAN LIVINGSTON SEAGULL HAD IT RIGHT!!!

IT WAS STRANGE THAT HE HAD DREAMS LIKE THAT. HE HAD NEVER BEEN IN A PLANE OR ANYTHING OF THE SORT.

ALL OF THE RELATIVES SAID THAT THEY WISHED THAT THEY HAD AN IMAGINATION LIKE HIS.

HIS GRANDMA WOULD SAY; THAT KID IS REALLY OUT THERE AND I WISH THAT I COULD JOIN HIM.

HE IS THE ONLY ONE AROUND HERE THAT IS HAVING ANY FUN AT ALL!

HIS GRANDMA WAS HIS BEST FRIEND. SHE REALLY SEEMED TO UNDERSTAND HIM AND HIS WEIRD WAYS. THEY WERE BOTH LEO'S.

SHE WAS STRANGE IN HER OWN WAYS TOO.

SHE AND GRANDPA LOVED TO DRINK THEIR BEER.

GRANDMA WAS A LITTLE EMBARRASSED BY HOW MUCH BEER THAT THEY DRANK.

SHE WOULD USE BEER CANS LIKE STONES WHICH WERE MORTARED TOGETHER AND SHE BUILT FOUNTAINS, BARBEQUES AND SERVING TABLES OUT OF THE CANS THAT SHE MORTARED TOGETHER.

SHE WOULD THEN PAINT THE BOTTOMS OF THE CANS DIFFERENT COLORS. THEY DID LOOK PRETTY GOOD IN A CHEESY SORT OF WAY.

THERE WAS ONLY SO MUCH THAT YOU COULD BUILD OUT OF BEER CANS THOUGH. HER WHOLE BACK YARD ENDED UP BEING BEER CANS AND BRICKS. IT LOOKED PRETTY GOOD.

THEY HAD TWO DOGS THAT ATE NOTHING BUT CANNED SKIPPY DOG FOOD.

JUST BEFORE TRASH DAY SHE WOULD GO TO THE PAINS OF PUTTING A BEER CAN IN EACH ONE OF THE DOG FOOD CANS OR CANS OF VEGETABLES.

THEY DIDN'T HAVE ALUMINUM BEER CANS IN THOSE DAYS SO HER TRASH CANS WERE ALWAYS VERY HEAVY AND MILES COULD HEAR THE TRASH MEN COMPLAIN AS THEY LIFTED THE HEAVY CANS. HE COULD HEAR THEM SAYING.

"WHO ARE THEM OLD FARTS TRYING TO KID"?

HE TOLD HIS GRANDMA ALL ABOUT HIS SOARING TRIPS OVER THE CITY. SHE SEEMED TO UNDERSTAND WHAT IT WAS LIKE.

SHE CALLED IT THE PETER PAN SYNDROME AND SHE ALWAYS WANTED TO KNOW WHAT HAPPENED AFTER HIS LATEST DREAM.

HE WOULD TELL HER ALL ABOUT THE DREAMS IN THE MORNING.

SHE WAS VERY MUCH INTO ART. SHE PAINTED QUITE A FEW SURREAL TYPE PAINTINGS INVOLVING SOARING.

MILES ALWAYS LOVED THEM. SHE REALLY DID UNDERSTAND.

HE WAS EXCEPTIONALLY SMART IN SCHOOL, BUT HE HAD HIS OWN RULES FOR SCHOOL.

FOR EXAMPLE; HE WOULD NOT BRING HOME ANY HOMEWORK.

ANYTHING THAT THEY STUDIED IN CLASS MILES WOULD GET STRAIGHT A'S ON IT.

HE RETAINED EVERYTHING THAT THE TEACHERS TAUGHT IN CLASS!

IT WOULD REALLY PISS OFF THE TEACHERS. THEY COULD NOT SEND HIM TO THE PRINCIPALS OFFICE, BECAUSE HE HAD NOT DONE HIS HOMEWORK. IT REFLECTED BACK ON THE TEACHERS CREDIBILITY AS A GOOD TEACHER.

THEY COULDN'T GRADE HIM ON HOMEWORK ALONE.

MILES WASN'T AFRAID TO TELL THEM SO EITHER.

HE RETAINED EVERYTHING THAT HE LEARNED IN CLASS AND THE TEACHERS KNEW IT. HIS APTITUDE TEST SCORES ALWAYS CAME BACK AS COLLEGE LEVEL. HE NEVER REALLY GRASPED ENGLISH GRAMMER VERY WELL THOUGH.

HE WOUND UP STARTING HIGH SCHOOL AT 13 YEARS OLD. IF HE DIDN'T KNOW IT. IT WAS BECAUSE THE TEACHER DIDN'T TEACH IT!

THE TEACHERS DID NOT WANT THE DEPARTMENT HEADS TO THINK THAT THEY WERE LAZY AND THAT WAS WHY THEY GAVE OUT ALL OF THAT HOMEWORK IN THE FIRST PLACE. THEY WERE LAZY.

THEY GAVE MILES SPECIAL ATTENTION BECAUSE THEY KNEW THAT HE WOULD RETAIN IT!

LOTS OF STUDY HALLS BY THE TIME HE GRADUATED.

HE ALMOST NEVER HEARD FROM HIS MOTHER AND THAT WAS ALRIGHT BY HIM. HE WAS VERY HAPPY WHERE HE WAS.

THERE WERE YEARS OF DREAM FLIGHTS OVER THE VALLEY.

AS TIME WENT BY HE WAS BEGINNING TO EXPAND HIS SOARING TO THE HOLLYWOOD HILLS. HIS GRANDMA MADE MANY TRIPS OVER THERE TO VISIT HER MOTHER. THIS WAS EXTRA FODDER FOR HIS SOARING DREAMS.

IT SEEMED THAT HE COULDN'T SOAR WHERE HE
HAD NEVER BEEN AT ALL.
HE DIDN'T HAVE TO FLY OVER IT TO KNOW WHAT
IT WAS LIKE TO FLY OVER IT THOUGH! HE JUST
IMAGINED IT.

TAKEN TO THE BEACH

HIS MOTHER SHOWED UP AND TOOK HIM AWAY FROM THE TREE FORTS AT HIS GRAND MOTHERS HOUSE.

MILES WAS NOT HAPPY AT ALL. HE LOVED THE WAY THAT THINGS WERE GOING BUT MOM HAD HER WAY.

SHE MOVED IN WITH ONE OF HER BOYFRIENDS INTO AN APARTMENT IN SEAL BEACH CALIFORNIA. SHE FELT THAT SHE NEEDED HER FAMILY BACK BECAUSE SHE WAS SOON TO BE MARRIED AGAIN. SHE DID MARRY HIM SOON AFTER THEY MOVED THERE.

ROBERT HAD THIS OLD BOAT WITH A BIG OLDSMOBILE ENGINE. IT WAS A PRETTY DEEP "V" HULL, AND WOULD TAKE THE OCEAN WAVES WELL.

IT WAS A CADILLAC OF ITS DAY. IT WAS A CHRIS CRAFT SHIP LAP HULL, AND IT WAS FAST. HELL! THAT BOAT WOULD HAUL ASS! IT JUST POUNDED IT'S WAY THROUGH THE WAVES. IT WAS A VERY HEAVY BOAT.

HE WAS LIKE A JECKLE AND HYDE KIND OF GUY. SOMETIMES HE WAS REAL NICE, AND SOMETIMES HE WAS REAL MEAN.

IT DEPENDED ON IF HE WAS DRUNK OR NOT! MOM LOVED HIM WHEN HE WAS SOBER.

THEY LIVED IN AN UPSTAIRS APARTMENT RIGHT ON THE BEACH. HE WOULD GET DRUNK AND GET MOM TO DRIVE HIM AROUND WHILE HE HELD A KNIFE TO HER THROAT! SHE REALLY KNEW HOW TO PICK'EM.

HE WOULD BEAT THE HELL OUT OF HER AND ABUSE THE ANIMALS TOO! HE WOULD GET UP IN THE MORNING, AND REALIZE WHAT HE HAD DONE, AND BEG FOR FORGIVENESS.

EVEN THE DAMN DOG FORGAVE HIM FOR THROWING IT OFF OF THE SECOND FLOOR BALCONY IN TO THE ALLEY BELOW.

MILES MOTHER WOULD FORGIVE HIM BECAUSE MOST OF THE TIME HE WAS VERY GOOD TO HER.

HE HAD A LITTLE CARPET CLEANING BUSINESS ON THE SIDE. MOM WROTE A LITTLE CATCH PHRASE FOR HIM, USING HIS NAME.

"CLEAN IT GOOD WITH ROBIN HOOD".

SHE ALWAYS SAID THAT HE WAS THE BEST LOVER. THAT SHOWS WHERE SHE HAD HER PRIORITIES.

ROBERT HAD NOTICED HOW AGILE THAT MILES WAS.

MILES WAS ABLE TO DO STANDING BACK FLIPS FLATFOOTED RIGHT ON THE SAND. HE HAD BEEN

IN A TUMBLING CLASS IN THE VALLEY, AND SEEMED TO BE AFRAID OF NOTHING.

THEY ALL GOT TOGETHER ONE DAY AND ROBERT TOOK THE FAMILY OUT WATER SKIING. MOM WOULDN'T EVEN TRY SHE SAID THAT SHE BRUISED TOO EASY.

HIS SISTER WAS A TERRIBLE KLUTZ TOO, BUT THEY TRIED, AND TRIED TO GET HER UP ON THOSE SKIS UNTIL THEY HAD USED UP MOST OF THE GAS.

HE SAID THAT MILES WANTED A TURN TOO!

SHE SAID: HE AINT GOING TO DO ANY BETTER AND SHE CRIED AND SOBBED UNTIL HE FINALLY PUT HIS FOOT DOWN.

HE SAID THAT IT WAS ALMOST TIME TO GO HOME LET MILES HAVE A TURN BEFORE WE RUN OUT OF GAS.

MILES TOOK TO IT RIGHT AWAY.

HIS FIRST ATTEMPT AT WATER SKIING HE WAS RIGHT UP ON THEM, AND WAS DOING STUNTS ON THE FIRST RIDE.

FINALLY THEY WERE OUT OF GAS AND HAD TO GO BACK IN. MILES ONLY GOT ABOUT TEN MINUTES ON THE SKIS. ROBERT PROMISED THAT THEY WOULD GO SKIING AGAIN SOON. HIS SISTER WAS FURIOUS THAT HE MADE IT LOOK SO EASY.

WITHIN A FEW DAYS OF PRACTICE, THEY ENTERED MILES IN THE "LONG BEACH TO CATALINA" ENDURANCE RACE. HE CAME IN AT FOURTH PLACE.

PRETTY GOOD FOR A BEGINNER. HE WAS A NATURAL AND A PLEASURE FOR HIS STEP-DAD TO HANG OUT WITH!

HE TAUGHT MILES ABOUT CARS AND HOW TO WORK ON THEM. MILES LEARNED AT AN EARLY AGE AS TO HOW AN INTERNAL COMBUSTION ENGINE WORKED. ALL ABOUT HOW TO TAKE IT APART, REPAIR IT, AND TO PUT IT BACK TOGETHER.

ALL OF HIS TEACHINGS WENT WELL WITH THE AUTO SHOP CLASSES THAT HE WAS TAKING IN HIGH SCHOOL. MILES EXCELLED IN CLASS BECAUSE OF ALL OF THE EXTRA ATTENTION AT HOME.

IN HIGH SCHOOL HE WAS ON THE VARSITY HIGH DIVING TEAM AT HUNTINGTON BEACH HIGHSCHOOL.

HE HAD THE ADVANTAGE OF THE TUMBLING CLASSES THAT HE HAD TAKEN WHILE HE WAS IN THE VALLEY AND OF COURSE HIS DREAMS, TO SEE HIM THROUGH HIS DIVES.

HE HAD ALREADY DONE ALL OF THEM MANY TIMES BEFORE DURING HIS DREAMS, SO HE HAD PLENTY OF PRACTICE.

HE USED TO GO ON DIVING EXCURSIONS WITH HIS CLOSE BUDDIES FROM THE DIVING TEAM AT HIGH SCHOOL.

SOMETIMES THEY WENT DOWN THE COAST AND IN TO MEXICO TO DIVE OFF OF THE HIGHEST CLIFFS THAT THEY COULD FIND THERE.

THE LOWEST DIVE POINTS WERE AT ABOUT 85 FEET AND THE HIGHEST POINT WAS AT ABOUT

115 FEET. NOBODY SEEMED TO WANT TO GO OFF OF ANYTHING HIGHER.

MILES WAS A THRILL A MINUTE KIND OF GUY. HE LOVED TO STAND ON THE EDGE OF THE CLIFF, WATCHING THE SURF COME IN AND GO OUT, HE WOULD TIME IT, SO THAT BY THE TIME HE GOT TO THE WATER, IT WOULD BE DEEP ENOUGH TO DIVE INTO.

THE FIRST TIME OUT. HE STOOD THERE FOR QUITE SOME TIME JUST WATCHING THE WAVES AND THROWING ROCKS SO THAT HE COULD GET THE TIMING RIGHT. HE WAS A VERY GOOD SHALLOW WATER DIVER. HE HAD A KNACK TO BE ABLE TO TIME THE DIVES SO THAT WHEN HE HIT THE WATER HE WAS ALREADY ROLLING IN KIND OF A "U" SHAPE. HE WAS IN AND RIGHT OUT AGAIN.

WHAT A RUSH TO DIVE OFF OF THE CLIFFS AS THE WATER RUSHES AWAY AND EXPOSES THE SAND BELOW. TIME TO GO! HE WOULD SAY AS HE DOVE OFF OF THE CLIFFS.

HE WOULD FLY LIKE A BIRD WITHOUT FEATHERS OR MORE LIKE A PENGUIN; ARMS ARCHED BACK IN A FULL LAYOUT LIKE HE WAS SKY DIVING AND PLUNGING INTO THE OCEAN BELOW.

LITERALLY HUNDREDS OF DIVES LIKE THAT. HE WOULD DIVE IN THEN SCURRY UP TO THE TOP AGAIN AND AGAIN.

HIS BUDDIES TOLD HIM THAT HE SHOULD BE A LITTLE MORE CAREFUL AND THAT ONE OF THESE DAYS HIS LUCK MIGHT RUN OUT!

HE WOULD ALWAYS SAY THAT THERE WAS NO LUCK TO IT! IT WAS TIMING. HE WAS RIGHT. MOM AND HER NEW HUSBAND BROKE UP AGAIN. THIS TIME IT WAS FOR GOOD!

SURFING

MILES GOT TO SPEND A SUMMER WITH HIS UNCLE BILLY.

HE WAS ONE OF THE OLD TIME SURFERS, THAT SURFED THE LONG BOARDS.

HE HAD SURFED THE OLD BALSA WOOD SURFBOARDS. THEY WERE HEAVY BUT PRETTY STRONG AND WOULD SUPPORT HIS ENORMOUS WEIGHT! HE WAS A BIG MAN.

HIS UNCLE TAUGHT HIM HOW TO SURF ON THE BIG CALIFORNIA SWELLS. HE STARTED OUT ON THE BIG BOARDS.

HIS UNCLE HAD GIVEN HIM AN OLD ALLEN SURFBOARD. IT WAS 9'6" LONG AND IT WAS KIND OF A GREENISH TINT FROM THE COLOR OF THE FIBERGLASS IN THOSE DAYS.

HIS BUDDIES CALLED IT "THE LOG". IT WAS SO HEAVY THAT IT USUALLY TOOK TWO OF THEM TO CARRY IT OUT TO THE BEACH.

HE HAD USED THE LOG FOR ABOUT SIX MONTHS WHEN ONE DAY HE HAD LET ONE OF HIS FRIENDS USE IT. HE BROKE IT IN HALF.

MILES CUT IT DOWN AND MADE TWO BELLY BOARDS OUT OF IT AND THEN MOVED QUICKLY TO THE SHORT BOARDS.

ON THE BIG BOARDS HE COULD RUN ALL OVER THE TOP OF THE BOARD FROM BOW TO STERN.

THE BIG BOARDS WERE THE EASIEST ONES TO HANG TEN TOES OVER THE NOSE. THEY WERE BY FAR THE MOST STABLE.

THE SMALLER BOARDS WERE QUICKER TURNING AND EASIER TO GET OUT OF THE WAY OF TROUBLE.

WHENEVER THERE WAS A STORM COMING THEN HE WAS THERE.

THE BIGGER THE SWELLS THE BETTER.

HE SPENT HIS YOUNG YEARS RIDING THE BIG SWELLS AND HAD NO FEAR OF THE OCEAN AT ALL!

MILES WENT OUT WITH HIS BUDDIES ONE AFTERNOON.

THERE WAS A STORM BLOWING IN AND THE WATER WAS UNSEASONABLY WARM BECAUSE OF THE PHOSPHORUS IN THE WATER.

IT WOULD MAKE IRIDESCENT STREAKS IN THE WATER WHEN YOU DRAGGED YOUR HAND THROUGH IT OR DISTURBED THE WATER IN ANY WAY.

IT WAS BEAUTIFUL AT NIGHT. WHEN THE WAVES STOOD UP TALL IN THE MOONLIGHT IT LOOKED LIKE A HUGE GREEN L.E.D. LIGHT!

THE SWELLS WERE RUNNING FROM TWENTY TO THIRTY FEET. THE SMALL CRAFT WARNINGS WERE OUT!

THEY ALL PADDLED OUT ABOUT FOUR MILES SO THAT THEY COULD CATCH THE BIG ONES. THAT WAS ONE OF THE BEAUTIES OF SEAL BEACH AREA. THE WATER WAS REAL SHALLOW FOR ABOUT THREE MILES OUT!

THERE WAS THIS HUGE JETTY THAT BELONGED TO THE NAVY. IT WAS A BREAK WATER FOR THE SHIPS THAT WERE INSIDE OF IT.

MILES AND HIS BUDDIES ALL TOOK OFF ON THE SAME WAVE. BEAUTIFUL LONG PACIFIC SWELLS. AS THEY STARTED GETTING CLOSER TO THE JETTY THE WAVES WERE STANDING UP TALLER AND TALLER.

THE WAVE WAS BEGINNING TO CLOSE OUT ON BOTH SIDES OF THEM, SO ALL OF THEM HAD TO GO STRAIGHT TOWARD THE JETTY. THEY ALL STEPPED BACK ON THEIR BOARDS SO THAT THEY WERE AT THE TOP OF THE WAVE WHEN IT HIT THE BREAK WATER.

THE WAVE DUMPED THEM OVER THE TOP OF THE JETTY AND DESTROYED ALL OF THEIR SURFBOARDS.

WHAT A RIDE! IT DOESN'T GET ANY BETTER THAN THAT!

THEY ALL CRAWLED UP ON TO THE JETTY AND HIKED BACK ON ABOUT TWO MILES OF ROCKS THAT WERE COVERED WITH BARNACLES EXCEPT FOR THE VERY TOPS OF THE ROCKS WHICH WERE PRETTY SMOOTH FROM ALL OF THE FISHERMEN THAT WENT OUT TO FISH EVERY DAY AND THEN BACK TO THE BEACH.

NOBODY WAS HURT BUT HIS MOM HAD TOLD HIS UNCLE ANYWAY. THIS WORRIED HIS UNCLE QUITE A BIT AND HE TOLD MILES THAT HE NEEDED TO HAVE MORE RESPECT FOR MOTHER OCEAN AND THAT HE WAS SIMPLY AN EXTREMELY LUCKY GUY.

HE SPENT A COUPLE MORE YEARS IN SEAL BEACH. THAT WAS WHERE THE BEST SURF WAS. HE SURFED ALL OF THE BEACH TOWNS. HUNTINGTON BEACH, SUNSET BEACH, THE TRESTLES AT THE MARINE BASE, AND OF COURSE INTO MEXICO.

HITCHHIKING WAS EASY IN THOSE DAYS, EVEN WITH A SURFBOARD.

IF IT GOT ANY BETTER THEN IT WAS PRETTY CLOSE BY. HE WORKED FOR ALL OF THE LOCAL SURFBOARD SHOPS. OLE, HOBBIE, DWAYNE AND ALLEN, AT REPAIRING SURFBOARDS AND BUILDING THEM TOO!

HE BECAME QUITE A FIBERGLASS WORKER. HE ALWAYS HAD MONEY BECAUSE HE WAS A HARD WORKER AND NOT AFRAID TO GET HIS HANDS DIRTY.

HE LIKED HAVING MONEY AND HATED BEING POOR. HIS CHILDHOOD WAS A TESTAMENT TO THAT.

HIS MOTHER MOVED FROM HUSBAND TO HUSBAND AND BOY FRIEND TO BOY FRIEND. SHE ALWAYS CAME OUT ON THE RAW END OF THINGS. SHE NEVER HAD ANY MONEY. MILES HATED BEING POOR AND ALWAYS KEPT A JOB BECAUSE OF IT!

HE FIRST LEFT HOME AT THE AGE OF 14 WHEN HIS MOTHER KICKED HIM OUT OF THE HOUSE.

JUST ANOTHER ONE OF HER TANTRUMS AFTER
LEAVING HER LATEST BOYFRIEND.

HE STUCK AROUND SEAL BEACH FOR AWHILE.
HE HAD A LITTLE HUT ON THE BEACH. THAT HE
HAD THATCHED TOGETHER SOME PANELS OF
PALM FRONDS SO THAT HE HAD FOUR SIDES AND
A LEAN-TO TYPE ROOF. HE THEN LASHED THEM
TOGETHER. IT MADE IT EASIER FOR HIM TO MOVE
HIS HUT UP AND DOWN THE BEACH. YOU HAVE
TO REMEMBER THAT IT WAS THE EARLY 60'S, AND
NOTHING LIKE IT IS ALLOWED NOW.

IT WAS NICE LIVING ON THE BEACH. IT MADE IT
SO THAT IF THE SURF WAS UP HE COULD MAKE
A QUICK RUN BEFORE GOING TO WORK AT THE
SURF SHOP.

THEY WERE PRETTY LENIENT WITH HIS COMINGS
AND GOINGS FOR THE SAKE OF SURFING. THEY
WOULD LET HIM USE THEIR SHOWER AND
BATHROOM FACILITIES BECAUSE HE DIDN'T
HAVE ANY OF THAT IN HIS HUT ON THE BEACH.
HE REALLY LEARNED TO LOVE HIS LITTLE HUT ON
THE BEACH. THERE WAS ALWAYS A PARTY GOING
ON IN THE EVENINGS. NIGHT SURFING WAS
ALWAYS A BLAST. THERE WAS ALWAYS SOMEONE
NEW THAT CAME BY AND SPENT THE NIGHT.

MOST EVERYBODY THAT CAME BY, BROUGHT
SOMETHING TO EAT. BEFORE NOT TOO MUCH
TIME WENT BY AND MILES NEVER HAD TO BUY
ANY FOOD AT ALL!

HE HAD THE IDEAL SITUATION. A PLACE FOR
EVERYONE TO HANG OUT!

HE WAS A REAL SURF BUM AND PROUD OF IT. IN A SENSE HE WAS HOMELESS BUT HE DIDN'T REALLY THINK OF IT THAT WAY.
HE REALLY WAS A FREE SPIRIT.
THE DREAMS HE WAS HAVING WHILE LIVING ON THE BEACH WERE WONDERFUL TOO. HE GOT INTO SOARING FROM SEAL BEACH CLEAR TO MEXICO. HE WAS ONE WITH THE SEAGULLS. YOU CAN'T REALLY EXPLAIN THE RUSH! ALL OF THAT SOARING WAS KEPT TO HIMSELF AND OF COURSE HIS GRANDMOTHER. HE LIKED HIS FRIENDS BUT HE REALLY WAS A LONER AT HEART.
THERE WAS A BOTTLE OF WINE ONCE IN A WHILE BUT NO DRUGS OR ANYTHING THAT THE COPS WOULD EVER BOTHER HIM ABOUT. THEY RARELY CAME OUT TO THE HUT ON THE BEACH. NOBODY REPORTED ANY NOISE.
BESIDES HE STILL WENT TO SCHOOL. EARLY MORNING SURFING, THEN SURF SHOP, THEN SCHOOL. THEN BACK TO THE SURF SHOP.
THE SURF SHOPS WOULD SPONSOR HIM ON MANY OF THE LOCAL SURFING CONTESTS. HE WAS A REAL HOT DOG WITH A BIG SET OF BALLS. MORE BALLS THAN BRAINS I THINK!
ONE OF HIS BEST FRIENDS TURNED OUT TO BE A VERY FAMOUS SURFER. "CORKY CARROL".
MILES WAS NEVER SO LUCKY AND CORKY CAME FROM A WEALTHY LOVING FAMILY AND GOT ANYTHING HE WANTED, SO HE HAD THE BEST OF EVERYTHING FOR SURFING.
SOMETHING HAD HAPPENED TO THE WEATHER THAT NEXT YEAR. THE SURF WAS QUITE A BIT

FLATTER THAN USUAL. MILES WAS BEGINNING
TO GET BORED.
IT WAS TIME TO LEAVE THE OCEAN FOR A WHILE.
THE SURF WAS WAY TOO GLASSY. IT WAS TIME
TO LOOK FOR OTHER ADVENTURES.
AT LEAST THE DREAMS WERE STILL GOOD.

THINKING IS THE BEST WAY TO TRAVEL

HE MOVED BACK TO THE SAN FERNANDO VALLEY AND TO HIS GRANDMOTHERS HOUSE WHERE HE GREW UP WITH THE TREE HOUSE. ONE OF HIS UNCLES HAD THE BIG ELM TREE TRIMMED BY A PROFESSIONAL TREE TRIMMING COMPANY.
THEY TOOK DOWN ALL OF THE TREE FORTS. MILES WAS BUMMED OUT! HE ASKED HIS GRANDMA. WHY DID YOU LET THEM TAKE DOWN THE TREE FORTS? SHE SAID THAT THE TREE TRIMMING COMPANY SAID THAT IT WAS UNSAFE!
OH WELL; AT LEAST HE COULD STILL DREAM ABOUT THE TREE FORT!
HE WENT OUT BACK AND LOOKED AT THE TREE THAT HE HAD SPENT SO MANY YEARS IN. HE SAW THE LAST OF THE RUNGS THAT THEY HAD LEFT BEHIND THE CLEATS THAT HE HAD LAG SCREWED INTO THE TREE WENT UP TO THE LOWER FORKS OF THE TREE.
HE SLEPT IN THE BACK YARD ON HIS FIRST NIGHT BACK. HIS DREAMS WERE AS VIVID AS HE HAD

REMEMBERED A FEW YEARS EARLIER. HE REALLY MISSED THE ELEVATION OF THE TREE FORT.

HE THOUGHT ABOUT THE BEACHES AND THE HUT THAT HE HAD LEFT BEHIND. HE DREAMED OF SOARING UP AND DOWN THE PACIFIC COAST LINE. THE THRILL OF SOARING WOULD ALWAYS BE HIS FONDEST MEMORY.

HE WOULD MISS ALL OF THE ACTION AT THE BEACHES. ESPECIALLY THE PARTIES ON THE BEACH AND THE PEOPLE THAT HE MET THERE.

HE TOOK OCCASIONAL TRIPS OVER THE MOUNTAINS TO SANTA MONICA BEACH BUT THEY WERE TINY SWELLS AND HE SOON BECAME BORED WITH THEM TOO.

HE WAS FEELING VERY ALONE AND SAD FROM THE LOSS OF THE TREE FORT AND THE LACK OF BIG WAVES.

HE THOUGHT TO HIMSELF OH WELL: NO MATTER WHERE YOU GO.

NOW IT WAS TIME FOR HIM TO EXPAND HIS HORIZONS, AND LOOK FOR ANOTHER ADVENTURE.

HE DISCOVERED A GROUP OF PEOPLE CALLED HIPPIES. THEY HAD SUCH A FREE LIFESTYLE THAT MILES DECIDED THAT HE WANTED TO CHECK IT OUT FOR HIMSELF.

HE USED TO TAKE TRIPS OUT TO GRIFFITH PARK OBSERVATORY TO PARTAKE IN THE FREE CONCERTS THERE. HE MET A COUPLE OF SWEET GIRLS THERE THAT TURNED HIM ON TO POT.

HE COULDN'T BELIEVE HOW COOL IT WAS TO EAT. THE MUNCHIES WERE OUTRAGEOUS AND

THE SEX WAS SOMETHING THAT HE HAD ONLY DREAMED IT MIGHT BE.

HE LEARNED THE MEANING OF BEING A HIPPIE! HIS GRANDPA SAID THAT HIS DEFINITION OF A HIPPIE WAS SOMEONE WHO LOOKED LIKE TARZAN, WALKED LIKE JANE AND SMELLED LIKE CHEETAH.

THE FLOWER CHILD MOVEMENT OF THE 60'S WAS A WORLD OF WONDER FOR HIM. "THINKING" REALLY WAS THE BEST WAY TO TRAVEL.

HE TOOK WAY MORE L.S.D. THAN HE EVER SHOULD HAVE AND EVEN VOLUNTEERED FOR SOME L.S.D. EXPERIMENTS AT THE LOCAL COLLEGE AT U.C.L.A. AFTER HE TURNED 18 YEARS OLD.

HE FINALLY FOUND A WAY TO SOAR LIKE HE DID WHEN HE WAS A KID OR AT LEAST TO FLOAT AROUND THE ROOM.

NONE OF THOSE DRUGS WERE ANYWHERE NEAR AS GOOD AS THOSE DREAMS WERE.

IT SEEMED THAT THE MORE DRUGS THAT HE DID THE LESS THAT HE COULD HAVE A QUALITY DREAM. THE DREAMS OF OLD WERE FADING FAST!

JUST ABOUT ALL THAT THE HALLUCINATIONS FROM THE L.S.D. DID, WAS TO MAKE WALLS, RUGS, HAIR, TREES, AND JUST ABOUT EVERYTHING ELSE LOOK LIKE THEY WERE BREATHING. YOU COULD EVEN HEAR THEM BREATHE.

SOME BUDDIES OF HIS HAD A HOUSE OUT IN CHATSWORTH.

IT WAS NICKNAMED "THE OWENSMOUTH HOUSE". IT WAS A REAL COOL PLACE TO PARTY.

THEY ALWAYS HAD BANDS THERE OR AT THE VERY LEAST A BUNCH OF GUYS JAMMING TOGETHER.
THERE WERE TWO HOUSES ON THE PROPERTY. THE FRONT MAIN HOUSE WAS LIKE A PALACE AND NONE OF THE PARTY PEOPLE WERE ALLOWED IN THAT HOUSE AT ALL. THE GUEST HOUSE OUT BACK WAS MAINLY FOR FAMILY MEMBERS.
THERE ALSO WAS A HUGE WORKSHOP/ GARAGE WITH A KITCHEN AND BATHROOM ATTACHED. THAT WAS THE PARTY ROOM AND IT WAS JUST OUTSIDE TO THE SWIMMING POOL AREA.
THAT WAS WHERE YOU CRASHED IF YOU WERE TOO STONED TO DRIVE HOME. IT WAS KIND OF A THREE TIERED THING. IF THE COPS CAME TO THE FRONT HOUSE THEN THE GUEST HOUSE AND THE PARTY HOUSE WERE WARNED AND THEY HAD PLENTY OF TIME TO PUT THINGS AWAY.
THESE GUYS WERE THE LOCAL CONNECTIONS FOR EVERY DRUG THAT YOU COULD EVER WANT! THEY WERE "THE" SAN FERNANDO VALLEY CONNECTION.
IN THE MID TO LATE 60'S IF YOU TOOK L.S.D., MESCALINE, SPEED, OR SMOKED POT! IT PROBABLY CAME FROM THEM.
I GUESS THAT WAS HOW THEY AFFORDED THAT HOUSE.
ONE OF THE HUNDREDS OF PARTY'S THAT MILES WENT TO THERE WAS A CHOCOLATE MESCALINE CAPPING PARTY.
MILES HAD DONE SO MANY HALLUCINOGENIC DRUGS THAT HE DIDN'T REALLY GET OFF ON THEM VERY WELL ANY MORE.

SO THE GUYS AT THE OWENSMOUTH HOUSE WOULD PUT HIM IN CHARGE OF CAPPING. HE USUALLY KEPT HIS WITS ABOUT HIM.

ALL OF THE GUYS THAT WERE CAPPING, WORE SCARVES OVER THEIR NOSES AND MOUTHS AND PUT BALLOONS OVER THEIR FINGERTIPS, TO KEEP FROM GETTING HIGH FROM OSMOSIS AND BREATHING THE DUST. IT ONLY WORKED FOR A LITTLE WHILE BEFORE EVERYBODY WAS WASTED.

MILES RODE HIS MOTORCYCLE OVER TO THE HOUSE BECAUSE HE FIGURED THAT HE WASN'T GOING TO HAVE TO DRIVE ANYWHERE THAT NIGHT BECAUSE OF WHAT HE WAS DOING FOR THEM.

HE SPENT MOST OF HIS TIME THERE ANYWAY. HE WAS USUALLY VERY CONSCIENTIOUS ABOUT GETTING STONED AND DRIVING. THAT WAS A DEFINITE NEGATIVE FOR HIM.

THEY WERE ALMOST THROUGH CAPPING UP THE MESCALINE WHEN SOMEONE PASSED HIM A JOINT. IT WASN'T LIKE ANYTHING THAT HE HAD EVER SMOKED BEFORE. IT TASTED LIKE SPEARMINT AND WHEN YOU WALKED ACROSS THE FLOOR IT WAS LIKE YOU WERE FLOATING. SORT OF LIKE A GHOST. YOU COULDN'T FEEL YOUR FEET TOUCHING THE FLOOR. YOU KIND OF HOVERED AROUND.

SOME FOOL THAT WAS AT THE CAPPING PARTY BROKE THE GOLDEN RULE OF THE HOUSE! HE LEFT THE PARTY AND WALKED DOWN THE STREET TO A CONVENIENCE STORE TO GET SOME MUNCHIES.

WHEN HE GOT THERE HE GOT PARANOID AND CALLED THE COPS OR THEY STOPPED HIM IN THE PARKING LOT! WHO REALLY KNOWS THE TRUTH. THE GUY THAT WENT WITH HIM TO MAKE SURE HE DIDN'T SCREW UP CALLED THE HOUSE AND TOLD THEM WHAT HE HAD DONE. THEY KNEW FOR SURE THAT THE COPS WERE COMING THIS TIME!

WELL IT WAS HELL AT THE OWENSMOUTH HOUSE AFTER THAT! THEY SCRAMBLED TO PUT AWAY ALL OF THE STUFF INTO THE STASH SPOTS AND EVERYBODY TOOK OFF. IT WAS A GOOD THING FOR THEM THAT THEY DIDN'T HAVE DRUG SNIFFING DOGS BACK IN THOSE DAYS.

MILES WAS REAL STONED FROM ALL OF THE MESCALINE AND THE P.C.P. OR ANIMAL TRANQUILIZERS THAT HE HAD JUST SMOKED.

NOW HE HAD TO TRY AND GET BACK TO VAN NUYS FROM CHATSWORTH ON HIS MOTORCYCLE.

HE DID NOT LOOK FORWARD TO IT.

HE STARTED OUT O.K., IN FACT IT WAS ALMOST PLEASURABLE. HE MADE IT DOWN THE FREEWAY TO HIS EXIT AND NOTICED THAT HIS HANDLEBARS WERE BEGINNING TO BEND A LITTLE.

THERE WAS NOTHING THAT HE COULD DO BUT TO KEEP ON GOING. THE FURTHER THAT HE WENT THE MORE THAT THE HANDLEBARS WERE BENDING. HE FINALLY ROUNDED THE LAST CORNER AND WAS ON HIS OWN STREET. NOW HE WAS LAYING ON THE GAS TANK AND WAS BARELY ABLE TO REACH THE PEDALS OR THE HANDLEBARS ANYMORE.

HE WAS IN LOW GEAR WHEN HE DROVE THROUGH THE GARAGE DOOR AND FELL OVER ON TO THE GARAGE FLOOR.

HE MADE IT! DON'T KNOW HOW BUT HE MADE IT! WHEN HE FINALLY GOT UP HE NOTICED THAT THE HANDLE BARS WERE NOT BENT! STRANGE. HOW IN THE HELL DID THAT HAPPEN? IT WAS A PRETTY TRIPPY DAY.

ROUND HOUSE

ON SOME OF THE TRIPS OVER COLDWATER CANYON DRIVE TO SANTA MONICA BLVD. HE NOTICED THAT THERE WAS A COOL 4-STORY ROUND HOUSE. THERE WAS A FOR RENT SIGN ON IT. IT WAS PRETTY PRICEY BUT IT HAD TWELVE MASTER SUITES, AND TWO KITCHENS.
IN THE MIDDLE OF THE HOUSE AT GROUND LEVEL WAS AN INDOOR SWIMMING POOL, AND THAT POOL WAS CONNECTED TO AN EVEN LARGER OUTDOOR POOL. KIND OF LIKE A BIG HOUR GLASS. THERE WERE HUGE PATIO'S AROUND TWO THIRDS OF THE HOUSE. THERE WAS A PAIR OF SLIDING GLASS DOORS THAT KEPT THE COLD AIR OUT, AS WELL AS KEEPING THE HOT AIR OUT IN THE SUMMER MONTHS. MILES REALLY WANTED TO RENT THIS PLACE.
HE STARTED OUT WITH 11 OF HIS MOST TRUST WORTHY FRIENDS, THEY WOULD SHARE ALL EXPENSES ON THE HOUSE.
WITH THE UTILITIES INCLUDED, IT CAME TO ONE HUNDRED DOLLARS A MONTH EACH. IT

SOUNDED LIKE A HELL OF A DEAL. THEY HAD PARTIES ALL OF THE TIME, WITH BANDS. PEOPLE FROM ALL AROUND HEARD ABOUT THE HOUSE AND DROPPED IN OCCASIONALLY.

MILES MADE HIS SHARE OF THE MONEY BY RUNNING TRIPS FOR THE OWENSMOUTH HOUSE.

THINGS WENT WELL FOR QUITE A WHILE. AS TIME WENT BY THE COST INCREASED TO TWO HUNDRED A MONTH EACH BECAUSE NOW THEY ONLY HAD SIX PEOPLE AND AS IT TURNED OUT THAT WAS MUCH BETTER.

NOT AS MANY PERSONALITIES TO DEAL WITH AND MUCH MORE ROOM TO BOUNCE AROUND IN THE HOUSE.

THE PARTIES WERE STILL GREAT! AND THERE WERE GIRLS HANGING AROUND ALL OF THE TIME.

THE HOUSE WAS THE COOLEST THING THAT HE HAD EVER GOTTEN INTO WITH OTHER PEOPLE.

THERE STARTED TO BE OCCASIONAL BATTLES OVER WHO WAS TO DO THE CLEANING AROUND THE HOUSE.

NATURALLY EVERYONE HAD TO CLEAN THEIR OWN TWO ROOMS BUT WHEN IT CAME TO THE KITCHEN AND THE REST OF THE HOUSE NOBODY WANTED TO CLEAN THEM EVEN IN EXCHANGE FOR RENT.

THEY FINALLY DECIDED TO GET A GIRL WHO NEEDED A PLACE TO STAY TO COME AND BE A HOUSE KEEPER IN EXCHANGE FOR RENT. SHE COULD HAVE ALL OF THE FOOD THAT SHE NEEDED

TOO. NO EXPENCES FOR HER SHE JUST DID THE CLEANING.

THE GIRL THAT THEY PICKED WAS A BIT OF A HORNY LITTLE SLUT.

IT WASN'T ALL BAD UNTIL PERSONALITIES BEGAN TO CLASH OVER THE GIRL AND WHO'S TURN IT WAS WITH HER.

NOBODY SEEMED TO WANT IT TO BE HER CHOICE.

MILES KNEW THAT THE GREAT HOUSE THAT THEY ALL HAD THE OPPORTUNITY TO BE A PART OF WAS COMING TO AN END.

THE GIRL HAD SLEPT WITH EVERYBODY THERE AND A FEW OF THE OTHER PARTY PEOPLE TOO! SHE MANAGED TO SPREAD THE CLAP TO EVERYONE AT THE HOUSE AT LEAST ONCE BEFORE THEY FINALLY FIGURED OUT WHO HAD IT.

DURING ONE OF THEIR PRETTY NOISY PARTIES TWO OF THE GUYS WERE ARGUING OVER THE GIRL WHEN ALL OF A SUDDEN MILES HEARD GUNSHOTS.

ONE OF THE GUYS WAS SHOOTING AT THE OTHERS FEET WITH A PISTOL THAT HE PICKED UP SOMEWHERE.

MILES WAS PISSED! ONE OF THE CONDITIONS TO LIVING AT THAT HOUSE WAS THAT THERE WOULD BE NO GUNS. GUNS BRING COPS!

THE NEXT THING WAS A SERIES OF EVENTS THAT STARTED WITH THE NEIGHBORS CALLING THE COPS OVER THE GUNSHOTS AND THE NEIGHBORS CALLING THE OWNERS AND HAVING THEM EVICTED FROM THE HOUSE.

THAT WAS THE END OF A WHOLE BUNCH OF FUN.

MILES WAS HAVING A RUN OF VERY POOR LUCK. HE HAD PICKED UP THREE KILOS OF POT FROM THE OWENSMOUTH PEOPLE.

HE HAD JUST THROWN IT IN TO THE BACK OF HIS STATION WAGON AND WAS ON HIS WAY TO DELIVER IT TO ONE OF HIS OWN CONNECTIONS.

HE ROUNDED A CORNER GOING INTO AN ALLEY IN VAN NUYS WHEN THE RED LIGHTS CAME ON BEHIND HIM. HE HAD THROWN THE KILO'S INTO THE BACK. SO HE COULD NOT REACH THEM.

OH WELL HE HAD TO PULL OVER AND TAKE HIS PUNISHMENT! FIRST OFFENCE HE THOUGHT MAYBE IT WON'T BE TOO BAD! MAYBE PROBATION. HIS MIND WAS RACING.

HE PULLED OVER IN TO THE ALLEY AND SHUT THE CAR OFF. THE COP WAS BY HIMSELF AND HE CAME UP TO THE CAR WINDOW AND SAID: IS THAT YOU MILES?

MILES WAS SURPRISED TO SEE ONE OF HIS OLD POT SMOKING BUDDIES FROM HIGH SCHOOL. HE WAS RELIEVED. THE COP SAID: SORRY TO HEAR ABOUT YOU LOOSING THAT HOUSE. I HEAR THAT IT WAS PRETTY COOL.

MILES TOLD HIM THAT A COUPLE OF BAD APPLES CAUSED THEM TO LOOSE THE HOUSE AND NOW THE OWNERS WON'T LET ANY YOUNG PEOPLE RENT THAT HOUSE ANY MORE. IT WAS TORN UP PRETTY BAD.

IT HAD JUST TURNED DARK WHEN HE GOT PULLED OVER AND THEY CHATTED FOR AWHILE WHEN THE COP SHINED HIS FLASHLIGHT INTO THE BACK OF THE WAGON.

HE SAID: WHAT DO YOU GOT IN THE BACK SEAT BUDDY? HE LOOKED AT THE COP AND SAID: NOW WHAT DO YOU THINK BUDDY? THE PACKAGES WERE SHINY RED AND SHINY GREEN CELLOPHANE. OBVIOUSLY FROM MEXICO.

HE SAID: I'LL TELL YOU WHAT. YOU GIVE ME ONE OF THOSE LITTLE PACKAGES YOU GOT THERE AND I'LL LET YOU GO!

NICE GUY! RIPPED HIM OFF FOR $50. WELL THERE IS A COP FOR YOU.

HE TOLD HIM THAT WAS GOOD ENOUGH FOR HIM NOT JUST GOOD! BUT IT WAS GREAT! AND THEY PARTED WAYS.

AS TIME WENT BY, THE BIG CITY WAS GETTING WORSE AND WORSE TO LIVE IN OR MAYBE IT WAS BECAUSE OF ALL OF THE DRUGS.

HE WAS BEGINNING TO GET PARANOID! IT JUST WASN'T AS MUCH FUN AS IT USED TO BE.

HE HAD SCORED SOME ORANGE SUNSHINE FOR ANOTHER ONE OF HIS CONNECTIONS. HE GOT 45 HITS FROM THE OWENSMOUTH HOUSE AND WAS ON THE WAY BACK TO THE VALLEY. IT WAS WAY AFTER DARK AND THE STREETS WERE LIT UP LIKE DAYLIGHT.

HE PULLED INTO A GAS STATION AND GASSED UP HIS WAGON. HE JUMPED BACK INTO THE CAR AND PULLED OUT FROM THE GAS STATION INTO THE LEFT HAND TURN LANE AND WAS SIGNALING

TO TURN LEFT. MILES WAS A VERY SAFE DRIVER NORMALLY. HE HARDLY EVER GOT PULLED OVER.

THE CAR ACROSS THE STREET FROM HIM HIT HIM WITH REAL POWERFUL QUARTZ LIGHTS AND FLASHED THEM ON AND OFF A COUPLE OF TIMES. THIS TEMPORARILY BLINDED HIM,

HE HAD PURPLE SPOTS FLASHING IN HIS EYES LIKE A FLASHBULB WENT OFF IN HIS EYES AND HE WENT AHEAD AND MADE THE LEFT TURN, EXCEPT THAT BECAUSE HE WAS BLINDED BY THE LIGHTS HE RAN OVER THE CENTER DIVIDER. WELL JUST BARELY CLIPPED IT! AND HERE CAME THE RED LIGHTS AGAIN.

THIS CRAP WAS GETTING OLD. HE PULLED OVER WHILE GRABBING THE BAGGIE WITH THE L.S.D. IN IT. HE TORE THE CORNER OFF OF THE BAGGIE WITH HIS TEETH AND SWALLOWED IT!

HE REALLY HADN'T DONE ANYTHING WRONG BUT THE COP WANTED TO FUCK WITH HIM ANYWAY. THE COPS TOLD HIM THAT HIS HEADLIGHTS WERE OFF! THAT'S WHY THEY PULLED HIM OVER.

THE COPS SEARCHED THE CAR AND ALL THAT THEY COULD FIND WAS THIS BAGGIE WITH THE CORNER TORN OFF. THEY GAVE HIM A SOBRIETY CHECK AND HE PASSED, BUT THEY KEPT MESSING WITH HIM FOR ABOUT 45 MINUTES. PLENTY OF TIME FOR THE ACID TO KICK IN.

HE WAS LOOKING AT THE COP WHEN HE NOTICED THAT THE COPS MUSTACHE AND HIS EYEBROWS LOOKED LIKE THEY WERE GROWING, AND BREATHING. HE WAS TRIPPING LIKE HE

HAD NEVER TRIPPED BEFORE. 45 HITS OF ACID.
I GUESS.
HE STARTED LAUGHING AT THE COP WHEN THEY
HANDCUFFED HIM!
THE NEXT THING THAT HE REMEMBERED WAS
THAT HE WAS RIDING HIS MOTORCYCLE AND
HE DIDN'T KNOW WHERE HE WAS GOING AND A
WEEK HAD GONE BY.

BURNED OUT!

THAT WAS ENOUGH FOR HIM! IT WAS TIME FOR A BADLY NEEDED CHANGE OF LIFESTYLE! HE HAD LEFT IN HIS CAR AND WOUND UP ON HIS BIKE. HE HAD TO GO BACK TO THE COP SHOP AND ASK THEM WHAT THEY DID WITH HIS CAR. THEY ASKED HIM. YOU MEAN TO TELL ME THAT YOU DON'T KNOW WHERE YOUR CAR IS YET!

I DON'T KNOW WHAT YOU WERE ON KID BUT YOU MAYBE SHOULD START THINKING ABOUT GETTING STRAIGHT. HE GAVE MILES THE ADDRESS OF THE IMPOUND LOT AND HE GOT HIS CAR BACK.

IT WAS GETTING REAL SCARY OUT THERE BECAUSE IT WAS THE REAL WORLD AND YOU COULD REALLY GET HURT IF YOU WEREN'T CAREFUL.

DRUGS WERE NOT THE ANSWER.

GETTING STRAIGHT MAYBE WASN'T SUCH A BAD IDEA AFTER ALL.

HE WAS AFRAID TO HANG OUT THERE TOO LONG. HE DIDN'T WANT TO END UP LIKE SO MANY OF HIS FRIENDS. BURNED OUT!

HE WAS ALREADY GETTING PRETTY CRISPY. HE NEEDED TO MOVE ON, AND GET CLOSER TO NATURE.

THAT WAS PROBABLY THE BEST THING ABOUT HIS USE OF L.S.D.

HE REALLY BECAME ONE WITH HIMSELF AND ONE WITH NATURE AS WELL. HE STARTED TO MAKE FREQUENT TRIPS OUT TO THE MOJAVE DESERT WHEN THE CENTURY PLANTS WERE BLOOMING JUST TO PARTAKE IN THE TRUE BEAUTY OF THINGS. PLANTS, AND ANIMALS ALIKE.

HE LOVED TO JUST SIT AND ENJOY THE BEAUTY OF THE STARS AT NIGHT AND THE MILLIONS OF SETS OF EYES LOOKING BACK AT HIM IN THE DARKNESS.

HE OCCASIONALLY TOOK SOME ACID WHILE HE WAS OUT THERE. IT KIND OF MADE A DULL TRIP A LITTLE NICER.

EVEN WITH THE BEAUTY OF THE DESERT AND TRIPPING WITH NATURE IT WAS TIME TO TAKE A BREAK!

HE TRIED AND FAILED TO MAKE DRUGS A LIFESTYLE. AT LEAST NOT FULL TIME ANYMORE!

HE LONGED FOR HIS DREAMS AGAIN. HE TRIED SLEEPING IN LATE, HE YEARNED FOR THE DREAMS OF OLD. HE WAS LOOSING IT!

THE DREAMS WERE EVADING HIM. THE DRUGS WERE TOO STRONG!

MOUNTAIN MAN

MILES ASKED HIS MOTHER TO CONTACT HIS DAD FOR HIM BECAUSE HE WANTED TO SEE IF HE COULD GET TO KNOW HIM.
HE HAD VERY LITTLE TIME WITH HIM WHEN HE WAS LITTLE AND DID NOT REALLY KNOW HIM AT ALL!
HIS MOM SPENT SO MANY YEARS LYING TO MILES ABOUT WHAT HIS FATHER DID TO HER. SHE WAS AFRAID THAT MILES WOULD LEARN THE TRUTH.
HIS GRANDMOTHER HAD ALREADY TOLD HIM ABOUT HIS MOTHER SCREWING AROUND WITH HIS FATHERS BEST FRIENDS AND HIS BROTHERS. THAT WAS THEIR SECRET! THAT WAS THE REAL REASON THAT MOM AND DAD DIVORCED.
SHE FINALLY CONSENTED AND CONTACTED HIS FATHER FOR HIM. SHE THOUGHT THAT HE NEEDED A FATHER FIGURE BADLY ENOUGH, TO LET HIM GO. SHE THOUGHT THAT THE DRUGS WERE EATING HIM UP.

SHE COULDN'T SEE THE FOREST FOR THE TREES
THOUGH. HIS SISTER HAD TAKEN SO MANY LEGAL
PRESCRIPTION DRUGS THAT SHE HAD OVERDOSED
OVER A DOZEN TIMES ALREADY. MILES HAD SAVED
HER LIFE ON SEVERAL OCCATIONS ALREADY.
MOM WAS SO NAIVE THAT SHE THOUGHT THAT
IT WAS ACCIDENTAL.
THEY WERE ALL ATTEMPTS AT SUICIDE. IT WAS
REALLY A CRY FOR HELP THAT NEVER CAME.
MOM JUST COULDN'T SEE THROUGH THE LIES.
MOM'S OPINION OF MILES WAS THAT HE WAS A
SCREW-UP. HE WAS THE ONE THAT WAS USING
THE "ILLEGAL" DRUGS.
MOM HAD TOLD THE KIDS THAT THEIR FATHER
DIDN'T WANT ANYTHING TO DO WITH THEM ALL
OF THEIR LIVES. IT WAS FUNNY THOUGH MILES
ALWAYS REMEMBERED THE MYSTERIOUS CHECK
THAT HIS MOM GOT EVERY MONTH.
IT WAS FROM THE FATHER THAT NEVER PAID
CHILD SUPPORT!
THIS WAS ONE LIE THAT SHE WAS GOING TO
HAVE TO BITE HER LIP ON.
MOM FINALLY CONTACTED HIS DAD AND HIS
FATHER WAS MORE THAN HAPPY TO HAVE HIS
BOY COME TO LIVE WITH HIM.
NOW MILES WOULD BECOME A MOUNTAIN
MAN!
HE AND DAD HIT IT OFF REAL GOOD. DAD WAS
A WELDER AND A REAL GOOD MECHANIC WHO
WORKED AT ONE OF THE LOCAL SAWMILLS IN
THE BEAUTIFUL MOUNTAINS OF NORTHERN

CALIFORNIA. PLUMAS COUNTY, NEAR MT. LASSEN.

SOON AFTER MILES ARRIVED DAD SAT HIM DOWN AND BROKE OUT A SHOE BOX. IN IT WAS RECEIPTS FOR ALL OF THE CHILD SUPPORT PAYMENTS THAT HE HAD BEEN MAKING FOR ALL OF THOSE YEARS.

MILES TOLD HIS POP THAT HE HAD ALREADY FIGURED THAT ONE OUT.

DAD SAID: THANK GOD FOR SMALL FAVORS.

MILES SPENT A YEAR WORKING IN THE WOODS AS A LOGGER, CAT SKINNER, CHOKER SETTER AS WELL AS VARIOUS OTHER TRADES. HE WAS TRYING TO FIND HIS CALLING. HE BECAME KIND OF A JACK OF ALL TRADES AND A MASTER OF NONE EXCEPT MAYBE MECHANICS, AND HEAVY EQUIPMENT OPERATOR.

DAD HAD REALLY BECOME A VERY GOOD FRIEND AND TEACHER TO HIM.

HE LOVED THE MOUNTAINS AND THE FRESH AIR AND THE WILDLIFE. HE FELT TRULY AT PIECE THERE. BETTER THAN DRUGS ANY DAY!

THE VIET NAM WAR WAS GOING FULL TILT NOW AND THEY WERE DRAFTING EVERYBODY THAT WASN'T MARRIED WITH CHILDREN.

MILES KNEW THAT HE WOULD BE DRAFTED SOON. HE WAS REAL LOW ON THE LIST FOR THE DRAFT.

HE HATED THE IDEA OF LEAVING THE MOUNTAINS BUT BECAUSE HE HAD LEARNED TO LOVE THEM SO MUCH.

THE MOUNTAINS WERE REALLY WHERE HE BELONGED. HE TOLD DAD THAT HE HAD TO RETURN TO THE VALLEY SO THAT HE COULD ATTEMPT TO GET A SCHOOL INSTEAD OF BEING A GRUNT IN THE MILITARY BECAUSE HE WAS DRAFTED.
HE TRIED THE NAVY FIRST AND THEY TURNED HIM DOWNED BECAUSE OF HIS SCHOOLING. HE THEN TRIED THE AIR FORCE. THE SAME THING HAPPENED THERE TOO!
THE ARMY ONLY WANTED GRUNTS AND THE MARINES WERE WILLING TO LET HIM TAKE AN APTITUDE TEST TO SEE WHAT HE WAS QUALIFIED FOR. SO THAT WAS THE PLAN.

OFF TO WAR!

BECAUSE OF HIS EXTENDED USE OF L.S.D. AND THE FACT THAT HE LOVED ALL THINGS. PLANTS AND ANIMALS ALIKE!
HE HAD BECOME A CONSCIENTIOUS OBJECTOR. THE THOUGHT OF KILLING ANYTHING REALLY BOTHERED HIM.
HE DECIDED TO ENLIST IN ORDER TO GET A SCHOOL. HE DID NOT WANT TO BE A GRUNT!
HE COULDN'T STAND THE THOUGHT OF SOME ASSHOLE TELLING HIM TO GO AND KILL ANOTHER HUMAN BEING.
WHAT IF THEY WERE JUST LIKE HIM AND THEY DIDN'T WANT TO KILL EITHER?
HE JUST HAD TO DO SOMETHING DIFFERENT AND STILL SERVE HIS COUNTRY. ALL OF THE YOUTH OF THOSE DAYS HAD A SENSE OF DUTY TOWARDS THEIR COUNTRY.
EVEN THOUGH HE WAS A BURNED OUT HIPPIE HE STILL LOVED HIS COUNTRY. YOU DON'T HAVE ENOUGH OF THAT WITH TODAY'S YOUTH.

BOOT CAMP WAS HELL FOR A HIPPIE! THEY SHAVED HIS HEAD INCLUDING THE MOLES THAT WERE GROWING THERE.

THE BLOOD RAN DOWN HIS NECK AND CLEAR TO THE FLOOR. HE HEARD THE BARBER SAY WOOPS TWICE. THEY STUFFED A BUNCH OF SULFUR IN TO THE WOUNDS TO STOP THE BLEEDING.

HE TOOK A LOT OF BEATINGS FOR HIS COUNTRY. THAT WAS HIS FIRST AND LAST EXPERIENCE WITH WATER-BOARDING. THEY BEAT HIM SO BADLY THAT THEY CAUSED HIM TO LOOSE 80% OF HIS HEARING. HE NEVER RATTED ON ANYONE AND ADVANCED IN RANK BECAUSE HE HAD KEPT HIS MOUTH SHUT.

HE HAD GOTTEN BOOT CAMP OUT OF THE WAY AND HAD LEARNED HOW PROUD HE WAS TO BE A MARINE. IT WAS REALLY MORE LIKE HE WAS "TERRORIZED" INTO SUBMISSION.

IT WAS FORCED DOWN HIS THROAT IN A BIG WAY BUT THE PRIDE TO HAVE SURVIVED THE WHOLE ORDEAL IS STILL A WONDERFUL THING TODAY.

THE DRILL INSTRUCTOR HAD A KNACK TO BRING OUT THE PRIDE IN THE TROOPS.

IT WAS A SONG THAT THEY SANG TO FEEL THE GLORY OF BEING AN AMERICAN.

IT WAS TO THE TUNE OF "GHOST RIDERS IN THE SKY".

THE DRILL INSTRUCTOR CAME OUT ONE EVENING AND SANG THE SONG. HE TOLD THE RECRUITS TO LEARN IT AND THE NEXT TIME THAT THEY GOT INTO FORMATION THEY HAD TO SING IT.

THEY ALL SAT DOWN THAT EVENING AND LEARNED THE WORDS FROM MEMORY. WE STILL HAVEN'T FORGOTTEN.

MARINE CORPS SONG
YOU CAN HAVE YOUR ARMY KHAKI'S
YOU CAN HAVE YOUR NAVY BLUES
NOW HERE'S ANOTHER UNIFORM I'LL INTRODUCE TO YOU
THIS UNIFORM IS DIFFERENT
IT'S THE FINEST EVER SEEN
THE GERMANS CALLED THEM DEVIL-DOGS
BUT THEIR NAME IS JUST MARINES

THEY TRAINED THEM DOWN IN DIEGO
THE LAND THAT GOD FORGOT
THE MOUNTAINS HIGH, THE RIVERS DRY, THE SUN IS BLAZING HOT
YOU CAN PEEL A MILLION ONIONS, AND TWICE AS MANNY SPUDS
AND WHEN YOU HAVE A LITTLE TIME
YOU MAY EVEN WASH YOUR DUDS

NOW LISTEN GIRLS I'LL TELL YOU, A STORY THAT IS TRUE
GET YOURSELF A GOOD MARINE
THERE IS NOTHING HE CAN'T DO
AND WHEN HE GETS TO HEAVEN
TO SAINT PETER HE WILL TELL
ANOTHER MARINE REPORTING SIR
I'VE SERVED MT TIME IN HELL

IF HE HAD TO DO IT OVER, HE PROBABLY WOULD HAVE GONE TO CANADA.

HE WAS VERY MECHANICAL MINDED, AND WENT FOR A 6300 AVIATION MECHANICS. HE PASSED ALL OF THE LOGIC TESTS, AND QUALIFIED FOR THE SCHOOLING.

HE WAS SHIPPED OUT TO TENNESSEE FOR HIS SCHOOLING.

MARCH EARLY IN THE MORNING, AND SCHOOL ALL AFTERNOON. IT WASN'T UNTIL THE COMPLETION OF THE SCHOOLING THAT HE FINALLY GOT SHORE LEAVE. HE DIDN'T KNOW ANYBODY THERE; SO HE JUST STAYED ON BASE.

HIS TURN TO SHIP OUT CAME AFTER NOT NEAR ENOUGH SCHOOLING.

HE WAS GOING TO DANANG AIR BASE VIET NAM!

HE ARRIVED LATE IN THE EVENING OF THE FIRST DAY. HE COULD HEAR MORTARS, RPGS AND GUNFIRE IN THE DISTANCE. IT WAS NOT A GOOD NIGHTS SLEEP.

THE MORNING CAME LIKE CANNON FIRE! THE SQUAD LEADER CAME IN AND GOT EVERYONE TO THEIR FEET. THEY WERE ALL GOING TO HAVE TO DO MESS DUTY FOR A COUPLE OF DAYS, UNTIL THEY COULD FIGURE OUT WHERE EVERYBODY WAS GOING.

JUST TO KEEP EVERYBODY PSYCHED UP FOR ACTION, THEY HAD EVERYONE JOG AROUND THE MESS HALL TO STAY IN SHAPE. THEY WERE ALL RUNNING TWO BY TWO BY TWO AROUND THE

MESS HALL, WHEN MILES STEPPED ON A FLOOR DRAIN.

HE FELT A SNAP! HE KEPT GOING THAT DAY, BUT WHEN HE GOT UP IN THE MORNING; HE COULD NOT PUT ON HIS BOOT! HIS FOOT WAS SWOLLEN LIKE A BALL.

HE WENT TO THE INFIRMARY WHERE THEY TOLD HIM THAT HE WAS THE LUCKIEST MAN ON BASE.

THEY TOLD HIM THAT HE WAS GOING TO BE PLACED IN CAUSALITY COMPANY, AND WAS GOING BACK TO THE UNITED STATES.

HE TRULY WAS A LUCKY GUY.

HE WAS SENT BACK TO THE UNITED STATES WITHOUT ANY INVOLVEMENT IN THE WAR SO FAR! HE GOT HIS G.E.D. OUT OF THE WAY.

HE HAD MADE LANCE CORPORAL OUT OF BOOT CAMP, AND BECAME THE SERIES HONOR MAN. HE WENT ON TO CORPORAL, AND TO SERGEANT. HE WAS A PRETTY SQUARED AWAY MARINE.

LIFE WAS PRETTY SMOOTH AT CASUALTY CO. MILES BECAME BORED WITH LIFE ON BASE.

HE WAS THANKFUL THAT HE WAS NOT GOING TO SEE ANY ACTION IN THE WAR.

HIS HEARING HAD GOTTEN WORSE FROM ALL OF THE BEATINGS THAT HE HAD RECEIVED IN BOOT CAMP.

HE WAS GOING TO STAY IN CASUALTY COMPANY UNTIL HE WAS DISCHARGED FOR HIS HEARING LOSS.

IT WAS PRETTY LAID BACK, JUST WAITING FOR HIS DISCHARGE. HE MADE SEVERAL NEW FRIENDS WHILE HE WAS THERE.

HE STARTED MAKING TRIPS BACK TO THE OWENSMOUTH HOUSE TO SCORE POT FOR HIS FRIENDS. THEY WERE MOSTLY OFFICERS.

MILES RECEIVED NOTICE THAT HE SHOULD SQUARE AWAY ALL OF HIS DEBTS, AND GET ALL OF THE ADDRESSES FROM HIS FRIENDS, BECAUSE HE WAS GOING HOME!

HE GAVE ALL OF HIS POT PARAPHERNALIA TO A COOK BUDDY OF HIS.

THE IDIOT COOK WENT AWOL THAT DAY, AND WAS SOON AFTERWARDS HE WAS CAUGHT AND ARRESTED FOR A BUNCH OF SEEDS AND STEMS THAT THEY HAD FOUND IN HIS LOCKER.

HE RATTED OUT MILES TO BEAT THE RAP THAT HE WAS CHARGED WITH!

THEY ARRESTED MILES AND CHARGED HIM WITH USE, POSSESSION, AND SALES OF MARIJUANA ON A MILITARY BASE.

SO NOW MILES HAD TO WAIT FOR A TRIAL.

WHILE WAITING FOR TRIAL HE RECEIVED 27 RECOMMENDATIONS FOR PROMOTION BUT THE POWERS TO BE FOUND HIM GUILTY OF ALL CHARGES AND SENTENCED HIM TO 8 MONTHS IN PRISON AND A BAD CONDUCT DISCHARGE.

MILES WAS OUTRAGED WITH ALL THAT HE HAD BEEN THROUGH AND NEVER RATTED ANYONE OUT WHEN HE HAD PLENTY OF GOOD REASON TO DO SO.

HIS GEAR WAS STOWED AWAY AND HE WAS SENT TO PRISON. HE SERVED HIS TIME WITHOUT INCIDENCE.

AFTER HE WAS THROWN INTO THE ICE BOX FOR HIS INITIATION TO PRISON. HE GOT A FULL ON CASE OF PNEUMONIA AND WAS RELEASED FROM THE ICE BOX.

HIS TIME WAS FINALLY UP AND IT WAS TIME TO RECEIVE HIS DISCHARGE. HE WENT BEFORE THE COMPANY COMMANDER.

THE COMMANDER SAID: WHILE LOOKING THROUGH YOUR MILITARY RECORD I SEE HERE THAT YOU ACCOMPLISHED QUITE A BIT.

HE TOLD MILES THAT HE SHOULD BE PROUD OF WHAT HE HAD ACHIEVED SINCE HE WAS IN THE CORPS. HE WAS A SQUARED AWAY MARINE AND HE HAD RECEIVED 27 RECOMMENDATIONS FOR PROMOTION.

HE WAS HOLDING THE DISCHARGE THAT MILES WAS PRAYING FOR. HE LOOKED MILES IN THE EYE AND SAID: I AM TEARING UP THIS DISCHARGE AND PUTTING YOU BACK TO DUTY.

ALL OF THE CHARGES HAVE BEEN DROPPED. YOU WILL LOSE ALL OF THE RANK THAT I KNOW YOU WORKED SO HARD FOR AND ALL OF THE PAY.

MILES SAID: WITH ALL DUE RESPECT SIR, YOU SHOULDN'T HAVE DONE THAT.

HE SENT HIM OFF TO ANOTHER COMPANY TO BE SHIPPED OUT ON THE FOLLOWING WEEK AS A GRUNT!

THERE WAS NO WAY THAT MILES WAS GOING TO BE A GRUNT!

MILES WENT AWOL THAT NIGHT! HE HAD A FRIEND IN THE LEGAL DEPARTMENT ON BASE. HE TOLD MILES THAT THE ONLY WAY THAT HE COULD GET AWAY FROM HAVING TO GO TO MILITARY PRISON AGAIN WAS TO COMMIT A FELONY IN A CIVILIAN TOWN AND DO AT LEAST 8 MONTHS IN JAIL.

BACK HOME

MILES WENT WITH THAT THOUGHT PATTERN.
HE GOT HIS CAR WHICH HAD BEEN STORED OFF
BASE AND PROCEEDED TO PLAN HIS RELEASE
FROM THE MILITARY.
EVEN THOUGH IT WOULD BE VERY EMBARRASSING
TO HIS FATHER HE PLANNED A ROBBERY AT A
SMALL LIQUOR STORE NEAR WHERE HIS DAD
LIVED. KELLY'S LIQUOR STORE, IN CANYON DAM
CALIFORNIA, NEXT TO LAKE ALMANOR.
HE TOOK A BIG KNIFE AND WENT TO THE PHONE
BOOTH RIGHT OUTSIDE OF THE LIQUOR STORE
AND CALLED THE COPS ON HIMSELF. THEN HE
WENT INSIDE AND ROBBED THEM.
HE MADE IT ABOUT TWO MILES BEFORE HE RAN
INTO THE ROAD BLOCK.
THEY TOOK HIM TO JAIL AND CHARGED HIM
WITH ARMED ROBBERY. HE WAS GIVEN A COURT
APPOINTED LAWYER WHO WAS KIND OF LIKE
MATLOCK!
MILES TOLD HIM ABOUT THE TREATMENT THAT
HE RECEIVED IN THE MILITARY AND THE FACT

THAT HE NEVER RATTED ANYONE OUT AND ABOUT HOW HE WAS RAILROADED INTO PRISON AND STRIPPED OF ALL PAY AND RANK AND THEN PUT BACK TO DUTY AS A GRUNT EVEN THOUGH HE WAS A CONSCIENTIOUS OBJECTOR TO THE WAR!

THE LAWYER WAS OUTRAGED AT WHAT OUR GOVERNMENT HAD DONE TO HIM.

HE TOLD MILES THAT HE COULD GET HIM OFF OF ALL CHARGES AND BACK INTO THE MILITARY IF HE WANTED.

MILES TOLD HIM "NO WAY" I NEED TO BE CONVICTED OF A FELONY AND DO 8 MONTHS IN JAIL. THE LAWYER WAS A GREAT MAN!

MILES RECEIVED HIS DISCHARGE. THIS TIME IT WAS AN UNDESIRABLE DISCHARGE. LIKE A "C" ON YOUR REPORT CARD.

HE SERVED HIS TIME IN JAIL. HE BECAME A TRUSTEE AT THE JAIL. AFTER WHAT THE MILITARY HAD DONE TO HIM THEY COULDN'T BELIEVE THAT HE HAD SUCH A GOOD ATTITUDE TOWARD LIFE.

HE FINISHED HIS TIME IN JAIL WITH EVERYBODY THERE BEING HIS FRIENDS.

LATER THE CHARGES WERE REDUCED TO A MISDEMEANOR. MILES DID NOT EVEN HAVE TO ASK HIS LAWYER TO DO IT.

HE WENT BACK TO WORK IN THE WOODS FOR THE SUMMER MONTHS, AND TO WORK IN UTAH AS A LIFT OPERATOR IN THE WINTER MONTHS. HE ALWAYS KEPT A STEADY JOB.

HE GOT INTO SKIING THE DEEP POWDER OF UTAH. WHAT A GREAT FEELING SKIING THROUGH THE UNTRACKED POWDER.

HE WAS A TOP TOWER LIFT OPERATOR. HE DID THAT SO HE WOULD BE ABLE TO GET MORE SKIING IN. IT WAS TURNING INTO A GREAT LIFESTYLE. THE WORK WAS EASY AND THE SKIING WAS GREAT!

HE WOULD GO TO THE LODGES TO PARTY IN THE EVENINGS, AND TO MEET THE GIRLS THAT WORKED IN THEM.

HE RAN INTO THIS REAL CUTE REDHEAD.

SHE WAS A FIERY LITTLE THING. THEY WERE IN BED ON THE FIRST NIGHT AND EVERY NIGHT AFTER THAT!

WITHIN TWO WEEKS THEY WERE MARRIED AND BEFORE HE EVEN HAD TIME TO THINK ABOUT WHAT HE WAS DOING SHE GOT PREGNANT. HIS MOM SET THEM UP WITH AN APARTMENT IN SALT LAKE CITY WHERE HE GOT A JOB AS A PAINTER.

HE WORKED FOR A FEW MONTHS AND SAVED UP SOME MONEY SO THAT THEY COULD MAKE THE MOVE BACK TO THE MOUNTAINS IN CALIFORNIA.

MILES WANTED TO MEET HER PARENTS SO THEY TOOK A TRIP TO IDAHO SO THAT SHE COULD SEE THEM TO SAY "LOOK AT ME" I'M MARRIED.

MILES AND HER DAD STRUCK UP A PRETTY GOOD FRIENDSHIP. HE HAD TOLD MILES THAT HE WAS A LIFER IN THE MILITARY AND THAT HIS DAUGHTER HAD EMBARRASSED HIM ON MANY OCCASIONS.

SHE WAS THE PUNCH CARD LITTLE WHORE AT EVERY BASE THAT HE SERVED ON.

HE WAS TRULY SURPRISED THAT SHE ENDED UP WITH SOMEBODY OF A WHITE PERSUASION.

MILES WAS SHOCKED BUT NOT COMPLETELY SURPRISED AT ALL!

THEY FINISHED THEIR VISIT. SHE DIDN'T EVEN HUG THEM GOODBYE.

ON HIS WEDDING DAY THEY WERE FUCKING LIKE A COUPLE OF MINKS. THEY WERE ON THE FIFTH TIME AROUND.

HE ASKED HER IF SHE WAS SORE?BECAUSE HE SURE WAS.

SHE SAID: NO WAY! I USED TO RUN WITH A BUNCH OF BIKERS BEFORE I MET YOU. SHE SAID PROUDLY, I HAVE DONE AS MANY AS FORTY AT A TIME! I NEVER GOT SORE!

MILES THOUGHT TO HIMSELF; FUCKING BIKERS!

SHE MUST HAVE BEEN LIKE LEATHER INSIDE! THEY SAY THAT YOU CAN'T WEAR IT OUT BUT I DON'T KNOW.

MILES TRIED TO MAKE IT WORK! HE STUCK IT OUT FOR ALMOST THREE YEARS THEY HAD ANOTHER KID THIS TIME A GIRL. SHE EVEN HAD AN I.U.D. AND STILL GOT PREGNANT AGAIN.

SHE HAD TRAINED HIM TO FUCK HER PRETTY GOOD BUT HE STILL COULDN'T KEEP UP WITH HER.

HE GOT A VASECTOMY TO ENSURE THAT HE DID NOT HAVE ANY MORE KIDS AND THAT WAS THE OPPORTUNITY THAT HE NEEDED.

WHILE HE WAS WORKING TWO JOBS TRYING TO SUPPORT THEM HE WOULD COME HOME BETWEEN JOBS AND PORK THE OLE LADY BECAUSE SHE SAID THAT SHE WASN'T GETTING ENOUGH.
HEAVEN HELP HIM, SHE GOT PREGNANT AGAIN! IT WAS A BLESSING REALLY. IT WAS A WAY OUT!
SHE LOVED IT! SHE WAS A HOPELESS NYMPHOMANIAC. IT TURNED OUT THAT SHE WAS TOO MUCH FOR HIM AND HE WOUND UP HAVING A MAJOR HEART ATTACK AT THE RIPE OLD AGE OF TWENTY-SIX. DIVORCE WAS THE ONLY ANSWER FOR HIS HEALTH.
HE TRIED TO MAKE IT IN TOWN BUT EVERY TIME THAT HE WANTED TO SEE THE KIDS. HE HAD TO SCREW HER FIRST! SOME PEOPLE MIGHT SAY WHAT A GREAT DEAL BUT MILES WAS DIEING.

GONE SKIING

HE BECAME A VEGETARIAN TO TRY AND GET HIS HEALTH BACK THEN HE BECAME A VERY PHYSICAL AND EXTREMELY ACTIVE PERSON AGAIN. NOT THAT TWO JOBS WEREN'T ENOUGH.

HE WENT BACK TO UTAH FOR SOME BADLY NEEDED REST FROM FUCKING. EVEN AFTER HE HAD LEFT HER AND HE HAD OTHER GIRLFRIENDS.

SHE STILL WANTED TO FUCK HIM. THOSE WERE HER CONDITIONS JUST SO HE COULD SEE HIS KIDS. SHE EVEN HAD ANOTHER BOYFRIEND ALREADY AND SHE STILL WANTED TO FUCK HIM.

HE HAD TO GET OUT JUST TO SAVE HIS OWN LIFE! ALL OF IT WAS AT THE EXPENSE OF HIS KIDS.

IT REMINDED HIM OF WHEN HE WAS A KID. IT WENT FULL CIRCLE AGAIN.

HE LOVED THE ADVENTURE OF SKIING THE UNTRACKED POWDER IN THE MOUNTAINS OF UTAH, BUT AT LAST THAT WASN'T ENOUGH! HE

TRIED ICE CLIMBING BUT THAT WASN'T ENOUGH EITHER!

HE MET A BEAUTIFUL GIRL NAMED CONNIE SHE WAS THE DAUGHTER OF THE OWNER OF THE SKI RESORT.

CONNIE WAS A REAL SWEETHEART. MILES COULD HAVE REALLY LOVED HER BUT THE TIMING WAS ALL WRONG.

HE NEEDED TO SEEK REAL ADVENTURE BEFORE HE DIED! HIS FATHER DIED AT THE VERY EARLY AGE OF 47 AND SO DID HIS GRANDFATHER. MILES FIGURED THAT HE PROBABLY ONLY HAD TWENTY OR SO YEARS LEFT.

HE NEEDED TO CRAM 20 YEARS WORTH OF ADVENTURE INTO AS FEW YEARS AS POSSIBLE OR WHATEVER YEARS HE HAD REMAINING.

ONE WITH THE EAGLES

HE RAN INTO A GROUP OF FOLKS THAT WERE INTO HIKING AND HANG GLIDING. THEY TOOK HIM TO A LOCAL BEGINNER HILL AND THEY WERE AMAZED AT HOW FAST THAT HE CAUGHT ON.
THEY ASKED HIM IF HE WAS SURE THAT HE HAD NEVER DONE IT BEFORE?
HE TOLD THEM, ONLY IN MY DREAMS! MILES GOT SO ADDICTED TO THE SPORT, THAT HE WENT AND BOUGHT HIS OWN KITE.
IT WAS A DELTA WING DESIGN, WITH A SUPER LIGHT WEIGHT CARBON FIBER FRAMEWORK. IT WAS A STATE-OF-THE-ART KITE IN THOSE DAYS.
THEY WOULD TAKE TRIPS WHERE THE WIND HAD A LOT OF UP DRAFTS AND SMOOTH ROLLING HILLS.
MILES SOARED LIKE AN EAGLE IN THE UP DRAFTS. THE FEELINGS WERE ONLY MATCHED BY THE DREAMS THAT HE USED TO HAVE, AS A YOUNG BOY. NO! THE DREAMS WERE STILL BETTER!

THE THRILL OF SOARING WAS BORNE INTO HIM.
HE WAS DESTINED TO SOAR WITH THE EAGLES
INTO ETERNITY. HE HAD HIS OWN DELTA WING
GLIDER NOW THAT COULD BE BROKEN DOWN FAR
ENOUGH TO TAKE IT ON LONG HIKES OR TO BE
STORED IF NECESSARY.
ONE MORNING HE AND HIS SOARING BUDDIES
LOADED THEIR TRUCK WITH THE SUPPLIES FOR
ALL OF THEM EXCEPT FOR ONE. HE WAS THE
DRIVER OF THE TRUCK.
THEY WANTED TO GO TO THE CLIFFS OVER THE
TOP OF CRYSTAL LAKE.
IT WAS BETWEEN QUINCY CALIFORNIA WHICH
WAS THE COUNTY SEAT AND TAYLORSVILLE
WHERE THEY ALWAYS HAD THE RODEO ON THE
FOURTH OF JULY.
THE CLIFFS WERE ABOUT A THOUSAND FEET
HIGHER THAN THE LAKE ITSELF. THE LAKE WAS AT
6000 FEET AND IT WAS ABOUT THREE HUNDRED
YARDS ACROSS THE LAKE.
THE OLD TALES ABOUT THE CLIFFS WAS THAT
THE INDIANS WOULD DIVE OFF OF THOSE
CLIFFS.
IT WAS THEIR WAY OF FLYING WITH THE
EAGLES.
AS FAR AS THE TALES GO MOST OF THEM DIDN'T
MAKE IT.
MILES LOVED TO DIVE, BUT THAT WAS WAY TOO
FAR OF A DIVE FOR HIM TOO.
THE LAKE WAS AN EXTINCT VOLCANO. IT WAS
MEASURED AT 7000 FEET DEEP. AMAZING. 1000
FEET BELOW SEA LEVEL AND THE WATER WAS

CRYSTAL CLEAR. THE LAKE WAS NEVER STOCKED WITH FISH BUT HAD SOME OF THE LARGEST GERMAN BROWN TROUT THAT HE HAD EVER SEEN. IT WAS FED BY UNDERGROUND CURRENTS.

THEY ALL WENT TO THE CLIFFS AND ONE AT A TIME THEY RAN OFF OF THE CLIFF AND CAUGHT THE UP DRAFTS. THE DRAFTS WOULD SOMETIMES TAKE THEM, AS MUCH AS 1000 FEET HIGHER. THE RUSH WAS MUCH BETTER THAN ANY DRUGS. THIS WAS THE BEGINNING OF A WHOLE SUMMER OF EXCITEMENT!

THEIR LAST TRIP TO THE TOP, WAS IN THE FALL. THE AIR WAS VERY STILL THAT DAY. MILES RAN OFF OF THE CLIFFS THAT DAY AND DROPPED ABOUT 500 FEET BEFORE HE GOT ENOUGH SPEED TO GET ACROSS THE LAKE AND DOWN THE OTHER SIDE INTO THE INDIAN VALLEY WHERE HE LIVED. THERE WAS USUALLY ENOUGH UP DRAFTS TO HANG OUT OVER THE LAKE FOR AWHILE BUT NOT ON THIS DAY! THEY ALL CONGREGATED AT THE BOTTOM OF THE HILL BUT ONE OF THEM DIDN'T SHOW.

AS IT TURNED OUT THAT HIS GLIDER FOLDED UP RIGHT AFTER HE JUMPED OFF OF THE CLIFF AND HE CRASHED ON THE ROCKS AT THE BOTTOM, 1000 FEET DOWN. THE FOREST SERVICE PUT UP A CABLE THE FULL LENGTH OF THE CLIFFS. THERE WERE WAYS AROUND IT BUT NOT REALLY WORTH IT!

THEY HAD A WONDERFUL MEMORIAL SERVICE FOR HIM. HE WILL ALWAYS RIDE HIGH IN THE SKY

FOREVER! THE GROUP JUST WENT THEIR OWN WAYS AND LOST TOUCH WITH EACH OTHER.
HE TRULY LOVED SOARING BUT IT WAS MUCH TOO DANGEROUS BY YOURSELF. HE CAREFULLY PACKED HIS GLIDER IN PLASTIC AND CANVAS AND PUT IT AWAY FOR LATER.

TAKE ME TO THE RIVER

MILES LOVED THE ICY COLD WATER OF THE FEATHER RIVER AND MANY TIMES HE WOULD GO DOWN THE RIVER TO A PLACE CALLED, "WHITE ROCKS". HE WOULD PRACTICE HIS HIGH DIVING THERE.

HE MET A LOT OF DOWN TO EARTH PEOPLE ON THE RIVER. IT WAS A WHOLE DIFFERENT CLASS OF PEOPLE DOWN RIVER.

WHEN HE RETURNED TO THE FEATHER RIVER, HE RAN INTO A GUY NAMED MARK. MARK HAD 22 ACRES OF BOTTOMLAND ALONG THE FEATHER RIVER. HE HAD SEVERAL FAMILIES THAT WERE LIVING ON THE PROPERTY WITH SEVERAL DIFFERENT RESIDENCES ON THE PROPERTY. IT WAS A REAL FUN PLACE TO BE. IT WAS SORT OF A COMMUNE.

THERE WERE ALWAYS B.B.Q'S AND SKINNY DIPPING PARTIES GOING ON. THEY PLAYED A FORM OF VOLLEY BALL THAT THEY LOVINGLY CALLED "JUNGLE BALL".

THERE WERE ALL HI-ENERGY TYPE PEOPLE LIVING THERE. THEY HAD THIS GREAT COMMUNITY GARDEN IN WHICH EVERYONE SHARED THE WORK ON.

THEY HAD TO HAVE AN EIGHT FOOT HIGH FENCE AROUND IT, IN ORDER TO KEEP THE DEER FROM RIPPING THEM OFF. IT WAS WELL WORTH THE EFFORT. THEY HAD A WONDERFUL GARDEN.

MARK HAD THIS OLD BROKEN DOWN CHICKEN COUP SLASH BARN ON THE PROPERTY, AND TOLD MILES THAT HE COULD LIVE THERE IF HE WANTED TO FIX IT UP. MARK TOLD HIM THAT EVEN IF HE MOVED, AFTER FINISHING HIS HOME. HE COULD HAVE ALL OF THE RENT FROM IT FOR 1 YEAR, JUST FOR BUILDING IT! MILES AGREED AND STARTED WORKING ON IT. HE SPENT MONTHS GOING UP TO OLD MINING SHACKS AND BRINGING DOWN THE BOARDS TO FINISH HIS CABIN.

THE PEOPLE WHO LIVED ON THE PROPERTY WERE HAVING A PARTY, WHEN HE MET THIS BEAUTIFUL YOUNG WOMAN NAMED ANGELA. WHAT A KNOCK OUT! SHE EVEN SEEMED TO HAVE SOME MORALS. NOTHING LIKE THE GIRLS THAT HE KNEW IN THE PAST.

HE STRUCK UP A WONDERFUL RELATIONSHIP WITH ANGELA. THEY SPENT QUITE A BIT OF TIME TOGETHER. SHE HELPED HIM WITH TEARING DOWN OLD BARNS, AND RE-BUILDING THE OLD CHICKEN COUP THAT THEY WOULD LIVE IN TOGETHER.

THEY FOUND AN OLD MINING SHACK WHICH HAD BEEN ABANDONED. IT HAD A WOOD BURNING

COOK STOVE IN IT. HE AND ANGEE MADE SEVERAL TRIPS UP TO THE OLD SHACK BRINGING THAT OLD STOVE OUT, A PIECE AT A TIME. IT WAS VERY HEAVY. THEY WORKED ON THE CABIN ALL SPRING AND SUMMER AND INTO THE NEXT FALL.

ANGELA WAS THE MOST BEAUTIFUL WOMAN THAT HE HAD EVER KNOWN, AT LEAST, ANY WOMAN THAT WAS HIS.

HE TOLD HIS BUDDY MARK THAT HE WAS AFRAID THAT HE WAS LOOSING HER .

HE TOLD MILES THAT YOU CAN'T LOOSE SOMETHING THAT YOU DON'T ALREADY HAVE!

THAT HURT A LITTLE, BUT NEVER THE LESS SHE BEGAN GROWING DISTANT.

SHE DIDN'T THINK MUCH OF MILES SMOKING POT!

SHE STARTED TAKING CLASSES AT THE COMMUNITY COLLEGE. SHE KEPT FINDING MORE AND MORE EXCUSES TO BE AWAY.

SHE WAS CRAWLING INTO A SHELL AND WAS VERY DEPRESSED AS WELL AS DEPRESSING TO BE AROUND.

MILES WAS PARTYING WITH MARK AND SOME OF HIS OTHER FRIENDS ONE AFTERNOON. THE SUBJECT WAS SAILING.

THEY STARTED TALKING ABOUT MULTI-HULLS, WHEN HE PERKED UP WITH ANTICIPATION.

THE CONVERSATION TURNED TO A SERIOUS DISCUSSION OF HOW THEY WOULD CARRY THIS TO THE NEXT LEVEL.

NOW THIS WAS POSSIBLY THE ADVENTURE THAT MILES WAS THINKING ABOUT! DREAMING ABOUT! WAITING FOR ALL ALONG.

MARK HAD A NICKNAME FOR EVERYONE HE KNEW. HE REFERRED TO MILES AS MILO; OR IF A POT DEAL WAS INVOLVED, HE WAS THEN REFERRED TO AS M.O.M. " MILES OSCAR MCGEARY ".

MILES STILL HAD CONNECTIONS IN L.A. AREA, WHERE HE WOULD GO TO, WHENEVER THEY NEEDED POT. IT WAS $50.00 A KILO BACK IN THOSE DAYS. HE ALWAYS WENT TO THE OWENSMOUTH HOUSE PEOPLE. IT WAS ALWAYS A FAST AND EASY SCORE.

MILES WAS REALLY GETTING DEEP INTO HIS FEELINGS FOR ANGELA. THEY WERE EVEN DISCUSSING MILES GETTING HIS VASECTOMY REVERSED. EVEN WITH EVERYTHING THAT HE WAS WILLING TO DO FOR THEIR RELATIONSHIP, ANGELA SEEMED TO BE DRIFTING A LITTLE MORE EVERY DAY. SHE WAS A PRETTY GOOD CHRISTIAN GIRL, AND MILES EXPERIENCE WITH THE DRUG WORLD SORT OF SCARED HER A BIT.

MILO LOVED REGGAE MUSIC. REAL STRANGE FOR A WHITE GUY BACK IN THOSE DAYS AND THE THOUGHT OF SAILING AROUND THE ISLANDS REALLY INTRIGUED HIM. BUT WHAT ABOUT ANGELA?

LET'S GO SAILING "THE LONG ROAD SOUTH".

MILO, MARK, AND BOBBO DISCUSSED THE IDEA OF PULLING THEIR RESOURCES TOGETHER, AND BUYING A SAILBOAT AND SAILING AROUND THE ISLANDS FOR A FEW YEARS. NOW THERE WAS AN ADVENTURE THAT MADE SENSE. FINDING ISLAND GIRLS!
MILO AND ANGEE WERE NOT GETTING ALONG VERY WELL AND HE DECIDED THAT HE AND ANGEE SHOULD SPEND SOME TIME APART.
THIS WAS PROBLY NOT THE BEST MOVE THAT HE EVER MADE.
WHERE WAS HE GOING TO FIND ANOTHER WOMAN LIKE ANGELA?
HE LEFT ANGEE A CAR SO THAT SHE COULD GET AROUND. HE REALLY LOVED HER BUT THOUGHT THAT SPENDING SOME TIME APART, WOULD BE A GOOD IDEA.
THUS; MILO, MARK, AND BOBBO GOT THEIR PRIVATE BUSINESSES SQUARED AWAY AND

HEADED TOWARD THE OCEAN AND ADVENTURES THAT MILO ONLY DREAMED OF IN THE PAST.

THEY FIRST MADE CONTACT WITH THE OCEAN ON THE GULF COAST AT CORPUS CHRISTI, TEXAS. THEY HAD BROUGHT A SUBSTANTIAL AMOUNT OF POT WITH THEM THAT THEY HAD GROWN AT THE FEATHER RIVER THAT YEAR AND WERE PARTYING WITH SOME OF THE LOCALS ON PADRE ISLAND. THEY INQUIRED ABOUT MULTI-HULLS, FOR SALE. THEY SAW QUITE A FEW OF THEM IN THE AREA.

THE PRICES WERE TOO HIGH FOR THEIR BLOOD. THEY INQUIRED AS TO WHERE THEY COULD FIND THE BEST PRICES ON BOATS, EVEN FIXER-UPPERS. THEY WERE TOLD THAT THE FLORIDA KEYS WAS THE BEST BET.

THEY CAMPED ON THE BEACH THAT NIGHT. IT WAS SUCH A SERENE AND BEAUTIFUL PLACE, AND THE OCEAN BREEZES WERE VERY COMFORTING. MILO WAS RUDELY AWAKENED IN THE MORNING BY BEING EATEN ALIVE BY SAND FLEAS AND HAVING A NASTY HANGOVER, AT THE SAME TIME.

MILES WAS FEELING VERY HUNG OVER, AND RUDE. HE TOLD THE OTHER THE OTHER GUYS THAT WILL BE THE LAST TIME THAT I WILL SLEEP ON THE BEACH AND LET YOU GUYS SLEEP IN MY TRUCK!

HE GOT DRUNK AGAIN AND LATER THAT DAY APOLOGIZED TO MARK AND BOBBO FOR BEING SUCH AN ASSHOLE. HE REALLY NEEDED TO MELLOW OUT!

THE NEXT MORNING THEY HEADED AROUND THE GULF COAST ON THEIR QUEST FOR A MULTI-HULL. THEY STOPPED AT ALL OF THE BOAT YARDS ALONG THE WAY.

THEY COULDN'T FIND ANY GOOD PRICES ON SAIL BOATS ANYWHERE! THEY SAW HUNDREDS OF BEAUTIFUL BOATS OF ALL TYPES.

MILO LISTENED TO ALL OF THEIR OPINIONS ABOUT MONO HULLS AND MULTI HULLS. THE MAJORITY OF THEM THOUGHT THAT MONO HULLED SAILBOATS WERE MUCH MORE SEAWORTHY THAN MULTI- HULLS.

A MONO HULL WOULD SURVIVE A FULL ON KNOCK DOWN AND EVEN CAN GET ROLLED ALL OF THE WAY OVER AND STILL COME UP BOBBING LIKE A CORK. THIS INFORMATION DID NOT ENTER MARKS MIND. MARK WAS AFTER THE ROOM ON MULTI HULLS AND HOW STABLE THAT THEY WERE ON THE WATER. SO THEY CONTINUED ON. MARK PROBABLY SHOULD HAVE HAD A MOTORBOAT MULTI HULL!

THERE WAS SIGNAGE ALONG THE HIGHWAY THAT REMINDED THEM THAT MARTI-GRAS WAS IN AFFECT. THEY ALL DECIDED THAT IT WAS PARTY TIME! AGAIN!

MILO TOOK SOME L.S.D. AND TRIPPED FOR A COUPLE OF DAYS SMOKING POT AND DRINKING WINE. HE GOT LAID BUT COULDN'T QUITE REMEMBER WHAT SHE LOOKED LIKE.

HE JUST HOPED THAT HE DIDN'T GET THE GIFT THAT KEEPS GIVING AND HE HOPED THAT IT

REALLY WAS A HER. IT WAS SORT OF AN "EASY RIDER MOMENT".

IT RUNS SHIVERS UP YOUR SPINE JUST THINKING ABOUT IT!

HUNG OVER AND SPACED OUT THEY SPLIT FROM NEW ORLEANS AND HEADED FOR THE FLORIDA KEYS WHILE THEY STILL HAD MONEY FOR A BOAT.

THIS TIME IT WAS THE MOST DIRECT ROUTE TO THE KEYS THE HWY ACROSS FLORIDA. "ALLIGATOR ALLEY". THIS WAS THE MOST BEAUTIFUL PLACE THAT MILES HAD EVER BEEN TO AS FAR AS NATURAL PRESERVED WILDLIFE HABITAT.

IT COULD GET DANGEROUS BUT IT WAS EXTREMELY BEAUTIFUL AT THE SAME TIME.

A TROPICAL PARADISE

AFTER A 4200 MILE CROSS COUNTRY TRIP THEY FINALLY ARRIVED IN KEY LARGO, FLORIDA TO EXPERIENCE THEIR FIRST TROPICAL SUNSET. GOD IT CERTAINLY WAS BEAUTIFUL! YOU COULD STAND IN ONE SPOT AND SEE A SUNRISE OVER THE OCEAN AND YOU COULD SEE A SUNSET OVER THE OCEAN. THE GULF COAST AND THE ATLANTIC OCEAN. BEAUTIFUL! SEA TO SHINNING SEA.
THE FIRST BOAT YARD THAT THEY STOPPED AT. THEY SAW IT!
A 30 FT. "PIVER" TRI-MIRAN SLOOP. THE BOATS NAME WAS "THE FERRET" OR [THE WANDERER]. SHE WAS SLEEK AND HAD PLENTY OF ROOM FOR THE THREE OF THEM.
THEY SAW THIS CURLY BLONDE HAIRED GUY DOING SOME SANDING, AND PAINTING ON HER. THE BOAT SEEMED TO BE IN THE FINISHING STAGES OF MINOR REPAIR. THEY ASKED HIM HOW MUCH DID HE WANT FOR IT? HE SAID THAT HE WANTED $2500.00 FOR HER.

THEY WENT AHEAD AND PURCHASED HER FROM HIM. HIS NAME WAS, "CAPTAIN RON".

THEY ASKED HIM WHY HE WAS SELLING HER SO CHEAP? HE TOOK THEM THROUGH THE BOAT AND SHOWED THEM SEVERAL SPOTS THAT NEEDED ATTENTION. THE GUYS THANKED HIM FOR BEING SO HONEST ABOUT THE DAMAGE TO THE BOAT. THEY HAD ALREADY BOUGHT IT, HE COULD HAVE TOLD THEM ANYTHING!

THEY PARTIED WITH HIM THAT NIGHT AND HE TOLD THEM MANY STORIES ABOUT SAILING HER ALL OVER THE BAHAMAS.

IT WAS VERY EXCITING TO HEAR ALL OF THE TALES AND HAIR RAISING SAILING ADVENTURES. THE BOAT GOING AIRBORNE AS IT FLEW OFF OF THE BACKSIDE OF A WAVE AND SO ON.

THEY WERE LEFT WONDERING IF THIS GUY WAS SOME SORT OF PIRATE OR SOMETHING WORSE. AT ANY RATE HE WAS A GOOD STORY TELLER.

THEY AWOKE THE NEXT MORNING AND SAID THEIR GOOD-BYE'S TO CAPTAIN RON.

THE BOAT YARD WAS TEAMING WITH ACTIVITY. THERE WERE PEOPLE WORKING ON ALL SORTS OF BOATS FROM FISHING BOATS TO CIGARETTE BOATS, CABIN CRUISERS, HOUSE BOATS, AND SAIL BOATS.

THEY BEGAN TEARING OFF THE DAMAGED FIBERGLASS AND RAN INTO MAJOR DRY ROT IN ONE OF THE CROSS ARMS! THEY KNEW WHAT TO DO THEY HAD ALL BEEN IN CONSTRUCTION FOR SEVERAL YEARS AND THIS WAS JUST ANOTHER

HOUSE TO THEM. A FLOATING HOUSE BUT NEVER THE LESS JUST ANOTHER HOUSE.

MARK AND BOBBO WERE CARPENTERS BUT MILO HAD EXPERIENCE WITH BUILDING FURNITURE AND FIBERGLASS. MARK AND BOBBO WANTED TO NAIL THE BOAT TOGETHER BUT MILO HAD LEARNED FROM THE OTHER BOAT OWNERS THAT TO PRE-DRILL AND SCREW WAS THE BEST CONSTRUCTION METHOD AND NOT TO USE STEEL SCREWS WHICH WERE CHEAP BUT TO USE BRASS OR BRONZE OR STAINLESS SCREWS INSTEAD. THAT WAS QUITE A BIT MORE EXPENSIVE BUT NECESSARY, FOR THE BEST QUALITY AND LASTING WORK.

THE BOAT WORK WAS GOING ALONG VERY WELL SO MILO DECIDED TO START LEARNING TO SAIL.

WHENEVER HE HAD THE OPPORTUNITY TO GO SAILING HE DID. HE WAS ALWAYS GETTING CALLED AWAY WHEN ANYONE WAS GOING OUT. MOST OF MILO'S WORK ON THE BOAT WAS FIBERGLASS AND THERE WAS ALWAYS "CURE TIME".

HE WOULD TAKE ADVANTAGE OF THOSE DOWN TIMES TO GO SAILING. HE HAD A STANDING REQUEST THAT WHEN ANYONE WAS GOING SAILING THAT HE WANTED TO GO. HE SPOTTED A COUPLE THAT WAS LIVING ABOARD THEIR SAILBOAT AT THE MARINA.

THEY HAD A COUPLE OF WINDSURFERS TIED OFF TO THE STERN OF THEIR BOAT. SEVERAL TIMES A

DAY THEY WOULD JUMP ON THEM AND PRACTICE TACKING UP AND DOWN THE CANAL.

MILES COULD SEE THAT IT WAS SIMILAR TO WHAT HE LEARNED OR RELEARNED ABOUT "THE WING LIFT THEORY" AND THAT YOU NEEDED TO THINK OF THE SAIL LIKE THIS.

YOU ARE NOT BEING PUSHED BY THE WIND BUT INSTEAD YOU ARE BEING SUCKED BUY THE LOW PRESSURE AREA ON THE FRONT SIDE OF THE SAIL. LIKE HANG GLIDING. THE LOW PRESSURE AREA ON TOP OF THE WING IS WHAT KEPT YOU FROM FALLING OUT OF THE SKY WHILE HANG GLIDING.

THAT SAME LOW PRESSURE AREA IS WHAT PROPELS A SAILING VESSEL.

MILES STRUCK UP A LASTING FRIENDSHIP WITH THE WINDSURFER FOLKS. THEY LET HIM BORROW THEIR WINDSURFERS WHENEVER HE WANTED TO AND HE BECAME A VERY GOOD WINDSURFER.

HE COULDN'T WAIT FOR THE CHANCE TO GET ON A BIG WAVE AND HAVE THE POWER TO JUMP OFF OF THE BACKSIDE OF IT AND TO ACTUALLY OUTRUN THE WAVES.

USING THE WING LIFT THEORY MAKES IT SO THAT YOU CAN STEER THE BOAT WITHOUT USING THE RUDDER. IT IS REAL HANDY TO KNOW IN CASE YOU LOOSE YOUR RUDDER. SIMPLY SHEET THE SAILS FOR THE DIRECTION THAT YOU WANT TO TRAVEL.

THE ONLY TIME THIS METHOD DOES NOT APPLY, IS WHEN YOU ARE RUNNING DIRECTLY DOWN WIND. WING & WING.

IN REALITY; IT APPLIES THEN TOO! YOU ARE BEING PUSHED TO A CERTAIN EXTENT. IT IS VERY IMPORTANT TO DOWNHAUL THE MAIN SAIL, OR ANY SAIL FOR THAT MATTER.YOU STRETCH IT TIGHT FROM TOP TO BOTTOM. IT MAKES FOR A VERY SHARP, CLEAN LEADING EDGE, AND KEEPS THE AIR THAT IS MOVING ACROSS THE FRONT OF THE SAIL, FROM GETTING DISTURBED.

HE GRASPED SAILING VERY QUICKLY AND BY THE TIME THAT THE BOAT WAS READY TO SAIL MILO KNEW WHAT TO DO. THEY PUT HUNDREDS OF HOURS INTO "THE FERRET" AND IT WAS NOW TIME TO GO SAILING.

THEY DID ALL OF THEIR LAST MINUTE PROJECTS AND SPLASHED HER INTO THE WATER. THEY WERE ALL EXCITED.

THEY PARTIED WITH THE PEOPLE OF THE BOATYARD THAT NIGHT. THEY HAD A GREAT TIME AND MILO DISCOVERED THAT MOST OF THEM WERE VERY GOOD PEOPLE.

THE NEXT MORNING THEY GOT UP AND THE WIND WAS BLOWING FROM 10 TO 15 MILES PER HOUR STRAIGHT ON SHORE OUT OF THE EAST. A PERFECT BEAM REACH.

MILES TOLD MARK THAT IT WAS A GOOD DAY TO SAIL AND SO THEY DECIDED TO SAIL DOWN THE KEYS TO SHAKE DOWN THE BOAT BEFORE GOING TO THE ISLANDS.

MILO HAD ALREADY SOLD HIS TRUCK AND STOCKED THE BOAT WITH FOOD. AFTER THE BOAT WAS STOCKED AND THE RIGGING WAS TUNED

THEY WENT OUT FOR THEIR FIRST SHAKE DOWN
CRUISE DOWN ISLAND.
MARK AND BOBBO HAD BEEN MAD AT MILO FOR
SPENDING SO MUCH TIME SAILING BUT NOW IT
WAS MILO'S TIME TO SHINE.

SHAKE DOWN

THEY MOTORED OUT OF THE CUT AND OUT
TOWARD THE INTER COASTAL WATERWAY. IT
WAS A FAIRLY CALM DAY BUT THE WIND WAS
BUILDING SLOWLY.
FINALLY ONE AT TIME THEY RAISED THE SAILS
AND MILO DOWN HAULED EACH ONE AS THEY
WERE RAISED. MARK, AND BOBBO THOUGHT
THAT MILO WAS FULL OF SHIT BECAUSE HE WAS
TAKING SO MUCH TIME RAISING THE SAILS AND
TUNING THE SAIL AT THE SAME TIME. AT THIS
POINT NEITHER MARK NOR BOBBO HAD EVER
SAILED OR EVEN READ A CHART? THEY DIDN'T
KNOW PORT FROM STARBOARD!
MARK CONSIDERED HIMSELF CAPTAIN AND
WANTED TO TAKE THE HELM. MILO SAID: THIS
IS FINE MARK BUT REMEMBER, YOU CAN'T DRIVE
IT LIKE A CAR. NOW GO AHEAD YOU HAVE TO
LEARN SOMETIME.
IN HIS THE FIRST FIVE MINUTES AT THE HELM
HE NEARLY FLIPPED THE BOAT! HE SCREAMED AT
MILO! WHAT DO I DO?

MILO LAUGHED AND LET ALL OF THE SAILS OUT AND THE BOAT BEGAN PLANEING AH SHIT! SHE WAS HAULING ASS, FRIGGIN SURFING.
MILO WAS YELLING YEA HAAA! AS MARK SURFED UP AND DOWN THE SWELLS. MILO WAS BARKING ORDER ABOUT THE SAILS AS MARK WAS TRYING TO DRIVE IT AROUND. PULL THE MAIN IN! LET IT OUT! LET THE JIB OUT! PULL IT IN! THEY HAD A HARD TIME GETTING MARK TO STEER IT IN A STRAIGHT LINE. MILO FINALLY SHOWED HIM HOW TO LOOK AT A COMPASS. AFTER SEVERAL MINUTES IT FINALLY GOT A LITTLE EASIER.
THEY HAD A GREAT DAY AND MADE IT QUITE A WAYS DOWN THE KEYS. HE KEPT TRACT OF WHERE THEY WERE ON THE CHARTS.
MARK POINTED TO ONE OF THE ISLANDS AND SAID: LETS GO ANCHOR OVER THERE. THE WATER IN THE COVE WAS BROWN AS DIRT.
HE TOLD MARK THAT THEY WOULDN'T HAVE TO WORRY ABOUT ANCHORING. THEY WOULD JUST RUN AGROUND IF THEY WENT THERE. MARK SCREAMED! I'M THE CAPTAIN OF THIS SHIP AND I SAID WE'LL GO OVER THERE!
SO BY ORDER OF THE CAPTAIN THEY WENT TOWARD THE KNOWN BAD WATER.
THE BOTTOM KEPT GETTING BROWNER AND BROWNER AND MILO WAS GRITTING HIS TEETH WAITING TO HIT BOTTOM WHEN ALL OF A SUDDEN! THEY HIT!

MARK WAS STANDING UP WHEN THE BOAT RAN AGROUND AND THE "G" FORCES THREW HIM INTO THE WATER.

HE STOOD UP IN KNEE DEEP WATER AND STARTED SCREAMING AT MILO. YOU PURPOSELY RAN MY BOAT AGROUND! YOU MOTHERFUCKER!

MILO RESOUNDED BACK AT MARK: YOU ROTTEN SON-OF-A-BITCH!

MILO WAS LAUGHING SO HARD THAT HE COULDN'T CONTROL HIMSELF.

DO YOU REALLY THINK THAT I PUT ALL OF THIS TIME AND EFFORT AND MONEY INTO THIS BOAT TO PURPOSELY WRECK IT! YOU IGNORANT BASTARD! HE CHUCKLED SOME MORE.

MARK THOUGHT ABOUT IT FOR A WHILE AND APOLOGIZED TO HIM BUT MILO DIDN'T FORGET!

THERE WAS AN EGO PROBLEM WITH HIM AND MARK.

MARK HAD THIS HITLER THING GOING. THERE HAD BEEN QUITE A BIT OF TENSION FOR SOME TIME ALREADY. THERE WAS NO SERIOUS DAMAGE JUST BARKED OFF A LITTLE FIBERGLASS FROM ONE OF THE SKAGGS.

MILO AND BOBBO JUMPED OFF OF THE BOAT AND PUSHED HER OUT TO SAFE ANCHORAGE. MILO SPOTTED A BAR ON THE ISLAND AT MARATHON KEY AND JUMPED IN TO THE DINGHY. HE TOLD MARK THAT HE WAS GOING TO GO HAVE A DRINK. SEE YA LATER.

MARK AND BOBBO SAID; WAIT A MINUTE!

WE WILL GO WITH YOU. THEY ALL LOADED INTO THE DINGY AND WENT TO SHORE. THEY ALL HUNG OUT IN THE BAR FOR QUITE AWHILE. MILO TOLD MARK THAT HE WAS GOING OUTSIDE FOR A WHILE.

ON HIS OWN

MILO HAD MADE UP HIS MIND THAT IT WAS TIME TO GO AND WENT BACK OUT TO THE BOAT AND GOT ALL OF HIS TOOLS AND PRIVATE GEAR. HE LEFT MARK A LETTER, WISHING HIM GOOD LUCK.

THIS JUST CAN'T WORK; I NEED TO CAPTAIN MY OWN SHIP. GOOD FUCKING LUCK ASSHOLE! THANKS FOR THE LESSON IN TRUST!

MILES WROTE OFF ALL OF THE EFFORT THAT HE HAD PUT INTO THE FERRET. WHAT HE HAD LEARNED WAS EXTREMELY VALUABLE TO HIM. HE WOULD HAVE A BOAT OF HIS OWN IN NO TIME. HE LOADED EVERYTHING INTO THE DINGHY AND WENT BACK TO SHORE. HE WENT TO A PHONE BOOTH AND CALLED A CAB AND HE HAD THE CAB DRIVER TAKE HIM BACK TO KEY LARGO.

THE CAB DRIVER DROPPED HIM OFF AT THE BOAT YARD WHERE HE HAD STARTED OUT.

LUCK WAS WITH HIM, AND HE RAN INTO ONE OF HIS NEW FRIENDS, THAT HE HAD MET THERE SEVERAL WEEKS BEFORE.

HIS BUDDY KEN AND HIS WIFE BARBIE SAID THAT HE COULD STAY ON THEIR BOAT UNTIL HE GOT BACK ON HIS FEET AND THAT ALL HE HAD TO DO WAS TO KEEP THE BILGE PUMPED AND TO KEEP HER CLEAN.

IT IS VERY IMPORTANT TO KEEP A BOAT CLEAN. IF THE COCKROACHES EVER GET STARTED YOU'LL NEVER GET RID OF THEM.

HE SAID; THANKS A LOT KEN THEN WENT ABOARD, AND JUST SAT THERE FOR AWHILE, CONTEMPLATING THE FEELING OF BEING ON A BOAT OF HIS OWN.

IT GAVE HIM A SENSE OF FREEDOM THAT HE HAD NEVER FELT BEFORE. LIKE HE WAS REALLY IN CONTROL OF HIS OWN DESTINY.

HE STAYED THERE UNTIL CLOSE TO SUNSET THEN WENT OUT TO THE COCKPIT AND JUST ENJOYED THE TROPICAL SUNSET THAT WAS TAKING PLACE.

THERE WAS A FIRE PIT UP ON SHORE WITH A BUNCH OF PEOPLE LAUGHING AND JUST HAVING FUN. ONE OF THE LADIES WAS WALKING BY THE BOAT AND ASKED MILO IF HE WANTED TO GO TO A BOAT YARD PARTY? MILO ACCEPTED AND THANKED THEM FOR ASKING.

IT WAS A GREAT PARTY AND MOST OF HIS NEW FRIENDS WERE THERE. IT WAS REALLY GOOD TO SEE THEM AGAIN. THEY HAD BECOME LIKE FAMILY TO HIM.

HE RECALLED THAT WHILE HE WAS WORKING ON THE FERRET EVERYONE WAS SURPRISED THAT HE WAS SUCH A HARD WORKER. THE PEOPLE OF THE

KEYS WERE PRETTY LAID BACK AND SOME MIGHT SAY THAT THEY ARE LAZY.

HE MADE A LOT OF FRIENDS, JUST FOR THAT REASON. MOST PEOPLE IN TROPICAL CLIMATES ARE PRETTY LAID BACK. YOU KNOW; NAPS IN THE AFTERNOON AND ALL THAT STUFF.

HE KNEW THAT HE BELONGED HERE. HE MET MANY NEW PEOPLE, ONE OF WHICH WAS CAPTAIN LEM.

HE HAD A BEAUTIFUL 60 FOOT CUTTER SLOOP NAMED PANACEA, A FAIRLY SHALLOW DRAFT CENTERBOARD SLOOP. IT WAS AN ALDEN DESIGN WOODEN BOAT. CAPTAIN LEM HAD A LOT OF FUNNY SEA STORIES AND WAS GREAT TO LISTEN TO.

HE KNEW SO MUCH ABOUT WOODEN BOATS THAT MILO WAS MESMERIZED FOR QUITE SOME TIME. HE WAS A WORLD OF KNOWLEDGE.

CAPTAIN LEM WOULD NEVER DO ANY SERIOUS SAILING AGAIN. HE WAS TOO OLD. HE DID KNOW EVERYTHING THAT THERE WAS TO KNOW ABOUT SAILING THOUGH.

ONE DAY WHILE THERE WAS A BOAT YARD PARTY GOING ON THERE WERE A FEW KIDS THAT WERE MINDLESSLY RUNNING AROUND AND JUST PLAIN HAVING FUN!

MILES AND CAPTAIN LEM WERE STANDING THERE WATCHING THEM WHEN MILES ASKED HIM; DON'T YOU WISH THAT YOU COULD HAVE THAT KIND OF ENERGY AGAIN? CAPTAIN LEM ANSWERED: NO, I DON'T RIGHTLY THINK SO.

IF I HAD THAT KIND OF ENERGY I WOULD HAVE TO HAVE THAT KIND OF MENTALITY. MILO LAUGHED; PRETTY TRUE STORY LEM.

ON THE WALL AT THE BOAT YARD WAS ANOTHER BOAT. A STEEL BOAT NAMED PARADOX.

TWO MEN OWNED IT. I ASKED THEM WHAT PARADOX MEANT AND ONE OF THEM ANSWERED WITH A SMILE ON HIS FACE TWO DOCKS BESIDE EACH OTHER.

MILO SAID: THAT'S REAL FUNNY BUT WHAT DOES IT REALLY MEAN? THE MAN ON THE BOAT LAUGHED AND SAID THAT IT MEANS THAT IT'S NOT WHAT IT APPEARS TO BE.

HE LATER FOUND OUT THAT THEY WERE GAY AND THEN HE REALLY UNDERSTOOD WHAT THEY MEANT BY PARADOX.

ANOTHER BOAT ON THE WALL, THAT HE THOUGHT REALLY MADE SENSE WAS NAMED "ICE MAKER". THE OWNER PAID FOR HIS CRUISING BY HAVING A DESALINIZATION PLANT ON BOARD AND SELLING ICE OR BARTERING FOR FOOD OR BOOZE.

HE ALSO HAD A RAIN WATER COLLECTION SYSTEM THAT REALLY WORKED GREAT! ICE IS REAL HARD TO COME BY OVER THERE. HE THOUGHT THAT WOULD BE A GREAT WAY TO PAY FOR SAILING AND ISLAND HOPPING.

HE WENT TO SEE HIS BUDDY WILLARD. MILO HAD MET WILLARD WHEN THEY WERE WORKING ON THE FERRET. WILLARD HAD A TRI-MIRAN TOO. WILLARD WAS A STRANGE COOKIE. MILO KNEW THAT WILLARD KNEW SOMETHING THAT MILO

NEEDED TO KNOW. NOT ONLY ABOUT SAILING BUT ALSO ABOUT LIFE IN THE KEYS IN GENERAL.

AFTER ALL; MILO WAS A SCAMMER AND SO WAS WILLARD. HE JUST WANTED IN ON THE ACTION.

WILLARD WAS A VERY GIVING PERSON AND MILO KNEW IT. HE WAS THE KIND OF GUY THAT WOULD STAND BY YOU THROUGH THICK AND THIN. A MAN WITH HONOR. A "SEMPER FI" KIND OF GUY.

MILO HAD THE TALENT THAT WILLARD NEEDED AND WILLARD HAD THE OPPORTUNITIES AND THE CONNECTIONS THAT MILO WANTED AND NEEDED.

WILLARD HAD A 36-FOOT PIVER TRI-MIRAN, SAILBOAT. HE HIRED MILO TO BUILD HIM SOME STASH SPOTS IN HIS SAILBOAT'S INTERIOR.

MILO KNEW THAT HIS REQUESTS WERE NOT WHAT ANY NORMAL PERSON WOULD ASK TO HAVE BUILT INTO THEIR BOATS. THEY WERE ALL HIDDEN SPOTS.

HE HAD THE STRONG FEELING THAT THE BOAT WAS TO BE USED TO SMUGGLE ITEMS IN AND OUT OF THE UNITED STATES.

HE TOLD WILLARD ABOUT HIS GIRLFRIEND ANGEE. HE TOLD WILLARD THAT HE WAS IN LOVE WITH HER AND THAT HE WANTED HER BACK.

WILLARD WARNED HIM ABOUT BEING ALONE WITH SOMEONE IN THE CONFINES OF A SAILBOAT FOR EXTENDED PERIODS OF TIME IS VERY STRENUOUS ON A RELATIONSHIP, TO SAY THE LEAST. ESPECIALLY ON A SMALL SAILBOAT.

HE TOLD MILO THAT HE SHOULD REMEMBER WHY THEY HAD SPLIT UP, IN THE FIRST PLACE.

HE WEIGHED ALL OF THE FACTS OUT IN HIS MIND, AND DECIDED TO GO AHEAD AND SEND FOR ANGEE. HE WAS LONELY AND WANTED HER BACK. THAT IS IF ANGEE WANTED TO COME OUT TO FLORIDA AT ALL!

HE CALLED HER, AND TOLD HER THAT HE MISSED HER, AND THAT HE WANTED HER WITH HIM.

IT TURNED OUT THAT ANGEE WAS REAL EXCITED ABOUT THE PROSPECTS, AND DEFINITELY WANTED TO GET OUT OF THAT CABIN WHERE HE HAD LEFT HER.

HE MADE ARRANGEMENTS FOR ANGEE TO BE AT THE PHONE AT THE RIGHT TIME, IT WAS A COMMUNITY PHONE AT THE CABINS BECAUSE THE PHONE COMPANY WOULD NOT PUT IN ANY OTHER LINES.

MILO MADE ARRANGEMENTS AND SPOKE TO HER ON THE PHONE.

ANGEE WAS GOING TO SELL THE CAR AND TAKE THE BUS TO KEY LARGO, FROM CALIFORNIA. ONE HELL OF A LONG TRIP ON A BUS.

HE TOLD HER ABOUT THE SAILBOAT THAT HE WAS STAYING ON AND WHAT HAD HAPPENED WITH MARK & BOBBO, AND THAT HE WANTED HER BACK WITH HIM. SHE WASN'T SURPRISED ABOUT MARK, AND BOBBO.

HE TOLD HER THAT THEY WOULD GO SAILING TOGETHER ON A BOAT LIKE THE ONE HE WAS STAYING ON. SHE AGREED, AND TOLD MILO THAT SHE WOULD BE THERE SOON.

THE BOAT THAT MILO WAS STAYING ON WAS A 28-FOOT "KINGS CRUISER". HE LOVED THE DESIGN AND HOW LOW AND SLEEK THAT SHE LOOKED IN THE WATER.

THE BOAT ONLY HAD 4'6" HEADROOM. YOU JUST HAD TO SIT.

THEY WERE ALL BUILT IN SWEDEN AND SAILED OVER TO THE UNITED STATES. VERY SEAWORTHY HULL DESIGN.

SHE LOOKED LIKE A SPORTS CAR ON THE WATER. HE THOUGHT THAT MAYBE THIS IS THE DESIGN THAT HE WOULD LIKE FOR HIS ULTIMATE CRUISER. REAL SLEEK ON TOP BUT MOST OF THE BOAT WAS UNDER WATER.

HE HAD NOT MET VERY MANY PEOPLE SINCE HE HAD BEEN THERE EXCEPT FOR THE BOAT YARD PEOPLE.

WILLARD OFFERED TO TAKE HIM OUT PARTYING FOR THE NIGHT. HE MET SEVERAL AVAILABLE SINGLE WOMEN SOME OF THEM WERE NASTY LITTLE SLUTS BUT A FEW OF THEM WERE NICE GIRLS.

HE WAS BEGINNING TO WONDER IF HE HAD DONE THE RIGHT THING BY SENDING FOR ANGEE AT ALL!

HE MET A BEAUTIFUL CANADIAN GIRL NAMED LUCY.

HE STRUCK UP A CONVERSATION WITH HER AND WAS BEGINNING TO GET ALONG WITH HER VERY GOOD. TOO GOOD!

LUCY TESTED MILO TO THE LIMIT OF HIS SELF DISCIPLINE.

JUST IMAGINE A HIPPIE WITH MORALS. GO
FIGURE.
THEY SAT IN THE ROOM HOLDING HANDS AND
LOOKING AT EACH OTHER LONGINGLY FOR A
COUPLE OF HOURS. HE COULDN'T TAKE IT ANY
MORE AND HE KISSED HER. SHE WAS VERY
RECEPTIVE TO HIM.
HE WAS SCARED TO DEATH! WHAT DID HE THINK
THAT HE WAS DOING?
HE COULD FALL IN LOVE WITH A GIRL LIKE THIS
ONE AND HE KNEW THAT ANGEE WAS TO ARRIVE
VERY SOON AND THAT HE FELT GUILTY THAT
HE HAD GONE THIS FAR WHEN ANGEE WAS SO
CLOSE.
HE BROKE HIS GRASP ON LUCY AND TOLD HER
THAT HE HAD A CONFESSION TO MAKE.
LUCY LOOKED INTO HIS EYES WITH A VERY
HAPPY SMILE ON HER FACE. THE SMILE FADED
TO SORROW AS HE EXPLAINED TO LUCY ABOUT
ANGEE.
I AM SO SORRY FOR LEADING YOU ON.
IF THINGS WERE DIFFERENT. I WOULD LOVE TO
SPEND SOME TIME WITH YOU BUT BECAUSE OF
MY FEELINGS FOR ANGEE I CAN'T LET THIS GO
ANY FURTHER. I AM VERY SORRY.
LUCY SEEMED STRUCK WITH SADNESS. IT SEEMED
THAT SHE HAD FINALLY FOUND SOMEONE THAT
SHE NEEDED AS A SOUL MATE TOO.
IT WAS ALMOST LIKE LOVE AT FIRST SIGHT.
ALTHOUGH THEY HAD ONLY KNOWN EACH OTHER
FOR A FEW HOURS THEY BOTH SOMEHOW FELT
BONDED.

IT WAS A TUFF THING FOR MILO TO DO, BUT HONESTY WAS ALWAYS THE BEST POLICY. THE TRUTH SHALL SET YOU FREE!

HE EXPLAINED TO LUCY, THAT IF HE HAD NOT ALREADY SENT FOR ANGEE, HE WOULD HAVE BEEN PROUD TO SEEK A RELATIONSHIP WITH HER. SHE WAS THE KIND OF GIRL THAT HE WAS REALLY AFTER.

IT WAS TOO LATE TO CHANGE. HE HAD TO BE HONEST WITH HER, AND WITH HIMSELF.

LUCY FELT THE SAME WAY, AND ALSO ADMIRED MILO FOR HIS HONESTY WITH HER. SHE TOLD HIM THAT IF IT DIDN'T WORK OUT, SHE WOULD BE THERE FOR HIM.

IN A DEMENTED WAY; HE REALLY WANTED HER AND NOT ANGEE. HE REMEMBERED HOW ANGEE WAS TREATING HIM BEFORE HE LEFT. ANGEE WAS SO BEAUTIFUL THOUGH. THERE WERE VERY FEW WOMEN AS BEAUTIFUL AS HER.

THEY PARTED FRIENDS AND HE WENT BACK TO THE BOAT TO GET SOME REST. ANGEE WAS TO ARRIVE TOMORROW. HE FELT GUILTY AS HELL FOR THE LITTLE THAT HE DID DO, HE JUST NEEDED TO PUT IT BEHIND HIM.

ANGEE IS HERE: LETS GO SHOPPING.

ANGEE ARRIVED ON SCHEDULE; "THE BIG GRAY DOG" DROPPED HER OFF BY THE BIG HOTEL IN TOWN. IT WAS OUT IN FRONT OF THE UNWINDER HOTEL. THEY WERE KNOWN FOR THEIR WET "T" SHIRT CONTESTS. MILO RAN TO HER AND HELD HER TIGHTLY.
SOMEHOW SHE FELT COLD TO HIM AT LEAST FOR THE MOMENT AT HAND. SHE WAS SO BEAUTIFUL THAT MILO HAD FORGOTTEN ALL OF THE BAD TIMES.
THEY GOT ANGEE'S STUFF OFF OF THE BUS AND WALKED OVER TO THE BOATYARD. SHE WAS SO BEAUTIFUL IN MILO'S EYES.
OH HELL! SHE WAS ALWAYS A FOX AND HE KNEW THAT HE SHOULD HAVE NEVER LEFT HER BEHIND. SHE COULD HAVE ANY MAN THAT SHE WANTED. MAKE NO MISTAKE ABOUT HER BEAUTY.
MILO HAD MADE A BIG MISTAKE BY LEAVING HER BEHIND. HE ONLY HOPED THAT HE COULD REPAIR

THE DAMAGE THAT HE HAD DONE WHEN HE LEFT HER IN THE FIRST PLACE.

MARK AND BOBBO HAD ALREADY USED UP MOST OF HIS MONEY SO IT WAS GOING TO BE DIFFICULT TO RAISE MONEY FOR A BOAT.

ANGEE AND MILO SPENT THE NEXT FEW DAYS GETTING REACQUAINTED AFTER THEIR SEPARATION OF A FEW MONTHS.

ANGEE WAS VERY WEARY AND LEERY OF HIM. AFTER ALL HE HAD JUST LEFT HER 3 MONTHS AGO!

WHAT DID HE THINK THAT SHE WAS SUPPOSED TO THINK ABOUT HIM! AFTER ALL OF THAT SHIT! AFTER MILO LEAVING HER THERE!

BUT BEING A FORGIVING SOLE WAS ONE OF ANGEE'S BETTER VIRTUE'S. OR MAYBE THIS WAS HER PAYBACK!

EVENTUALLY SHE DID FORGIVE HIM FOR LEAVING AS WELL AS ADMITTING THAT SHE HAD NOT BEEN THE MOST ROMANTIC PERSON IN THE LAST DAYS BEFORE HE DECIDED THAT HE WAS GOING TO LEAVE AND EVEN BEFORE THEN.

THEY SPENT THE NEXT FEW DAYS GETTING REACQUAINTED AGAIN AND MAKING LOVE AT EVERY OPPORTUNITY THAT HE COULD FIND AN EXCUSE FOR.

LIFE WAS WONDERFUL AGAIN AND THEY REALLY LOVED THE BOAT THAT THEY WERE BABY-SITTING. THEY ASKED IF THE BOAT WAS FOR SALE AND THEY WERE TOLD THAT ALL BOATS ARE FOR SALE, BUT THEY WERE ASKING TOO MUCH FOR THE ONE THAT THEY WERE STAYING ON SO

THEY ABANDONED THE IDEA OF BUYING THAT ONE.

AFTER GETTING THE BUGS OUT OF THEIR RELATIONSHIP, THEY GOT TO THE BUSINESS AT HAND. GETTING A BOAT!

THEY CHECKED OUT THE LOCAL MARINA'S FOR SEVERAL DAYS. FINALLY THEY SPOTTED THIS LITTLE WOOD POWERBOAT.

FIRST BOAT

IT WAS A 25 FOOT, OWENS, CABIN CRUISER.
IT WAS MADE OUT OF MARINE PLYWOOD AND IT
HAD A CHEVY 327 V-8. CORVETTE ENGINE! MILO
KNEW ABOUT THAT ENGINE VERY WELL SO THEY
DECIDED TO GO AHEAD AND LOOK INTO BUYING
HER.
THE BOAT WAS OWNED BY A LITTLE OLD LADY.

HER HUSBAND HAD DIED A FEW MONTHS
BEFORE.
THAT LITTLE BOAT WAS HER HUSBANDS PRIDE
AND JOY. HE SPENT ALL OF HIS SPARE TIME,
TINKERING WITH HER ENGINE AND TRYING TO
KEEP UP WITH THE BRIGHT WORK.
HE SPENT SO MUCH TIME WITH THE BOAT THAT
SHE WAS ALMOST JEALOUS OF IT! OH HELL! SHE
WAS!
THAT DAMN BOAT WAS TEARING THEM APART
AND THERE WAS NOTHING THAT SHE COULD DO
ABOUT IT!

FINALLY; THE OLD MAN DIED AND SHE WAS STUCK WITH THE BOAT THAT SHE HAD HATED ALL THESE YEARS. NOW SOMEHOW SHE WAS STRANGELY ATTRACTED TO THIS LITTLE BOAT! PERHAPS SHE JUST WANTED TO FEEL CLOSE TO WHAT HER HUSBAND HELD SO DEARLY TO HIM.

SHE FINALLY DECIDED TO PUT HER UP FOR SALE BECAUSE THE DOCK RENT WAS PRETTY HIGH AND THE BOAT WAS LOOKING A LITTLE TATTERED.

SHE SPOTTED ANGEE AND MILO LOOKING AT THE BOAT. SHE ASKED MILO IF HE KNEW ABOUT BOATS? HE LOOKED AT HER AND SAID: ENOUGH, I GUESS.

SHE WAS ASKING FOR $ 1500.00 FOR THE BOAT BUT THAT WAS A LITTLE OUT OF THEIR BUDGET SO MILO OFFERED HER $ 1000.00 FOR THE BOAT AND POINTED OUT THE WORK THAT NEEDED TO BE DONE. THE WOMAN SAID: YOU DON'T HAVE TO TELL ME ABOUT BOAT'S NEEDING WORK YOUNG MAN!

MY HUSBAND WAS ALWAYS WORKING ON THIS BOAT SOMETIMES I THINK THAT HE LOVED THIS BOAT MORE THAN HE LOVED ME!

SHE TOLD THEM TO GO AHEAD AND TAKE THE DAMN BOAT FOR A THOUSAND DOLLARS AND GOOD LUCK TO YOU LITTLE LADY! AS SHE GLARED ANGEE STRAIGHT IN THE EYE.

THEY WENT TO THE BANK AND WITHDREW THE MONEY THAT THEY NEEDED FOR THE BOAT AND A LITTLE EXTRA FOR GAS. THEN RETURNED TO THE MARINA WHERE THE BOAT WAS.

THE BOAT WAS QUITE COMFORTABLE WITH IT'S STANDING HEADROOM BUT A LITTLE EXPENSIVE TO MOVE AROUND.

THEY KNEW THAT THE GOAL AT HAND WAS TO FIND A SAILBOAT THAT WOULD BE A COMFORTABLE CRUISER.

THE FIRST PROJECT AT HAND FOR THE TIME BEING WAS TO START ON A MAINTENANCE PROGRAM ON THE PRESENT RESIDENCE. THE CABIN-CRUISER!

THEY DROVE THEIR BOAT TO THE BOATYARD THAT MILO HAD STARTED OUT AT IN THE FIRST PLACE.

THEY KNEW HIM PRETTY WELL AT THE BOATYARD. HE WAS RESPECTED THERE! HE WAS KNOWN FOR BEING A HARD WORKER.

HE HAD WORKED ON SEVERAL BOATS WHILE WORKING ON THE FERRET WITH MARK AND BOBBO.

WHEN HE HAD RUN OUT OF MONEY HE NEEDED SIDE WORK JUST TO GET BY. THE OWNERS OF THE BOATYARD ALWAYS HAD A BOTTOM TO BE PAINTED OR SOMETHING TO BE DONE AROUND THE BOATYARD.

HE MANAGED TO KEEP THEM IN FOOD, SPIRITS, AND SUPPLIES.

THEY DOCKED THEIR CABIN CRUISER ALONG THE WALL! IT WAS ROUGH CORAL WALL SO THEY REALLY NEEDED GOOD FENDERS.

THEY WENT TO THE LOCAL MARINE STORE AND PURCHASED SEVERAL OF THE GOLDEN BOAT SAVERS. AT LEAST YOU WOULD HAVE THOUGHT

THAT THEY WERE MADE OUT OF GOLD, FOR WHAT THEY COST!

THEY GOT BUSY SANDING, SCRAPING, CAULKING, VARNISHING, AND PAINTING, THE ENTIRE INSIDE AND OUT OF THE BOAT. SHE WAS QUITE PRETTY AND A PLEASURE TO LIVE ON.

THEY HAD JUST SPLASHED HER BACK IN THE WATER AND MOVED HER BACK ON THE WALL. MILO FIRED UP THE ALCOHOL STOVE TO MAKE SOME COFFEE.

THE TOP BLEW OFF OF THE BURNER AND STRAIGHT ALCOHOL HIT THE CEILING IN THE GALLEY!

MILO SCREAMED! FIRE! THE ENTIRE CABIN WAS ENGULFED WITH FLAMES! IT WAS HELL ON THE WALL TODAY!

THEIR NEIGHBORS REACTED IMMEDIATELY AND HE HAD ALL OF THE FIRE EXTINGUISHERS THAT HE NEEDED AND WAS ABLE PUT THE FIRE OUT WITH MINOR DAMAGE. WHAT A MESS! FIRE EXTINGUISHER JUICE EVERYWHERE.

THE CURTAINS WERE BURNED UP. ANGEE DIDN'T LIKE THEM ANYWAY. SO MUCH FOR WASTED TIME.

THEY JUST NEEDED TO PAINT THE INSIDE AGAIN! ANOTHER, COUPLE MORE COATS OF PAINT COULDN'T HURT ANYWAY.

THEY FINALLY GOT HER REPAINTED AND LOOKING MIGHTY PRISTINE! HE WANTED TO START SPREADING OUT THEIR SEARCH AREA.

ANGEE AND MILO DECIDED TO TAKE A TRIP UP THE INTERCOSTAL WATERWAY TO MIAMI TO TRY AND FIND THEIR DREAM BOAT!
LOTS OF BOATS ON THAT RIVER! AND A HELL OF A LOT OF CANALS TOO! THEY CAME UP TO THIS TURN-TABLE BRIDGE THAT WAS LOW TO THE WATER. HE BLEW HIS CONCH SHELL HORN THREE TIMES! THE BRIDGE OPENED AND HIS EYES LIT UP!

THEY FOUND HER

HE SPOTTED THIS BEAUTIFUL LITTLE 28-FOOT MONO-HULL RAFTED ALONG-SIDE A HOUSEBOAT ON THE MIAMI RIVER.
IT WAS A KING'S CRUISER DESIGN SWEDISH BUILT WOODEN BOAT!
HE PULLED UP TO THE LITTLE SAILBOAT AND RAFTED ALONG SIDE HER. SHE HAD A FOR SALE SIGN ON HER. HE LOOKED HER OVER PRETTY GOOD.
THE BOAT HAD BEEN GUTTED FROM FIRE. PROBABLY ONE OF THOSE ALCOHOL STOVES AND SOMEONE HAD RE-RIBBED HER FROM BOW TO STERN. THERE NOW WAS A RIB EVERY 4 TO 5 INCHES. IT WAS REALLY QUITE A STURDY HULL. IT WOULD BE A GOOD STARTING POINT.
HE WENT INTO THE BOAT-YARD, WHERE THE BOAT WAS DOCKED, AND QUESTIONED SOME OF THE GUYS THAT WERE WORKING THERE, ABOUT THE SAILBOAT.

THEY DIRECTED HIM TO THE MARINE SUPPLY
STORE ON THE PROPERTY. MILO MET JIM AND
MARY. THE OWNERS OF THE BOAT-YARD.
JIM TOLD HIM THAT THE OWNER OF THE
SAILBOAT WANTED $2000.00 CASH FOR THE
BOAT AND THAT THE BOAT HAD BEEN THERE FOR
QUITE SOME TIME.
THE GUY THAT OWNED THE BOAT HAD BOUGHT
IT FROM SOME CUBANS THAT HAD BEEN USING
IT AS A FISHING BOAT. THEY WERE THE ONES
THAT FOUND THE BOAT AND RAISED HER TO
SAIL AGAIN SOMEDAY.
THEY HAD TAKEN ONE OF THE REAR HATCHES
AND TURNED THE AREA INTO A THROUGH HULL
AREA FOR AN OUTBOARD MOTOR. THEY HAD
CUT RIGHT THROUGH THE PLANKS AND FIBER
GLASSED THIS OPEN HOLE TO THE OCEAN.
THEY HAD PAINTED HER DARK BLUE AND RED
WITH YELLOW TOE RAILS. SHE WAS PRETTY
UGLY SITTING THERE AND WOULD PROBABLY BE
THERE FOR A WHILE LONGER.
NOT MANY WANT-TO-BE SAILORS ON THE MIAMI
RIVER. ESPECIALLY NOT LOOKING FOR A JUNKER
LIKE THAT ONE! MILO RECOGNIZED THE HULL
DESIGN AND WAS CONVINCED THAT SHE WOULD
SAIL AGAIN!
HE DIDN'T HAVE THE CASH FOR THE BOAT AND
ASKED JIM IF HE NEEDED ANY HELP AT THE BOAT
YARD.
HE TOLD JIM OF HIS CARPENTRY AND FIBERGLASS
AND PAINTING SKILLS AND THE FACT THAT HE
HAD WORKED FOR HOBIE AND ALLEN AND OLE

SURFBOARD SHOPS. JIM SAID: WELL HELL YES!
WHERE HAVE YOU BEEN ALL THIS TIME?

SO HE WENT TO WORK ON THIS TUGBOAT THAT
JIM WAS RE-FURBISHING. HE WAS GIVEN A LOW
WAGE BUT HE WAS ALLOWED TO DOCK HIS BOAT
THERE FOR FREE BECAUSE HE WAS WORKING FOR
JIM.

HE WORKED ON THE TUG FOR A COUPLE OF
MONTHS DOING A LITTLE BIT OF EVERYTHING
BUT MOSTLY FIBERGLASS WORK.

THE TUG WAS NEXT TO A SAILBOAT THAT
WAS JUST IN THE BEGINNING STAGES OF THE
BUILDING PROCESS.

THE OWNER OF THE SAILBOAT TOOK NOTICE
OF MILO'S WORK ON THE TUG AND APPROACHED
HIM TO ASK IF HE WOULD WORK FOR HIM TOO!
MILO NEEDED MORE MONEY SO HE AGREED TO
WORK FOR HIM AS WELL.

IT WAS A 65 FOOT KETCH RIGGED SAILBOAT THAT
WAS GOING TO BE USED AS A CHARTER BOAT. IT
WAS A HIGH FREEBOARD FLUSH DECK. IT WOULD
TAKE TWENTY PEOPLE. 20 PAYING CUSTOMERS AT
A TIME.

HE LEARNED A GREAT DEAL ABOUT RIGGING AND
BUILDING BOATS IN GENERAL FROM THE OWNER
BUILDER OF THAT BOAT.

THIS JOB WOULD BRING HIM ENOUGH MONEY TO
BUY THE SAILBOAT THAT HE WANTED. IT DIDN'T
TAKE LONG AT ALL, AND HE HAD THE MONEY TO
BUY THE LITTLE BURNED OUT SAILBOAT.

HE BEGAN WORKING ON IT EVERY DAY AFTER
WORK AND ON WEEKENDS. WHEN HE FIRST

TORE INTO IT! HE WASN'T SURPRISED TO FIND BARNACLES BETWEEN THE LAYERS OF WOOD ON THE CABIN TOP.

THE BOAT HAD TO SPENT QUITE SOME TIME ON THE BOTTOM! THIS BOTHERED MILO FOR AWHILE. HE SHOOK THE THOUGHT OFF!

THE BOAT YARD WAS REALLY A WRECKING YARD OF BOATS, AND PARTS, AND MILO BECAME A REAL JUNK COLLECTOR TO COME UP WITH THE PARTS THAT HE NEEDED FOR HIS NEW TREASURE.

ANGEE BUSIED HERSELF WITH SEWING SEAT COVERS AND DRAWING PICTURES OF HOW SHE WANTED THE INTERIOR OF THE BOAT TO LOOK.

AFTER SEVERAL MONTHS OF INTENSE WORK ON THE LITTLE BOAT IT WAS TIME TO NAME THE BEAUTIFUL SLEEK LITTLE BOAT.

THEY THOUGHT ABOUT IT LONG AND HARD AND CAME UP WITH THE NAME "SNAP-DRAGON".

A SUITABLE NAME FOR SUCH A BEAUTIFUL AND DELICATE LOOKING CRAFT.

THEY HAULED THE BOAT OUT OF THE WATER AND RE-PAINTED HER HULL AND TOP SIDES. THEY RE-FIT HER RUDDER AND MADE SURE THAT THE KEEL WAS NOT GOING TO FALL OFF!

SPLASH! BACK IN THE WATER AGAIN. HE GROUND ALL OF THE OLD FIBERGLASS AND PAINT OFF OF HER DECK AND INSTALLED NEW TOE RAILS AND RUB RAILS THEN PUT SEVERAL LAYERS OF FIBERGLASS ON THE DECKS AND CABIN-TOP.

SHE WAS REALLY COMING TOGETHER NOW! IN THE NEXT FEW WEEKS: HE STEPPED THE MAST AND TUNED THE RIGGING.

IT WAS TIME TO ORDER THE SAILS. HE FOUND A GREAT DEAL ON SAILS FROM A PLACE CALLED BACON & ASSOCIATES.

THEY DEALT IN GENTLY USED SAILS, FROM RACING BOATS THAT WERE EXPERIMENTING WITH DIFFERENT SAIL CONFIGURATIONS. THE OWNER OF THE BIG CHARTER BOAT THAT HE WAS WORKING ON HAD TOLD HIM HOW TO ORDER THE SAILS. THE HEIGHT, THE LUFF, AND THE FOOT OF THE SAIL.

THEY BOUGHT ALL OF THE SAILS THAT THEY NEEDED, AND SOON IT WOULD BE TIME TO GIVE HER A SHAKE DOWN CRUISE, BACK TO KEY LARGO.

THE BOATYARD THAT THEY WERE LIVING AT WAS IN THE FLIGHT PATH OF MIAMI INTERNATIONAL AIRPORT. VERY NOISY. THEY COULDN'T WAIT TO GET OUT OF THERE!

MILO FINISHED WITH HIS OBLIGATIONS ON THE TUG AND THE SAILBOAT, AND PUT THE CABIN CRUISER UP FOR SALE. HE HAD ALSO REPAINTED THE CABIN CRUISER AND PUT A NEW COAT OF VARNISH ON THE BRIGHT WORK.

IT DIDN'T TAKE HIM VERY LONG TO FIND TO FIND A BUYER FOR THE CABIN CRUISER THAT THEY HAD BEEN LIVING ON FOR ALMOST A YEAR. SHE WAS QUITE COMFORTABLE, WITH 6 FT. HEAD-ROOM. ANGEE AND MILO ENDED UP HAVING FREE RENT FOR JUST OVER A YEAR, AND MADE A FEW BUCKS TO BOOT! IT EVEN PAID FOR THE SAILBOAT!

ANGEE AND MILO WOULD REALLY MISS THAT HEADROOM WHEN THEY MOVE TO THE "SNAP-

DRAGON". SHE ONLY HAD 5 FEET 2 INCH HEADROOM, AND THAT WAS AFTER MILO LOWERED THE FLOOR BOARDS ABOUT TEN INCHES. HE HAD TO NOTCH ALL OF THOSE BOARDS, TO FIT ALL OF THOSE NEW RIBS THAT WERE ADDED.

YOU JUST HAD TO SIT DOWN A LOT! OUTDOOR LIVING WAS WHAT IT WAS ALL ABOUT ANYWAY. LIFE IN THE TROPICS.

MILO CONTACTED HIS FRIEND, "CAPTAIN RON", THE GUY THAT THEY HAD BOUGHT THE FERRET FROM, AND HE CAME TO HELP MILO SAIL HER BACK TO KEY LARGO.

CAPTAIN RON TOLD HIM THAT HE HAD DONE A VERY GOOD JOB OF PUTTING HER TOGETHER, HE SAID: "NO HURRY", BUT YOU SHOULD THINK ABOUT BEEFING UP THE RIGGING A BIT. JUST BE CAREFUL IN HEAVY WINDS BRO.

IT TOOK JUST A BREATH OF WIND TO GET HER UP TO HULL SPEED; 10 TO 12 KNOTS OF WIND, DROVE HER AT 7 $\frac{1}{2}$ KNOTS. VERY IMPRESSIVE!

IT WAS A GREAT ADVENTURE THAT WAS IN STORE, FOR THE SNAPDRAGON, ONE THAT MILO WOULD NEVER FORGET, AS LONG AS HE LIVES. IT WAS A BEAUTIFUL SAIL THAT DAY.

THE SNAPDRAGON WAS FLAWLESS SHE WOULD SAIL SO CLOSE TO THE WIND THAT YOU WOULD THINK THAT YOU WERE SAILING STRAIGHT INTO THE WIND. 28 DEGREES OFF OF THE WIND.

MOST BOATS WILL SAIL AT A COMFORTABLE 45 DEGREES OFF OF THE WIND. WHEN YOU CAN SAIL AS CLOSE AS THE SNAP DRAGON, TO THE WIND YOU COULD CERTAINLY WIN SOME RACES.

MILO WILL BE ABLE TO HAVE SOME GOOD STORIES FOR HIS GRAND CHILDREN SOMEDAY. CAPTAIN RON AND MILO SAILED HER UP THE CANAL TO THE BOAT-YARD IN KEY LARGO. EVERYONE LOOKED AT THE BEAUTIFUL SLEEK SNAPDRAGON AS SHE EASILY NAVIGATED THE CANAL. UNDER SAIL ALONE, SHE DOCKED PERFECTLY.

THE ADVENTURE BEGINS

EVERYONE APPLAUDED AS HE TIED HER OFF TO THE DOCK FOR THE FIRST TIME. ANGEE WAS IN LOVE WITH THE BOAT. IT WAS AS MUCH A PART OF ANGEE, AS IT WAS HIS.

THEY BOTH SLAVED TO GET TO THIS DAY IN TIME. FINALLY! A SAILBOAT OF THEIR OWN.

HE PUT TWO HUGE DEEP CYCLE CATERPILLAR BATTERIES UNDER HER FLOORBOARDS, AND SECURED THEM, IN CASE OF A KNOCKDOWN; HEAVEN FORBID!

ANGEE AND MILO BOUGHT ALL OF THE CHARTS FOR THE BAHAMAS, FLORIDA STRAIGHTS, AND THE CARIBBEAN. THEY GOT ALL OF THE WIRES SECURED INTO HARNESSES AND MADE THEM WATER TIGHT CONNECTIONS. SALT WATER IS BRUTAL ON ELECTRICAL WIRING.

THEY HAD A TWO-BURNER GIMBALED PROPANE STOVE AND 12-VOLT LIGHTS. THEY BOUGHT AN AM / FM STEREO CASSETTE, WITH A C.B. RADIO BUILT IN, AND A GOOD RACK OF TAPES, & WATERPROOF SPEAKERS.

ALL SET! THEY STARTED BUYING CANNED GOODS. THEY PEELED OFF THE LABELS AND MARKED THEM WITH PERMANENTE MARKERS AND DIPPED THEM IN WAX AND PUT THEM UNDER THE FLOORBOARDS, AND SEATS.

FINALLY, THEY COULD NOT GET ANY MORE FOOD ON THE BOAT.

THE MORE WEIGHT SHE HAD THE BETTER SHE SAILED AND MUCH MORE STABLE TOO!

SHE FELT VERY SECURE WITH THE WATERLINE SO LOW TO THE WATER. THE HEAVIER THAT SHE WAS THE MORE ABLE SHE WAS TO POINT TO WINDWARD.

SEVERAL COUPLES WERE GETTING READY TO GO CRUISING TO THE BAHAMAS. SO ANGEE AND MILO DECIDED THAT IT WOULD BE THE SAFEST FOR THEM TO GO WITH A GROUP.

HE GOT A HOLD OF CAPTAIN RON AGAIN. HE WAS JUST A LITTLE WAYS DOWN THE KEYS AT HIS SLIP IN ANOTHER MARINA. HE WAS AT THE LORELEI MARINA AT ISLAMORADA.

MILO NEEDED TO KNOW A LITTLE MORE ABOUT NAVIGATION! THEY WERE LEAVING THE NEXT DAY AND HE NEEDED A CRASH COURSE!

HE BOUGHT A BOTTLE OF RUM AND A CASE OF COKE AND THEY STUDIED CHARTS ALL NIGHT LONG.

CAPTAIN RON TAUGHT HIM ABOUT SET AND DRIFT. HOW FAR THE CURRENT TAKES YOU PER HOUR AND LEE-WAY; WHEN YOU ARE SAILING TIGHT INTO THE WIND, HOW MUCH YOUR BOAT BLOWS SIDEWAYS. DEAD RECKONING, WHEN

A COURSE IS COMPUTED AT A CERTAIN SPEED THE SPOT ON THE FACE OF THE EARTH WHERE YOU THINK THAT YOU ARE IN LONGITUDE AND LATITUDE.

IT WAS A LONG NIGHT AND HE WANTED TO BE SURE EVERYTHING WAS GONE OVER CORRECTLY. CAPTAIN RON TESTED HIM ON ALL DIFFERENT POSSIBILITIES AND MILO PASSED WITH FLYING COLORS. HE SAID: YOU DON'T HAVE TO WORRY ABOUT IT BRO; I'LL KEEP AN EYE OUT FOR YOU.

HE WAS READY FOR TOMORROW NIGHTS TRUE TEST! THE FIRST CROSSING!

CAPTAIN RON HAD A CHARTER GOING THAT SAME DAY.

ALL OF THE BOATS SAILED OUT TO THE REEF. THAT WOULD BE THE TAKE-OFF POINT THAT NIGHT

THEY ALL HOISTED THEIR SAILS JUST AFTER SUNSET AND SAILED TOWARD GUN CAY CUT BAHAMAS.

A NORTHEASTER WAS BLOWING AT ABOUT TWENTY KNOTS.

THE GULF STREAM TRAVELS AT ABOUT THREE KNOTS FROM SOUTH TO NORTH SO WHEN THE WIND BLOWS OUT OF THE NORTH AT FIFTEEN TO TWENTY KNOTS IT CANCELS THE DRIFT OF THE GULF STREAM.

MILO HAD TO TAKE TWO REEF POINTS IN THE MAINSAIL IN ORDER TO KEEP FROM GETTING KNOCKED DOWN. IT JUST MAKES THE SAIL SHORTER AND SHORTER. THE SNAPDRAGON WAS VERY TENDER TO HIGH WINDS. SOMETIMES

HE THOUGHT THAT HER MAST WAS TOO TALL UNLESS THE WINDS WERE VERY LIGHT. THEN HE WANTED ALL OF THE SAIL THAT HE COULD GET! HE PICKED A STAR ON THE HORIZON AND SAILED DIRECTLY AT IT BECAUSE HE WAS SAILING FROM WEST TO EAST.

THE SNAPDRAGON HAD THE ADVANTAGE OF BEING ABLE TO SAIL VERY TIGHT INTO THE WIND. SO THEY DID NOT HAVE TO TACK FOR THE WHOLE CROSSING. TACKING AT NIGHT CAN BE DANGEROUS ANYWAY.

DURING THE CROSSING ANGEE WAS BELOW PRAYING AND MAKING CUBAN COFFEE FOR MILO. THEY WERE POUNDING TO WINDWARD PRETTY HARD. IT WAS NOT VERY COMFORTABLE FOR ANGEE AT ALL.

HE KEPT GETTING SLAPPED IN THE FACE. HE THOUGHT MAYBE THERE WAS A LOOSE PIECE OF SHEET LINE OR SOMETHING SO HE TURNED ON HIS FLASHLIGHT AND LOOKED OVER ALL OF THE RIGGING BUT HE COULDN'T FIND ANY LOOSE HALYARDS ANYWHERE. HE GOT SLAPPED AGAIN AND HE SHINED THE FLASHLIGHT AROUND AGAIN BUT NO LUCK! THERE WAS SOMETHING VERY ILLUSIVE GOING ON!

AS THE SUN CAME UP IN THE MORNING HE SAW THE SILHOUETTE OF AN ISLAND, THERE IT WAS! "GUN CAY, CAT CAY CUT". HE REALLY NEVER UNDERSTOOD WHY THEY CALL THEM CAY'S, THEY WERE JUST ISLANDS TO HIM.

HE LOOKED INTO THE FOOT WELL OF THE COCKPIT AND SAW THE REASON THAT HE KEPT FEELING LIKE HE WAS GETTING SLAPPED.

THERE WERE AT LEAST A HALF DOZEN FLYING FISH IN THE COCKPIT! HE HAD BEEN LOOKING IN THE WRONG PLACE ALL OF THE TIME.

HE LAUGHED AND POINTED THEM OUT TO ANGEE THEN THEY BOTH LAUGHED! HE THREW THEM OVERBOARD AND SHRUGGED HIS SHOULDERS.

HE SAILED IN TO THE CUT AND DROPPED HIS ANCHORS THEN DOVE IN AND MADE SURE THAT THEY WERE SECURE FOR THE REST OF THE DAY AND THAT NIGHT.

IT WAS WHAT THEY CALLED, A BIMINI ANCHORAGE.

MILO ALWAYS PRACTICED DIVING HIS ANCHORS IN. A GOOD HABIT TO GET INTO WHILE SAILING ANYWHERE THAT THERE IS A LOT OF CURRENT!

YOU PUT ONE ANCHOR OFF OF THE BOW AND LET YOUR ANCHOR LINE WAY OUT! ABOUT 500 FEET THEN DROP ANOTHER ANCHOR OFF OF THE STERN AND PULL YOURSELF UP TO ABOUT 200 FEET FROM THE BOW. THEN YOU FEED THE REAR ANCHOR THROUGH THE CHALK AT THE BOW. THEN THE BOAT CAN SWING FROM SIDE TO SIDE AND NOT DRAG ANCHOR.

AFTER SETTING HIS ANCHORS HE SAT IN THE COCKPIT AND LOOKED UP AT THE RIGGING AND THERE WAS SEAWEED HANGING FROM THE SPREADERS AND ALL OVER THE BAGGY WRINKLES WHICH ARE THE CHAFE GUARDS FOR THE SAILS !

HE WAS KNOCKED DOWN AFTER ALL!

DURING THE TRIP HE HAD TAKEN A FEW WAVES INTO THE COCKPIT.

IT WAS A GOOD THING THAT IT WAS SELF-BAILING AND THAT HE WAS WEARING A HARNESS BECAUSE OPEN SEAS WERE COMING THROUGH THE COCKPIT FROM TIME TO TIME DURING THE CROSSING AND WASHING HIM FROM ONE SIDE OF THE COCKPIT TO THE OTHER.

THANK GOD! WE MADE IT! WE DRUG OUR SPREADERS THROUGH THE WATER AFTER ALL. WE ARE SO LUCKY! ANGEE TOLD HIM. WELL WHY DO YOU THINK THAT I WAS DOWN BELOW PRAYING?

THEY JUST WANTED TO SOAK UP THE BEAUTY OF THE WATER AND THIS PLACE IN GENERAL. WHILE SWIMMING AROUND HE SPOTTED SOME CONCH ON THE BOTTOM.

CONCH FRITTERS FOR DINNER! OH BOY! THOSE SEA SNAILS ARE THE BEST EATING THINGS IN THE OCEAN AND THEY ARE EASY TO CATCH TOO!

ABOUT THREE HOURS LATER THE OTHER BOATS STARTED ARRIVING.

THEY ALL WERE ALL SURPRISED TO SEE THE SNAPDRAGON ANCHORED AND WAITING FOR THEM. THE FRITTERS WERE ALREADY COOKING AND ANGEE AND MILO WERE TREATING.

CAPTAIN RON RAFTED ALONG SIDE OF THE SNAPDRAGON. HE KNEW THAT MILO HAD ANCHORED PROPERLY.

THEY ALL GOT TOGETHER THAT EVENING AND PLAYED MUSIC AND SMOKED POT UNTIL VERY LATE. WHAT A BEAUTIFUL FIRST DAY IT WAS WONDERFUL TO BE ALIVE!

THE NEXT MORNING HE WOKE UP FREEZING HIS ASS OFF! WHAT THE HELL! THIS IS SUPPOSED TO BE THE TROPICS!

HE MADE A POT OF CUBAN COFFEE. THAT WARMED UP THE CABIN FOR A WHILE. HE DRANK HIS COFFEE AND NOTICED STEAM ON THE WATER.

HE OPENED THE HATCH TO GET A BETTER LOOK. ANGEE! HE SCREAMED! LOOK OUT OF THE HATCH!

SHE GOT UP AND LOOKED AND TO HER AMAZEMENT THERE WAS TWO INCHES OF SNOW ON THE DECK OF THE BOAT!

MILO GOT RIGHT OUT AND WASHED IT OFF WITH SALT WATER AND THOUGHT TO HIMSELF. PARADISE. BAH!

THE SNOW WAS ALL OVER THE ISLAND. IT WAS BEAUTIFUL THOUGH. HE THOUGHT TO HIMSELF: GOD I HOPE I NEVER SEE THAT AGAIN IN THE BAHAMAS!

IT TURNED OUT THAT WAS THE YEAR THAT ALL OF THE CITRUS CROPS FROSTED IN FLORIDA!

A FEW DAYS LATER IT WARMED UP VERY NICELY AND IT WAS TIME TO SAIL AGAIN.

THIS TIME; THE GREAT BAHAMA BANKS! IT WAS ABOUT A HUNDRED-MILE STRETCH OF PRETTY DEAD WATER. NO FISH TO SPEAK OF AND THE WATER WAS PRETTY SHALLOW.

THERE WAS SOMETHING ABOUT THIS PLACE AND TIME THAT MILO DIDN'T LIKE. HE DIDN'T KNOW WHAT IT WAS EXACTLY BUT HE DIDN'T LIKE IT! IT WAS LIKE A DESERT IN THE OCEAN!

ANGEE AND MILO WERE SAILING ALONG WITH A FRIEND WHO WAS SOLOING HIS OWN BOAT. IT WAS SAFER TO SAIL IN TEAMS.

THEY SET SAIL ON A BEAM REACH, AND AS THE DAY WENT BY THE WIND CLOCKED AROUND TO THE POINT THAT THEY WERE HARD INTO THE WIND! IT WAS STARTING TO BLOW HARD FROM THE DIRECTION THEY WERE TRYING TO GO. SOUTH! NORMALLY YOU TAKE THE NORTHRELY WINDS TO BLOW SOUTH. THEN TAKE THE SOUTH WINDS BACK HOME.

THE WIND WAS SLOWLY BUILDING ALL DAY. FINALLY THE WIND WAS SO STRONG THAT MILO HAD TO ROUND UP INTO THE WIND TO REEF THE MAIN SAIL AGAIN.

HE BROUGHT THE BOAT AROUND ON COARSE AND CONTINUED SAILING. HE WAS VERY UNCOMFORTABLE BEATING SO HARD INTO THE WIND! YOU ARE SUPPOSED TO KEEP THE WIND TO YOUR BACKS!

HE WAS SITTING DOWN DRINKING CUBAN COFFEE AND EATING A PIECE OF HOBO BREAD WHEN HE LOOKED UP AT THE MAST AND IT WAS AN "S" SHAPE.

SLAPPED DOWN AGAIN!

IN A MATTER OF HALF A SECOND THE MAST
SNAPPED IN HALF AND FELL INTO THE WATER.
THERE WAS ABOUT A FIVE-FOOT SWELL AND THE
WATER WAS ABOUT FIFTEEN FEET DEEP.
THE PIECE OF THE MAST THAT WAS IN THE WATER
WAS HITTING THE BOTTOM AND THE RAGGED
END WAS HITTING THE BOTTOM OF THE BOAT!
TRYING TO PUNCH A HOLE IN THE BOTTOM.
INSTANT HELL! HE THREW IN THE ANCHOR AND
PROCEEDED TO CUT ALL OF THE RIGGING FREE.
FINALLY SAFE FOR NOW; THEY WERE WORRIED
THAT THEIR BUDDY WOULDN'T NOTICE THEIR
TURMOIL UNTIL IT WAS TOO LATE.
LUCK HAD IT WITH THEM AND HE NOTICED THAT
THEY DIDN'T HAVE A MAST ANYMORE. HE TURNED
AROUND AND RESCUED THEM. FORTUNATELY FOR
HIM IT WAS A DOWN WIND RESCUE.
HE TOWED ANGEE AND MILO BACK TO GUN CAY.
HE STUCK AROUND LONG ENOUGH TO MAKE SURE
THE BOAT WAS SECURE AND TURNED AROUND

AND SAID: I GOT TO GO DOWN SOUTH SEE YA LATER. GOOD LUCK MILO.

IT WAS NECESSARY FOR HIM TO GET AS FAR SOUTH AS HE COULD AS SOON AS HE COULD. IT IS A GOOD PRACTICE TO KEEP THE WIND TO YOUR BACK. TODAY HE WAS GOING TO HAVE TO BEAT IT THOUGH!

AT GUN CAY AGAIN. MILO WAS TRYING TO RIG A WAY THAT HE COULD USE HALF OF THE MAST AND CONTINUE ON. IT WAS NO USE.

HE COULD RIG IT GOOD ENOUGH TO GET HOME BUT NOT GOOD ENOUGH TO CRUISE THE ISLANDS. THEY WERE SITTING ON THE BOAT WONDERING WHAT THEY SHOULD DO NEXT WHEN A POWER BOAT OFFERED TO TOW THEM TO BIMINI HARBOR. AT LEAST THERE WERE PEOPLE THERE! THEY ACCEPTED.

THE RESCUE BOAT'S NAME WAS "TIBBARON". HE TOLD THE CAPTAIN OF THE 46 FOOT HATTERAS THAT HIS HULL SPEED WAS 7 $\frac{1}{2}$ KNOTS. THE TIBBARON'S CAPTAIN SAID: OK SKIPPER AND THEY WERE TOWED TO BIMINI.

MILO CALCULATED TIME AND DISTANCE TO BIMINI HARBOR THEY WERE THERE SO FAST THAT HE CHECKED TIME AND DISTANCE AGAIN AND WAS SURPRISED AT AN AMAZING 10 $\frac{1}{2}$ KNOTS.

ANGEE WAS SO BUMMED OUT THAT SHE WANTED TO RIDE ON THE POWER BOAT.

IT WAS A LONELY TRIP FOR MILO. HE SAW HER ON THE POWER BOAT, DRINKING COCKTAILS, AND WAVING AT HIM FROM TIME TO TIME.

WELL AT LEAST IT DIDN'T TEAR THE BOAT UP. THE TIBBARON TOWED THE SNAPDRAGON TO WHERE THEY ANCHORED.

THE CAPTAIN SAID THAT HE DIDN'T HARDLY NOTICE THAT IT WAS THERE. THEY SAID THEIR GOODBYES AND LEFT THEM FOR WHO KNEW HOW LONG AT THAT POINT.

ABOUT A WEEK HAD GONE BY, AND MILO WAS STANDING ON THE DECK ONE DAY AND SAW CAPTAIN RON SAILING IN WITH ONE OF HIS CHARTERS.

HE WAVED HIS ARMS AT CAPTAIN RON AND ASKED HIM FOR A RIDE BACK TO KEY LARGO. CAPTAIN RON SAID; SURE. HE COULD USE A CREW MEMBER AND THAT HE WOULD HELP HIM FIND A MAST AND HELP HIM STEP IT WHEN THEY GOT BACK!

HE RELUCTANTLY LEFT ANGEE BEHIND TO TAKE CARE OF THE SNAPDRAGON. HE KISSED ANGEE GOOD-BYE, AND LEFT WITH CAPTAIN RON.

HE RAN A FEW LOCAL CHARTERS WITH CAPTAIN RON, AND EARNED ENOUGH MONEY TO BUY ANOTHER MAST AND RIGGING FOR THE SNAPDRAGON. HE SCRAMBLED TO FIND ALL OF THE PARTS, AND PIECES AND MORE EXTRAS THAT HE COULD POSSIBLY NEED. THERE ARE NO PARTS STORES OUT ISLAND, OR AT LEAST VERY FEW.

FINALLY; THE MAST, RIGGING AND MORE FOOD WE'RE READY AND CAPTAIN RON HAD ANOTHER CHARTER TO BIMINI HARBOR WHERE HE HELPED

MILO STEP THE MAST AND WISHED HIM GOOD LUCK AGAIN.
NOW THE RIGGING ON THE SNAPDRAGON WAS NOT AS FRAIL AS THE NAME! IN FACT QUITE STOUT NOW.

BACK IN THE SADDLE

ANGEE AND MILO SAILED OUT OF BIMINI HARBOR WITH ANTICIPATION IN THEIR HEARTS. THEY WERE ABOUT A MONTH AND A HALF BEHIND SCHEDULE AT THIS POINT. THEY SPENT ALL DAY AND ALL NIGHT GOING ACROSS THE BAHAMA BANKS AGAIN.

IN THE MORNING THEY CLEARED THE BANKS INTO DEEP BLUE WATER, AND THEY SAILED THAT DAY TO NASSAU BAHAMAS.

AS THEY APPROACHED THE ENTRANCE OF THE CHANNEL AT PARADISE ISLAND. THE WIND WAS RIGHT ON THEIR NOSE SO THAT THEY HAD TO TACK BACK AND FORTH TO MAKE IT IN TO THE CHANNEL.

THERE WAS A CRUISE SHIP THAT WAS STANDING OFF SHORE AND THE CAPTAIN WAS WATCHING THE SNAPDRAGON FIGHTING TO GET IN TO THE CUT.

THE CAPTAIN GOT IMPATIENT AND DECIDED TO COME IN ANYWAY. MILO WAS ON HIS LAST TACK TO MAKE THE CUT WHEN THE CRUISE SHIP

STARTED BLOWING HIS HORN WARNING THAT
HE WAS COMING THROUGH.

HE SHOULD HAVE KNOWN THAT WHILE UNDER
SAIL YOU HAVE THE RIGHT-OF-WAY.

MILO SAW THAT HE WAS GOING TO BE SMASHED
BY THE CRUISE SHIP BEFORE HE COULD MAKE
IT THROUGH THE CUT SO HE CAME ABOUT AND
HEADED BACK OUT AS THE CRUISE SHIP CAME IN
TO THE CUT. THE SHIP WAS BLOWING ITS HORN
CONSTANTLY AS IT PULLED UP TO THE DOCK.

HE CAME ABOUT ONE MORE TIME AND EASILY
MADE IT INTO PORT THAT TIME. HE SAILED TO AN
ANCHORAGE, INSIDE THE CUT AND DROPPED HIS
SAILS AND HIS ANCHOR. MILO AND ANGEE GOT
INTO THEIR DINGY AND ROWED TO SHORE.

HE AND ANGEE WERE WALKING DOWN THE DOCK
PAST THE SPOT WHERE THE CRUISE SHIP WAS
DOCKED WHEN HE SPOTTED THE CAPTAIN OF
THE CRUISE SHIP.

HE WALKED UP TO THE CAPTAIN AND SAID:
AREN'T YOU SUPPOSED TO GIVE THE RIGHT-OF-
WAY TO A VESSEL UNDER SAIL?

THE CAPTAIN SAID: YOU MEAN TO TELL ME THAT
YOU ARE MAKING A TRIP LIKE THIS WITHOUT
A MOTOR? MILO SAID: THAT IS CORRECT
CAPTAIN.

THE CAPTAIN APOLOGIZED TO MILO FOR PUTTING
HIM IN HARMS WAY AND OFFERED HIM AND
ANGEE A JOB ON THE CRUISE SHIP. MILO AS A
NAVIGATOR AND ANGEE AS A GALLEY WORKER.
THEY THANKED THEM FOR THE OFFER AND SAID
THAT THEY WERE ON THEIR FIRST CRUISE AND

THAT MAYBE SOMETIME IN THE FUTURE THAT COULD WORK OUT. THEY TOOK ONE OF HIS CARDS.

THEY LEFT THE SHIP AND WENT TO THE LOCAL FARMERS MARKET AND PURCHASED LOTS OF KEY LIMES A WHOLE STALK OF FRESH GREEN BANANA'S THEN WENT BACK TO THE SNAPDRAGON FOR A GOOD NIGHTS SLEEP.

THEY GOT UP IN THE MORNING AND MILO SPOTTED SOME CONCH ON THE FLOOR OF THE ANCHORAGE AND DOVE THEM UP FOR LATER.

THEY PULLED ANCHOR AND HEADED OUT OF THE SOUTH CUT OF THE HARBOR, AND THEN FURTHER SOUTH HEADED TOWARD ELUTHERA, AND CAT ISLAND ON THE ATLANTIC SIDE. EVERY DAY WAS TRULY PARADISE. WARM TROPICAL BREEZES, FRESH COCONUTS AND ALL OF THE FRESH FISH ANYONE COULD WANT.

EASY DAY SAILS TO EVERY ISLAND. JUST A COUPLE OF HOURS EACH DAY. IT JUST DOESN'T GET ANY BETTER.

THEY WERE WORKING THEIR WAY FURTHER AND FURTHER SOUTH ALONG THE PRESENT CHAIN OF ISLANDS. JUST A FEW MILES EACH DAY. NICE AND EASY.

WEEKS OF WONDERFUL DAY SAILS TO MANY DIFFERENT ISLANDS ALONG THE CHAIN. SOME INHABITED SOME NOT. SOMETIMES THEY WOULD STAY A FEW DAYS AND SOMETIMES LONGER.

ONE AFTERNOON HE AND ANGEE WERE SAILING ALONG A VERY RAGGED SET OF ISLANDS WHEN

THEY DECIDED THAT WERE GOING TO RUN OUT OF DAYLIGHT SOON.

THEY DECIDED THAT THEY WOULD SAIL INTO A CUT THAT HAD A NICE ANCHORAGE WITH PLENTY OF NATURAL ROCKS AROUND THE LITTLE COVE AND THEY WOULD BE SAFE FROM THE ATLANTIC SWELLS.

SO THEY SAILED AT HULL SPEED INTO THE CUT WHICH HAD ALMOST AN EQUAL CURRENT IN THE OPPOSITE DIRECTION.

THE BEGINNING OF THE END

THE WORST DID HAPPEN. THE CUT WAS LIKE A RIVER INLET AND OUTLET TO THE ISLANDS THAT THE WATER SURROUNDED.
IT WAS VERY FAST MOVING WATER UNTIL IT HIT HIGH TIDE THEN IT WAS THE SAME THING WHEN THE TIDE WAS RUNNING OUT.
IT TOOK ALMOST TWO HOURS TO GET INTO THE CUT. IT WAS ALMOST DARK WHEN THEY FINALLY ANCHORED AND BREATHED A SIGH OF RELIEF.
IT WAS A PEACEFUL LITTLE COVE WITH A WHITE SAND BOTTOM. A WONDERFUL PLACE TO BE AFTER BEATING SO HARD GETTING IN THERE; OR SO THEY THOUGHT!
THEY DROPPED THEIR ANCHORS, AND RELAXED FOR THE NIGHT.
ABOUT TWENTY MINUTES AFTER THEY ANCHORED. A 30' CIGARETTE BOAT PULLED UP BESIDE THEM.
THEY WERE VERY ABRUPT WITH THEM AND BANGED THEIR BOAT VERY HARD. REALLY RUDE GUYS!

THAT OCEAN GOING DEEP "V" HULL WAS OBVIOUSLY BEING USED FOR SOME SORT OF SMUGGLING OPERATION.

THE MEN ON BOARD TOLD HIM TO GET THE FUCK OUT OF THERE! NOW! , OR THEY WILL HAVE A PROBLEM!

MILO LOOKED AT THEM AND SAID THAT HE DID NOT WANT ANY PROBLEM WITH THEM AND THAT THEY WOULD LEAVE AT SUNRISE, NO PROBLEM! WE ARE VERY TIRED FROM THE SAIL TODAY.

THEY SAID; YOU'VE BEEN WARNED! AND LEFT. MILO WAS LEFT WITH A TERRIFYING SINKING FEELING!

ABOUT TEN O'CLOCK THAT EVENING, MILO WAS AWAKENED BY THE SAME GUYS DRAGGING HIM OUT OF BED BY ONE ANKLE.

HE WAS KICKING AT THEM WITH NO AVAIL. THEY PROCEEDED TO PISTOL WHIP HIM, AND WHEN THEY WERE THROUGH, HE WAS LAYING THERE COVERED WITH BLOOD.

THEY MADE HIM WATCH AS THEY ALL BRUTALLY RAPED ANGEE SEVERAL TIMES!

EACH OF THE THREE OF THEM MADE EYE CONTACT WITH HIM, AS THEY EACH SCREWED HER IN THE PUSSY AND IN THE ASSHOLE.

MILO FELT SO SORRY FOR HER; DESPAIR SWEPT OVER HIM,

BUT HATE WAS KING. HE HATED THEM MORE THAN HE WAS SORRY FOR ANGEE. ALL HE COULD THINK OF WAS PAYBACK!

WHEN THEY WERE THROUGH THEY SAID; NOW! GET OUT OF HERE!

THEY WERE LUCKY TO BE ALIVE!

HE WAS BEATEN TO A PULP! HATE WAS EATING HIM.

ALL OF THEIR FACES WERE ON HIS MIND AS HE PULLED ANCHOR AND THEY SAILED AWAY INTO THE NIGHT!

ANGEE AND MILO CRIED TOGETHER ALL NIGHT, AS THEY SAILED AROUND IN CIRCLES FOR THE ENTIRE NIGHT.

ANGEE WAS SOBBING UN-CONTROLLABLY AND HE ASKED HER WHAT HE COULD DO TO COMFORT HER.

SHE SAID: JUST STAY THE FUCK AWAY FROM ME ASSHOLE!

IF YOU WERE HALF A MAN YOU WOULD HAVE STOPPED THEM!

MILES WAS THINKING ABOUT BEING A CONSCIENTIOUS OBJECTOR.

HOW COULD HE THINK THAT WAY ANY MORE AFTER WHAT HAD JUST HAPPENED TO HIM AND ANGEE.

NOW HE WAS CHANGED FOREVER. SOMEDAY THEY WOULD PAY!

MILO WAS DEVASTATED! HE WANTED TO HOLD HER AND TRY TO MAKE IT BETTER BUT ANGEE WOULD HAVE NOTHING TO DO WITH HIM.

HE KNEW THAT THE DAY WOULD COME WHEN HE WOULD HAVE A GUN FOR PROTECTION FROM PEOPLE THAT THEY HAD JUST ENCOUNTERED. HE NEVER DREAMED THAT HE WOULD EVER NEED A GUN IN PARADISE!

HE SAID TO HIMSELF; PAYBACK IS A MOTHER FUCKER! HE SCREAMED INTO THE DARK, I'LL GET YOU MOTHERFUCKERS!

HE WAITED ON ANGEE HAND AND FOOT! HE DID ALL THE COOKING AND CLEANING BUT HE JUST COULDN'T GET ANGEE OUT OF HER SLUMP. HE THOUGHT TO HIMSELF; IS THIS THE BEGINNING OF THE END FOR THEM?

SEVERAL MORE WEEKS WENT BY AND ANGEE SEEMED TO BE PULLING OUT OF HER SLUMP A LITTLE.

THEY CONTINUED TO SAIL DOWN ISLAND AND FINALLY MADE IT TO THE JUMENTOS CAYS OR AS KNOWN BY THE LOCALS "THE RAGGED ISLANDS".

THERE WAS A CAY NAMED NURSE CAY. BEAUTIFUL COVES FOR ANCHORING PATCHES OF WHITE SAND BEACHES.

THIS WAS AS CLOSE AS THEY WOULD GET TO PARADISE!

FINALLY ANGEE. WE MADE IT! PARADISE. THERE WAS NOBODY THERE BUT THEM.

ANGEE WAS STRUCK WITH AN OVERWHELMING FEELING OF FEAR! SHE JUST COULDN'T HELP BUT REMEMBER THAT TERRIBLE NIGHT! THERE WERE NO PEOPLE HERE! JUST LIKE BEFORE!

THE WAVE OF FEAR FINALLY PASSED AND ANGEE WAS HAPPY TO BE THERE AGAIN. SORT OF.

ANGEE AND MILO HUNG AROUND AND EXPLORED THE ISLAND FOR A FEW WEEKS. HE FOUND SOME GREAT CONCH BEDS, AND LOTS OF LOBSTER TOO!

ONE DAY: HE WAS SAILING AROUND THE ISLAND IN THE SAILING DINGY, AND NOTICED A CUT IN THE ROCKS THAT HE HAD NOT SEEN BEFORE. HE SAILED CAREFULLY TOWARD THE CUT AND MANAGED TO SLIP INTO ANOTHER COVE.

THERE WAS BEAUTIFUL WHITE SAND BEACHES ALL AROUND. THIS COULD BE THE PERFECT HURRICANE ANCHORAGE HE THOUGHT.

CLIFFS OF JAGGED ROCKS SURROUNDED THE COVE. THE CUT WAS ABOUT EIGHT FEET WIDE AND AT HIGH TIDE AND THE RIGHT CONDITIONS HE COULD SLIP THE SNAPDRAGON THROUGH THE CUT. SHE WAS ONLY SEVEN AND A HALF FEET WIDE.

HE SAILED THE DINGY UP ON TO ONE OF WHITE SAND BEACHES AND STEPPED OUT OF THE DINGY ON TO THE BEACH. THE SAND WAS WARM ON HIS FEET, BUT IT FELT DIFFERENT SOMEHOW.

HE LOOKED DOWN AT HIS FEET AND NOTICED THAT THE SAND WAS ABOUT HALF POT SEEDS. THIS REALLY EXCITED HIM, BECAUSE IT WAS COMMON FOR BALES OF POT TO DRIFT UP INTO THESE COVES.

LUCKY DAY

WAS THIS GOING TO BE HIS LUCKY DAY AFTER ALL!

THAT WAS ONE OF THE REASONS THAT HE CAME TO THIS STRIP OF ISLANDS IN THE FIRST PLACE! IT WAS REALLY TO GO BALE HUNTING, AND IT WAS HIS TURN TO GET WEALTHY!

HE HIKED UP THE RAGGED ROCKS TO GET A BETTER LOOK AT THE COVE FROM A MORE AERIAL VIEW. MILO LOOKED DOWN INTO THE COVE AND WAS FLABBERGASTED AT THE SIGHT OF IT.

THERE HAD TO BE AT LEAST A THOUSAND NURSE SHARKS IN THE COVE.

IT'S A SPAWNING GROUND FOR NURSE SHARKS! NO WONDER THEY CALLED IT NURSE CAY.

HE GOT A REAL UNEASY FEELING ABOUT ALL OF THESE SHARKS. HE HAD AFTER ALL BEEN DIVING THESE WATERS FOR WEEKS NOW!

AFTER SHAKING OFF THE MOMENT OF FEAR HE LOOKED OVER THE SHORE LINE AND SPOTTED ONE!

A BALE! A BALE! HE SHOUTED. HE SCURRIED DOWN THE ROCK CLIFFS BACK TO THE DINGY. HE CLIMBED IN AND ROWED THE DINGY OVER TO WHERE THE BALE WAS. THE SHARKS WERE VERY CURIOUS ABOUT THE DINGY, AND FOLLOWED IT CLOSELY.

NURSE SHARKS ARE NOT REAL AGGRESSIVE. THEY ARE MAINLY JUST CURIOUS.

MILO VERY CAREFULLY STEPPED OFF OF THE BOW OF THE DINGY ONTO THE BEACH. HE DRAGGED THE BALE TO THE DINGY AND THREW IT IN. IT WAS VERY HEAVY BECAUSE IT WAS SOAKED WITH SEA-WATER.

HE VERY CAREFULLY STEPPED BACK INTO THE DINGY AND SHOVED OFF WITH ONE OF THE OARS. HE RIGGED THE SAIL AND GOT THE HELL OUT OF THERE!

HE SAILED BACK AROUND THE SMALL CAYS AND BACK TO THE SNAPDRAGON. AS HE APPROACHED ANGEE NOTICED THE BALE AND ASKED HIM WHAT IT WAS?

HE TOLD HER THAT IT WAS AN ENGINE FOR THE SNAPDRAGON. IT WAS SATELLITE NAVIGATION. IT WAS ENOUGH MONEY TO CRUISE FOR YEARS! HE SHOVED THE BALE INTO WHERE THE ENGINE WOULD NORMALLY BE SITTING. BELOW THE COCKPIT.

IT WAS TIME TO GO HOME. THE CANNED GOODS WERE ALMOST GONE, THE PROPANE WAS ALMOST GONE TOO! IT WAS ALL DOWN WIND GOING HOME.

BLOWING HOME

ANGEE AND MILO BATTENED DOWN THE HATCHES AND PREPARED TO SAIL A MARATHON SAIL HOME. THIS TIME THEY STAYED ONLY TO THE ATLANTIC SIDE OF THE ISLANDS. IT WAS EASIER OPEN WATER TO NAVIGATE IN.
THEY SAILED BACK THROUGH THE CHAIN OF ISLANDS THAT THEY FOUND SO VERY EXCITING ON THE WAY DOWN ISLAND. THEY JUST BLEW THROUGH THEM AND ESPECIALLY WHERE ANGEE WAS RAPED.
MILES POINTED IT OUT TO ANGEE AND TOLD HER THAT HE WOULD NEVER FORGET THIS SPOT. NEVER!
AS THEY WERE PASSING THE SPOT, ANGEE WAS STONE SILENT. YOU COULD JUST SEE THE FEAR IN HER EYES.
MILO THOUGHT TO HIMSELF; I FEEL YOUR PAIN SWEETHEART. I'LL BE BACK!
NEXT STOP NASSAU! IT WAS A WONDERFUL SAIL BACK TO NASSAU.

THEY PICKED UP SOME COCONUT RUM, BANANAS AND LIMES. HE DOVE UP A COUPLE OF CONCH AND MADE A BATCH OF CONCH SALAD FOR THE TRIP.

HE HAD GOTTEN INTO THE HABIT OF TOWING THE DINGY BEHIND THE SNAPDRAGON WITH A NICE LONG PAINTER. IT MADE MUCH MORE ROOM ON THE DECK OF SUCH A SMALL BOAT.

THE PAINTER WAS ABOUT A 50 FOOT LONG PIECE OF NYLON ROPE THAT KEPT THE DINGHY WELL AWAY FROM THE BOAT. HE DECIDED TO TOW IT FOR THE LAST LEG OF THE JOURNEY.

THEY SET OUT OF NASSAU RUNNING WING & WING DOWN WIND ACROSS THE GREAT BAHAMA BANKS AND TOWARD THE CAT CAY, GUN CAY CUT.

THE SEAS WERE BUILDING QUITE HIGH. IN FACT, THEY WERE AS HIGH AS THE MAST OF THE SNAPDRAGON. 29 FEET AND HIGHER.

THE SNAPDRAGON WAS A VERY LOW FREEBOARD BOAT WHICH WAS WHY SHE LOOKED SO SLEEK IN THE WATER.

SHE WAS RUNNING DOWN-WIND SO FAST THAT SHE WAS BEGINNING TO START SURFING DOWN THE FACES OF THE WAVES.

THIS PRESENTED A BIG PROBLEM WITH THE DINGY.

IT WAS GETTING AIRBORNE WHEN THE SNAPDRAGON HIT THE BOTTOM OF THE TROUGH BETWEEN THE SETS OF WAVES.

HE NEEDED TO MAKE A CHOICE AND FAST!

EITHER CUT THE DINGHY LOOSE OR GET IT ON BOARD FAST!

FINALLY! HERE IT CAME! LIKE A BOMB FALLING OUT OF THE SKY!

IT SMASHED INTO THE BACK STAY WITH SUCH FORCE THAT THE WHOLE BOAT SHOOK VIOLENTLY. HE CALLED OUT TO ANGEE TO TAKE THE TILLER. HE WANTED TO TRY AND GET IT ON BOARD.

ANGEE WAS SCARED TO DEATH AND DIDN'T KNOW IF SHE COULD HANDLE THE BOAT IN THAT ROUGH OF SEAS BUT THERE WASN'T ANY CHOICE AND SHE TOOK THE TILLER.

HE IMMEDIATELY GRABBED THE DINGY WHICH WAS ALREADY HUNG UP AND SNAGGED ON THE RIGGING. HE GRABBED A HOLD OF IT AND DRUG IT ON TO THE STERN OF THE BOAT. IT BEAT THE HELL OUT OF HIS LEGS AS HE TRIED TO PULL IT ON BOARD FROM AROUND THE BACKSTAY.

BLEEDING PROFUSELY ALL OVER THE STERN OF THE BOAT HE WAS SLIPPING AROUND ON THE STERN IN HIS OWN BLOOD! HE FINALLY GOT IT SECURED AND GASPED TO CATCH HIS BREATH.

ANGEE WAS AS WHITE AS A SHEET! SHE YELLED! PLEASE TAKE THIS TILLER OUT OF MY HANDS. I CAN'T DO THIS ANY MORE! HE TOOK THE TILLER AGAIN AND ANGEE TENDED TO HIS WOUNDS.

ONE HELL OF A SAIL THAT DAY. THE WIND AND THE CURRENT TO THEIR BACKS. THEY MANAGED 12 $\frac{1}{2}$ KNOTS ON THAT CROSSING! WHAT A RIDE! A LOT OF DRIFT!

SO MUCH FOR BEING LAZY AND NOT PUTTING THE DINGHY ON BOARD TO START WITH.

FINALLY BACK AT GUN CAY. THEY PREPARED THE SNAPDRAGON FOR HER LAST CROSSING.

THEY TOOK ADVANTAGE OF THE CURRENT TO GET OUT OF THE CUT AND STOOD OFF SHORE UNTIL WELL AFTER SUNSET. THEY HAD JUST STARTED OFF SHORE, WHEN A U.S. COAST-GUARD CUTTER CAME ALONG SIDE OF THE SNAPDRAGON.

THE CAPTAIN OF THE CUTTER ANNOUNCED OVER HIS P.A. SYSTEM; PREPARE TO BE BOARDED!

MILO WAS HALF PANICKED BECAUSE THEY HAD ABOUT A HUNDRED POUNDS OF POT ON BOARD!

THE SNAPDRAGON WAS SO LOW IN THE WATER THAT SHE LOOKED MORE LIKE A SURFBOARD. MILO STOOD IN THE COCKPIT WITH HIS ARMS SPREAD APART.

THERE WAS LIGHTING FLASHING AND THE SEAS WERE BUILDING. FINALLY THE CAPTAIN ANNOUNCED OVER THE LOUDSPEAKER.

"HAVE A SAFE TRIP SKIPPER", AND DISAPPEARED JUST AS FAST AS HE HAD APPEARED.

MILO SIGHED WITH RELIEF, AND SET A COURSE FOR KEY LARGO.

THERE WAS SO MUCH DRIFT WITH THE WIND COMING OUT OF THE SOUTHEAST THAT THEY COULD NOT MAKE KEY LARGO WITHOUT BEATING THEMSELVES TO DEATH. THEY DECIDED TO HEAD FOR MIAMI'S BISCAYNE BAY INSTEAD.

THEY SAILED RIGHT PAST THE COASTGUARD STATION, AND INTO THE ANCHORAGE FOR THE NIGHT.

WHEN THEY AWOKE IN THE MORNING, THE WIND HAD COME AROUND FROM THE NORTH AGAIN

AND THEY HEADED DOWN THE INTERCOSTAL
WATERWAY TO KEY LARGO, WING AND WING.
THE CROSSING WENT WELL. IT WAS NICE TO BE
BACK IN KEY LARGO AGAIN.

BACK TO HOME PORT

IT WAS PARTY TIME! THEY SAW ALL OF THEIR OLD FRIENDS AND EXCHANGED STORIES ABOUT THEIR ADVENTURES.
ANGEE AND MILO KEPT THE STORY OF HER BEING RAPED TO THEMSELVES.
THERE WERE SEVERAL DAYS OF PARTYING WITH SEVERAL GROUPS OF FRIENDS. IT WAS NICE TO SEE THE POSITIVE FEELINGS COME BACK TO ANGEE AGAIN.

MILO FOUND A BUYER FOR THE POT AND THEY WERE $50,000 RICHER.
CAPTAIN RON CAME BY ONE DAY AND ASKED MILO TO HELP HIM WITH A CHARTER. MILO WAS THE ONLY ONE THAT CAPTAIN RON TRUSTED. AFTER ALL, HE HAD TRAINED HIM. MILO WASN'T AFRAID OF HIGH SEAS.
MILO WAS WORRIED ABOUT ANGEE'S MENTAL WELL BEING, FROM THE EXPERIENCE IN THE BAHAMAS.

ANGEE ASSURED MILO THAT SHE WOULD BE ALL RIGHT AND THAT HE SHOULD GO WITH RON ON THE CRUISE AND MAKE SOME MONEY. HE WENT WITH CAPTAIN RON ON THE CHARTER.

IT WAS A GROUP OF 6 LESBIANS. THAT WAS PRETTY KINKY!

THERE WAS A LOT OF CROTCH LICKING GOING ON WITH THOSE HORN DOG GIRLS. IT WAS QUITE AN EXPERIENCE FOR MILO.

HE HAD NOT SEEN ANYTHING LIKE THAT SINCE THE SIXTIES. THEY CRUISED AROUND FOR ABOUT 10 DAYS AND THEN BACK TO KEY LARGO AGAIN.

AS THEY WERE MOTORING DOWN THE CANAL WHERE CAPTAIN RON'S SLIP WAS. ALL OF THE GIRLS WERE NAKED AS JAY-BIRDS, LAYING AROUND ON DECK,

THEY WERE ALL SUNNING THEIR CROTCHES WHEN THEY CRUISED BY THE SNAP-DRAGON. THE PEOPLE ALONG THE WALL AT THE BOAT YARD WERE WHOOPING AND WHISTLING AS THEY WENT BY.

ANGEE JUST GLARED AT THE GIRLS ON THE BOAT AS IT WENT BY.

MILO HELPED CAPTAIN RON DOCK THE BOAT AND THEN WENT TO EXPLAIN TO ANGEE ABOUT THE NAKED GIRLS.

ANGEE GOT MAD ABOUT THE GIRLS AND WOULD NOT BELIEVE A WORD HE SAID BUT IT WAS ONLY AN ACT.

EVIDENTLY ANGEE HAD BEEN DOING SOME SAILING OF HER OWN WITH ONE OF HIS BEST FRIENDS! WHILE HE WAS OFF ON CHARTERS.

ANGEE JUST USED THE GIRLS FROM THE CHARTER AS AN EXCUSE AND WOULDN'T LISTEN TO HIS EXPLANATION.

THEY ARGUED ABOUT THE BOAT AND THE FACT THAT SHE DECIDED TO LEAVE HIM WHEN SHE WAS RAPED!

ANGEE JUST TOOK HER HALF OF THE MONEY THAT THEY GOT FROM THE BALE, AND GOT MILO TO PAY HER FOR HER HALF OF THE SNAP DRAGON AND THEN LEFT HIM. NEVER TO SEE HIM AGAIN.

FUNNY; ALL OF THAT TIME TOGETHER AND JUST TO HAVE IT END LIKE THIS WAS A TOTAL SHOCK BUT HE KNEW IN HIS HEART THAT SOMETHING WAS UP.

THE DAY BEFORE ANGEE WAS RAPED WAS THE LAST TIME HE HAD MADE LOVE TO HER. HE WAS SWEPT WITH LOSS AND LONELINESS. HE WEPT FOR WEEKS AND EVERY NIGHT HE WAS ALONE.

THE LAST THING THAT HE HEARD WAS THAT ANGEE WENT SAILING WITH JOEY. SHE NEVER KNEW HOW BADLY THAT SHE HAD BROKEN MILO'S HEART!

HE THOUGHT ABOUT A GUN AND REALIZED THAT IF HE HAD A WEAPON, HE WOULD AT LEAST HAVE HAD A FIGHTING CHANCE AND MAYBE HE WOULD STILL HAVE ANGEE OR THEY COULD BOTH BE DEAD RIGHT NOW!

WHEN EVER HE STOPPED TO THINK ABOUT ANGEE, HE CRIED HIS HEART OUT OVER THE

LOSS HE SUFFERED. HE TRIED DESPERATELY TO PULL HIMSELF OUT OF HIS SLUMP. IT WAS VERY HARD ON HIM.

MILO HUNG OUT WITH HIS FRIENDS AND DATED ALL OF THE AVAILABLE WOMEN THAT HE HAD THE CHANCE TO MEET. HE TOOK ALL OF THEM SAILING OUT TO THE REEFS AND TO SOME OF THE CLOSE BY ISLANDS. HE WAS LOOKING FOR THE RIGHT WOMAN TO CRUISE WITH.

HE SPREAD HIMSELF ALL OVER THE FLORIDA KEYS. HE NEVER DID FIND LUCY AGAIN, ALTHOUGH HE DID THINK OF HER OFTEN. SHE WAS THE ONLY ONE THAT WAS REAL! AT LEAST HE THOUGHT SO.

HE HAD FRIENDS IN HIGH PLACES IN FLORIDA CITY AND IN THE KEYS. HE WENT TO WORK AS A CARPENTER FOR A GOOD FRIEND OF HIS BUDDY WILLARD.

WILLARD TOLD HIS BUDDY "SHORTY" ABOUT MILO'S ABILITY TO BUILD STASH SPOTS THAT YOU COULDN'T FIND THEM WITH THE NAKED EYE. THEY WERE ALL MAGNETIC DOORS.

SHORTY KEPT MILO BUSY FOR BETTER THAN A YEAR DOING VARIOUS PROJECTS FOR HIM. HE SUPPLIED HIM WITH A CAR, AND ALL OF THE POT THAT HE WANTED, AND $ 200.00 A DAY.

MILO WANTED SOME OF THAT EASY MONEY THAT HIS BUDDY WILLARD WAS GETTING OR AT LEAST A CHANCE AT IT!

FINALLY HIS BUDDY WILLARD INTERVENED IN HIS BEHALF BECAUSE HE KNEW THAT MILO HAD A LOT OF FRIENDS IN THE KEYS AND MORE

IMPORTANTLY A LOT OF BUYERS THAT WILLARD WOULD GET A PIECE OF THE ACTION WITH ANYWAY.

MILO JUST NEEDED TO USE DISCRETION ABOUT WHERE HIS POT CAME FROM. HE WAS ABLE TO STEP INTO THE BEST SUPPLIER HE HAD EVER MET AND HE WASN'T ABOUT TO SCREW THIS ONE UP!

HE STARTED WITH SMALLER AMOUNTS 3 TO 5 POUNDS OF HIGH GRADE SENSE FROM JAMAICA. PURPLE BUD. OUTRAGEOUS, STICKY, WEED.

IT WAS FRONTED TO HIM AT THE RATE OF $ 350.00 PER POUND. HE SOLD THE POT FOR $100.00 PER OUNCE COMING OUT TO $1600.00 PER POUND. $1250.00 PROFIT PER POUND. HE TURNED OVER 3 TO 5 POUNDS PER WEEK. A HANDSOME INCOME FOR A SINGLE GUY AND LATER THEY INCREASED THE AMOUNT.

HE BECAME A SPONSOR FOR A LOCAL REGGAE / ROCK BAND.

HE DROVE AN MG MIDGET. THE TRUNK WOULD HOLD 30 POUNDS EASILY. HE DECIDED TO PARTNER UP WITH CAPTAIN RON TO DO SOME LARGER FASTER AMOUNTS.

HE AND CAPTAIN RON BEGAN RUNNING TRUNK LOADS OF THE SENSE TO GEORGIA AND SOUTH CAROLINA. THEY CONTINUED DOING TRUNK LOADS EVERY WEEK UNTIL ONE WEEK. ONE OF CAPTAIN RON'S FRIENDS, BURNED THEM.

THEY BOTH LOST THEIR ASSES AND CAPTAIN RON BURNED HIM FOR HIS SHARE OF THE LOSS.

THAT WAS THE END OF THAT CONNECTION, AND A LONG FRIENDSHIP TOO.

HE VOWED TO NEVER HAVE ANY MORE DEALINGS WITH CAPTAIN RON AGAIN. ESPECIALLY AFTER CAPTAIN RON SHOT AT HIM AND ACCUSED HIM OF STEALING SOME OF HIS POT. WHAT A JERK!

HE DECIDED TO TAKE A BRAKE FROM DEALING FOR A WHILE.

HE WANTED TO GO SAILING AGAIN. HE THOUGHT ABOUT ANGEE AGAIN AND ABOUT BUYING A GUN.

HE WENT TO A GUN STORE IN MIAMI. HE TOLD THE GUNSMITH THAT HE WAS LOOKING FOR A GUN FOR HIS SAILBOAT. THE GUNSMITH SHOWED HIM MANY PISTOLS THAT WERE VERY GOOD AT CLOSE RANGE. BUT MILO HAD SOMETHING ELSE IN MIND.

HE TOLD THE GUNSMITH THAT HE WANTED A 20 GAGE SEMI-AUTOMATIC SHOTGUN. HE ALSO WANTED A BOX OF SHELLS, LOADED WITH SLUGS AND ANOTHER BOX WITH DOUBLE OO BUCK SHOT AND ALL NEEDED TO BE MAGNUM LOAD SHELLS.

THE GUNSMITH SAID: ISN'T THAT A LITTLE LARGE FOR A COMPACT SAILBOAT?

MILO SIMPLY SAID THAT HE HAD SOMETHING IN MIND AND THAT HE THOUGHT THAT THIS WOULD WORK OUT BEST FOR HIS NEEDS.

HE WENT BACK TO KEY LARGO AND WENT DOWN BELOW IN THE SNAPDRAGON. HE PULLED OUT THE SHOTGUN AND BEGAN TO WEEP FOR THE LOSS OF ANGEE. HE PROCEEDED TO DISMANTLE THE SHOTGUN.

HE WENT FOR A WALK IN THE MANGROVES AND FOUND A GNARLY CHUNK OF LIGNUM VITTIE. IT IS THE HARDEST WOOD IN THE FLORIDA KEYS. HE WENT BACK TO THE SAILBOAT AND BEGAN TO CARVE A PISTOL GRIP FOR THE SHOTGUN.

THE SHOTGUN WOULD HOLD FIVE SHELLS, SO THE CHAMBER HAD TO STAY.

HE SAWED THE BARREL OFF JUST $\frac{1}{2}$ INCH PAST THE CHAMBER AND ROUNDED IT OFF WITH A FILE. HE SHAPED THE GRIP SO THAT IT WOULD BE COMFORTABLE TO SHOOT WITH EITHER HAND.

I SURE WOULDN'T WANT TO BE ON THE RECEIVING END OF THAT LITTLE BEAUTY!

FINALLY! PROTECTION ON THE HOME FRONT! HE INSTALLED A BRACKET ON THE FORWARD SIDE OF THE MAST STEP.

THE MAST STEP IN THE SNAP DRAGON WAS ACTUALLY AN ARCH THAT WAS LAMINATED STRIPS OF WHITE OAK. IT WAS ABOUT A FOOT THICK AND WENT OVER THE "V" BIRTH. THE BRACKET COULD NOT BE SEEN FROM THE HATCHWAY.

HE STAYED IN KEY LARGO AND PARTIED WITH ALL OF HIS OLD FRIENDS AND THEN RAN A FEW CHARTERS ON HIS OWN.

HE WORKED ON THE SNAPDRAGON SOME MORE, AND MANAGED TO GET STANDING HEADROOM AFTER 3 YEARS OF BENDING OVER LIKE A HUNCHBACK! GOD IT'S NICE TO STAND UP AGAIN.

HE DID NOT WANT A STEADY WOMAN. ACTUALLY HE DID NOT WANT TO FALL IN LOVE AGAIN AT ALL!

HE COULDN'T STAND THE PAIN! HE TRIED FOR A WHILE AND SHOPPED AROUND QUITE A BIT BUT IT DIDN'T WORK OUT!
NONE OF THEM WERE AS GOOD AS ANGEE.
HE RESTOCKED HIS BOAT WITH CANNED GOODS AND INSTALLED SOME MORE ADVANCED NAVIGATIONAL AIDS.
HE BOUGHT AN OUTBOARD MOTOR FOR HIS SAILBOAT AND GOT A LIGHTER WEIGHT SAILING DINGHY. HE THEN HAULED THE BOAT AGAIN, AND REPAINTED HER BOTTOM .
SPLASH! IN THE WATER AGAIN. RIGGING TUNED AND WIND STEERING INSTALLED AND WORKING.

ALMOST TIME TO GO SAILING AGAIN.

WORD WAS GOING AROUND THE BOATYARD THAT
HE WAS GOING TO SOLO TO THE BAHAMAS.
A FEW LOCAL GIRLS WERE LOOKING FOR A FREE
RIDE TO THE BAHAMAS. THEY ASKED HIM IF HE
WANTED A CREW. HE THOUGHT ABOUT IT FOR
AWHILE AND SAID: NOT THIS TIME LADIES.
HE DIDN'T TELL ANYONE WHEN OR WHERE HE
WAS GOING.
HE JUST DISAPPEARED INTO THE NIGHT.
A WONDERFUL CROSSING TO GUN CAY, CAT CAY
CUT. HE STAYED ONE NIGHT AND SAILED EARLY
THE NEXT MORNING FOR NASSAU BAHAMAS.
THE WIND STEERING WAS A GOD SENT GIFT. IT
WORKED PERFECTLY. HE WAS ACTUALLY ABLE TO
GET A FEW NAPS ALONG THE WAY.
HE ARRIVED IN NASSAU QUITE REFRESHED. HE
DOCKED HIS BOAT, AND WENT OVER TO PARADISE
ISLAND TO DO A LITTLE GAMBLING AT ONE OF
THE CASINO'S THERE.

HE WAS HAVING GREAT LUCK ON THE CRAP TABLES WHEN HE NOTICED A BEAUTIFUL BAHAMIAN GIRL.

HE SMILED AT HER AND SHE SMILED BACK AT HIM. SHE PUT HER ARM AROUND MILO AND SMILED AGAIN.

HE ASKED HER IF SHE WAS HIS GOOD LUCK CHARM?

SHE GIGGLED AND SAID THAT SHE WAS WHATEVER HE WANTED HER TO BE.

SHE HAD BEAUTIFUL GREEN EYES. VERY RARE FOR BLACK GIRLS. SHE STAYED AT HIS SIDE FOR THE ENTIRE EVENING.

HE DID QUITE WELL AT THE CRAP TABLES BUT FINALLY TOO TIRED TO KEEP UP AND KEEP HIS EYES OPEN ANY LONGER.

HE TOLD THE PRETTY BAHAMIAN GIRL THAT HE HAD TO GO BACK TO HIS BOAT AND THAT HE HAD A WONDERFUL TIME.

SHE LOOKED HIM IN THE EYES. SHE WAS JUST GLOWING WITH BEAUTY AND ASKED MILO IF SHE COULD STAY WITH HIM THAT NIGHT.

HE HAD ONLY SLEPT WITH A BLACK GIRL A COUPLE OF TIMES BEFORE. HIS FRIEND WILLARD HAD TAKEN MILO TO A PLACE THAT HE KNEW OF AND GOT HIM LAID A FEW TIMES BY SOME BLACK GIRLS IN MIAMI.

HE WAS EXTREMELY AROUSED BY HER PROPOSITION AND ACCEPTED.

HE DIDN'T KNOW IF SHE WAS A HOOKER OR NOT. IT DIDN'T REALLY MATTER ANYWAY. SHE DIDN'T ASK FOR ANY MONEY.

THEY WALKED ARM IN ARM TO THE BOAT DOCK. HE STEPPED ON BOARD AND HELD HIS HAND OUT FOR THE BEAUTIFUL WOMAN OF COLOR. HE HELPED HER BELOW, AND TO THE "V" BIRTH WHERE SHE BEGAN TO UNDRESS.

HER SKIN WAS LIKE BLACK SILK. SHE WAS EVEN MORE BEAUTIFUL WITH HER CLOTHES OFF.

SHE HAD ABSOLUTELY NO BODY FAT! SHE HELPED HIM TAKE OFF HIS CLOTHES. WHILE SHE HELPED HIM GET THEM OFF SHE WAS GENTLY STROKING HIS HARD BODY. IT WAS SO EROTIC THAT HE COULD NOT CONTROL HIMSELF ANY LONGER.

BOTH WERE COMPLETELY NAKED NOW. HE SAT BACK ON THE "V" BIRTH AND LAID BACK. SHE TOOK HIM INTO HER AND VERY GENTLY MADE LOVE TO HIM.

HE WAS VERY APPRECIATIVE OF HER EFFORTS AND TOLD HER THAT HE HAD NEVER HAD A LOVER LIKE HER BEFORE.

SHE SMELLED SO CLEAN. HE DOVE INTO HER AGAIN AND AGAIN UNTIL SHE FINALLY CLIMAXED TOO! SHE HAD NEVER DONE THAT BEFORE. BLACK MEN DIDN'T PARTAKE IN ORAL SEX.

HE CRAWLED INTO BED BESIDE HER AND THEY SLEPT THE REST OF THE NIGHT PEACEFULLY.

THE NEXT MORNING HE WOKE UP AND THERE SHE WAS. HE RECALLED THE NIGHT BEFORE AND WAS IMMEDIATELY AROUSED AGAIN. HE LEANED OVER TO HER AND KISSED HER GENTLY.

SHE AWAKENED AND SMILED AT HIM. SHE FELT HIS HARDNESS AND ASKED HIM TO MAKE LOVE

TO HER AGAIN. THEY MADE LOVE ONE MORE TIME AND WHEN THEY WERE BOTH SPENT.

THEY DECIDED THAT THEY OUGHT TO GO AND GET SOMETHING TO EAT.

HE WAS A LITTLE WEAK NOW. WHOEVER SAID THAT MAKING LOVE WAS NOT WORK!

THEY WERE FAMISHED AND ATE LIKE LITTLE PIGS. AFTER EATING THEY WALKED AROUND TOWN. THEY WENT TO THE FARMERS MARKET AND GOT SOME FRUIT AND VEGGIES LOTS OF KEY LIMES AND BANANAS AND THEN HEADED BACK TO THE BOAT.

THEY GOT BACK TO THE BOAT AND LOADED ALL OF THE GROCERIES ON THE BOAT AND TOPPED OFF THE WATER. SHE LOOKED AT HIM AND SAID: MY NAME IS GLORIA.

THERE WAS STARK SILENCE!

THEY HAD SPENT OVER TWENTY-FOUR HOURS TOGETHER, MADE LOVE SEVERAL TIMES AND BECAME VERY ATTACHED, AND DIDN'T EVEN KNOW EACH OTHERS NAMES YET!

HE LAUGHED AND ANNOUNCED THAT HE WAS VERY SORRY AND TOLD HER THAT HIS NAME WAS MILO AND I AM VERY GLAD TO MEET YOU TOO! THEY LAUGHED TOGETHER.

SHE ASKED HIM WHEN HE WAS LEAVING. HE TOLD HER THAT HE WASN'T SURE THAT HE WANTED TO LEAVE AT ALL.

THIS MADE GLORIA VERY HAPPY.

GLORIA ASKED MILO IF SHE COULD GO WITH HIM.

HE HELD HER CLOSE AND LOOKED HER IN THE EYES. HE SAID: ANY OTHER TIME HE WOULD SAY YES BUT THIS TIME HE WAS ON A MISSION DOWN ISLAND.

SHE ASKED IF HE WOULD STOP ON THE WAY BACK. HE TOLD HER THAT NASSAU WAS ALWAYS A STOP OVER AND THAT HE WOULD LOOK HER UP ON THE WAY BACK.

SHE SAID: DO YOU PROMISE? HE SAID: YES I DO.

HE ASKED HER IF SHE WOULD SPEND THE REST OF THE NIGHT WITH HIM SO THAT THEY COULD MAKE LOVE SOME MORE.

SHE SMILED AND SAID: BUT OF COURSE I WILL. THEY MADE LOVE ALL NIGHT AGAIN AND AWOKE EARLY THE NEXT MORNING. HE MADE SOME ESPRESSO.

THEY DRANK COFFEE AND ATE BREAKFAST. FINALLY HE TOLD GLORIA THAT HE HAD TO GO NOW.

IT WAS A LITTLE TENSE FOR THE MOMENT BUT GLORIA KNEW THAT HE WOULD RETURN. HE DID PROMISE.

MILO SWORE THAT HE WOULD BE BACK AGAIN. HE RAISED THE MAIN SAIL AND TIED IT OFF AND DOWN HAULED IT NICE AND TIGHT.

HE THEN GRABBED THE LOOSE END OF THE SHEET LINE AND STEPPED UP ON TO THE DOCK. HE KISSED HER GOOD-BYE AND STEPPED BACK ON TO THE BOAT. HE PULLED IN THE SHEET LINE A FEW YARDS, GRABBED THE TILLER AND SAILED

AWAY FROM THE DOCK AWAY FROM NASSAU AND TOWARD ELUTHRA ONCE AGAIN.

HE HAD FINALLY MADE UP FOR ALL OF THE LOVE MAKING THAT HE MISSED OUT ON WHEN ANGEE LEFT HIM.

HE DIDN'T KNOW WHAT IT WAS BUT HE SOMEHOW FELT OBSESSED OR POSSESSED. HE WASN'T QUITE SURE. AS THE DAYS WENT ON HE STARTED THINKING ABOUT ANGEE AND THAT TERRIBLE NIGHT!

HE WISHED THAT HE COULD SOMEHOW CHANGE THE WAY THAT EVERYTHING TURNED OUT.

ULTIMATELY HE KNEW THAT HE COULDN'T BUT MAYBE THERE WAS SOMETHING THAT HE COULD DO. SOMETHING EVIL!

HE WAS NEARING THE SPOT WHERE ANGEE WAS RAPED. THE TIME WAS RUNNING ABOUT THE SAME. THE CURRENT WAS RUNNING OUT AND IT WAS ALMOST DARK. HE DECIDED TO STAY OFFSHORE AND WAIT UNTIL MORNING.

HE WANTED THE ELEMENT OF SURPRISE ON HIS SIDE.

HE STOOD OFFSHORE GOING IN CIRCLES ALL NIGHT. HE HAD DASTARDLY PLANS FOR TOMORROW.

THE SHOW DOWN!

THE NIGHT SKY WAS STARTING TO TURN TO
MORNING SKY WHEN HE HEADED INTO THE CUT.
HE HAD A PERFECT BEAM REACH GOING INTO THE
CUT. THE CURRENT WAS RUNNING INTO THE CUT
TOO. ALTHOUGH IT WAS ALMOST HIGH TIDE.
AS HE SAILED INTO THE CUT HIS STOMACH
KNOTTED UP. THEN HE SPOTTED THEM! OFF TO
HIS RIGHT!
HE JUMPED BELOW AND GRABBED HIS GUN. HE
TURNED AND SAILED HARD INTO THE WIND, HE
GOT TO THE OPPOSITE SIDE OF THE ANCHORAGE
AND TACKED STRAIGHT TOWARD THE CIGARETTE
BOAT.
THEY WERE STILL SLEEPING AT THIS POINT.
THE SNAPDRAGON WAS ALMOST STEALTH GOING
THROUGH THE WATER. HE SAILED UP ALONG
SIDE OF THE CIGARETTE BOAT AND STALLED THE
SNAPDRAGON INTO THE WIND.
HER SAILS WERE FLAPPING AND MAKING QUIET
A RACKET WHEN TWO OF THE CREW POKED THEIR
HEADS OUT OF THE FORWARD HATCH.

THEIR EYES GOT VERY LARGE WHEN THEY MADE
EYE CONTACT WITH MILO. THEY REMEMBERED
WHO HE WAS!

MILO LEVELED HIS SAWED OFF SHOTGUN AT
THEIR HEADS, AND LET THEM HAVE IT! BAM!
BOTH OF THEIR FACES SEAMED TO DISAPPEAR
INTO RED AS THEY WENT DOWN LIKE SACKS OF
POTATOES.

ANOTHER GUY STUCK HIS HEAD OUT OF THE
CENTER HATCH. HE REMEMBERED HIM TOO! BUT
HE WAS TOO LATE AND MILO SHOT HIM TOO!
POINT BLANK RIGHT IN THE FACE!

INSTANT RED AND DOWN HE WENT! MILO COULD
HEAR ALL OF THEM MOANING AND YELLING FOR
EACH OTHER'S HELP. THEY WERE ALL BLINDED
BY THE BLOOD IN THEIR FACES AND SOME EYES
MISSING TOO, NO DOUBT!

HE JUMPED ON BOARD WITH HIS SHEET LINE
IN HAND. HE TIED IT OFF QUICKLY TO THEIR
CABIN-TOP HAND-RAIL, AND WENT THROUGH
THE BOAT.

THEY WERE NOT DEAD YET! AS HE WENT THROUGH
THE BOAT HE WAS SLIPPING IN WHAT LOOKED
LIKE BUCKETS OF BLOOD! IT WAS LIKE SNOT
THAT HE WAS SKATING ON BAREFOOTED.

HE FOUND ALL OF THEM HUDDLED TOGETHER
AND THEIR FACES HALF GONE.

ONE OF THEM ASKED MILO WHAT HE WAS GOING
TO DO WITH THEM?

HE TOLD THEM THAT HE WAS GOING TO DO WHAT
"THEY" SHOULD HAVE DONE!

YOU HAVE ALREADY RUINED MY LIFE HE SAID.
NOW IT IS YOUR TURN TO DIE!
ONE AT A TIME, HE PUT HIS GUN TO EACH OF
THEIR HEADS AND PULLED THE TRIGGER, UNTIL
THEY ALL WERE DEAD!
EXECUTION STYLE!
HE WENT BACK ABOARD THE SNAPDRAGON, AND
RE-LOADED THE GUN WITH MAGNUM SLUGGERS.
HE WENT BACK ABOARD THE CIGARETTE BOAT,
AND WENT BELOW.
STILL SLIPPING AROUND IN THE BLOOD HE BLEW
HOLES IN THE BOAT BELOW THE WATERLINE.
THOSE MAGNUM LOADS DID A FINE JOB OF
MAKING HOLES IN THINGS. HE DISCONNECTED
THE POSITIVE BATTERY TERMINAL OF THE
BATTERY SO THAT THE BILGE PUMP COULD NOT
WORK. THE BOAT WOULD GO DOWN IN ABOUT
FIFTEEN FEET OF WATER.
HE UNTIED THE SHEET LINE AND STEPPED BACK
ON TO THE SNAPDRAGON. HE JIBBED THE MAIN
AROUND AND SAILED BACK OUT OF THE CUT.
NOBODY EVER KNEW THAT HE WAS THERE!
HE LOOKED OVER HIS SHOULDER AS HE WAS
SAILING OUT OF THE CUT SAYING TO HIMSELF
PAYBACK IS A MOTHERFUCKER! ROT IN HELL! YOU
SONS OF BITCHES!
HE DIPPED OUT A FEW BUCKETS OF SEA WATER
TO WASH OFF ALL OF THE BLOOD THAT HE HAD
SKATED AROUND ON. CLEAN AGAIN. HE HAD A
GREAT FEELING OF ACCOMPLISHMENT. PEACE AT
LAST!

HE SAILED A FULL DAY FURTHER SOUTH AND THEN RESTED FOR A FEW DAYS.

HE STAYED ON THE BOAT THE FIRST NIGHT WITHOUT GOING TO SHORE. THE NEXT DAY HE WENT INTO TOWN AND TOPPED OFF HIS WATER JUGS AND PICKED UP SOME FRESH LIMES AND COCONUTS.

HE STOWED HIS GEAR AGAIN AND SET SAIL FOR THE BIG ISLAND OF ANDROS. IT TOOK HIM THREE MORE DAYS TO GET TO SOUTH ANDROS. IT WAS JUST ACROSS THE BAY FROM CONGA TOWN.

THE COOL BREEZE CLUB

HE SAILED INTO LISBON CREEK AND UP TO A DOCK IN FRONT OF THE COOL BREEZE CLUB. HE COULD HEAR REGGAE MUSIC PLAYING IN THE CLUB.

THERE HE MET JASON AND VERA. THEY TREATED HIM LIKE THEIR LONG LOST SON. WONDERFUL PEOPLE. HIS FIRST NIGHT AT THE DOCK VERA SERVED HIM SOME CURRIED GOAT.

HE HADN'T EATEN ANY RED MEAT IN QUITE SOME TIME, BUT HE DIDN'T WANT TO HURT THEIR FEELINGS SO HE ATE SOME AND DISCOVERED THAT IT WAS QUITE A GOOD TASTING DISH. MILO HAD FORGOTTEN HOW GOOD TASTING RED MEAT COULD BE.

MILO SETTLED DOWN AFTER HIS MEAL AND HAD A CIGARETTE. HE HAD JUST FINISHED HIS SMOKE WHEN THE LIGHTS WENT OUT.

THEY WERE OUT FOR QUITE SOME TIME WHEN JASON CAME BACK INTO THE ROOM. HE ASKED MILO IF HE KNEW ANYTHING ABOUT GASOLINE

ENGINES. MILO JUMPED UP AND SAID: SURE THING MAN.

ON THE WAY OUT TO THE GENERATOR ROOM HE SPOTTED A WINDSURFER TUCKED BETWEEN TWO BUILDINGS.

THERE WERE SOME GREAT LOOKING REEFS JUST OUTSIDE OF THE CUT GOING INTO LISBON CREEK, AND HE WAS THINKING ABOUT SAILING ON THEM.

THEY FINALLY GOT TO THE GENERATOR ROOM. MILO DISCOVERED THAT IT WAS JUST A LOOSE COIL WIRE. IT WAS UP AND RUNNING IN JUST A FEW MINUTES.

ON THE WAY BACK TO THE COOL BREEZE CLUB HE ASKED JASON ABOUT THE WINDSURFER. JASON TOLD MILO THAT IT BELONGED TO ONE OF HIS REGULAR CUSTOMERS, NAMED WILLARD W.

MILO SAID: I KNOW WILLARD. I'VE DONE A LOT OF CARPENTRY WORK FOR HIM. HE WENT ON TO TALK ABOUT WILLARD'S TRI-MIRAN SAILBOAT.

FINALLY JASON REALIZED THAT THEY WERE TALKING ABOUT THE SAME PERSON.

JASON SAID THAT WILLARD JUST NEEDED TO STORE IT SO THAT HE WOULDN'T HAVE TO HAUL IT BACK AND FORTH.

FINALLY JASON SAID THAT HE COULD USE THE WINDSURFER AND THAT HE WAS SURE THAT WILLARD WOULDN'T MIND AT ALL.

HE PACKED UP THE WINDSURFER SAIL AND WISH BOOMS, AND WENT DOWN TO THE BEACH. HE RIGGED THE SAIL AND LAUNCHED RIGHT OFF OF THE BEACH.

IT WAS A PERFECT BEAM REACH STRAIGHT OUT TO THE REEF. HE SAILED OUT TO THE DARK BLUE WATER BEYOND THE REEF. HE JIBBED THE SAIL AROUND AND HEADED BACK TOWARD SHORE.

HE POPPED THE CENTERBOARD OUT OF THE TRUNK AND PUT THE SLING OVER HIS LEFT ARM.

HE WAS HAVING THE RIDE OF HIS LIFE! WATER WAS SQUIRTING OUT OF THE TRUNK LIKE A GIGANTIC ROOSTER TAIL. SAILING ACROSS JUST INCHES OF WATER AND LOOKING AT THE REEF GO BY. HE SPOTS SOMETHING OFF TO HIS LEFT AND IT DIDN'T LOOK TOO INVITING.

HE STEERED OVER TOWARD IT AND QUICKLY STEERED AWAY FROM IT. IT WAS ABOUT A TWELVE TO FOURTEEN FOOT HAMMERHEAD SHARK AND HE WAS FOLLOWING HIM RIGHT ACROSS THE REEF,

NO DOUBT WAITING FOR A TASTY SNACK! HE LOOKED DOWN AT HIS FEET, AND SAID: FEET'S DON'T FAIL ME NOW.

HE LEANED BACK ON HIS SAIL TO GET SOME MORE WIND. HE WAS DOING FIFTEEN TO TWENTY KNOTS, AND THE SHARK WAS RIGHT THERE.

HE WAS NEARING THE BEACH AND THE SHARKS BELLY WAS STARTING TO DRAG BOTTOM KICKING UP SILT.

THE SHARK TURNED, AND LEFT FOR DEEPER WATER.

MILO, IN THE MEANTIME SAILED THE WINDSURFER RIGHT UP ON TO THE SAND, DROPPED THE SAIL AND FELL TO THE GROUND

EXHAUSTED AND PRETTY DAMN SCARED FROM THE ORDEAL.

HE SAT THERE CATCHING HIS BREATH AND STARTED THINKING ABOUT AN INCIDENT IN KEY LARGO. SORT OF A DREAM SEQUENCE.

HE WAS TRYING OUT A NEW SNORKEL AND MASK AT THE ANCHORAGE OUTSIDE OF THE AIRSTRIP IN KEY LARGO.

HE WAS SNORKELING TOWARD THE CANAL TO CHECK OUT THE BOTTOM FOR OBSTRUCTIONS THAT COULD CAUSE A SCREW UP WHILE TRYING TO SAIL INTO THE CANAL.

HE HAD THE SPEAR FROM HIS HAWAIIAN SLING, AND WAS TAPING ALONG THE BOTTOM, CHECKING THE DEPTH AS HE MOVED ALONG THE BOTTOM. HE CAME ALONG THIS FAIRLY LARGE CLEAR SPOT ABOUT TWENTY BY THIRTY OR IT LOOKED THAT BIG WITH THE MAGNIFICATION OF THE WATER.

HE TOUCHED IN THE MIDDLE WITH HIS SPEAR AND NOTICED ALL AROUND HIM THAT THERE WAS A BIG CIRCLE OF CLOUDY WATER.

ALL OF A SUDDEN, IT LOOKED LIKE A BIG GREEN PIMPLE WAS ERUPTING FROM THE BOTTOM.

HIS HEART WAS POUNDING WITH ANTICIPATION OF WHAT WAS ABOUT TO HAPPEN.

THIS HUGE SPOTTED EAGLE RAY FLEW OUT FROM UNDER HIM FLAPPING HIS WINGS IN SLOW MOTION AND DISAPPEARED INTO THE DISTANCE AWAY FROM THE ANCHORAGE.

AS HE FADED BACK INTO HIS IMMEDIATE REALITY CHECK. HE AGAIN REALIZED HOW LUCKY THAT HE REALLY WAS, MANY TIMES OVER.

HE SHOOK OFF THE FEARS OF THE MOMENT AND ROLLED UP THE SAIL AND PACKED UP THE LANYARDS AND WISH BOOMS.

HE TOOK THEM BACK TO JASON'S PLACE AND TOLD HIM OF WHAT JUST HAPPENED TO HIM.

JASON JUST LAUGHED FOR A MOMENT AND GREW QUITE SOLEMN AND TOLD MILO A STORY ABOUT A COUPLE OF THEIR LOCAL DIVERS.

IT SEEMS THAT THEY WERE THERE TRYING TO SPEAR ONE OF THE BIG JEW-FISH THAT HUNG OUT NEAR THE FRESH WATER SPRING, WHICH IS AT THE SAME AREA WHICH HE JUST CAME FROM. THE PLACE WAS WHAT WAS CALLED A "BLUE HOLE".

THEY BOTH GOT A SHOT INTO THE JEW-FISH. IT WAS QUITE BLOODY AND THE HAMMERHEAD CAME OVER TO CHECK IT OUT.

ONE OF THE BOYS HAD A HOLD OF ONE OF THE SPEARS AND WAS TRYING TO KEEP THE FISH FROM GOING DEEP INTO THE SPRING AND FROM GETTING AWAY.

THE BOY WAS IN A CLOUD OF BLOOD WHEN THE SHARK TOOK HIM.

THEY NEVER FOUND ANYTHING OF THE BOY'S BODY AND NOBODY DIVES OUT THERE ANYMORE. AT LEAST NONE OF THE LOCALS.

AFTER HEARING THAT STORY MILO FELT VERY LUCKY. ON ANY NORMAL DAY HE WOULD HAVE FALLEN IN TO THE WATER TRYING TO PULL A

STUNT LIKE THAT. LUCK MUST HAVE BEEN IN THE CARDS.

HE WAS STARTING TO THINK ABOUT GLORIA AGAIN. WHAT A BEAUTY!

HE TOLD JASON ABOUT GLORIA. JASON WAS SURPRISED THAT MILO WOULD BE INTERESTED IN A BLACK GIRL. JASON SAID THAT SHE MUST BE VERY SPECIAL. MILO SAID: YES MAN.   SHE IS INCREDIBLY BEAUTIFUL.

SHE HAS A WONDERFUL PERSONALITY. YOU ARE A LUCKY MAN MILO. HE THOUGHT TO HIMSELF. I GUESS I AM LUCKY NOW.

HE TOLD JASON THAT HE WOULD SEE HIM AGAIN IN THE NEAR FUTURE AND THAT WILLARD WAS RIGHT ABOUT YOU AND VERA. YOU ARE GREAT FOLKS. YOU REALLY MADE ME FEEL AT HOME.

MILO HAD DINNER WITH JASON AND VERA THAT EVENING AND SET SAIL WITH THE CURRENT IN THE MORNING. LEAVING LISBON CREEK WITH THE THOUGHT OF RETURNING SOON.

HE HAD THE CURRENT TO HIS BACK WHICH MADE FOR SOME LONG DISTANCE DAYS. NO TACKING NECESSARY GOING NORTH.

A COUPLE OF STOPS AND A FEW DAYS LATER. HE WAS APPROACHING NASSAU HARBOR, PARADISE ISLAND AND GLORIA.

HE REALLY MISSED HER. HE THOUGHT TO HIMSELF. I COULD REALLY LOVE A WOMAN LIKE THAT!

A SOLE MATE. HE SAILED THE SNAPDRAGON UP TO THE DOCK AND TIED HER OFF. HE PUT ON THE

SPRING LINE AND FENDERS AND PAID THE DOCK-
MASTER.

IT WAS TIME TO FIND GLORIA. HE STASHED HIS
SHOTGUN IN ONE OF MANY OF HIS STASH PLACES
THAT HE HAD BUILT IN TO THE SNAPDRAGON.
POT STASH, MONEY STASH AND GUN STASH.

HE WALKED OVER THE BRIDGE TO PARADISE
ISLAND AND TO THE CASINO WHERE HE HAD
MET GLORIA. THE CASINO WAS VERY BUSY WITH
TOURISTS AND IT MADE IT HARD TO FIND
ANYONE.

HE STOPPED AT THE CRAP TABLES AND STARTED
BETTING THE LINE. HE WAS DOING VERY BADLY
WHEN ALL OF A SUDDEN HIS LUCK CHANGED.

HE LOOKED AROUND AND KEPT PLAYING AND
WINNING WHEN HE FELT A WARM PAIR OF LIPS
KISSING THE BACK OF HIS NECK. HE KNEW WHO
IT WAS AND TURNED AROUND AND KISSED
GLORIA ON THE LIPS VERY PASSIONATELY.

THE CUSTOMERS APPLAUDED AND HE AND GLORIA
LEFT THE TABLES AND SAT AT THE BAR.

GLORIA LOOKED HIM IN THE EYES AND AS TEARS
WELLED UP IN HER EYES, SHE SAID: I KNEW THAT
YOU WOULD COME BACK FOR ME.

HE LOOKED AT GLORIA AND ASKED HER IF SHE
WOULD LIKE TO GO SAILING FOR A COUPLE OF
MONTHS? GLORIA HESITATED FOR A MINUTE
AND SAID: I WAS HOPING THAT YOU WOULD
TAKE ME HOME WITH YOU.

HE LOOKED HER IN THE EYES AND TOLD HER,
YOU BET I WILL SWEETHEART, BUT IF YOU DON'T
MIND I WOULD REALLY LIKE TO TAKE THIS

OPPORTUNITY TO REALLY GET TO KNOW YOU THOROUGHLY AND THEN I WILL BE MORE THAN HAPPY TO MARRY YOU PROPER. I REALLY THINK THAT I LOVE YOU.

I JUST WANT TO MAKE SURE.

GLORIA SAID: I THINK THAT I LOVE YOU TOO MILO.

WELL THEN LET'S GO SAILING LOVER. THEY LEFT THE BAR HAND IN HAND.

THEY WENT TO WHERE GLORIA LIVED AND HE MET GLORIA'S MOTHER. BEATRICE. SHE TOLD HIM THAT GLORIA COULDN'T STOP RAVING ABOUT HIM AND NOW SHE COULD UNDERSTAND WHY.

GLORIA TOLD HER MOTHER THAT SHE WAS GOING SAILING WITH MILO FOR A COUPLE OF MONTHS AND THAT THEY WOULD STOP AND SEE HER ON THE WAY BACK TO THE UNITED STATES.

HER MOTHER WAS A LITTLE CONCERNED THAT GLORIA WAS RUSHING A BIT TOO QUICKLY INTO ROMANCE!

SHE SAID: YOUR FATHER WAS A BLONDE HAIRED WHITE MAN AND HE LEFT ME BEFORE YOU WERE BORN.

GLORIA TOLD HER MOM THAT SHE WAS JUST FOLLOWING HER HEART. HER MOM SAID: I KNOW HONEY, I FOLLOWED MINE TOO.

GLORIA AND MILO STOCKED THE SNAPDRAGON WITH FRESH WATER AND CANNED GOODS THEN WENT BACK TO MOM'S HOUSE FOR GLORIA'S CLOTHES. TOMORROW THEY WOULD GO SAILING IN TO THE FUTURE.

IT WAS A BEAUTIFUL TROPICAL DAY. A PERFECT SAILING DAY.

THEY LOADED ALL OF GLORIA'S SUPPLIES ON BOARD THE LITTLE BOAT AND HEADED SOUTH ONCE AGAIN. GLORIA KEPT LOOKING OVER THE SIDE AS THEY WERE SAILING ALONG. SHE KEPT GETTING GOOSE BUMPS.

MILO ASKED HER; WHAT'S A MATTER HONEY? ARE YOU COLD? SHE JUST SMILED AND SAID: IT'S NOTHING. I'LL BE ALRIGHT.

GLORIA WASN'T MUCH OF A WATER PERSON. WHENEVER MILO WENT INTO THE WATER TO SHOOT A LOBSTER OR A FISH SHE WAS ALWAYS SCARED TO DEATH THAT SOMETHING WOULD HAPPEN TO HIM. SHE WOULD ALWAYS BE WAITING AS HE CAME TO THE SURFACE. SHE WOULD BREATHE A SIGH OF RELIEF EVERY TIME MILO SURFACED FROM A DIVE.

GLORIA WAS RAISED IN THE BAHAMAS BUT SHE HADN'T SEEN MUCH OF THEM AT ALL. MILO HAD SEEN ALMOST ALL OF THE OUT ISLANDS, AND KNEW HIS WAY AROUND THEM VERY WELL BY NOW.

MANY PLACES THAT THEY STOPPED THE PEOPLE REMEMBERED HIM, BECAUSE HE WAS SO GIVING TO THE CHILDREN. HE ALWAYS HAD A KIND WORD, OR A FEW COINS FOR THE KIDS. GLORIA LOVED IT WHEN THEY MADE LANDFALL. SHE REALLY WAS A LAND LOVER.

THE SNAP DRAGON WAS GROWING SMALLER EVERY DAY. GLORIA WAS GROWING MORE, AND MORE, IMPATIENT. SHE GOT TO THE POINT OF

PUTTING OFF GOING BACK TO THE BOATAND TO THE POINT OF ANNOYANCE.

ADMITTEDLY; THE BOAT WAS PRETTY SMALL. WORSE THAN A SMALL TRAVEL TRAILER. YOU COULDN'T JUST STEP OFF WHENEVER YOU WANTED TO.

MILO SENSED THAT THIS WASN'T GOING TO WORK OUT AFTER ALL.

THEY DAY SAILED AROUND THE OUT ISLANDS FOR A COUPLE MORE WEEKS. BY THE TIME THAT THEY GOT BACK TO NASSAU, SHE WAS READY TO JUMP SHIP! SHE HAD NOT EVEN BEEN TO BLUE WATER YET!

HE SAILED UP TO THE DOCK AND TOOK DOWN THE SAILS AND THEN STOWED THE GEAR. HE BAGGED THE SAILS BECAUSE HE PLANNED TO STAY FOR A FEW DAYS BEFORE GOING BACK TO THE KEYS.

GLORIA STARTED PACKING ALL OF HER STUFF AND HE KNEW WHAT SHE WAS UP TO. SHE WASN'T A SAILOR AND SHE WASN'T GOING ANY FURTHER ON THIS TRIP OR ANY OTHER TRIP ON THE WATER.

SHE PUT ALL OF HER STUFF ON THE DOCK AND LOOKED AT HIM. TEARS WERE IN HER EYES. SHE SAID: I JUST CAN'T DO IT! YOU DO UNDERSTAND DON'T YOU?

HE TOLD HER THAT THIS WAS THE REASON THAT I WANTED TO GO ON A CRUISE WITH YOU. I NEEDED TO FIND OUT IF YOU HAD ANY SEA LEGS. IT'S O.K. SWEETHEART BUT WOULD YOU MIND

MAKING LOVE TO ME JUST ONE MORE TIME FOR OLD TIMES?

SHE GRABBED A HOLD OF HIM AND THEY WENT BELOW AND MADE LOVE UNTIL MORNING. IN THE MORNING SHE CALLED A CAB TO COME AND GET HER AND HER STUFF. SHE TOLD HIM THAT HE SHOULD LOOK HER UP WHENEVER HE WAS IN NASSAU.

THE CAB TOOK HER AWAY AND HE COULD ONLY THINK OF ADVENTURE. IT WAS TIME TO MAKE SOME MONEY. BIG MONEY.

"SMUGGLING"

WHEN I WAS A YOUNG BOY , MY FATHER SAID TO ME
A DOCTOR OR A LAWYER , THAT'S WHAT MY BOY SHOULD BE
I'LL BUY HIM BOOKS , AND SEND HIM TO SCHOOL
AND WHEN HE GROWS UP , HE'LL BE NOBODY'S FOOL
MY MOTHER BROKE INTO THE CONVERSATION
SHE SAID: I BEG TO DISAGREE
A WORLD FAMOUS POLITICIAN THAT'S WHAT MY BOY SHOULD BE
AND AFTER MANY YEARS OF HONEST POLITICAL WORK , AND
WHEN HE GETS TO CONGRESS IN THE FALL
HE WON'T HAVE TO DO ANYTHING AT ALL
I SAID ; WAIT A MINUTE MOM , WAIT A MINUTE DAD
I'M GOING TO BE A PIRATE , GOING TO LIVE DOWN IN THE KEYS
GOING TO BUY A BOAT & SMUGGLE DOPE

AND LIVE JUST HOW I PLEASE
I'LL RUN GRASS IN THE MOONLIGHT
AS THE COASTGUARD CHASES ME
A PIRATE. THAT'S WHAT I'M GOING TO BE
MY SISTER SAID THAT SHE WAS TALKING TO
SOME OF MY FRIENDS ALOUD
SHE SAID: RUMOR IN THE LOCKER ROOM , IS YOU
ARE WELL ENDOWED
WHY NOT GET OFF OF YOUR ASS BIG BROTHER ,
AND GET YOURSELF A FUN JOB ,
WHY NOT BE A PROSTITUTE , AND SELL OFF THAT
LITTLE BOD
WELL , I SAID: THAT'S A BETTER IDEA THAN MOM
& DAD HAD
BUT I'M GOING TO BE A PIRATE , GOING TO LIVE
DOWN IN THE KEY'S
GOING TO BUY A BOAT , AND SMUGGLE DOPE ,
AND LIVE JUST HOW I PLEASE
I'LL RUN GRASS IN THE MOONLIGHT , AS THE
COASTGUARD CHASES ME , A PIRATE , THAT'S
WHAT I'M GOING TO BE
WELL ; I NEVER WAS A DOCTOR OR A LAWYER
THAT JUST WASN'T MY CUP OF TEA
AND I NEVER WAS A PROSTITUTE , THOUGH IT
DIDN'T SOUND BAD TO ME
I STILL LOVE MY FAMILY THOUGH ; THEY STUCK
WITH ME , THROUGH AND THROUGH
NOW THEY'RE HERE IN FLORIDA , AND THEY ARE
WORKING AS MY CREW
NOW WE ALL ARE PIRATES , WE LIVE DOWN IN
THE KEYS

WE GOT A BOAT WE SMUGGLE DOPE , AND WE
LIVE JUST HOW WE PLEASE
WE RUN GRASS IN THE MOONLIGHT , AND WE
RUN IT BY THE TON AND WE DO IT FOR THE
PIRATE IN EVERYONE .

AFTER HIS FAILED LOVE AFFAIR WITH GLORIA
AND THE FACT THAT SHE HAD RUN HIM ALMOST
COMPLETELY OUT OF MONEY. HE DECIDED THAT
HE HAD BETTER GO AND SEE HIS BUDDIES IN
THE KEYS AGAIN.
HE HAD KEPT ALL OF HIS BUYER CONNECTIONS.
THE ONLY PROBLEM WAS THE SUPPLY PROBLEM.
HE NEEDED TO MAKE SOME QUICK CASH, AND
SMUGGLING SEEMED LIKE THE EASIEST THING
TO DO . HE GOT A BRAIN-STORM AND CONTACTED
A WELDER FRIEND OF HIS .
 HE HAD HIM BUILD A TORPEDO TO BE TOWED
BEHIND HIS SAILBOAT UNDER WATER.
THE TORPEDO WAS WEIGHTED WITH LEAD SO
THAT IT WOULD SINK SLOWLY TO THE BOTTOM
. IT HAD A MAGNETIC TETHER SO IF THE COAST-
GUARD CAME TOO CLOSE TO HIM. HE COULD
RELEASE THE TORPEDO AND NOT GET CAUGHT.
THE TORPEDO WAS FITTED WITH A TIMER
SO THAT AFTER 24 HOURS THE TIMER WOULD
INFLATE AN AIR BAG THEN THE TORPEDO
WOULD FLOAT TO THE SURFACE AND SEND OUT
A HOMING SIGNAL.
YOU COULD THEN RETURN AND RECOVER IT. THERE
WAS A WATER-TIGHT HOLD IN THE TORPEDO
WHICH COULD BE PACKED FULL OF GRASS.

HE DECIDED TO TRY A WORKING SHAKE DOWN CRUISE FOR HIS NEW TORPEDO. HE RE-STOCKED THE SNAPDRAGON WITH CANNED GOODS, AND HEADED FOR SOUTH ANDROS ISLAND [LISBON CREEK].

IT WAS A GREAT COUPLE OF WEEKS OF SAILING. HE DID NOT STOP AT PARADISE ISLAND THIS TIME. HE DIDN'T WANT TO RUN INTO GLORIA. HE ALSO SAILED PAST THE SPOT WHERE ANGEE WAS RAPED.

TEARS WELLED UP IN MILO'S EYES AS HE SAILED PAST. HE COULD FEEL THE HATE SURGE THROUGH HIS BODY, BUT THEN HE RELAXED IN THE THOUGHT THAT THEY WERE ALL GONE NOW!

HE SAILED UP TO THE DOCK AT THE COOL BREEZE CLUB AND SPOTTED JASON OUT ON THE PATIO. THEY HUGGED AND SHOOK HANDS.

IT WAS TRULY GREAT TO SEE HIM AGAIN. HE WAS FAMILY NOW. JASON AND VERA ALWAYS TREATED MILO LIKE THEIR OWN LONG LOST SON.

MILO WORKED ON HIS BOAT DOING SOME NEEDED MAINTENANCE PROJECTS. AS THE DAYS WENT BY JASON APPROACHED HIM AS TO HIS REAL REASON FOR BEING THERE. HE WAS WAITING FOR THE RIGHT OPPORTUNITY TO TALK TO JASON ABOUT LOOSE BALES.

HE TOLD JASON THAT HIS BUDDY WILLARD HAD FOUND A FEW BALES IN THAT AREA. JASON JUMPED UP AND SAID: THAT'S WRONG MAN!

I AM THE ONE THAT FOUND ALL OF THE BALES AND I SPLIT THEM WITH WILLARD AND HE TOOK

THEM TO FLORIDA SOMEWHERE. MILO WAS VERY GRATEFUL TO JASON FOR THE INFORMATION.
HE SAID TO JASON. COME OVER TO THE DOCK WITH ME. MILO GRABBED THE END OF THE TETHER AND RELEASED THE MAGNETIC CLAMP.
HE PULLED THE TORPEDO OVER TO THE CRANE ON THE DOCK, THAT JASON USED FOR OFF LOADING SUPPLIES FOR THEIR RESTAURANT. HE STARTED CRANKING THE TORPEDO OUT OF THE WATER UNTIL HE GOT IT ALL OF THE WAY UP ON THE DOCK.
JASON LOOKED AT IT AND SAID: WHAT IS IT MAN! MILO LAUGHED A LITTLE AND SAID THAT HE FIGURED THAT THIS WAS THE SAFEST WAY TO MOVE POT TO THE STATES.
JASON WAS TRULY SURPRISED. HE SAID: THIS IS A BEAUTIFUL THING THAT YOU HAVE DONE HERE MAN!
HOW MANY POUNDS CAN WE GET IN THERE? MILO SMILED, AND SAID: LET'S FIND OUT BUDDY.
BECAUSE JASON LIVED THERE HE ROAMED THE BEACHES ALL OF THE TIME. HE WAS ALSO THE HONORARY MAYOR. ANYBODY THAT FOUND ANY POT BROUGHT IT TO JASON.
JASON WAS [THE MAN] IN LISBON CREEK.
JASON HAD PLENTY OF POT STOCK PILED AND MILO SAID: WELL LET'S SEE WHAT YOU GOT. SOME OF IT WAS JUST STINKY OLD SEA WEED AND A BUNCH OF IT WAS REAL GOOD BUDS. WHEN HE TOLD JASON WHAT HE COULD GET FOR IT. HE WAS A LITTLE DISAPPOINTED THAT HE HAD NOT GOTTEN MORE BEFORE.

HE WARNED JASON THAT IT WAS NOT COMPLETELY FOOL PROOF AND THAT SHIT HAPPENS. THE WHOLE IDEA IS THAT YOU DON'T GO TO JAIL. THAT IS O.K. MAN, JASON SAID.

THEY PACKED THE POT INTO SMALLER PLASTIC BAGS, AND FILLED THE TORPEDO WITH THE BEST OF THE BUDS. THEY MANAGED TO GET 300 POUNDS IN IT WITH A LITTLE ROOM TO SPARE. JASON SAID: THIS IS PRETTY HEAVY DOESN'T IT SLOW YOU DOWN? MILO SAID: YOU CAN NOT HARDLY TELL THAT IT IS THERE.

JASON AND MILO LOWERED THE TORPEDO INTO THE WATER AND HOOKED THE TETHER UP. IT IS TIME TO HAVE A BEER. JASON SAID: THIS TIME IT IS ON ME.

THAT WAS RARE FOR JASON BECAUSE OF BEING SO FAR OUT ISLAND HE ALMOST NEVER BUYS THE BEER. WELL: AFTER ALL JASON STOOD TO MAKE A GOOD CHUNK OF MONEY OUT OF THIS EFFORT.

JASON AND MILO SAT UP LATE INTO THE EVENING DRINKING BECK'S BEER AND TALKING ABOUT THE OLD DAYS WHEN YOU COULD JUST LOAD THE POT ON YOUR BOAT AND JUST SAIL RIGHT INTO THE U.S.

THE MORNING CAME AND VERA HAD MADE BREAKFAST FOR ALL OF THEM. HE HAD A LONG WAY TO GO.

TRIPS LIKE THIS ONE WERE GOING TO HAVE TO BE PRETTY MUCH "NON STOP" EXCEPT FOR A FEW STOPS AT OUT ISLAND ANCHORAGES FOR SLEEP.

HE RAISED THE MAINSAIL AND DOWN-HAULED
IT. JUST HABBIT. THEN STOWED THE REST OF
THE LOOSE GEAR. IT WAS TIME TO GO. HE SAID:
I LOVE YOU GUYS AND I WILL SEE YOU VERY
SOON. BY THE WAY. KEEP YOUR EYES OPEN FOR
MORE BALES.
HE THEN SAILED AWAY FROM THE DOCK AND OUT
TOWARD BLUE WATER. THAT WAS THE SAFEST
WAY TO GO. GET ON ONE TACK AND SET THE
WIND STEERING AND TAKE IT EASY.
THIS WORKED VERY WELL FOR MILO AND HE RAN
MANY TRIPS TO THE ISLANDS SUCCESSFULLY.
OVER THE NEXT YEAR HE BROUGHT BACK ABOUT
A TON OF POT TO THE U.S.
HIS FINAL TRIP WITH THE TORPEDO HE WAS IN
THE MIDDLE OF THE GULF STREAM AND IT WAS
IN THE MIDDLE OF THE NIGHT. WHEN HE WOULD
USUALLY MAKE HIS CROSSINGS.
HE WAS SAILING ALONG IN A PRETTY VIOLENT
STORM AND HE LOOKED OVER HIS SHOULDER
JUST AS A COAST-GUARD PULLED ALONG SIDE. HE
WAS REAL SURPRISED AND HIT THE MAGNETIC
RELEASE.
THE COAST-GUARD VESSEL ANNOUNCED THAT
HE SHOULD PREPARE TO BE BOARDED.
THE SEAS WERE ABOUT TEN TO TWENTY FEET
AND IT WAS PRETTY NASTY OUT! THEY CRUISED
ALONG SIDE OF HIM FOR AWHILE. HE STOOD
UP IN THE COCKPIT AND HELD HIS HANDS OUT
PALMS UP, AND YELLED!
WHAT DO YOU WANT ME TO DO? A COUPLE
OF MINUTES WENT BY, AND THE COAST-

GUARD VESSEL ANNOUNCED: HAVE A SAFE TRIP SKIPPER!

THIS SOUNDS FAMILIAR HE THOUGHT . IT REMINDED HIM OF HIS FIRST TRIP TO THE BAHAMAS .

HE FINISHED HIS CROSSING TO THE KEYS AND ANCHORED FOR THE NIGHT . BY THE TIME HE GOT BACK TO THE AREA WHERE HE DROPPED THE TORPEDO. THE GULF STREAM HAD TAKEN IT TOO FAR NORTH .

HE THOUGHTTO HIMSELF; WELL IT WAS NICE WHILE IT LASTED . HE HAD MADE A HELL OF A CHUNK OF MONEY.

HE IMAGINED THAT SOMEONE IN EUROPE WOULD PROBABLY FIND IT. EASY COME EASY GO HE THOUGHT.

IT WAS TIME FOR HIM TO COME UP WITH A NEW SCAM TO GET QUALITY POT BACK TO THE UNITED STATES. THIS TIME HE DIDN'T WANT TO INVOLVE THE COAST-GUARD AT ALL.

HE TOOK A FEW TRIPS TO JAMAICA TO SEEK QUALITY POT FOR SHIPMENT TO THE UNITED STATES. "SENSE" THERE WAS A LOT OF MONEY IN PROFIT PER POUND .

HE COULD BUY THE POT AT THE POT FARM FOR SEVEN DOLLARS PER POUND. BY THE TIME HE GOT IT TO THE COAST IT WAS FORTY DOLLARS PER POUND AFTER PAYING OFF THE POLICE AND EVERYONE ELSE WITH THEIR HANDS OUT.

HE HAD HIS WELDER BUDDY FASHION TWO COLLARS TO FIT OVER THE PROPELLER-SHAFTS ON CRUISE SHIPS. AFTER THE SHIPS DOCKED HE

WOULD DIVE ON THE SHIPS AND ATTACH THE COLLARS TO THE SHAFTS. THE WATER IN THE MIAMI HARBOR WAS PRETTY MURKY AND IT WAS PRETTY EASY PUTTING THE COLLARS ON. THEY BECAME WEIGHTLESS WHEN YOU TOOK THEM UNDER WATER.

THE SHIP WOULD THEN SAIL OVER TO JAMAICA, WHERE HE WOULD HAVE A LOCAL DIVER REMOVE THE COLLARS. THEY WOULD PACK THEM WITH POT, AND RE-ATTACH THEM THEN LET THE SHIP TAKE THEM BACK TO THE UNITED STATES , AND DOCK IN THE MIAMI HARBOR .

HE WOULD THEN DIVE ON THE SHIP AGAIN AND REMOVE THE COLLARS .

THE WATER IN MIAMI WAS MURKY ENOUGH THAT HE COULDN'T BE SEEN DIVING ON THEM . HE HAD A BOAT IN A SLIP NEAR-BY WHERE HE TOOK THE COLLARS TO. THIS WAS THE EASIEST SCAM YET!

HE WAS REALLY RACKING UP FREQUENT FLYER MILES TO JAMAICA AND BACK. IN FACT HE HAD TO START A LEGITIMATE BUSINESS TO COVER HIS TRIPS TO JAMAICA .

HE STARTED BUYING ART FROM JAMAICA. MOSTLY CARVINGS.

LUCK WAS RUNNING WITH HIM IN ALL OF HIS ENDEAVORS.

HE COULD BUY THE ARTWORK SO CHEAP THAT THERE WAS ALMOST AS MUCH PROFIT IN THE ARTWORK AS THERE WAS IN THE POT BUSINESS. IF HE WERE SMART HE SHOULD HAVE STUCK WITH THE ART!

ONE DAY MILO WENT TO SEE THE CRUISE SHIP COME INTO PORT AND WATCHED IN DISMAY AS THE COASTGUARD SWARMED AROUND THE SHIP . THEY HAD EVIDENTLY HAD A PROBLEM WITH THE PROPELLER SHAFTS BEING OUT OF BALANCE.

THEY DOVE ON THEM AND FOUND THE PROBLEM. WOOPS! SO MUCH FOR THAT SCAM!

IT WAS IN ALL OF THE PAPERS. MILO HEARD ALL OF HIS BUDDIES TALKING ABOUT IT AND WONDERING WHY THEY HADN'T THOUGHT OF IT.

HE SOLD OFF ALL OF HIS ARTWORK TO A DEALER OF CARIBBEAN ARTWORK. HE MADE A TIDY PROFIT AND BAILED OUT OF THAT BUSINESS ALSO .

HE STILL HAD HIS MG MIDGET CONVERTIBLE FOR HIS NEXT SCAM, AND HE STILL HAD HIS BUDDY "SHORTY".

HE BOUGHT HIGH GRADE SENSE FROM SHORTY, FOR $350 PER POUND, AND TOOK TRUNK LOADS OF THIRTY POUNDS AT A TIME TO KNOXVILLE TENNESSEE.

THERE HE SOLD IT ONE POUND AT A TIME , FOR $2000 PER POUND.

A TIDY PROFIT OF ALMOST $50,000 PER TRIP AND DIDN'T EVEN HAVE TO WORRY ABOUT THE COASTGUARD. THE CAR WAS SO SMALL THAT HE WAS NEVER SUSPECTED OF ANYTHING .

THIS WORKED FOR QUITE A WHILE. AT LEAST UNTIL HIS CONNECTION GOT BUSTED!

MILO DIDN'T TAKE ANY CHANCE OF GETTING CAUGHT. HE JUST TURNED AROUND AND DROVE

BACK TO THE KEYS AND SOLD IT THERE FOR VERY LITTLE PROFIT. SO MUCH FOR THAT IDEA .

HE WAS A LOVER OF MUSIC AND HAD BEEN SPONSORING A LOCAL BAND IN THEIR MUSICAL ENDEAVORS . THERE HE MET TEDDY TED HAD CONNECTIONS IN NEW YORK.

MILO SUPPLIED TRUNK LOADS OF HIGH GRADE POT FOR TED FOR A VERY SMALL PROFIT SO THAT TED COULD MAKE GOOD MONEY AND THEY DID BUSINESS FOR A COUPLE OF YEARS.

THROUGH MOST OF HIS MANY SCAMS. A TRULY TRUSTED FRIEND, GOOD TIMES AND BAD .

THE SNAP DRAGON WAS GETTING A LITTLE RUN DOWN. HE TOOK THE MAST DOWN AND MOVED THE BOAT THROUGH ONE OF THE CUTS TO THE GULF SIDE. HE TOOK A JOB FOR AWHILE AS A BARTENDER AT THE CARIBBEAN CLUB IN KEY LARGO.

ONE NIGHT: ONE OF THE LOCAL GIRLS TOOK HIM HOME WITH HER FOR A NIGHT OF SEX. IT WAS THE FIRST NIGHT THAT HE HAD NOT SLEPT ON HIS BOAT IN QUITE AWHILE.

HE WAS VERY UNCOMFORTABLE. HE WASN'T USED TO NO MOTION OF THE OCEAN.

THEY WENT BACK TO THE BAR IN THE MORNING TO GET A RED BEER FOR THE HANG OVER. THE BAR TENDER SAID: YOU'RE ALL RIGHT!

MILO SAID: WHY SHOULDN'T I BE? HE SAID: WE THOUGHT THAT YOU MUST BE DEAD! THE BARTENDER SAID: I DON'T KNOW HOW TO TELL YOU THIS MAN, BUT YOUR BOAT WAS SUNK LAST NIGHT!

HE JUMPED UP! AND SAID: WHERE AT? THE BAR TENDER SAID THAT IT IS RIGHT OUT THERE, WHERE THAT BUOY IS. RIGHT WHERE IT WAS ANCHORED.

HE HAD AN AWFUL SINKING FEELING. SO MANY GOOD TIMES AND SO MANY HARD TIMES AND SO MUCH HISTORY.

HE WENT OUT TO THE DOCK AND STRIPPED TO HIS SHORTS AND JUMPED IN AND SWAM OUT TO THE BOAT.

HE DOVE UNDER TO WHERE THE BOAT WAS SUNK. THE CABIN TOP WAS BARELY UNDERWATER. HIS POT STASH WAS FLOATING IN THE CABIN.

HE SWAM AROUND THE BOAT AND SPOTTED THE DAMAGE. THERE WERE A COUPLE OF PLANKS CRACKED ABOVE THE WATERLINE.

IT TURNED OUT THAT SOMEONE HAD GOTTEN A NEW SPEED BOAT AND DECIDED TO GO HIGH SPEED THROUGH THE ANCHORAGE.

HE HIT THE BOAT SO HARD THAT IT FOLDED THE FRONT OF HIS BOAT UP THEN HE WENT IN CIRCLES AROUND THE BOAT TRYING TO WAKE SOMEONE UP. AS IF THEY WOULDN'T WAKE UP TO THAT!

HE MADE SO MANY WAVES FROM GOING AROUND AND AROUND. THAT HE SUNK THE BOAT. IF HE HAD JUST LEFT. IT WOULD HAVE BEEN O.K.

MILO GOT SOME FRIENDS TOGETHER AND GOT AN AIR BAG AND A BIG BILGE PUMP, THEY FILLED THE AIR BAG FIRST UNTIL THE DECK HATCHES WERE AWASH ABOVE WATER AND PUMPED THE

REST WITH THE BILGE PUMP AND RAISED THE
BOAT.

THE BREAK WAS ABOVE THE WATER LINE. IT WAS
AN EASY FIX EXCEPT FOR THE ELECTRONICS.

THE SNAP DRAGON WAS HISTORY. ALL OF THE
ELECTRONICS WERE TRASHED. HE REPAIRED THE
PLANKS AND PAINTED HER HULL BUT IT WAS
NOT THE SAME. IT WOULD BE LIKE STARTING
ALL OVER AGAIN.

HE SOLD THE BOAT AND MOVED INTO AN
APARTMENT. IT WAS BUMMER TIMES FOR AWHILE.
THE WHOLE BOAT THING WAS A WASH OUT!

MILES HAD BOUGHT A 36 FOOT SHARPIE DESIGN
SCHOONER FROM A COUPLE OF LESBIANS. HE
HAD MORE MONEY THAN HE REALLY NEEDED AT
THE TIME, AND THE GIRLS NEEDED MONEY. HE
BOUGHT THE BOAT FROM THEM, AND STOCKED
THE BOAT WITH RESIN, GLASS, GRINDING DISCS,
AND ACETONE.

HE PUT THE BOAT IN THE MANGROVES IN THE
MIDDLE OF THE NIGHT. HE JUST SAVED IT FOR
A RAINY DAY. JUST IN CASE.

WHEN HE FIRST STARTED OUT AT THE BOAT YARD
THE LESBIANS PUT ON SOME PRETTY GRAPHIC
SHOWS ON THE DECK OF THEIR BOAT. PRETTY
KINKY STUFF.

HE WAS THINKING ABOUT GOING BACK TO
CALIFORNIA TO RE-CONNECT WITH HIS KIDS
AGAIN. HE HAD MANAGED TO SAVE ABOUT
$200,000.00. HE HAD SPENT FAR MORE THAN HE
HAD LEFT. MAYBE THIS WOULD BE A GOOD TIME
TO GET OUT OF THE BUSINESS.

BIG FALL!

HE WAS APPROACHED BY ONE OF HIS ACQUAINTANCES FROM HIS OLD SMUGGLING DAYS. HE WANTED HIM TO CAPTAIN A FISHING BOAT TO COLOMBIA FOR HIM. HE SAID THAT HE WOULD PAY HIM $30,000.00 TO TAKE THE BOAT THERE AND THEN THEY WOULD FLY HIM HOME. HE THOUGHT ABOUT IT FOR A MINUTE AND SAID: WELL I GUESS THAT WOULD BE SAFE ENOUGH! HE WAS READY TO GIVE UP THE BUSINESS ALL TOGETHER. HE FIGURED THAT HE WOULD DO THIS ONE MORE SAFE THING, WITH NO CHANCE OF GETTING BUSTED. JUST DELIVER THE BOAT. HE HAD TO TIE UP LOOSE ENDS, SO HE TALKED TO HIS BUDDY TED.

TED AND MILO HAD BEEN PARTNERS FOR SEVERAL YEARS.

MILO WAS THE CONNECTION TO THE SUPPLIERS AND TED WAS THE CONNECTION TO THE BUYERS. THEIR RELATIONSHIP WAS ONE OF TRUST. THEY

NEVER STEPPED ON EACH OTHER'S TURF. THEY
BOTH MADE GREAT MONEY TOGETHER.

HE TOLD TED THAT HE HAD TO GO ON A MISSION
DOWN SOUTH AND HE GAVE HIM HIS SAFETY
DEPOSIT BOX KEY.

HE TOLD HIM, THAT IF ANY EMERGENCY HAPPENED
HE WOULD CALL HIM WHEN HE WANTED TED TO
GO TO THE BOX AND GET A COUPLE THOUSAND
OUT AND SEND IT TO WHERE EVER HE WAS.

TED SAID: NO PROBLEM HERE MAN, YOU ARE IN
GOOD HANDS.

MILO KNEW THAT THE BOAT WAS GOING TO BE
USED FOR POT SMUGGLING BUT, WHY SHOULD
THAT MATTER TO HIM? AFTER ALL, HE WASN'T
GOING TO BRING IT BACK ANYWAY.

HE HAD MET MANNY ON A PREVIOUS SMUGGLING
TRIP WITH HIS BUDDY GREG TO THE BAHAMAS.
HE HAD BROUGHT BACK A SMALL LOAD OF POT
FOR MANNY. HE DID NOT KNOW AT THAT TIME
THAT MANNY WAS GOING TO USE HIS PROFITS
FROM THAT TRIP TO FINANCE THIS TRIP TO
COLUMBIA.

THE TRIP FOR MANNY CAME OFF WITHOUT A
HITCH.

MILO AND GREG SAILED INTO PORT RIGHT UNDER
THE NOSE OF THE COASTGUARD INTO BISCAYNE
BAY.

THEY HAD MORE BALLS THAN BRAINS. THEN
THEY SAILED UP THE INTER-COASTAL WATERWAY
TO KEY LARGO.

HE HAD MADE TEN GRAND FOR HIS PART ON THAT
TRIP.   WHO KNOWS WHAT MANNY MADE.

BOB AND MILO MET MANNY AT MIAMI HARBOR. MANNY SHOWED BOB AND MILO THE BOAT.
IT WAS FILTHY, AND WAS IN REAL BAD NEED OF REPAIR. THE INJECTORS WERE CLOGGED, AND THE FUEL TANKS WERE FOWLED.
THERE WAS MUCH MECHANIC WORK NEEDED BEFORE THE BOAT COULD TAKE THAT LONG OF A TRIP. THAT'S WHY MILO BROUGHT BOB IN TO THE PICTURE.
BOB WAS A HELL OF A MECHANIC, IF ANYONE COULD FIX HER UP BOB COULD!
HE AND BOB DROVE UP TO MIAMI HARBOR WITH TOOLS IN HAND. THEY WORKED ALL DAY AND ALL NIGHT AND FINALLY GOT THE BOAT RUNNING GREAT! A SET OF INJECTORS WOULD HAVE BEEN NICE BUT MANNY SAID THAT WE SHOULD TRY AND DO IT BY JUST CLEANING THEM INSTEAD.
BOB WASN'T REAL HAPPY BECAUSE HE DIDN'T KNOW HOW MUCH SHIT WAS STILL IN THE FUEL TANKS. HE CHANGED THE FILTERS AND BOUGHT FOUR NEW ONES JUST IN CASE.
MILO WAS SO IMPRESSED WITH BOB'S MECHANICAL ABILITY THAT HE OFFERED BOB HALF OF THE FEE TO COME TO COLOMBIA WITH HIM.
BOB SAID THAT WOULD BE GREAT FOR HIM TOO. BECAUSE HE NEEDED THE MONEY ANYWAY AND HE TOO LIKED THE IDEA OF MAKING A NICE CHUNK OF MONEY WITHOUT ANY RISK OF GETTING BUSTED. HE ALSO LIKED THE THOUGHT OF ANOTHER ADVENTURE TOO!

THE BOAT WAS LOADED WITH PROVISIONS AND ICE, BEER, RUM ETC. MILO AND BOB WANTED TO TAKE THE BOAT ON A SHAKE DOWN CRUISE OUT TO THE GULF STREAM AND BACK BUT MANNY SAID THAT THEY DIDN'T HAVE ENOUGH TIME FOR THAT!

THEY NEEDED TO GO NOW IN ORDER TO MEET WITH THEIR SUPPLIERS IN COLOMBIA ON TIME.

MILO LOOKED AT THE NAME ON THE BACK OF THE BOAT.

IT SAID "EL PARIA" ON THE STERN, AND BOTH SIDES OF THE BOW.

HE ASKED MANNY WHAT "EL PARIA" MEANT IN SPANISH?

MANNY TOLD HIM THAT IT MEANT TO BE SICK, OR IN BAD CONDITION.

BOY: DID THEY HAVE THAT RIGHT!

"EL" IS THE MASCULINE FOR "THE" AND "PARIA" MEANING IN BAD CONDITION. I GUESS IT MEANS THE MAN IN BAD CONDITION OR THE BAD MAN.

THEY DEPARTED FROM MIAMI HARBOR AND HEADED DOWN THE INNER-COASTAL WATERWAY DOWN TO THE KEYS THEN JUMPED ACROSS TO GUN CAY, CAT CAY, CUT. IN THE BAHAMAS.

THEY WENT ACROSS THE BAHAMA BANKS TO NASSAU AND RESTED FOR A FEW DAYS. MILO LOOKED AROUND WHILE HE WAS IN THE CASINO BUT NEVER DID SEE GLORIA THERE. HE REALLY MISSED THAT SWEETHEART OF A GIRL.

THEN THEY PROCEEDED TOWARD GREAT INAGUA.

THE ISLAND WAS THE LAST OUTPOST BEFORE THE CROSSING THROUGH THE WINDWARD PASSAGE AND ON TO THE MAIN LEG OF THEIR JOURNEY ACROSS THE CARIBBEAN SEA AND ON TO ARUBA.

ON THEIR APPROACH TO THE ISLAND OF GREAT INAGUA ONE ENGINE SHUT DOWN. THE INJECTORS WERE CLOGGED AGAIN!

THEY LIMPED INTO PORT ON ONE ENGINE. THEY PULLED INTO PORT, WITH THE ENGINES SMOKING LIKE HELL AND RUNNING REAL BAD!

CUSTOMS CAME RIGHT OUT TO THE BOAT. THEY ASKED IF THEY HAD ANY WEAPONS ON BOARD THEY SAID YES AND TURNED THEM OVER TO THE AUTHORITIES. THEY TOOK THEM AND QUESTIONED EVERYBODY ABOUT WHERE THEY WERE ALL GOING.

THEY ALL TOLD THE POLICE THAT THEY WERE JUST DELIVERING THE BOAT TO A FISHING COMPANY IN COLOMBIA. THEY WERE SATISFIED BUT STILL HELD ALL OF THE WEAPONS FOR THEM UNTIL THEY WERE READY TO LEAVE THEIR ISLAND.

SOME OF THE YOUNG BAHAMIAN GIRLS CAME UP TO THE DOCK NEXT TO THE BOAT. ONE OF THEM HAD ON A LONG DRESS AND WAS QUITE ATTRACTIVE. SHE SQUATTED DOWN BY THE BOAT AND SPREAD HER KNEES APART EXPOSING HERSELF TO MILO AT HEAD LEVEL! SHE WAS SO CLOSE THAT HE COULD ALMOST SMELL IT!

SHE DIDN'T HAVE ANY UNDERWEAR ON!
HE RESISTED HER PROPOSITION BECAUSE SHE WAS SO YOUNG. NOT MUCH OLDER THAN HIS OWN DAUGHTER HE THOUGHT. PROBABLY IN HER VERY EARLY TWENTIES HE THOUGHT.
SHE ONLY WANTED $20 FOR SEX SO HE GAVE HER $20 FOR DOING HIS LAUNDRY INSTEAD.
WHEN THE GIRL RETURNED WITH THE LAUNDRY LATER THAT DAY. THE GIRL SEEMED A LITTLE PUT OUT! IT SEEMED THAT SHE REALLY WANTED THE SEX INSTEAD. A LITTLE WHITE MEAT!
MOST OUT ISLAND GIRLS ARE LOOKING FOR AN AMERICAN TO TAKE THEM AWAY FROM THE CRAPPY LIFE THAT THEY HAVE TO LIVE THERE. MOST ARE VERY POOR.
MILO WAS AFRAID THAT IF THEY HUNG AROUND TOO LONG. HE WOULD TAKE THE YOUNG BAHAMIAN GIRL'S OFFER AND GIVE IT TO HER. HE THOUGHT ABOUT GLORIA. HE WONDERED IF HE WOULD EVER SEE HER AGAIN.
THEY NEEDED MORE REPAIRS TO MAKE SURE THAT THERE WERE NO MORE PROBLEMS FOR THE LONGEST AND MOST DANGEROUS PART OF THE JOURNEY.
ON THE ISLAND, WAS A SALT MINE HE NEVER SAW SO MUCH SALT IN HIS LIFE. "THE MORTON SALT COMPANY". IF YOU EVER GET SEA SALT, THIS IS WHERE IT COMES FROM. QUITE AN OPERATION.
THEY NEEDED SUPPLIES, ICE, AND PARTS FOR THE DIESEL ENGINES. EVERYONE THEY ASKED SAID:

GO TO MORTON SALT COMPANY! ANYTHING THAT YOU NEED. MORTON SALT COMPANY!

THEY TOOK A LOCAL CAB. IT WAS A VERY RUSTED OUT OLD CHEVY WITH NO DOORS. THE CAB DRIVER ASKED THEM IF THEY WANTED ANY POT. HELL YES THEY SAID! THEY SCORED ENOUGH FOR A COUPLE OF WEEKS.

SO THEY WENT TO THE SALT COMPANY AND GOT ALL OF THE SUPPLIES THAT THEY NEEDED. THEY WERE VERY SURPRISED THAT THEY WOULD HAVE EVERYTHING.

THE YOUNG GIRLS WERE AT THE DOCK TO BID THEM ALL FAREWELL; MILO COULDN'T GET THE PICTURE OF THAT PRETTY YOUNG GIRL OUT OF HIS MIND FOR QUITE SOME TIME, IN FACT, I GUESS HE NEVER DID! SHE REMINDED HIM OF GLORIA. WHAT A FOX!

THEY WERE ON THE WAY AGAIN, BUT HE WAS STILL HAUNTED BY THE BOATS PERFORMANCE.

HE WAS TOLD THAT THE BOAT WOULD DO 14 KNOTS AND WITH ALL OF THE ISLAND HOPING AND BREAKDOWNS, GOING AGAINST THE CURRENT AND THE WIND THEY NEVER HAD A CHANCE TO REALLY CHECK IT OUT! THEY HAD NO ACCURATE MEASUREMENT OF THE SPEED THE BOAT WAS CAPABLE OF.

THE BOAT DIDN'T EVEN COME CLOSE TO THAT 14 KNOTS.

THE BOTTOM WAS FOWLED UP TO THAT POINT SO THEY HAD CLEANED IT WHILE THEY WERE IN GREAT INAGUA. IT SEEMED A LITTLE FASTER, BUT NOT MUCH!

No Matter Where You Go

THOSE POOR ENGINES HAD TO WORK REAL HARD TO PUSH THAT BIG BARGE BOTTOM ACROSS THE WATER. THE ONE THING THAT THE BOAT DIDN'T HAVE WAS A KNOT LOG AND THAT DISTURBED HIM A GREAT DEAL!

AS THEY WERE GOING THROUGH THE WINDWARD PASSAGE HE COULD SEE THE LIGHTS OF CUBA TO HIS RIGHT AND HAITI AND THE DOMINICAN REPUBLIC WERE TO HIS LEFT.

THE CUBANS ON BOARD WERE VERY NERVOUS AND ASKED HIM TO STEER A LITTLE FARTHER AWAY FROM CUBA. HE LAUGHED AND HEADED FURTHER OUT TO SEA.

HE WAS STILL HAUNTED BY THEIR SPEED. IT WAS VERY HARD TO JUDGE THE SPEED OF A STINK POT POWER BOAT MAKING ALL THAT NOISE AND SMELL.

ARUBA

NEXT STOP ARUBA HE TOLD THE CREW.
FIGHTING THE CURRENT ALL OF THE WAY. THEY
WOULDN'T SEE ANY-MORE LAND FOR THE NEXT
1,000 MILES.
NOW THEY HAD TO HIT AN ISLAND THAT WAS
ONLY TWENTY MILES WIDE AND LONG.
IT WAS TOUGH NO MATTER HOW GOOD YOU
WERE. IT WOULD BE NICE TO KNOW YOUR SPEED
AT LEAST!
MILO WAS A VERY GOOD NAVIGATOR. HE PRIDED
HIMSELF ON JUDGING SET, DRIFT, CURRENTS
AND SPEED.
IT WAS THE SPEED THAT REALLY BOTHERED
HIM.
HE HAD NO HISTORY TO DRAW FROM IN ORDER TO
REALISTICALLY PLOT THEIR SPEED. YOU REALLY
HAVE TO KNOW HOW FAST THAT YOU WENT AT
LEAST ONCE IN THE LIFE OF EACH BOAT. YOU
JUST CAN'T DEPEND ON SOMEONES LIES TO GET
YOU THERE.

THE CURRENT WAS FROM STARBOARD TO PORT AT TWO AND A HALF KNOTS AND IN A DISTANCE OF 1000 MILES THAT IS QUITE A BIT OF DRIFT. IF YOU KNOW YOUR SPEED THE DRIFT IS EASY TO FIGURE.

THE ISLAND OF ARUBA WAS ONLY 20 MILES WIDE. MISS-JUDGING THE SPEED BY ONLY ONE KNOT COULD THROW YOU OFF BY UP TO FIFTY MILES. PLENTY OF DISTANCE TO COMPLETELY MISS THE ISLAND WITHOUT EVEN SEEING IT.

HE BEGAN COMPUTING TIME SPEED AND DISTANCE TO THE ISLAND. HE KNEW THAT THE BOAT WASN'T DOING 14 KNOTS AS A-MATTER-OF-FACT AS HE LOOKED OVER THE SIDE HE HAD THE FEELING THAT HIS SAILBOAT WITH NO MOTOR WAS EVEN FASTER THAN THIS TUB EVER WENT! HIS SAILBOAT WAS CAPABLE OF DOING 7 $\frac{1}{2}$ KNOTS EASY. SO HE STARTED THERE. HE TOLD THE CREW THAT AT 7 KNOTS THEY WOULD ARRIVE IN ARUBA IN ABOUT 14 MORE DAYS.

TWO DAYS WENT BY AND HE ADJUSTED THE COMPASS COURSE FOR SIX KNOTS. AFTER A FEW MORE DAYS ON THAT HEADING THE CREW WAS CONCERNED THAT MILO WASN'T THE CAPTAIN THAT THEY THOUGHT HE WAS.

WHEN HE ORDERED THEM TO CHANGE COURSE AGAIN THEY BEGAN TO PANIC.

THE MORE THAT HE LOOKED AT THE WATER PASSING BY THE BOAT HE DECIDED TO ALTER THE COURSE AGAIN. THIS TIME HE RE-FIGURED FOR 5 $\frac{1}{2}$ KNOTS AND CHANGED COURSE AGAIN.

HE KNEW FROM EXPERIENCE THAT YOU SHOULD NEVER CHANGE COURSE WITHOUT A POSITIVE FIX ON YOUR POSITION. THEY NEVER DID HAVE A GOOD FIX ON THEIR POSITION.

HE CONTINUOUSLY THROUGHOUT THE TRIP CHECKED THE DEPTH SOUNDER, AND AS HE RAN THROUGH POCKETS OF SHALLOWER WATER, THEN HE COULD GET A PRETTY GOOD IDEA AS TO WHERE THEY WERE. HE WAS JUST FOLLOWING THE POCKETS OF SHALLOWS ACROSS THE BOTTOM.

THE CREW WAS REALLY WORRIED BY NOW BUT NOBODY ON BOARD KNEW THE OCEAN LIKE HE DID AND THEY HAD NO CHOICE BUT TO TRUST IN HIM. LIKE IT OR NOT EVERYONE WAS ALONG FOR THE RIDE.

HE DECIDED TO CONSULT HIS CHAPMAN'S GUIDE TO PILOTING AND SEAMANSHIP. HE DISCOVERED HOW TO FIGURE THEIR SPEED ACCURATELY.

HE HAD PUDY "THE COOK", GO TO THE BOW OF THE BOAT, AND ON HIS COMMAND HE WOULD DROP A PIECE OF BREAD INTO THE WATER. HE WOULD TIME IT FROM BOW TO STERN.

THEY DID IT DOZENS OF TIMES. HE HAD THE FEELING THAT ARUBA WAS NOT THAT FAR AWAY. THEY WERE GETTING CLOSE MILO FIGURED. HE DIDN'T WANT TO MAKE ANY MISTAKES AT THIS POINT.

THE SPEED COMPUTED AT 4 KNOTS, OR FIVE-MILES PER HOUR. FUCKING SLOW HE THOUGHT! HE HAD A GOOD IDEA BY NOW AS TO WHERE THEY WERE BUT KEPT IT TO HIMSELF. HE ORDERED THEM TO CHANGE THE COMPASS COURSE AGAIN,

THIS TIME BY 60 DEGREES. HE HAD ALREADY PASSED IT!

WELL IF THEY HAD NOT CHANGED COURSE THEN THEY WOULD HAVE NEVER SEEN IT AT ALL! THIS THREW THE CREW INTO PANIC!

MANNY SAID TO MILO. ARE YOU SURE YOU KNOW WHAT YOU ARE DOING CAPPY?

MILO SAT MANNY DOWN WITH THE CHART AND EXPLAINED TO HIM THAT THIS WAS HIS D.R. OR DEAD RECKONED POSITION AND THAT PUT THEM RIGHT HERE AND PUT HIS FINGER ON THE CHART. THEN HE PUT ANOTHER FINGER ON THE CHART AND SAID: ARUBA IS RIGHT HERE. SO ALL WE HAVE TO DO IS HEAD THIS WAY TO GET THERE.

MANNY SAID: WHAT DOES D.R. MEAN?

MILO TOLD HIM THAT MEANS THE WAY I FIGURE IT! I RECKON THAT WE ARE HERE! SO RELUCTANTLY THEY CONTINUED ON THE NEW COURSE.

THE SEA SPRAY HAD DRENCHED EVERYONE ON BOARD AND MILO WAS REAL IRRITABLE BECAUSE HE HAD A HUGE BOIL OR SEA SORE ON HIS ASS CAUSED BY SEA WATER BEING ON HIS LEVI'S AND KEEPING HIS ASS WET FOR A WEEK STRAIGHT AND HE COULDN'T SIT DOWN ANY MORE.

ANY TIME ANYONE WOULD QUESTION HIM ABOUT WHERE THEY WERE. HE WOULD SNAP AT THEM AND TELL THEM NOT TO BOTHER HIM. FINALLY THE BOIL CAME TO A HEAD AND POPPED!

HE LOST ALL OF THAT PUSS TENSION AND HE COULD THINK STRAIGHT AGAIN.

A HALF DAY LATER MANNY CAME TO HIM AND SAID: THE CREW IS REALLY WORRIED CAPPY! THEY WANT TO KNOW FOR SURE WHEN WE WILL GET THERE!

MILO WAS AT THE HELM WITH A BIG SMILE ON HIS FACE WHEN MANNY ASKED HIM. ARE YOU GOING CRAZY? WHY ARE YOU SMILING?

HE SAID: MANNY. LOOK STRAIGHT AHEAD, DO YOU RECOGNIZE THAT PIECE OF LAND? THAT ISLAND RIGHT OVER THERE.

MILO KNEW THAT MANNY HAD BEEN TO THAT ISLAND BEFORE AND WOULD RECOGNIZE IT!

MANNY LOOKED THROUGH THE BINOCULARS FOR QUITE AWHILE AND THEN HE STARTED LAUGHING AND SINGING AND YELLED! LAND HO! "ARUBA"!

THE ENTIRE CREW WAS DANCING AROUND THE DECKS WITH JOY. THEY WERE CHANTING IN THEIR NATIVE CUBAN LANGUAGE. THE CA-PI-TAN DID IT! THE CA-PI-TAN DID IT!

THEY CRUISED INTO PORT FOR A BADLY NEEDED REST!

IT TOOK 14 $\frac{1}{2}$ DAYS AT 5 MILES PER HOUR. WHAT A FUCKING SLOW TRIP! 1100 MILES. INCLUDES PASSING THE ISLAND AND FIGHTING THE CURRENT ALL OF THE WAY.

HE THOUGHT TO HIMSELF; IT'S A GOOD THING IT'S A ONE-WAY TRIP!

AFTER THAT TRIP THE FIRST TASK AT HAND WAS TO FIND SOME POT. THEY HAD RUN OUT SEVERAL DAYS EARLIER. THEN THE MOST IMPORTANT THING! PARTY, PARTY, PARTY, PARTY.

THEY DOCKED THE BOAT AND CALLED GREG TO COME WITH SOME MORE MONEY. HE FLEW OUT OF MIAMI THE NEXT MORNING AND ARRIVED IN ARUBA ON MILO'S BIRTHDAY.

TODAY WAS MILO'S BIRTHDAY. HE WAS THIRTY-TWO YEARS YOUNG TODAY.

HE AND MILO SAT DOWN TO A LONG TALK. MILO TOLD HIM OF THE NAVIGATIONAL PROBLEMS AND THE SPEED OF THAT PIECE OF SHIT!

MILO ALSO EXPLAINED TO HIM THAT THE BOAT WOULD NOT HOLD ENOUGH FUEL TO MAKE IT FROM SANTA-MARTA BACK TO THE UNITED STATES.

GREG "THE MANAGER OF THE TRIP" TOLD HIM THAT HE WOULD MAKE SURE THAT THE BOAT TOOK ON EXTRA FUEL BEFORE DEPARTING FOR THE U.S.

HE TOLD GREG THAT IT WASN'T HIS PROBLEM ANYWAY BUT MAKE SURE THAT THEY HAVE ENOUGH FUEL, SO THAT THEY WOULD HAVE A FIGHTING CHANCE OF MAKING IT!

WITH ALL OF THE DISCUSSIONS COMPLETE IT WAS PARTY TIME! THEY ALL PARTIED AND GAMBLED THE REST OF THE DAY.

GREG CALLED SANTA-MARTA TO SECURE A GUIDE FOR MILO. HE THEN FLEW BACK HOME.

MILO TOLD MANNY THAT TODAY WAS HIS BIRTHDAY AND THAT HE WANTED TO GET LAID. MANNY SAID: NO PROBLEM CAPPY!

SO MANNY AND MILO GOT A CAB AND STARTED BAR- HOPPING AROUND THE ISLAND.

MANNY HAD BEEN TO ARUBA SEVERAL TIMES
IN THE PAST AND KNEW WHERE ALL OF THE
HOOKERS WERE.

THEY GOT TO THIS LITTLE BAR WHERE THERE
WAS SOME LOCAL TALENT "HOOKERS".

MILO PICKED OUT THE ONE HE WANTED AND
WENT WITH HER INTO THE BACK ROOM.

SHE HAD HER WAY WITH HIM A COUPLE OF
TIMES. SHE SURE LIKED TO SWALLOW OR MAYBE
SHE JUST ACTED LIKE IT BECAUSE IT WAS HIS
BIRTHDAY. THEN THEY RETURNED TO THE BAR
WHERE MANNY AND THE OTHERS WERE.

THEY DRANK QUITE A BIT, AND MILO WAS
FEELING PRETTY SICK SO HE WENT TO THE
BATHROOM AND STUCK HIS FINGER DOWN HIS
THROAT TO GET RID OF SOME OF THE BOOZE.

HE WENT BACK OUT INTO THE BAR WHERE MANNY
WAS DRINKING WITH SOME OF THE OTHER
HOOKERS. MANNY SAID: LETS GO TO ANOTHER
BAR THAT HE KNEW OF.

HE AGREED. SO THEY SPLIT FOR DESTINATIONS
UNKNOWN TO MILO.

THEY GOT TO THE NEXT BAR AND HE SAW A
BEAUTIFUL COLOMBIAN GIRL AND TOLD MANNY
THAT HE WANTED THAT ONE TOO!

MANNY ARRANGED IT FOR HIM. IT WAS TIME TO
DRINK SOME MORE.

AFTER A COUPLE MORE HOURS HE WANTED SOME
MORE. HE GOT IT!

THAT POOR GIRL REALLY HAD TO WORK AT IT TO
GET HIM OFF BUT SHE MANAGED AND MILO WAS
HAPPY FOR A WHILE LONGER. THE NEXT GIRL

HE WENT FOR GOT HIM IN THE BACK ROOM AND BEGAN UNDRESSING HIM. HE WAS STINKING DRUNK BY NOW.

SHE PULLED OUT HIS PECKER AND LOOKED AT IT FOR A MINUTE THEN SAID: CONYO SENIOR! MUY MACHO CA-PI-TAN! AND HAD HER WAY WITH HIM TOO!

HE DID NOT REMEMBER MUCH AFTER THAT! HE WOKE UP IN THE MORNING WITH A SPLITTING HEADACHE.

MANNY WAS YELLING! CA-PI-TAN RAINBOW MAN! CA-PI-TAN RAINBOW MAN!

MILO SAID: WHAT THE FUCK ARE YOU TALKING ABOUT?

MANNY SAID: THE LAST FEW PLACES WE STOPPED AT LAST NIGHT, THE GIRLS WERE CALLING YOU CA-PI-TAN RAINBOW MAN!

MILO WENT TO TAKE A LEAK AND HE LOOKED AT HIS PECKER AND THEN STARTED LAUGHING! HE THOUGHT TO HIMSELF. I MUST HAVE HAD FUN AND I SEE WHAT THEY WERE TALKING ABOUT! "RAINBOW PECKER"! FIVE DIFFERENT COLORED RINGS.

HE AND MANNY WENT TO A LOT OF BEACH PARTIES ON ARUBA STILL WAITING FOR CAPTAIN BRUCE TO ARRIVE.

HE WAS TO BE THEIR GUIDE TO SANTA MARTA. AFTER A MONTH OF HANGING OUT AND PARTYING CAPTAIN BRUCE FINALLY SHOWED UP. SO MUCH FOR BEING IN A BIG HURRY TO LEAVE IN THE FIRST PLACE.

HE BROUGHT A LARGE BAG OF COCAINE WITH HIM FOR THE TRIP FROM ARUBA TO SANTA-MARTA. THE GUYS THAT SENT MILO ON THE MISSION WARNED HIM THAT HE SHOULD KEEP THE COCAINE AWAY FROM MANNY.
HE HAD A TENDENCY OF LOOSING IT WHILE UNDER THE INFLUENCE OF THAT CRAP! HE GETS REAL WEIRD.

COLUMBIA

IT WAS TIME TO GO SO THEY WENT OUT INTO
THE HARBOR AND SWUNG THE COMPASS FOR THE
LAST TIME. THEY SEEMED TO HAVE A PROBLEM
GETTING A BEARING ON A KNOWN COMPASS
COURSE.
IT TOOK ALL NIGHT TO GET TO SANTA-MARTA.
AS A MATTER-OF-FACT THEY WERE WELL INTO
THE NEXT AFTERNOON BEFORE THEY ARRIVED.
BEAUTIFUL WHITE SAND BEACHES, AND A LITTLE
TRASH ON THE OCEAN FLOOR. EVEN SO, QUITE
NICE.
THERE WAS A LITTLE POINT THAT STUCK OUT.
IT WAS CALLED: "AQUADEIENTE". PROBABLY
SPELLED IT WRONG.
THEY HAD A GLASS BOTTOM SUBMARINE THERE
IT WAS ACTUALLY A BOAT THAT WAS MADE TO
LOOK LIKE A SUBMARINE. IT WAS THE BIGGEST
ATTRACTION THERE.
MILO TOOK A CRUISE ON THE GLASS BOTTOM
SUB. THERE WERE TONS OF FISH AROUND THOSE
WATERS. A GREAT PLACE TO GO FISHING.

EVERYONE CLEARED CUSTOMS, THEN HE AND MANNY WERE ESCORTED TO A LOCAL HOTEL WHERE BOB AND MILO WOULD STAY FOR THE NEXT MONTH.

BOB WANTED NOTHING TO DO WITH MANNY AND HIS FRIENDS.
HE JUST PLAIN DID NOT TRUST THEM.
AS IT WAS HE DID HAVE A GOOD REASON TO NOT TRUST THEM. THEY HAD THE OPINION THAT BOB WAS GOING TO TURN THEM IN TO THE AUTHORITIES.
MILO THOUGHT THAT IT WAS THE COCAINE THAT WAS TALKING. THEY WERE EVEN TALKING ABOUT KILLING HIM AT ONE POINT.
ONE DAY BOB WENT TO MILO AND TOLD HIM THAT HE WANTED OUT! NOW!
MILO KNEW ENOUGH SPANISH BY NOW THAT HE KNEW THAT BOB HAD A GOOD REASON TO BE WORRIED. HE TOLD BOB THAT HE WOULD DO WHAT HE COULD. JUST HANG ON BUDDY.
MILO TOOK MANNY ASIDE AND EXPLAINED TO HIM THAT BOB WASN'T NEEDED ANYMORE AND THAT HE SHOULD SEND HIM BACK HOME.
MANNY SAID: I DON'T HAVE THE MONEY TO SEND HIM BACK!
THAT REALLY GOT MILO WONDERING WHAT THEY HAD PLANNED FOR HIM TOO!
MILO SAID: WHAT DO YOU MEAN! YOU DON'T HAVE THE MONEY!
MANNY SAID: THAT THE TRIP HASN'T BEEN PAID FOR YET!

HE ASKED MANNY: THEN HOW IN THE HELL ARE WE GOING TO GET BOB HOME?

MANNY SAID: BOB WILL HAVE TO COME UP WITH HIS OWN MONEY TO GET HOME.

BOB HAD USED UP ALL OF HIS MONEY JUST GETTING TO SOUTH AMERICA. HE TOLD MILO THAT HE WOULD DO ANYTHING TO GET BACK HOME.

MILO SAID: WHAT ABOUT YOUR GUN? YOU SHOULD GET ENOUGH MONEY OUT OF THAT, TO GET HOME.

HE ASKED CAPTAIN BRUCE IF HE COULD HELP HIM SELL THE GUN. IT WAS A NICKEL PLATED 38 REVOLVER. THERE SHOULD BE PLENTY OF MONEY THERE.

CAPTAIN BRUCE SAID THAT HE WOULD DO THE BEST HE COULD AND A COUPLE OF DAYS LATER HE CAME BACK WITH A PLANE TICKET TO MIAMI.

BOB WAS HAPPIER THAN HELL THAT HE WAS GOING HOME AND MILO THOUGHT ABOUT CALLING TED ABOUT SENDING HIM SOME MONEY TOO!

MILO DIDN'T REALLY WANT TO TAP INTO HIS OWN MONEY TO GO HOME, BESIDES HE WAS HAVING FUN WITH THE HOOKERS.

HE DECLINED CALLING FOR MONEY AND DECIDED TO STAY AND DO HIS PART OF THE MISSION. AFTER ALL HE STILL HAD A CAPTAIN TO TRAIN.

BOB DID MAKE IT OFF O.K. BUT MILO DID WORRY ABOUT HIM BECAUSE OF THE THINGS THAT HE HAD OVERHEARD ABOUT THEM KILLING HIM.

ALTHOUGH HE DIDN'T KNOW IT AT THE TIME, IT WOULD BE A LONG TIME BEFORE MILO WOULD MEET BOB AGAIN.

IT WAS PARTY TIME AT THE HOTEL.

PROSPECTIVE SELLERS WOULD BRING UP SAMPLES OF THEIR POT AND ASK MILO HOW MUCH HE COULD SELL IT FOR.

PART OF THE DEAL THAT MILO HAD WITH THE SMUGGLING TRIP WAS TO HELP THEM SELL IT WHEN THE POT MADE IT BACK TO THE UNITED STATES.

MOST OF THEM WERE NOT HAPPY WITH WHAT HE WOULD TELL THEM ABOUT THEIR POT. MOST OF IT WAS GARBAGE IN HIS OPINION.

NO PROBLEM GETTING HIGH THOUGH. IT SEEMED THAT ANY OF THE POT THAT WAS ANY GOOD THEY DIDN'T HAVE ENOUGH OF IT TO MAKE A TRIP OUT OF IT.

HE GOT REAL TIRED OF DIFFERENT HOOKERS EVERY NIGHT. HE ASKED MANNY IF HE COULD GET JUST ONE TO HANG ONTO FOR THE ENTIRE STAY.

MANNY ARRANGED IT FOR HIM AND IT WORKED OUT PRETTY GOOD FOR AWHILE.

THAT IS UNTIL HE GOT THE CLAP! HE PICKED THE WRONG ONE! SHE WAS NICE ENOUGH AND ALL BUT SHE HAD PLENTY OF OTHER CUSTOMERS EVEN WITH THE CLAP!

MANNY TOOK MILO INTO TOWN AND GOT HIM A SHOT OF PENICILLIN AND A FEW DAYS LATER THE DRIPPING STOPPED AND HE WAS ALL RIGHT AGAIN.

MILO HAD BEEN A WANT-TO-BE VEGETARIAN AND FISH EATER FOR A FEW YEARS BY NOW BUT THE CUBAN AND COLOMBIAN PEOPLE HE WAS PARTYING WITH HAD NO RESPECT FOR THAT TYPE OF LIFE-STYLE NOR DID THEY CARE ABOUT WHAT HE ATE.

ONE DAY WHEN A BUNCH OF THE LOCAL HOOKERS WERE AT THE HOTEL ROOM THEY WERE COOKING A PIG'S HEAD IN A BIG POT. EVERY-ONE WAS SITTING AROUND DOING LINES, SMOKING POT AND CHICKLE A DERIVATIVE OF COCAINE. IT TASTED LIKE DIESEL FUEL.

THEY WERE ALL WIRED UP AND TALKING LIKE FOOLS. THEY WERE ALL WHACKED OUT ON THE DRUGS THAT THEY WERE DOING AND NOT PAYING ANY ATTENTION TO THE POT OF FOOD ON THE STOVE.

ALL OF A SUDDEN. MILO LOOKED UP AT THE POT WITH THE PIG'S HEAD IN IT. THEN HE PUT HIS FINGER UP TO HIS MOUTH AND LOUDLY SAID: SHHHHHHHH! EVERY-ONE LOOKED AT HIM.

THE PIG'S HEAD HAD FLOATED UP ON ONE SIDE SO THAT ONE EAR AND ONE EYE WERE STICKING UP OUT OF THE POT AS IF IT WERE LISTENING AND WATCHING THEM.

HE SMILED AND SLOWLY POINTED TOWARD THE POT ON THE STOVE. THEY ALL LOOKED AT THE PIG'S HEAD AND STARTED LAUGHING.

THIS REALLY BROKE THE ICE FOR HIM AND THE COLOMBIAN PEOPLE HE WAS PARTYING WITH. THEY WOULD NO LONGER KID HIM ABOUT EATING PORK OR RED MEAT.

THESE PEOPLE WERE DOING MORE AND MORE COCAINE EVERYDAY. SMOKING IT WAS THE NORM.

THE COLOMBIANS WERE VERY FILTHY HYGIENE WISE. THEY ALL WOULD WIPE THEIR ASSES AND THROW THE SHITTY PAPER ON THE FLOOR BESIDE THE TOILET.

MILO WAS ALWAYS CLEANING UP AFTER THEM. YOU WOULD HAVE THOUGHT THAT THEY HAD NEVER USED INDOOR PLUMBING BEFORE! AS IT TURNED OUT. THE SEPTIC SYSTEMS IN COLUMBIA WOULD NOT HANDLE ANY TOILET PAPER AND MILO WAS WORKING AT BEING HYGIENIC FOR NOTHING.

EVERYONE WAS TRYING TO MAKE HIS OR HER OWN INDIVIDUAL DEAL WITH MILO AND EACH TRIED TO CUT EVERYONE ELSE OUT OF THE DEAL! THEY WERE ALL BACKSTABBING EACH OTHER FOR THE DEAL.

IT WAS AFTER SEVERAL WEEKS OF MEETING POTENTIAL SPONSORS OF THEIR SMUGGLING OPERATION THAT HE MET PAPA LUCHIO.

HE WAS PART OF THE COCAINE CARTEL IN COLOMBIA. A VERY POWERFUL MAN.

PAPA LUCHIO BOUGHT THE CONTRACT FOR THE SMUGGLING OPERATION.

MILO WAS MOVED TO PAPA LUCHIO'S HOME IN THE COUNTRY NEAR SANTA MARTA.

PAPA LUCHIO WAS A BAD MAN. HE HAD HIS OWN PRIVATE ARMY AND HAD THE REGULAR ARMY IN HIS BACK POCKET!

HE HAD HOOKERS AT HIS HOUSE ALL THE TIME.

MILO NEVER WORRIED ABOUT NEEDING SEX WHILE HE WAS THERE. IT WAS PARTY TIME ALL THE TIME.

ONE EVENING MILO WAS WATCHING A BUNCH OF OLD PORN BETA-MAX TAPES.

THERE WERE THESE TWO GUYS THAT WERE TAKING TURNS FUCKING THIS PRETTY GIRL IN THE ASS. THERE IS SOMETHING WEIRD ABOUT THESE COLOMBIANS, THEY ALL HAD A THING ABOUT FUCKING IN THE ASS.

THIS GUY WAS GETTING DOWN REAL HARD ON HER ASS WHEN HE GRABBED HER BY THE HAIR AND JERKED HER HEAD BACK REAL HARD.

YOU COULD SEE THE PAIN IN HER EYES WHEN HE DID THAT TO HER. HE THEN TOOK A SHARP KNIFE AND SLICED HER THROAT AND SPRAYED BLOOD ALL OVER THE CAMERA. THE TAPE ENDED. MILO WAS IN SHOCK! WHAT HAS HE GOTTEN HIMSELF INTO.

HE QUESTIONED ONE OF THE GUYS THERE ABOUT THE TAPE THAT HE HAD JUST WATCHED.

THEY ASSURED HIM THAT IT HAD NOTHING TO DO WITH THESE PEOPLE THAT HE WAS WORKING FOR.

AT PAPA LUCHIO'S HOME WAS A COCAINE KITCHEN.

THEY SHOWED HIM ALL OF THE STEPS THAT WENT INTO MAKING THE COCAINE.

FIRST THEY PICK THE COCA LEAVES AND THEN THEY PUT THEM INTO A METAL 55 GALLON DRUM.

THEN THEY FILL THE DRUM WITH DIESEL FUEL OR KEROSENE. THEN THEY PUT THE DRUM ON A LOW FIRE AND COOKED IT FOR SEVERAL DAYS OR UNTIL THE RESINS SEPARATED AND FLOATED TO THE TOP.

THEN THEY SKIMMED THE TOP OFF. THAT PRODUCT IS CALLED "CHICLY". SNOTTY GUM!

IT WAS KIND OF LIKE GUM. THEY TAKE THE CHICLY, AND PUT IT INTO A LARGE STAINLESS STEEL CONTAINER, AND FILL THE CONTAINER WITH ACETONE.

THE ACETONE TURNS THE GUM BACK INTO A LIQUID AGAIN. THEY STIR IT GENTLY FOR SEVERAL HOURS. THEN THEY POUR THE LIQUID THROUGH A LARGE METAL FILTER.

THEY PRESS THAT THEN THEY LET THE ACETONE WITH THE RESIDUE EVAPORATE.

THE LEFT OVER PRODUCT IN THE METAL SIEVE IS STILL CALLED CHICLY. THEY LET THAT DRY AND SMOKE IT LIKE CRACK! THAT TASTES LIKE DIESEL FUEL. PRETTY HORRIBLE STUFF.

THAT STUFF NEVER MAKES IT TO THE U.S. ALL OF THE LEFT OVER GOES ON TO BECOMING THE GOOD SHIT!

THE EVAPORATED PRODUCT IS THEN WASHED AGAIN IN ACETONE AND THEN IS POURED THROUGH A PAPER SIEVE TO SEPARATE MORE OF THE IMPURITIES OUT OF THE CHICLY AND THEN

PRESSED TO GET MOST OF THE ACETONE OUT. THEN IT IS LEFT TO EVAPORATE AGAIN.

THEN THEY TAKE THAT RESIDUE AND PUT PETROLEUM EITHER IN IT AND POUR THAT LIQUID THROUGH A LARGE PAPER FILTER. IT IS PRESSED AGAIN. THE PRODUCT LEFT IN THE FILTER IS COCAINE.

THE MORE WASHES OF EITHER. THE MORE PURE THE COCAINE. THEY PRESS THE FILTER AND THE SUBSTANCE WITHIN INTO BLOCKS AND LET IT COMPLETELY EVAPORATE.

ALL OF THAT CHEMICAL PROCESS REALLY MAKES YOU WONDER WHY PEOPLE PUT THAT SHIT UP THEIR NOSES.

PAPA LUCIO WAS SHIPPING COCAINE TO THE U.S. IN MANY DIFFERENT WAYS. SOME TIMES IT WAS AIR DROPS USING OLD U.S. BOMBERS.

THE ONE THAT REALLY SCARED MILO THE MOST WAS THAT THEY HAD TAKEN A BABY THAT HAD DIED AT BIRTH. THEY TOOK ALL OF THE GUTS OUT OF THE CORPSE AND PACKED THE CHEST CAVITY AND ABDOMINAL AREA WITH THE WHITE SHIT! THEN THEY HAD A WOMAN GO THROUGH A PUBLIC AIR TERMINAL AND FLY COMMERCIAL TO MIAMI.

THE WHITE SHIT WAS PASSED ON TO THE WAITING ASS HOLES AT THE OTHER END.

MILO WAS VERY DISAPPOINTED WITH THE NEW PEOPLE WHO HAD TAKEN OVER THE CONTRACT FOR THE POT TRIP.

HE NEVER TOOK KINDLY TO PEOPLE WHO DEALT IN COCAINE ANYWAY. THEY WERE ALL USERS AND CROOKS!

PAPA LUCIO MUST HAVE SENSED THAT MILO WAS UNHAPPY WITH WHAT HE HAD RECENTLY SEEN.

HE CALLED FOR MORE HOOKERS TO COME OUT TO THE RANCH AND ENTERTAIN HIM FOR THE REST OF HIS STAY AT THE RANCH.

THEY SENT OUT FOUR LADIES FOR MILO TO PLAY WITH AS HE CHOOSES. HE WOULD SPEND MOST OF THE DAY IN THE SWIMMING POOL, PLAYING WITH THE GIRLS.

THEY NICKNAMED HIM "NEPTUNA" BECAUSE HE SPENT SO MUCH TIME UNDER WATER.

HE BEGAN TO GET BORED WITH THE GIRLS. HE WANTED TO BE LOVED, NOT JUST GETTING SEX ANYTIME HE WANTED IT!

HE SLEPT WITH ALL FOUR OF THEM EVERY NIGHT. IT WAS GETTING PRETTY KINKY. THEN HE COMPLETELY LOST INTEREST .

HE WANTED NO MORE OF IT! HE TOLD PAPA LUCIO THAT HE WAS READY TO GO HOME. PAPA LUCIO TOLD HIM THAT HE WOULD BE GOING HOME SOON PLEASE JUST RELAX. MILO WAS GETTING MORE AND MORE UNSURE OF THESE PEOPLE.

MILO STARTED READING THE HOROSCOPES IN THE MIAMI HERALD. THE PAPER WAS BROUGHT TO THE RANCH EVERY DAY. HE HAD BEEN IN COLOMBIA FOR THREE MONTHS NOW.

HE WAS READING THE HOROSCOPES ONE DAY AND IT SAID THAT HE WAS GOING TO TRAVEL

AND THAT HE WOULD FIND COMFORT IN THE WRITTEN WORD.

WELL: MILO WAS NOT INTO RELIGION AND HE CERTAINLY WAS NOT INTO READING! HE DISMISSED THE READING OF THE HOROSCOPE.

THE ONLY PROBLEM WAS THAT THE SAME PREDICTION KEPT REPEATING EVERY DAY AND TRAVEL WAS ALWAYS IN THE PICTURE.

FINALLY THE DAY CAME. MANNY, PUDY, AND FOUR OTHER COLOMBIANS CAME UP TO HIM AND SAID: O.K. CAPTAIN, IT'S TIME TO GO!

HIJACKED

HE STOOD UP HAPPY AS HELL AND SAID: LET ME GET MY STUFF AND I'LL BE RIGHT WITH YOU.
HE GOT HIS STUFF TOGETHER AND WENT OUT TO WHERE MANNY AND THE REST OF THEM WERE WAITING. HE SAID: WELL LET'S GO.
THEY TOOK HIM OUT TO WHERE THE BOAT WAS DOCKED.
MANNY SAID: WE HAVE DECIDED THAT WE WANT YOU TO TAKE THE BOAT BACK TO THE UNITED STATES!
MILO SAID: I'M NOT GOING TO DO IT! IT IS SUICIDE IN THAT PIECE OF SHIT!
YOU WILL HAVE TO DO IT OVER MY DEAD BODY!
AT THAT POINT ALL OF THEM PULLED THEIR WEAPONS, AND TOLD HIM THAT HE DIDN'T HAVE ANY CHOICE!
HE WAS GOING TO DO IT! OR DIE!
HE WAS ESCORTED TO THE BOAT AT GUNPOINT! THEY ALL LOADED UP ONTO THE BOAT AND CRUISED OFF INTO THE NIGHT.

MANNY TOLD HIM THAT IF THEY MADE IT TO THE U.S. OK THAT HE WOULD MAKE ¼ MILLION DOLLARS.

THE THOUGHT OF THE MONEY WAS OK BUT FREEDOM WAS WHAT MILO WANTED TO KEEP.

HE RESIGNED HIMSELF TO THE FACT THAT HE HAD TO DO THIS THING. LIKE IT OR NOT!

MILO ASKED, WHAT ABOUT THE FUEL THAT IS NEEDED TO MAKE SURE WE GET TO THE UNITED STATES?
ONE OF THE GUYS ON BOARD SAID THAT THEY WOULD TOP US OFF WHEN THEY LOADED THE BOAT WITH THE POT.
HE KNEW THAT JUST TOPPING OFF WASN'T ENOUGH FUEL TO MAKE IT THERE. HE TOLD THEM THAT ISN'T ENOUGH TO MAKE IT THERE!
THE GUY SAID: WE WILL GIVE YOU ALL THE FUEL WE HAVE. DON'T WORRY ABOUT IT!
THEY TRAVELED FOR SEVERAL HOURS IN THE OPPOSITE DIRECTION OF HOME. MAKING IT FURTHER AWAY AND NEEDING MORE FUEL TO MAKE THE TRIP.
SEVERAL HOURS INTO THE NIGHT THEY ARRIVED AT THE SPOT WHERE THEY WERE LOADED WITH 10,000 POUNDS OF POT.
THAT FILLED ALL OF THE ICE HOLDS AND THERE WERE EVEN BALES ON DECK! HE DIDN'T KNOW WHAT THEY WERE THINKING. AFTER THEY HAD LOADED ALL OF THE POT ON BOARD MILO ASKED

WHERE THE FUEL WAS AND THEY SAID THAT WE
WOULD HAVE TO MAKE IT WITH THE FUEL THAT
WE HAD!

NOW THEY HAD TAKEN THEM IN THE OPPOSITE
DIRECTION FOR HALF OF A DAY AND STILL NO
FUEL!

THEY SHOWED MILO WHERE THEY WERE ON
THE CHART AND DEPARTED WITH ALL OF THE
WEAPONS. LEAVING ALL OF THE CREW AT THE
MERCY OF THE OCEAN AND MILO.

HE WONDERED IF MAYBE THEY WERE BEING SENT
AS A DECOY FOR YET ANOTHER LOAD AND THAT
WAS WHY THEY DIDN'T GIVE THEM ANY FUEL.

THEY MOTORED OFF INTO THE NIGHT TOWARD
THE UNITED STATES. THIRTY DAYS TO GO.

THE NEXT DAY WAS VERY CALM AND MILO
BROUGHT THE BOAT TO A STOP AND PROCEEDED
RIGGING THE MAST AND SAIL THAT HE HAD
BROUGHT JUST IN CASE OF AN EMERGENCY.

HE WAS A DIE HARD SAILOR AND BROUGHT THE
RIGGING FOR SAILS JUST IN CASE SOMETHING
HAD GONE WRONG AND THEY LOST ALL OF THEIR
POWER.

HE FIGURED AT THE VERY WORST THAT IT WOULD
MAKE A GOOD STEADYING SAIL.

NOT ONLY WERE THEY GOING TO LOOSE THEIR
POWER BUT THEY NEEDED BETTER FUEL MILEAGE
JUST TO GET PAST CUBA.

THEY HOISTED THE SAILS AND PROCEEDED ON
THEIR COMPASS COURSE TOWARD THE YUCATAN
CHANNEL. THEY WERE HEADING NORTHEAST

SKIRTING THE PEDRO BANKS OR AT LEAST HE THOUGHT SO!

ALL OF A SUDDEN THE DEPTH SOUNDER ALARM WENT OFF!

HE STOPPED THE BOAT AND BROKE OUT THE CHARTS. HE FOUND THE AREA WHERE IT SHOWED THEIR DEPTH.

THEY WERE 60 MILES OFF COURSE!

HE DIDN'T SEE HOW THAT WAS POSSIBLE. HE KNEW THEIR SPEED AND HAD FIGURED THEIR DRIFT.

HE WENT TO THE COMPASS AND STARRED AT IT FOR A FEW MINUTES THEN SLID THE DRAWER OPEN THAT WAS NEXT TO THE COMPASS AND FOUND THE PROBLEM.

ALL OF THE MECHANIC TOOLS WERE IN THE DRAWER! HE BEGAN THROWING TOOLS ACROSS THE CABIN IN DISGUST!

WHEN HE HAD GOTTEN ALL OF THE TOOLS OUT OF THERE HE DISCOVERED THAT THE COMPASS WAS ABOUT 40 DEGREES OFF.

HE DIDN'T KNOW IF THERE WAS PERMANENT DAMAGE TO THE COMPASS OR NOT.

HE CORRECTED THEIR COURSE AND CONTINUED ON THEIR WAY.

A MASSIVE SCHOOL OF DOLPHIN WAS OFF TO PORT. HE WATCHED THEM AND HIS COMPASS AND THE DEPTH SOUNDER VERY CLOSELY.

THE ALARM WAS GOING ON AND OFF FOR HOURS THEN ALL OF A SUDDEN THE SCHOOL OF DOLPHINS VEERED TOWARD STARBOARD RADICALLY!

HE KNEW THAT SOMETHING WAS WRONG.
THE ALARM WASN'T SHUTTING OFF ANYMORE
AND THE WATER WAS DANGEROUSLY SHALLOW.
HE THOUGHT WELL IT'S DO OR DIE AND DECIDED
TO FOLLOW THE DOLPHINS.
HE TURNED TO STARBOARD AND FOLLOWED THE
DOLPHINS FOR ABOUT AN HOUR WHEN THE
DEPTH SOUNDER ALARM FINALLY SHUT OFF.
HE LOOKED AT THE DEPTH AND WAS AMAZED TO
SEE THAT THEY WERE IN 230 FEET OF WATER.
HE WAS TOTALLY RELIEVED! HE LOOKED OUT FOR
THE DOLPHINS TO THANK THEM FOR THEIR HELP
BUT ALL OF THEM HAD DISAPPEARED.
THANKS GUYS MILO SAID TO HIMSELF YOU WERE
LIFE SAVERS BUDDIES.

THE GOOD THING WAS, NOW HE REALLY KNEW
WHERE HE WAS.

MILO WAS REMINDED OF STORIES THAT HE HAD
HEARD OF DOLPHINS LEADING SAILORS AWAY
FROM DANGEROUS REEFS, THEREFORE SAVING
THE LIVES OF MANY SAILORS. NOW THEY HAD
PROVEN THEMSELVES TO HIM. HE WOULD NEVER
DOUBT THEIR VALUE AGAIN.
NOW THAT THEY WERE CLEAR FROM IMMEDIATE
DANGER, HE AND THE CREW WOULD SPEND MANY
DAYS ON THE SAME OLD BORING COURSE. AT
LEAST THAT IS WHAT HE HAD HOPED FOR.
TWO DAYS AFTER THE EXPERIENCE WITH THE
DOLPHINS, THE SEAS STARTED BUILDING UP.

OH GREAT! HE THOUGHT. I COULDN'T GET THESE GUYS TO HOLD A STEADY COURSE IN GOOD WHETHER, NOW WITH SAILS UP RUNNING WING & WING IN FOUL WEATHER AND A FOLLOWING SEA WILL BE THE REAL TEST!

LUCHINO WAS AT THE HELM. HE WAS BY FAR THE WORST HELMSMAN OF THE GROUP.

HE WAS ON A NIGHT WATCH AT THE HELM WHEN ALL OF A SUDDEN THERE WAS A HELL OF A RACKET.

MILO BURST OUT OF BED THINKING THAT THEY RAN AGROUND OR SOMETHING. IT TURNED OUT THAT LUCHINO HAD FALLEN ASLEEP AT THE WHEEL.

THE SAILS WERE TIED OFF FOR A WING & WING DOWN WIND RUN. WHEN HE FELL ASLEEP.

THE BOAT ROUNDED UP AND WAS GOING STRAIGHT INTO THE WIND. WITH THE SAILS WINGED OUT!

THE PRESSURE WAS TOO MUCH FOR THE RIGGING AND DISS-MASTED THE BOAT.

MILO GOT EVERYONE UP AND THEY PULLED ALL OF THE RIGGING FROM THE WATER AND TIED IT FAST.

HE THEN WENT TO LUCHINO AND GRABBED HIM BY THE THROAT AND STARTED STRANGLING HIM.

THE REST OF THE CREW PULLED MILO OFF OF HIM. MANNY SAID TO MILO, WHAT DO YOU THINK YOU'RE DOING MAN?

MILO REPLIED, WE ARE RIDING FOR A BIG FALL!
IS THAT WHAT YOU WANT? ARE YOU READY TO
GO BACK TO CUBA MANNY?
MILO SAID: THAT THEY HAD ENOUGH FUEL TO
GET TO JAMAICA
SAFELY.
LETS THROW THIS SHITTY POT THAT WON'T
EVEN GET YOU HIGH OVER THE SIDE! LETS GO
TO JAMAICA INSTEAD AND ARRIVE SAFE AND
ALIVE!
MANNY SAID THAT HE COULDN'T DO THAT. HE
WOULD HAVE TO TAKE A FALL OR MAKE IT WITH
THE LOAD.
MILO TOLD MANNY THAT THEY WEREN'T GOING
TO MAKE IT BECAUSE THEY DIDN'T HAVE ENOUGH
FUEL. HE KNEW THAT WHEN THEY HAD LEFT
WITHOUT TAKING ON MORE FUEL.
WE ARE ABOUT TWO OR THREE DAYS SHORT OF
FUEL. WE WILL WIND UP DRIFTING OFF SHORE
OF CUBA!
MILO ASKED MANNY, ARE YOU SURE THAT YOU
ARE READY TO GO BACK HOME TO CUBA? WE DON'T
HAVE ENOUGH FUEL TO GET PAST CUBA!
WE CANNOT WAIT UNTIL WE RUN OUT OF FUEL
BEFORE WE THROW OUT THE POT! IT WILL JUST
DRIFT ALONG WITH US!
MANNY SAID: HE HAD FAITH THAT MILO COULD
THINK OF SOMETHING TO GET THEM THROUGH
THIS ORDEAL.
ALL THAT MILO COULD THINK OF WAS THAT THEY
HAVE BEEN RIDING FOR THE BIGGEST FALLS OF
THEIR POOR MISERABLE LIVES.

HE NOW KNEW THAT HE WOULD HAVE TO DO SOMETHING SO VERY DESPERATE THAT IF HE GOT CAUGHT HE WOULD SPEND THE REST OF HIS LIFE IN PRISON OR THE DEATH SENTENCE!

HE WAS NOT SURE THAT HE HAD IT IN HIM!

HE THOUGHT ABOUT ANGEE AND FIGURED OH WHAT THE HELL!

MILO HAD HIS COURSE SET FOR THE YUCATAN CHANNEL.

WHEN HE GOT CLOSE ENOUGH AND HAD ONLY ONE DAY OF FUEL LEFT HE WOULD HAVE TO KILL THE WHOLE CREW AS THEY CHANGED WATCHES.

IT WAS NOT WHAT HE WANTED TO DO BUT IT WAS HIS LIFE AT STAKE TOO!

THEY KEPT ON THEIR COURSE FOR A FEW MORE DAYS. HE KEPT A CLOSE EYE ON THE FUEL CONSUMPTION. HE WATCHED THE HABITS OF MANNY AND THE OTHERS VERY CLOSELY.

TIMING WOULD HAVE TO BE CRITICAL IF HE WAS TO SUCCEED IN KILLING THEM ALL, WITHOUT THE OTHERS HEARING WHAT WAS GOING ON.

MILO CHANGED THE WATCHES TO TWO HOUR WATCHES. THAT WAY HE COULD TAKE CARE OF ALL OF THEM IN THE DARKNESS OF NIGHT.

MILO PUT HIMSELF BETWEEN EACH WATCH SO THAT EVERYONE KNEW THAT THEY WERE GOING TO SEE HIM AT SHIFT CHANGE.

HE WOULD WAIT UNTIL EACH MAN WENT TO THE SIDE TO TAKE A PISS BEFORE STARTING THEIR SHIFT.

HE WOULD KICK EACH MAN OVER THE SIDE WHEN THEY HAD THEIR DICKS IN THEIR HANDS. NOBODY

WOULD EVER HEAR THEIR CRIES FOR HELP OVER THE NOISE OF THE DIESEL ENGINES.

THEN HE WOULD WAIT UNTIL THE NEXT SHIFT CHANGE AND DO IT AGAIN AND AGAIN UNTIL THEY ALL WERE GONE.

HE WOULD THEN THROW ALL TRACES OF THE POT OVER-BOARD AND CONTINUE ON UNTIL HE WAS PICKED UP BY THE COASTGUARD.

HOPEFULLY IT WOULD BE THE U.S. COASTGUARD!

HE DECIDED TO RIG THE MAIN SAIL AGAIN SO THAT THEY WOULD NOT HAVE TO RUN AT FULL THROTTLE AND ALSO POSSIBLY FOOL THE COAST GUARD INTO THINKING THAT IT WAS A SAILBOAT!

THEY HAD AN OLD A.M. RADIO ON BOARD HE DECIDED TO USE THAT AS A RADIO DIRECTIONAL FINDER.

HE TUNED IT INTO A STATION THAT WAS ALL-SPANISH, AND HAD MANNY TELL HIM WHERE IT WAS BEING BROADCAST FROM.

HE FINALLY FOUND A HAVANA STATION AND FIGURED OUT EXACTLY WHERE THEY WERE.

JUST ONE MORE DAY BEFORE MILO WOULD HAVE TO DO HIS DASTARDLY DEED!

YOU COULD CUT THE TENSION ON BOARD WITH A KNIFE!

THEY WERE SO CLOSE TO CUBA THAT YOU COULD SEE THE CUBANS PRAYING THAT THEY MADE IT.

LITTLE DID THEY KNOW WHAT MILO HAD IN STORE FOR THEM!

THEY WERE ROUNDING THE YUCATAN CHANNEL.
MILO KNEW THAT THIS WAS THE NIGHT! IT WAS
TIME TO START KILLING FOR HIS OWN LIFE!
MILO TOOK THE FIRST SHIFT. MANNY WAS TO
FOLLOW IN TWO HOURS.
THE TWO HOURS WERE UP AND MILO WOKE
MANNY. MANNY WENT TO THE SIDE AND PULLED
OUT HIS PECKER TO TAKE A PISS LIKE HE ALWAYS
DID BEFORE EACH SHIFT.
MILO WAS VERY NERVOUS BUT MOVED TOWARD
MANNY SLOWLY.
HE WAS JUST ABOUT TO JUMP TOWARD HIM
WHEN THEY WERE HIT WITH A POWERFUL
SPOTLIGHT! MANNY TURNED TO MILO WHOM
HAD STOPPED PROGRESS BY NOW.
BECAUSE OF THE CIRCUMSTANCES AT THIS
POINT HE SAID: CAPPY! WHAT'S GOING ON?
MILO TOLD HIM WELCOME TO CUBA MANNY!
THIS IS THAT BIG FALL THAT I WAS TELLING
YOU ABOUT!

CUBA

IT WAS A CUBAN GUNBOAT! THE BOAT LIT UP LIKE A CHRISTMAS TREE AND IT WAS COVERED WITH MEN IN UNIFORM CARRYING A.K.47'S!
THEY BOARDED THE "EL PARIA" AND CUFFED EVERYONE.
MILO LOOKED OVER AT MANNY AND SAID: GOD HELP YOU MANNY, YOU DON'T KNOW HOW LUCKY YOU REALLY ARE!
IT WAS THE LAST RUN FOR "EL PARIA".
THE GUN BOAT TOOK THEM IN TOW.
MILO AND THE CREW ARRIVED ABOUT FOUR HOURS LATER AT THE NORTHERN MOST POINT OF CUBA.
THAT WAS THE 19 MILES THAT MILO NEEDED TO ASSURE THAT THE CUBANS WOULD NOT BE ABLE TO BOARD THEM. THE CUBANS WENT PAST THE 12 MILE LIMIT TO STEAL THE BOAT FROM THE AMERICANS.

AFTER REACHING SHORE THE CUBANS UNLOADED ALL OF THE POT AND TOOK ALL OF THE CREW

MEMBERS ONE AT A TIME AND TOOK THEIR PICTURES IN FRONT OF THE POT! THEN ONE FINAL PICTURE OF THEM ALL TOGETHER.

THEY WERE MOVED TO THE FIRST INTERROGATION POINT.

THE HEAD GUARD IN CHARGE SPOKE TO MANNY FIRST.

MILO OVERHEARD MANNY TALKING TO THE GUARD,

HE WAS SAYING SOMETHING TO THE AFFECT THAT THE CAPTAIN WAS RESPONSIBLE FOR THE WHOLE THING.

HE WAS RATTING OUT CAPPY RIGHT FROM THE START! THEY THEN TOOK HIM OFF IN PRIVATE.

THEY SPOKE FOR A LONG TIME AND THEN MANNY WAS RETURNED TO THE REST OF THE CREW.

MANNY TOLD MILO THAT HE THOUGHT THAT THEY WERE GOING TO BE RELEASED BECAUSE WE WERE TOO FAR OFF SHORE AND THEY SHOULD NOT HAVE COME AFTER US!

MILO THOUGHT THAT THIS WAS TOO GOOD TO BE TRUE AND AS IT TURNED OUT IT WAS!

HE WAS NOW SURE THAT HE WAS TO BE HERE FOR A LONG TIME!

MILO WAS VERY TIRED AND NEEDED A LONG REST. HE WAS GOING TO GET ALL OF THE SLEEP THAT HE COULD STAND!

MILO THOUGHT TO HIMSELF. THIS "IS" THE BEGINNING OF THE END!

THE BIGGEST FALL OF MY LIFE! THE BIGGEST FALL OF ALL OF OUR LIVES.

THE DREAM

IT STARTS IN SORT OF A COUNTY FAIR ATMOSPHERE. MILO WAS WALKING THROUGH A CIRCULAR BOARDWALK AREA, AND SAW AN EXHIBIT THAT REALLY ATTRACTED HIS ATTENTION, BECAUSE IT WAS SO UNIQUE. IT REMINDED HIM OF A GAME SHOW SCENE.

THERE WAS A LARGE OVAL SHAPED POND WITH A SHIP'S BELL AT ONE END, AND THERE WAS A ROPE HANGING FROM THE BELL TO THE WATER.

THE OVAL POND HAD AN OVAL ISLAND IN THE MIDDLE. THE ISLAND WAS BEAUTIFULLY DECORATED WITH EXOTIC FLOWERS AND PALM TREES, WHICH IS WHAT ATTRACTED HIM IN THE FIRST PLACE.

HE STEPPED UP ONTO THE STAGE AREA.
TO HIS AMAZEMENT, HE SAW A FULL MAN SIZED ROOSTER STANDING THERE! RIGHT IN FRONT

OF HIM. HE SEEMED SO REAL THAT HE COULD ALMOST SMELL HIM!

THE ROOSTER SAID: COME ON OVER HERE MILO. MILO WAS FLABBERGASTED! NOT ONLY COULD HE SPEAK, BUT ALSO HE WAS A REAL ROOSTER!

HE SAID OK MILO; THIS IS YOUR LIFE. MILO WAS SO SURPRISED THAT HE COULDN'T KEEP HIS EYES AND EARS OFF OF HIM. HE SAID: MILO THIS IS A QUESTION AND ANSWER GAME.

I'LL ASK THE QUESTIONS AND YOU HAVE TO FIND THE ANSWERS. EVERY TIME YOU ANSWER MY QUESTION I'LL SWIM TO THE BELL AND RING IT AND THEN RETURN TO ASK YOU ANOTHER QUESTION. HE SAID: ARE YOU READY? MILO SAID: YES.

HE SAID: "MILO" WHAT HAVE YOU DONE WITH YOUR LIFE SO FAR? MILO SAID: WHAT DO YOU MEAN? HE SAID: WHAT SORT OF WORK DO YOU LIKE TO DO?

HE SAID THAT HE WAS MOST EXPERIENCED WITH PAINTING AND CARPENTRY BUT HE LIKED BEING "CAPTAIN" OF HIS OWN SHIP AND SAILING AROUND THE CARIBBEAN.

THE ROOSTER SAID: THAT'S GREAT! HE THEN JUMPED INTO THE WATER AND SWAM AT AN AMAZING SPEED TO THE BELL AND RANG IT LOUDLY ONCE AND SWAM BACK.

HE CLIMBED OUT OF THE WATER, AND WALKED OVER TO MILO.

HE PUT HIS WARM WET WING OVER HIS SHOULDER LIKE A GOOD FRIEND WOULD. THE SMELL THAT WAS COMING OFF OF THAT WET ROOSTER WAS GROSSE! SOMETHING WAS KEEPING HIM THERE AND THE SMELL WAS BECOMING A MORE FRIENDLY SMELL.

HE SAID: THAT WAS GOOD MILO. NOW; WHAT WOMAN DID YOU LOVE MORE THAN ANY OTHER? AND WHAT MADE HER DIFFERENT FROM ALL THE OTHERS?

HE THOUGHT ABOUT IT FOR A WHILE AND SAID: "ANGELA" WAS THE ONE THAT HE HAD LOVED THE MOST AND THERE WERE TWO THINGS DIFFERENT ABOUT HER FROM ALL THE OTHERS. [1] SHE IS A GOOD CHRISTIAN. [2] SHE IS A CAPRICORN.

THE ROOSTER SAID: THAT'S GREAT! AND JUMPED INTO THE WATER AGAIN AND SWAM AROUND TO THE BELL AND RANG IT TWICE.

HE CAME BACK AGAIN AND PUT HIS WARM WET WING OVER HIS SHOULDER AGAIN. HE SAID: MILO, NOW FOR PART THREE.

WHAT DO YOU WANT TO DO MORE THAN ANYTHING IN THE WORLD, TO MAKE YOU HAPPY?

HE TOLD THE ROOSTER THAT THERE WASN'T ANY DOUBT ABOUT THAT ANSWER! HE WANTED TO BE WITH HIS CHILDREN AGAIN.

THE ROOSTER GOT REAL EXCITED, AND SAID: PERFECT!
HE JUMPED INTO THE WATER AGAIN, AND SWAM AROUND TO THE BELL,
THIS TIME HE SWAM SO FAST THAT A TWENTY FOOT ROOSTER TAIL CAME UP FROM HIS FEET AS HE SWAM.
HE GOT TO THE BELL, AND THEN HE RANG IT VERY LOUDLY, THREE TIMES AND THEN RETURNED TO PUT HIS WARM WET WING OVER HIS SHOULDER ONCE AGAIN.

NOW THEY FACED THE PANEL ON THE STAGE.
THE PANEL HAD ALL OF THE LETTERS OF THE ALPHABET ON IT.

THE ROOSTER SAID; MILO, THIS IS THE FOURTH AND MOST IMPORTANT PART OF YOUR GAME OF LIFE.
HE SAID: WHAT IS THE #1 MOST IMPORTANT THING IN LIFE?

HE THOUGHT AND THOUGHT AND JUST COULDN'T COME UP WITH THE ANSWER. THE ROOSTER SAID: MILO, YOU ARE A GOOD AND GIVING PERSON. SO I AM GOING TO GIVE YOU A HINT.
MILO ALL YOU HAVE TO DO IS PUNCH THE LETTER "C".

SO MILO PUNCHED THE LETTER "C" AND SIRENS AND BELLS WENT OFF!
THE PANEL SPIT OUT A PIECE OF PAPER. A PHONE NUMBER WAS ON IT.

THE ROOSTER SAID: OK MILO ALL YOU HAVE TO DO TO WIN THE GAME OF LIFE IS TO GO TO ONE OF THE PHONE BOOTHS OVER THERE AND CALL THIS NUMBER FOR THE ANSWER.

HE WAS VERY EXCITED AND RAN TO THE PHONES. THEN HE FELT THROUGH HIS POCKETS AND NOTICED THAT HE DIDN'T HAVE ANY MONEY, LET ALONE CHANGE FOR THE PHONE.

MILO WALKED BACK OVER TO THE ROOSTER FEELING VERY DEJECTED.
HE TOLD THE ROOSTER THAT HE DIDN'T HAVE ANY MONEY FOR THE ANSWER.

THE ROOSTER TOLD HIM THAT YOU DON'T REALLY NEED ANY MONEY FOR THE ANSWER, BUT YOU CERTAINLY WILL HAVE TO PAY BEFORE YOU PLAY.

HE WOKE UP SWEATING!
"THE DREAM" WOULD HAUNT HIM ALMOST DAILY
FOR YEARS TO COME. SO MUCH FOR THE FIRST
NIGHT IN CUBA!

MILO AND THE REST OF THE CREW WERE
TRANSPORTED ACROSS COUNTRY TO A PLACE
CALLED G-2 "INTERROGATION".

G-2 INTERROGATION

MILO MET THIS LIEUTENANT NAMED WALTER. HE WAS VERY WELL EDUCATED AND QUITE SOFT SPOKEN. AS A MATTER OF FACT HE HAD BEEN EDUCATED IN THE UNITED STATES.

HE GAVE MILO A PACK OF CIGARETTES AND TOLD HIM TO GO AHEAD AND LIGHT UP. HE ASKED HIM IF HE COULD SEE THE PALMS OF HIS HANDS HE ASKED WHAT KIND OF WORK HE DID. HE TOLD HIM THAT HE WAS A PAINTER AND A CARPENTER. WALTER SEEMED TO DOUBT MILO'S STORY ABOUT BEING A CARPENTER OR A PAINTER UNTIL HE SAW THE CALLUSES ON HIS HANDS, EVEN THOUGH THEY WERE ALMOST GONE. THE SALT WATER HAD ALMOST ELIMINATED ALL OF HIS CALLUSES.

HE QUESTIONED MILO FOR A COUPLE OF HOURS. HE ASKED HIM ABOUT THE SIGN THAT WAS ABOVE THE STEERING STATION ON THE BOAT. MILO LAUGHED, AND SAID: THAT WAS NOTHING.

WALTER SAID: BUT THE SIGN SAID: THAT THE NEXT PERSON THAT FELL ASLEEP WOULD DIE!

OH THAT! MILO SAID: I WAS PISSED OFF AT LUCHINO, AND I PUT IT UP THERE SO THAT NO-ONE WOULD MAKE THAT MISTAKE AGAIN. NOTHING MORE THAN THAT!

WALTER TOLD MILO THAT IN CUBA WE BURN ALL OF THE MARIJUANA WE FIND!

MILO TOLD WALTER THAT THEY BURN IT ALL IN THE UNITED STATES TOO! JUST ONE JOINT AT A TIME!
A BIT OF A SMART ASS ANSWER THAT IRRITATED WALTER SOMEWHAT.

WALTER SENT HIM BACK TO HIS CELL AND HE COULD HEAR THEM CALL FOR THE OTHER GUYS ON THE CREW ONE AT A TIME UNTIL FINALLY THEY HAD TALKED TO EVERYONE AT LEAST ONCE!

THEY WOULD THEN RE-QUESTION WHOM EVER THEY WANTED TO UNTIL THEY GOT ALL OF THE CORRECT ANSWERS.
MILO HOPED THAT IT WAS THE TRUTH THAT THEY WERE REALLY AFTER BUT SOMEHOW HE DOUBTED IT. IT WAS ALL POLITICAL!

THE FOOD WAS TERRIBLE! BUT MILO WAS VERY HUNGRY AND ATE IT ALL ANYWAY. THEY PUT ANOTHER GUY IN THE CELL WITH HIM. HE

WAS FRIENDLY ENOUGH TO MILO BUT HE WAS DEFINITELY A COMMUNIST!

MILO HAD THE SUSPICION THAT HE WAS INTERROGATING HIM TOO!
AFTER HOURS OF TALKING TO EACH OTHER THEY WOULD CALL HIS CELL MATE OUT OF THE ROOM AND TALK TO HIM TOO! SOME OF THE QUESTIONS WALTER ASKED MILO JIVED WITH THE QUESTIONS HIS CELL MATE WOULD ASK.

THE INTERROGATIONS CONTINUED FOR WEEKS AND WALTER KEPT MILO IN CIGARETTES THE WHOLE TIME.

HE COULD HEAR PUDY AND MANNY BEING TORTURED! THEY WOULD SCREAM AND BEG FOR MERCY. HE COULD HEAR THEM BEING BEATEN ALMOST DAILY. MILO WAS REAL HAPPY TO BE AN AMERICAN AT THIS POINT! HE DIDN'T REALLY CARE WHAT HAPPENED TO MANNY AND THE REST OF THEM. AFTER ALL, THEY DID HIJACK HIM.

HE TOLD WALTER THAT HE WAS A VEGETARIAN AND HE HAD BEEN FOR SEVERAL YEARS. AT THAT POINT MILO DID NOT GET ANY MORE VEGETABLES WITH HIS FOOD. IT TURNED INTO HELL AT G-2.

FINALLY, ALL OF THE INTERROGATIONS WERE FINISHED! THEY SHIPPED HIM TO ANOTHER PRISON SOMEWHERE IN THE INTERIOR OF CUBA.

AT THIS POINT HE GOT HIS FIRST HAIRCUT. THEY SHAVED HIS HEAD JUST LIKE THE MARINE CORPS DID. THAT WASN'T SO BAD BECAUSE HE HAD SO MANY RATS IN HIS HAIR FROM NOT BEING ABLE TO COMB IT FOR OVER A MONTH. NOW THERE WASN'T ANY MORE MOLES TO LOOSE EITHER.

WHEN THEY WERE SHAVING HIS BEARD HE STARTED GROWLING AT THE BARBER AND WHEN HE WENT NEAR HIS MUSTACHE HE WENT OFF! HE EXPLODED WITH RAGE CALLING THEM ALL COMMIES. "DEATH TO THE COMMIES"!

THEY TACKLED MILO AND HELD HIM DOWN AND SHAVED HIM. THEY DID NOT REALIZE WHAT HIS MUSTACHE MEANT TO HIM. HE HAD WORN IT FOR HIS ENTIRE LIFE THUS FAR! IT WAS HIS IDENTITY

HE IMMEDIATELY STOPPED EATING ANYTHING AT ALL! HE DECIDED THAT HE WOULD SHOW THOSE COMMIE BASTARDS WHAT LENGTHS AN AMERICAN WOULD GO TO AND TO GET WHAT THEY WANTED! YEAH RIGHT!

THE COMMIES DON'T CARE! BUT THE COMMIES DON'T WANT TO HAVE AN AMERICAN DIE WHILE IN THEIR CUSTODY EITHER.

EVERY MORNING HE COULD HEAR GUNSHOTS GOING OFF! HE ASKED ONE OF THE INMATES

WHAT THEY WERE ALL ABOUT? THEY TOLD HIM THAT WAS A FIRING SQUAD!

THEY WERE EXECUTING SOMEONE EVERY MORNING! THE WALLS ON THE PRISON WERE ABOUT THREE FEET THICK OF SOLID ROCK AND MORTAR THEN STUCCO ON THE OUTSIDE OF THAT. THEY PUT THE MEN THAT THEY WERE GOING TO EXECUTE AGAINST THE OUTSIDE OF THE WALL ON HIS CELL BLOCK. YOU COULD HEAR THE BULLETS HIT THE WALL. PRETTY SCARY. JUST THREE FEET AWAY AND THEY WERE DIEING!

HE LEARNED THAT THERE WERE 10 MILLION PEOPLE ON THE ISLAND OF CUBA AND THAT ONE-QUARTER OF THE POPULATION WAS IN PRISON.

COMBINADO DEL ESTE

STILL NO CONTACT WITH THE OUTSIDE WORLD!
STILL NO TRIAL! WHAT WAS GOING TO HAPPEN
TO HIM WAS ANYBODY'S GUESS!
FINALLY HE WAS MOVED AGAIN. IT WAS TO A
PRISON NEAR HAVANA. IT WAS THE LARGEST
CITY ON THE ISLAND.

THE NAME OF THE PRISON WAS "COMBINADO
DEL ESTE".
HE WAS PLACED IN A CELL BLOCK WITH JAMAICANS,
COLOMBIANS, PEOPLE FROM DOMINICAN
REPUBLIC, AND LAST BUT NOT LEAST, HIS FELLOW
AMERICANS! MILO COULD FINALLY EAT AGAIN.

AT LAST! SOMEONE TO TALK TO. HE WAS PUT INTO
A CELL WITH TWO JAMAICANS, ONE GUY FROM THE
DOMINICAN REPUBLIC AND TWO AMERICANS.

THE JAMAICANS NAMES WERE, JOHNNY AND
CHENNY OR "CLEMENT".

THE DOMINICANS NAME WAS RAUAL. THE AMERICANS NAMES WERE, BOB "FANTASMA" FANTY FOR SHORT AND DOUG. LATER NICKNAMED "THE MEPBROMATO MAN" MEPBROMATO "MEPS" WERE A CUBAN VERSION OF REDS. THEY GAVE THEM TO THE PEOPLE THAT HAD AGGRESSIVE TENDENCIES.

THEY ALL WELCOMED MILO WITH OPEN ARMS. AFTER A COUPLE OF DAYS WITH HIS NEW FOUND FRIENDS, MILO TRULY KNEW WHO THE LOSERS WERE!

THE JAMAICANS WERE REALLY COOL GUYS WHICH JUST WERE AT THE WRONG PLACE AT THE WRONG TIME.
THE AMERICANS WERE HOPELESS EXCUSES FOR HUMAN BEINGS.

MILO TOLD FANTY THE STORY OF BEING HIJACKED AND BEING TAKEN AT GUNPOINT TO THE BOAT.

FANTY WAS A THREE TIME LOOSER AND DID NOT BELIEVE A WORD OF IT. HE TOLD HIM TO LAY DOWN AND LICK HIS NUTS, BECAUSE HE WAS GOING TO BE THERE A LONG TIME.

FANTY WAS A PIMP IN THE MIAMI AREA. MILO COULD NEVER UNDERSTAND HOW ANY WOMAN COULD LET ANY GUY MAKE A PROFIT ON THE SHITTY JOB THAT THEY HAVE TO PUT UP WITH BEING HOOKERS.

FANTY WAS THAT TYPE THOUGH. A USER FROM THE WORD GO!

HE CLAIMED THAT HE WAS THE PROTECTOR OF THE GIRLS.

THAT WOULD HAVE BEEN ALL RIGHT EXCEPT FOR THE FACT THAT HE WAS A WOMAN HIMSELF AND COULDN'T FIGHT FOR SHIT!

THE FIRST NIGHT WAS OVER AT COMBINADO DEL ESTE.

THAT DREAM! HE DIDN'T KNOW WHY HE KEPT HAVING IT.

THE SIGHT OF THE PRISON WAS ALMOST SURREAL. THE WHOLE THING OTHER THAN THE DOORS THEMSELVES WERE ALL MADE OUT OF CONCRETE. CONCRETE WINDOWS AND CONCRETE BARS AND NO GLASS. WHAT SO EVER.

THE WEATHER WAS OUTSIDE. THAT WAS THE WEATHER INSIDE. IF IT WAS BLOWING RAIN OUTSIDE, THEN IT WAS BLOWING RAIN INSIDE. AT LEAST THERE WAS FRESH AIR.

THE MATTRESSES WERE ALL MADE OUT OF TORN UP RAGS AND PUT INTO A BIG SACK. YOU COULD HAVE A MATTRESS MADE IN EXCHANGE FOR AMERICAN CIGARETTES.

THE FIRST THING THAT MILO DID WAS TO GET AS COMFORTABLE OF A MATTRESS AS POSSIBLE.

MILO NOW KNEW THAT HE WAS GOING TO HAVE TO TURN THIS VERY BAD THING IN TO SOMETHING PRODUCTIVE.
HE STARTED READING EVERYTHING THAT HE COULD GET HIS HANDS ON.

WHAT WAS THE MEANING BEHIND THIS OUTRAGEOUS DREAM? MILO WAS BEGINNING TO THINK THAT HE SMELLED LIKE FEATHERS!

THE SOUND OF IRON GATES IN THE MORNING CLANGING AND BANGING AS THEY ALL OPENED. WHAT A TERRIBLE SOUND!
THEY WERE BRINGING BREAD AND ABOUT A SHOT GLASS OF COFFEE FOR EACH OF THEM. THAT WAS BREAKFAST! ALL RIGHT THEN, BREAD AND WATER! OH BOY.

THE BREAD WAS ABOUT THE ONLY THING THAT WAS FRESH IN THAT DUMP.
HE TRIED TALKING TO HIS CELL MATES, INQUIRING ABOUT ANYONE GETTING RELEASED IN RECENT TIME.

THEY ALL LAUGHED AT HIM AND TOLD HIM THAT THE LAST TIME THAT ANYONE WAS RELEASED. THEY LET EVERYONE OUT OF PRISON AT THE SAME TIME.
THAT WAS DURING THE MARIEL BOAT LIFT.

FIDEL CASTRO HATED RONALD REGAN AND MADE NO ATTEMPT TO COMMUNICATE WITH HIM. BESIDES

WE WERE ABOUT TO GO TO WAR IN GRANADA AND THE CUBANS WOULD BE FIGHTING THAT WAR.

IT WAS NOT A GOOD TIME TO GET RELEASED FROM CUBA. ANY RELEASE WOULD HAVE TO BE POLITICALLY MOTIVATED. FAT CHANCE!

IT WAS FINALLY THE FIRST DAY FOR MILES TO GO TO SEE THE PEOPLE AT THE U.S. INTEREST SECTION.
HE WAS HOPING THAT SOME OF HIS FRIENDS IN FLORIDA WOULD BE ABLE TO SEND HIM SOME CARE PACKAGES, OR AT LEAST SOME MONEY TO BUY CIGARETTES WITH. HE COULDN'T CONTACT TED YET!
HE WENT INTO THE INTEREST SECTION WITH THREE OF THE OTHER PRISONERS.
THE WOMAN AT THE INTEREST SECTION WAS VERY HATEFUL TOWARD THE AMERICANS THAT WERE THERE.

MILES ASKED HER WHY THEY MADE SUCH A BIG DEAL ABOUT THE VICTIMLESS CRIME OF MARIJUANA.

SHE BECAME OUTRAGED! AND SAID THAT HER BROTHER WAS KILLED OVER A MARIJUANA DEAL. FANTY TOLD HER THAT HER BROTHER SHOULD HAVE KILLED THE COP!

SHE TOLD HIM THAT HER BROTHER WAS THE COP!

IT WAS NOT A VERY PLEASANT VISIT FOR ANY
OF THE AMERICANS AFTER THAT ORDEAL. FANTY
WAS A REAL CROWD PLEASER.
MILO WAS ABLE TO SEND OFF HIS FIRST LETTERS
OF MANY THAT WOULD GO OUT IN THE FUTURE.
THEY WOULD ALL SEE THE BITCH AT THE
INTEREST SECTION ONCE A MONTH.

OVER THE NEXT FEW WEEKS HE MET THE REST
OF THE LOSERS IN HIS CELL BLOCK. THERE WAS
A LOT OF BLACK MARKET TRADE GOING ON,
BETWEEN THE AMERICANS AND THE CUBANS
IN THE ADJACENT CELL BLOCK.

AMERICAN CIGARETTES WERE THE BIG TRADE
ITEMS. DEODORANT WAS ANOTHER GOOD TRADE
ITEM.
YOU COULD GET FOUR PACKS OF CUBAN
CIGARETTES FOR ONE PACK OF AMERICAN.

THAT DREAM AGAIN! IT ENDS IN A DIFFERENT
SPOT EVERY TIME.
IT JUST DOESN'T MAKE ANY SENSE. THERE IS
NO REAL END TO IT!
TODAY WAS A NEW DAY FOR HIS DREAMS.
HE STARTED HAVING DREAMS OF ESCAPING.

AT LEAST THERE WAS HOPE AGAIN.
SEVERAL TIMES HE MANAGED TO GET TO THE
BEACH ON THE NORTH SHORE AND GET A WIND
SURFER FROM ONE OF THE RESORTS. ALTHOUGH
THE WINDSURFING FELT REAL ENOUGH HE NEVER

MADE IT TO THE UNITED STATES HE WOULD ALWAYS END UP WITH A ROOSTER WITH HIS WING OVER HIS SHOULDER. HE WAS A REAL FRIEND.

EVERY DAY; THEY WOULD SERVE THE MAIN DISH WITH RICE. CHICKEN BONES WITH RICE. "CHICKEN AND RICE" OR THEY WOULD SERVE RICE AND ROCKS "BEANS AND RICE", OR FISH BONES AND RICE; "FISH AND RICE". YOU GET THE IDEA! NO MEAT, JUST BONES!

ONE DAY HE WAS EATING SOME RICE AND ROCKS WHEN HE BIT INTO A PIECE OF GRAVEL "HENCE THE NAME RICE AND ROCKS".
IT SHATTERED ONE OF HIS MOLARS AND HE HAD TO GO TO THE DENTIST TO HAVE IT PULLED. IT TOOK DAYS TO FINALLY SEE A DENTIST.

THEY WOULD NOT TRY TO SAVE YOUR TEETH. THEY WOULD ONLY PULL THEM TO KEEP YOU FROM BEING IN PAIN BUT NO PAIN KILLER TO PULL THEM EITHER!

ON THE WAY BACK FROM GETTING ONE OF HIS TEETH JERKED OUT. HE SAW AN AREA WHERE THERE WERE A FEW HUNDRED CHICKENS RUNNING AROUND IN A FENCED YARD.

THERE WAS A GUY CHASING ONE OF THE CHICKEN'S AROUND THE YARD, WITH A CLEAVER! HE COULDN'T CATCH IT SO HE THREW THE

CLEAVER AT THE CHICKEN THE CLEAVER STUCK IN THE SIDE OF THE CHICKEN AND KILLED IT!

HE ASKED A CUBAN INMATE THAT WAS CLOSE BY WHO BUTCHERED THE CHICKENS THERE?

THE CUBAN TOLD HIM THAT IT WAS THE GUY RUNNING AROUND WITH THE CLEAVER, A MENTAL PATIENT!
THAT MADE PERFECT SENSE TO HIM BECAUSE HE COULDN'T MAKE ANY SENSE OF HOW THEY BUTCHERED THEIR CHICKENS THERE!

IT WAS AS IF THE CHICKEN WAS LAYING ON THE TABLE PLUCKED BUT WITH HEAD AND FEET AND GUTS STILL IN TACT AND A CLEAVER WAS USED TO RANDOMLY CHOP IT UP INTO LITTLE CHUNKS. THEN THE LARGER CHUNKS OF MEAT WERE TAKEN OUT FOR SOMETHING ELSE, HENCE THE NAME "CHICKEN BONES AND RICE".

EVERY ONCE IN AWHILE THEY WOULD SERVE WHOLE FISH. MACKEREL I THINK! AGAIN GUTS AND ALL, DEEP FRIED UNTIL THE SKIN WAS CRUNCHY.

A TEN INCH FISH WOULD GIVE YOU ABOUT TWO OUNCES OF FISH BY THE TIME YOU THROW AWAY WHAT WAS NO GOOD. WHAT WAS LEFT THOUGH, WAS PRETTY GOOD. MILO STARTED EATING THE CRUNCHY FINS OF THE FISH. EVEN THE FINS WERE BECOMING TASTY TREATS.

THERE WAS THIS OTHER MEAT THAT THEY GOT. THE TEXTURE WAS LIKE A WELL-COOKED POT ROAST, NOT ALL BAD. THE COLOR WAS BRIGHT RED AFTER IT WAS COOKED. THE AMERICAN INMATES CALLED IT "WONDER MEAT".

THEY WONDERED WHAT IT WAS!
MILO INQUIRED WITH SOME OF THE CUBAN PRISONERS AS TO WHAT KIND OF MEAT THAT WAS.
THE BEST ANSWER THAT MILO COULD GET WAS. PENGUINA OR "PENGUIN".
MILO HAD NEVER HEARD OF ANYONE EATING THEM BUT EVIDENTLY THE CUBANS DO!

THEY WOULD SEND THE CUBAN FISHING FLEET TO THE ANT-ARTIC AND KILL MILLIONS OF THE LITTLE CREATURES. AS WELL AS DOLPHINS, AND SHARKS. REAL PREDATORS.

SOME OF THE FOOD THAT THEY SERVED WAS ANYBODY'S GUESS AS TO WHAT IT WAS, IN FACT MOST OF IT!

SOMETIMES WHEN THE FOOD WAS EDIBLE. FIGHTS WOULD BREAK OUT FOR LARGER PORTIONS OF THE CRAP! "WONDER-FOOD"

THE PRISONERS KIND OF SEPARATED EACH OTHER BY LANGUAGE.
ALL SPANISH SPEAKING GUYS ATE TOGETHER WHERE THEY SERVED THE CHOW AND THE

AMERICANS ATE IN THE HALLWAYS OR IN THEIR OWN CELLS AS IF THEY DIDN'T SPEND ENOUGH TIME IN THEM AS IT WAS!

MOST OF THE AMERICANS AND THE COLOMBIANS WOULD GO OUTSIDE ONCE A MONTH TO PLAY IN THE SUNLIGHT FOR A COUPLE OF HOURS.
REALLY ALL THEY DID WAS TO GO OUTSIDE LONG ENOUGH TO GET A PRETTY GOOD SUNBURN AND THEN SUFFER FOR A WEEK OR SO FROM ALL OF THE FUN. THEY WOULD DO IT AGAIN AND AGAIN.

IT WOULD HAVE BEEN DIFFERENT FOR MILO IF HE WERE ABLE TO GO OUT A LITTLE EVERY DAY BUT ONCE A MONTH WAS OUT OF THE QUESTION. HE GOT PRETTY WHITE IN THERE.

ONE DAY MILO AND CHENNY "THE JAMAICAN" WERE STANDING IN THE CHOW LINE. CHENNY HAD BEEN WORKING ON HIS SPANISH AND SAID TO ONE OF THE COLOMBIANS WHO WAS SITTING AND EATING.

HE PROUDLY EXCLAIMED: "TO COMER MIAIRDE" "YOU EAT SHIT".
THE COLOMBIAN JUMPED UP AND STARTED FIGHTING WITH CHENNY.
MILO WAS FRIENDLY WITH THE COLOMBIANS AND TOLD HIM TRANQUILLO "TAKE IT EASY". NO INTENDO MALLOW PALAVER.

"HE DOESN'T MEAN ANYTHING BAD BY HIS WORDS".

MILO SAID: INTENDE: YO COMER MIERDA, TO COMER MIERDA, TOTAL PERSONA'S AQUI COMER MIERDA, COMIDA ES MIERDA.
LOOSELY TRANSLATED MEANS.
I EAT SHIT, YOU EAT SHIT, AND EVERYBODY HERE EATS SHIT. THE FOOD IS SHIT! WITH THAT THE COLOMBIANS ALL STARTED LAUGHING. THEY JUST DIDN'T KNOW THAT CHENNY WAS TRYING TO BE FUNNY.

I GUESS BECAUSE EVERYONE AGREED. PEACE WAS THERE AGAIN. AT LEAST FOR A WHILE.
ONE EVENING JOHNNY AND CHENNY WERE PLAYING ON THE BOTTOMS OF SOME PLASTIC BUCKETS. THEY WERE SINGING "BONGO MAN" BY JIMI CLIFF. SLOWLY ALL OF THE PRISONERS EVOLVED TO THE CELL WHERE THEY WERE PLAYING.
IT WAS ONE OF THE BEST NIGHTS AT THE COMBINADO DEL ESTE' WHILE HE WAS THERE.
THEY WERE ACTUALLY ABLE TO MAKE SOMETHING GOOD COME FROM ALL OF THE BAD. EVEN IF IT WERE ONLY FOR ONE DAY.

WHEN THINGS WENT SMOOTHLY IN THE CELL BLOCK, THEY WOULD ALLOW THE INMATES TO WATCH TELEVISION. LOTS OF CUBAN PROPAGANDA!

EVERY ONCE IN AWHILE THERE WOULD BE A GOOD MOVIE IN SPANISH OF COARSE.
THEY WERE WATCHING THE NEWS ONE DAY AND SAW THIS AMERICAN GUY WHO HAD JUST HIJACKED AN AIRPLANE FROM TEXAS TO CUBA.

HE WALKED DOWN THE STAIRS FROM THE PLANE TO THE GROUND THEN KNEELED DOWN AND KISSED THE GROUND OF CUBA THEN ANNOUNCED THAT FIDEL CASTRO WAS HIS IDLE AND HE WANTED TO STAY IN CUBA, AND BECOME A COMMUNIST! MORE PROPAGANDA!

THE AMERICANS MUMBLED LOUDLY. NOT BEING ABLE TO UNDERSTAND HOW ANYONE COULD WANT TO LIVE IN THIS GOD FORSAKEN PLACE!

A COUPLE OF MONTHS WENT BY AND HIS IDOL FIDEL CASTRO THREW HIM IN PRISON WITH THE REST OF THE AMERICANS THAT MADE THE MISTAKE OF COMING TO THEIR COUNTRY.

MILO WAS OUTRAGED THAT THEY WOULD PUT A COMMUNIST SYMPATHIZER IN GENERAL POPULATION WITH THE FREE WORLD OF MEN EVEN AS BAD AS THEY WERE, LOVED AMERICA. THE HIJACKER BEFRIENDED A FEW OF THE COLOMBIANS.

ACTUALLY HE BRIBED THEM WITH SOME OF THE THINGS THAT HE GOT FROM THE UNITED STATES. CIGGS, CANDY ETC. THEY IN TURN WOULD LET

HIM GO TO THE FRONT OF THE CHOW LINE AND GET WHAT HE WANTED FIRST. HE WAS THE LAST ONE TO COME TO THE COMBINADO DEL ESTE' AND HE DEFINITELY WAS NOT WELCOME BY THE AMERICANS THAT WERE THERE.

THIS DID NOT SIT WELL WITH MILO, COMMIE HATER THAT HE WAS. SO AFTER A COUPLE OF DAYS OF THIS BLATANT ARROGANCE.
MILO DECIDED THAT "ENOUGH WAS ENOUGH" AND HE WAS GOING TO DO SOMETHING ABOUT IT!

THE WANT-TO-BE COMMIE GOT HIS FOOD IN THE SAME FASHION THAT HE HAD BEEN DOING FOR THE FEW DAYS PRIOR, BY GOING TO THE FRONT OF THE LINE. ON THE WAY BACK TO HIS CELL HE WAS JUST ABOUT TO WALK PAST MILO WHEN MILO SNAPPED!

MILO KNOCKED THE TRAY OUT OF HIS HANDS AND GRABBED HIM BY THE ADAMS APPLE WITH ONE HAND AND STARTED BEATING HIS FACE WITH THE OTHER HAND. THIS WENT ON FOR JUST A SHORT TIME WHEN THE OTHER INMATES REALIZED THAT MILO WAS GOING TO KILL HIM!

FINALLY CHENNY AND JOHNNY MILO'S CELLMATES PULLED MILO OFF OF HIM. LATER THAT DAY, MILO WAS TAKEN TO INTERROGATION TO FIND OUT WHAT HAD HAPPENED. MILO TOLD

THEM THAT THE GUY WAS A COMMIE LOVER, AND THAT IF THEY LEFT HIM THERE THAT HE SURELY WOULD BE KILLED IF NOT BY ME THEN SURELY BY ANOTHER ONE OF THE AMERICANS THERE. WE HAVE NOTHING TO LOOSE!

SO THEY TOOK HIM OUT OF POPULATION WITH THE AMERICANS, COLOMBIANS, JAMAICANS, ETC. AND PUT HIM WITH CUBAN POPULATION IN PRISON.

CHENNY AND JOHNNY WERE THE GROWERS OF THE POT THAT WAS ON THE BOAT THAT THEY GOT BUSTED ON. THEY JUST WANTED TO COME ON THE BOAT TO PROTECT THEIR INVESTMENT. IT WAS 40 FOOT SPEED BOAT THAT THEY TOOK FROM JAMAICA TOWARD THE WINDWARD PASSAGE. BETWEEN CUBA AND HAITI.

THE NAVIGATOR SET THE AUTOPILOT ON THE BOAT AND THEN WENT BELOW TO HAVE SEX WITH HIS GIRLFRIEND.
SOMEHOW THEIR COARSE CHANGED OR THEY MADE A NAVIGATION MISTAKE AND THEY HIT CUBA IN THE MIDDLE ON THE SOUTHWEST SIDE OF THE COUNTRY! THAT IS SOME BAD NAVIGATING!

THEY RAN AGROUND IN THE MIDDLE OF THE NIGHT, ON A SAND BEACH AT FULL SPEED. THE BOAT WAS HOPELESSLY STUCK. THEY TOOK ALL OF THE POT OFF OF THE BOAT, AND STASHED IT

HIGH UP ON THE BEACH. THEY DIDN'T REALIZE THAT THEY WERE EVEN IN CUBA, AT THAT POINT.

THEY WALKED AROUND FOR A COUPLE OF DAYS AND FINALLY FOUND SOME PEOPLE. THE PROBLEM WAS THAT THE PEOPLE ONLY SPOKE SPANISH, AND THEY WERE IN CUBA! WOOPS!
THE CAPTAIN OF THEIR BOAT WAS A CUBAN AMERICAN NAMED MARTAIN AND COULD SPEAK SPANISH FLUENTLY.

CHENNY HATED MARTIN FOR SCREWING UP LIKE THAT! HE LOST ALL OF HIS POT, AND HIS FREEDOM TO BOOT. CHENNY WAS ABOUT AS BUMMED OUT AS I HAVE EVER SEEN ANYBODY BE.

ONE DAY CHENNY AND JOHNNY PLANNED TO TAKE HIS LIFE OR AT LEAST MAKE HIM WISH THAT HE WERE DEAD OR WAS ABOUT TO DIE.
THEY ASKED MILO TO GO TO MARTIN'S CELL AND BRING HIM DOWN TO THEIR CELL AND TO TELL HIM THAT CHENNY WANTED TO TALK TO HIM. SO HE CAME PEACEFULLY TO THE CELL AND MILO WALKED OUTSIDE THE CELL.

SUDDENLY CHENNY SLAMMED THE CELL DOOR AND PULLED OUT A HANDMADE KNIFE THAT HE HAD BEEN WORKING ON FOR QUITE SOME TIME AND WAS ABOUT TO CHOP HIM UP WHEN THE GUARDS ARRIVED TO RESCUE HIM. LUCKY GUY!

THEY THREW CHENNY AND JOHNNY INTO THE SWEAT BOX. IT WAS A CELL, BARELY TALL ENOUGH TO SIT UP IN. IT HAD NO VENTILATION TO SPEAK OF. THEY WERE KEPT THERE FOR ABOUT A MONTH. THEN THEY WERE RETURNED TO THEIR CELL AND WARNED NOT TO TRY THAT AGAIN!

POOR CHENNY WAS SO PERSECUTED BY THE CUBANS.
HE GOT NOTHING FROM THE JAMAICAN INTEREST SECTION.
HE HAD THIRTEEN CHILDREN BACK HOME.
THERE WERE ABOUT FOUR DIFFERENT MOTHERS BETWEEN THE KIDS.

CHENNY WOULD NOT GIVE UP HIS KIDS TO THEIR MOTHERS. HE THOUGHT THAT ALL WOMEN ARE WHORES AND NOT FIT TO RAISE HIS CHILDREN.
HIS MOTHER WAS TAKING CARE OF HIS KIDS AT THAT POINT. SO MUCH FOR WHORES.

THE DAYS WERE LONG AND THE NIGHTS WERE LONGER. MILO HATED THE AMERICANS THAT WERE IN HIS CELL. HE COULD NOT STAND EVEN TRYING TO COMMUNICATE WITH THEM.
HE STARTED SLEEPING ALL DAY WHILE ALL OF THE JERKS TOOK THEIR CUBAN DRUGS FOR THEIR FAKE CONDITIONS. THEY WERE PRETTY SLOPPY PEOPLE.

THE DREAMS WERE MILO'S ONLY HOPE FOR SANITY. HE WAS NOW HAVING TWO COMPLETELY DIFFERENT DREAMS EVERY NIGHT!

THE ESCAPE DREAMS, AND THE ROOSTER DREAMS.

MILO WAS TRYING TO PUT THE DREAMS ALL TOGETHER.

"THE LETTER C" HE THOUGHT ABOUT IT OVER AND OVER.

CUBA, CAPRICORN, CARPENTER, CAPTAIN, CHRISTIAN, AND CHILDREN. THERE WAS SOMETHING MISSING THAT MILES COULDN'T GRASP.

MILO WAS DETERMINED TO TRY AND MAKE A GOOD THING HAPPEN FROM THIS TERRIBLE EXPERIENCE THAT WAS HAPPENING TO HIM NOW!

MILO HAD NEVER READ BOOKS VERY MUCH IN THE PAST.

MAYBE HE REALLY WOULD FIND COMFORT IN THE WRITTEN WORD.

HE DECIDED THAT HE WAS GOING TO EDUCATE HIMSELF WHILE HE WAS THERE.

MILO BECAME VERY FAST AT READING, AND WAS UP TO A BOOK A DAY. HE HAD NEVER REALIZED BEFORE, HOW SATISFYING A GOOD BOOK COULD BE.

THEY CAN TAKE YOU TO OTHER PLACES AND OTHER WORLDS.

ALL OF THE BOOKS IN THE WORLD WOULDN'T STOP THOSE DREAMS FROM COMING EVERY DAY. MILO WAS BEGINNING TO LOOK FORWARD TO THEM. THE ENDING WAS GETTING CLOSER AND CLOSER. THE ROOSTER BECAME A CLOSE FRIEND TO MILO.

THE MONTHS WERE FLYING BY WITH ALL OF THE GOOD BOOKS THAT THEY HAD THERE. MILO THOUGHT THAT HE MUST HAVE READ ALL OF THE ENGLISH WRITTEN BOOKS IN CUBA BY NOW.

ONE DAY MILO GOT A MESSAGE FROM MANNY. HE WAS THE GUY THAT HIJACKED HIM IN THE FIRST PLACE AND THAT MILO DIDN'T GET A CHANCE TO KILL.
IT WAS FUNNY THAT HE NEVER HAD ANY DREAMS OF FINISHING THE JOB WITH MANNY, AND THE REST OF THEM.
THERE MUST HAVE BEEN A PURPOSE TO THAT.
I GUESS THAT HE COULD HAVE BEEN SERVING TIME FOR MURDER AS WELL.

MANNY HAD WORKED HIS WAY UP TO TRUSTEE. MILO MET WITH MANNY AT THE GATE BETWEEN THE CUBAN POPULATION, AND THE AMERICANS.
MILO WAS STILL REAL PISSED OFF AT MANNY FOR BEING IN THIS GOD AWFUL PLACE. HE ASKED HIM HOW HE LIKED BEING BACK IN CUBA NOW? YOU SHOULD HAVE LISTENED TO ME YOU

BASTARD. MANNY SAID: YOU ARE RIGHT CAPPY. I SCREWED UP.

MANNY WAS GOING TO SPEND THE REST OF HIS NATURAL LIFE IN PRISON AT COMBINADO DEL ESTE.
MANNY WAS AFTER FAVORS FROM MILO. HE KNEW THAT MILO HAD ABOUT $200,000.00 BACK AT THE UNITED STATES. HE ASKED MILO IF I CAN GET YOU OUT WOULD YOU SEND ME SOME MONEY ONCE IN A WHILE?

MILO ASKED HIM, HOW IN THE HELL ARE YOU GOING TO DO THAT!
HE TOLD MILO THAT, ALL HE HAD TO DO WAS TO TELL THEM THAT HE DID HIJACK HIM.

HE SAID: THAT HE WAS THERE FOR LIFE ANYWAY AND THAT HE WAS SORRY FOR ALL OF THE TROUBLE THAT HE CAUSED HIM AND HE SAID THAT HE REALIZED NOW THAT HE WAS RIGHT ABOUT THROWING THE POT OVERBOARD.
MILO TOLD HIM THAT IF HE COULD PULL THAT OFF HE WOULD BE HAPPY TO SEND HIM SOME MONEY OCCASIONALLY.
MILO SNICKERED TO HIMSELF. FUCK THAT PIECE OF SHIT! HE WILL NEVER GET ANYTHING FROM ME EVER!

MANNY WAS TRUE TO HIS WORD.
AFTER MILO WAS ALREADY THERE FOR ALMOST TWO YEARS. HE FINALLY TOLD THE TRUTH.

RELEASED

ABOUT A MONTH LATER THE LIEUTENANT THAT WAS IN CHARGE OF THE AMERICANS CAME TO MILO'S CELL AND TOLD HIM TO WRAP UP HIS PROPERTY. HE WAS GOING HOME! MILO WAS YELLING I'M GOING HOME I'M GOING HOME THANK GOD! I'M GOING HOME!

MILO WAS THE LAST AMERICAN TO BE THROWN IN PRISON THERE AND HE WAS THE FIRST TO BE RELEASED! THE REST OF THE AMERICANS WERE IN AWE OF HIS BEING RELEASED SO SOON.

THEY TOOK MILO OUT OF THE PRISON THAT DAY AND PUT HIM IN A HALFWAY HOUSE TO AWAIT HIS PLANE TICKET OF WHICH HIS MOTHER HAD TO PAY FOR.

THE CUBAN GOVERNMENT APOLOGIZED TO MILO FOR THE MISUNDERSTANDINGS AND FOR ANY PAIN THAT HE MAY HAVE HAD TO ENDURE.
THEY TOLD HIM THAT HE WAS WELCOME IN THEIR COUNTRY, WHENEVER HE WANTED TO RETURN.
MILO GRACIOUSLY DID NOT ACCEPT. HE NEVER WOULD.

HE WAS LOOKING FORWARD TO, GOING TO THE BANK AND WITHDRAWING ALL OF HIS MONEY FROM HIS SAFETY DEPOSIT BOX AND GETTING THE HELL OUT OF FLORIDA AND GOING TO SEE HIS KIDS AGAIN.

MILO FLEW TO MIAMI INTERNATIONAL AIRPORT AND BREEZED RIGHT THROUGH CUSTOMS AND RIGHT OUTSIDE TO CATCH A CAB.

IT WAS A LONG RIDE BACK TO KEY LARGO A LITTLE OVER A HUNDRED MILES. MILO HAD THE CAB TAKE HIM TO WHERE HE HAD LEFT HIS CAR.

IT WAS THE PLACE WHERE MILO ONCE LIVED WITH SOME OF HIS VERY GOOD FRIENDS. HE KNOCKED ON THE DOOR AND WHEN HIS OLD GIRL-FRIEND SAW HIM SHE WAS PETRIFIED. SHE LOOKED LIKE SHE HAD SEEN A GHOST! SHE HAD A NEW BOYFRIEND NOW.

SANDY ASKED HIM IF THIS WAS HIS FIRST STOP?
HE SAID: YES. SANDY SAID: THEN YOU DON'T
KNOW.

MILO SAID: KNOW WHAT? SHE SAID THAT TED
LEFT TOWN ABOUT TWO WEEKS AFTER YOU DID.

SHE SAID: I KNOW THAT YOU WERE PARTNERS
AND THAT HE HAD ACCESS TO YOUR MONEY.
HE WAS SPENDING MONEY LIKE CRAZY BEFORE
HE LEFT. HE NEVER CAME BACK AND NOBODY
KNOWS WHERE HE WENT.
MILO SAID: GOD I TRUELY HOPE THAT YOU ARE
WRONG ABOUT HIM. ALTHOUGH HE HAD NEVER
RECIEVED ANY LETTERS FROM HIM OR IN HIS
BEHALF.

MILO SPENT THE NIGHT AND WAS TO GO TO THE
BANK THE NEXT DAY.
HIS HEART WAS POUNDING WITH ANTICIPATION
OF WHAT HE WAS GOING TO FIND OUT
TOMORROW. HE HARDLY SLEPT AT ALL.

MORNING CAME AND HE WENT TO THE BANK WITH
HOPE IN HIS HEART. HE GAVE THE BANK MANAGER
HIS NAME AND ACCOUNT NUMBER. THE MANAGER
LOOKED PERPLEXED AT MILES AND QUESTIONED
ACCESS TO HIS SAFETY DEPOSIT BOX.

THE MANAGER SAID THAT HIS RENT ON THE BOX
HAD NOT BEEN PAID FOR OVER A YEAR AND THAT
IT WAS EMPTY.

MILO'S HEART SANK INTO DEPRESSION. HE SAID THANKS ANYWAY.

MILO TOOK TO THE BOTTLE FOR ABOUT A WEEK. SOME FRIENDS HAD TAKEN UP A COLLECTION FOR HIM AT ONE OF THE LOCAL RESTAURANTS THAT HE USED TO EAT AT REGULARLY. THEY HAD A FIVE GALLON WATER BOTTLE FULL OF COINS THAT THEY WERE GOING TO SEND HIM IN CUBA BUT HAD NEVER GOTTEN AROUND TO SENDING IT.

HE RAN OUT OF MONEY REAL FAST AND IT WAS TIME TO GET HIS SHIT TOGETHER AGAIN.

SO HE PICKED HIMSELF UP, DUSTED HIMSELF OFF AND GOT READY TO START ALL OVER AGAIN.

HE MADE A TRIP OUT TO THE MANGROVES WHERE HE HAD PULLED THE TRAILER WITH THE OLD SHARPIE ON IT THAT HE HAD BOUGHT FROM THE LESBIANS A YEAR OR SO EARLIER.

HE LOOKED FOR A COUPLE OF HOURS AND ALMOST GAVE IT UP FOR LOST TOO!

THE MANGROVES HAD GROWN MUCH MORE THAN HE THOUGHT THAT THEY WOULD. FINALLY HE SPOTTED HER. ALL OF THE RESIN AND FIBERGLASS WAS STILL THERE!
NOBODY HAD FOUND HER. THANK GOD FOR SMALL FAVORS.

HE HAD LOST HIS CAR BECAUSE THE LANDLORD
WANTED IT OUT OF THERE BUT AT LEAST HE
STILL HAD THE BOAT!
IT WAS NOW TIME TO GO BACK TO A BIKE
AGAIN!

HE GOT A HOLD OF ANOTHER ONE OF HIS OLD
FRIENDS THAT HAD A TRUCK.
JOEY SAID: I THOUGHT THAT YOU WERE GOING
TO DIE THERE.

MILO TOLD HIM THAT EVERYONE THOUGHT THE
SAME THING.
THEY GOT A CHAIN SAW AND BLAZED A PATHWAY
OUT TO THE NEAREST ROAD.

THE OLD BOAT

JOEY ASKED HIM HOW HE THOUGHT OF THIS
PLACE. HE TOLD HIM THAT HE WANTED IT IN A
SAFE PLACE WHERE IT WOULDN'T GET STOLEN.
JOEY SAID: WELL YOU CERTAINLY FOUND THE
RIGHT PLACE.
I HAD NO IDEA THAT IT WAS HERE AND I
WONDERED WHERE IT WAS AFTER YOU GOT
BUSTED. EVERYBODY DID.
MILO TOLD HIM THAT HE WAS GLAD THAT IT
WAS NEVER FOUND!

THEY GOT THE BOAT OUT AND DRUG IT TO AN
OLD FRIENDS PLACE TO WORK ON IT. LOTS OF
WORK TO DO. MILES GOT A JOB AT THE BOAT
YARD AGAIN PAINTING BOTTOMS ON BOATS.
THAT WAS WHERE HE HAD STARTED OUT IN THE
BEGINNING.
HE THOUGHT OH WELL: NO MATTER YOU GO.

HE WENT BACK TO ONE OF HIS OLD CONNECTIONS THAT HE USED TO SELL TO. HE ASKED HIM IF HE COULD SELL POT FOR HIM. IT WAS A ROUGH LIVING TO SELL POT OUT OF A BICYCLE!
BETWEEN THAT AND WORKING OUT OF THE BOAT YARD, HE MANAGED TO GET ENOUGH MONEY TOGETHER TO BUY THE SMALL THINGS THAT HE NEEDED TO PUT THE BOAT TOGETHER AGAIN.

FINALLY THE BOAT WAS FINISHED AND IT WAS TIME TO SELL HER.

HE TOLD EVERYBODY THAT HE KNEW ABOUT THE BOAT BEING FOR SALE. ONE DAY HE GOT THE NEWS THAT ONE OF HIS OLD CONNECTIONS WANTED TO BUY HER.
MILO MET WITH HIS OLD BUDDY DANNY AND THEY SETTLED ON THE PRICE OF $14,000.00 AND 5 POUNDS OF HIGH GRADE POT.

MILO TOOK THE POT AND THE MONEY AND BOUGHT AN OLDER DODGE VAN MOTOR HOME CONVERSION.
IT WAS ALL HE NEEDED TO GET BACK HOME TO CALIFORNIA, HIS KIDS, FAMILY AND VERY OLD FRIENDS. IT WAS TIME TO GO.

HE KNEW THAT HE WAS GOING TO BE RETURNING TO THE WORK FORCE AGAIN.
HE HAD NOT FORGOTTEN HOW TO WORK. HE BOUGHT ALL OF THE TOOLS THAT HE THOUGHT HE WOULD NEED FOR ANY JOB HE MIGHT

CHOOSE. HE HAD A LOT OF STORIES FOR HIS OLD BUDDIES.
HE WAS REALLY LOOKING FORWARD TO THE RIDE HOME.

HE SAID GOODBYE TO THE ONES THAT HE WANTED TO AND HEADED OUT OF TOWN. HE THOUGHT TO HIMSELF; WHAT A HORRIBLE WASTE OF TIME. TEN YEARS OF HIS LIFE AND ALL HE HAS TO SHOW FOR IT IS A MOTOR HOME AND A FEW POUNDS OF POT.

HE HAD MET A GUY IN CUBA THAT LIVED IN VIRGINIA NEAR COLONIAL WILLIAMSBURG. HE NEEDED A LITTLE MORE CASH TO MAKE EVERYTHING COME TOGETHER LIKE HE WANTED.

HE SOLD A COUPLE OF POUNDS THERE AND HEADED OUT FOR CALIFORNIA ONCE AGAIN. HE CHANGED THE OIL, TRANSMISSION FLUID, PLUGS, AND OTHER FLUIDS.

HE WAS SO ANXIOUS TO SEE HIS KIDS AGAIN. HE WAS SURE THAT THEY HAD FORGOTTEN HIM BY NOW SO HE REALLY HAD A LOT OF CATCHING UP TO DO. HE SAID GOODBYE TO HIS OLD PRISON BUDDY THAT HAD JUST BEEN RELEASED FROM CUBA JUST A YEAR AFTER MILO HAD.
JESSIE JACKSON HAD GONE TO CUBA, AND WAS ABLE TO GET ALL OF THE REST OF THE AMERICANS RELEASED FOR SOME POLITICAL FAVORS.

AS HE WAS PULLING OUT ON TO THE FREEWAY HE SPOTTED A GUY HITCHING A RIDE TO OKLAHOMA.
MILO FIGURED THAT HE COULD USE THE HELP DRIVING. THEY SMOKED POT, AND DRANK BEER AND TRADED OFF DRIVING TO THE MOST SOBER OF THE TWO.

THEY DROVE ALMOST A THOUSAND MILES NON STOP AND PULLED INTO CATOOSA OKLAHOMA. THEY WENT TO A K.O.A. CAMPGROUND.

THIS WAS THE TOWN WHERE THE HITCH HIKER LIVED.
WHEN HE CHECKED IN TO THE CAMP GROUND THE LADY AT THE OFFICE TOLD HIM THAT HE WASN'T GOING TO LIKE IT IN THIS TOWN.
HE TOLD HER THAT HE WAS NOT GOING TO STAY AND HE WAS LEAVING TOMORROW. MILO WAS DEAD TIRED AND NEEDED ABOUT 15 HOURS SLEEP.

THE HITCH-HIKER LEFT HIM THERE AFTER MILO GAVE HIM A LITTLE STASH. HE WENT TO SLEEP. NO DREAMS THAT NIGHT! TOO TIRED.

BACK IN JAIL

ABOUT MIDNIGHT THE VAN DOORS WENT FLYING OPEN AND A COP DRUG HIM OUT OF BED BY ONE FOOT OUTSIDE AND ON TO THE GRASS.
THE COP HELD HIM DOWN ON THE GROUND WITH A PISTOL TO THE BACK OF HIS HEAD!
HE TOLD MILO NOT TO MOVE OR HE WOULD BLOW HIS HEAD OFF! THE COP WAS SHACKING SO BAD THAT HE WAS AFRAID THAT THE GUN MIGHT GO OFF ACCIDENTALLY.
HE LOOKED OVER TO HIS RIGHT AND THERE WAS THE HITCH-HIKER ON THE GROUND BESIDE HIM. MILO SCREAMED. "MY BABIES"! THE COPS WENT STRAIGHT TO THE STASH SPOT AND GOT ALL OF HIS POT.
THE HITCH HIKER SNITCHED HIM OFF! THEY TOOK MILO TO JAIL AND HE NEVER SAW THE HITCH-HIKER AGAIN.

MILO SAT ON HIS BUNK AND HE WAS THINKING ABOUT THE LAST TEN YEARS, AND ALL OF THE TRIALS AND TRIBULATIONS OF THE PAST. HE

THOUGHT ABOUT ANGELA AND HER BEING RAPED.
HE THOUGHT ABOUT CUBA AND THE LOSS OF
EVERYTHING.
HE SAID TO HIMSELF, GOD PLEASE HELP ME.
HE WENT TO SLEEP THAT NIGHT. THAT DREAM
AGAIN!

MILO WAS WALKING THROUGH A CIRCULAR
BOARDWALK AREA , AND SAW AN EXHIBIT THAT
REALLY ATTRACTED HIS ATTENTION BECAUSE IT
WAS SO UNIQUE .
IT REMINDED HIM OF A GAME SHOW SCENE .

THERE WAS A LARGE OVAL SHAPED POND WITH A
SHIP'S BELL AT ONE END AND THERE WAS A ROPE
HANGING FROM THE BELL TO THE WATER .

THE OVAL POND HAD AN OVAL ISLAND IN
THE MIDDLE . THE ISLAND WAS BEAUTIFULLY
DECORATED WITH EXOTIC FLOWERS AND PALM
TREES , WHICH IS WHAT ATTRACTED MILO IN
THE FIRST PLACE .

HE STEPPED UP ONTO THE STAGE AREA.
TO HIS AMAZEMENT , HE SAW A FULL MAN SIZED
ROOSTER STANDING THERE! RIGHT IN FRONT OF
HIM .

THE ROOSTER SAID: COME ON OVER HERE MILO
THIS HAS BEEN A LONG TIME COMING.
MILO WAS FLABBERGASTED ! NOT ONLY COULD
HE SPEAK , BUT HE WAS A REAL ROOSTER! HE

WAS EVEN MORE REAL THAN THE PAST DREAMS
WERE.

HE SAID OK MILO THIS IS YOUR FINAL GAME
OF LIFE . MILO WAS SO HAPPY THAT HE JUST
COULDN'T KEEP HIS EYES AND EARS OFF OF HIM
.
OK MILO THIS IS A QUESTION AND ANSWER
GAME. YOU KNOW THE DRILL.

I'LL ASK THE QUESTIONS AND YOU HAVE TO
FIND THE ANSWERS. EVERY TIME YOU ANSWER
MY QUESTION I'LL SWIM TO THE BELL AND RING
IT AND THEN RETURN TO ASK YOU ANOTHER
QUESTION.
ARE YOU READY ? MILO SAID: YES .

HE SAID "MILO" WHAT HAVE YOU DONE WITH
YOUR LIFE SO FAR ?
MILO SAID: WHAT DO YOU MEAN?
THE ROOSTER SAID: WHAT SORT OF WORK DO
YOU LIKE TO DO?

MILO SAID THAT HE WAS MOST EXPERIENCED
WITH PAINTING AND CARPENTRY BUT HE
LIKED BEING "CAPTAIN" OF HIS OWN SHIP AND
SAILING AROUND THE CARIBBEAN. I DON'T LIKE
CUBA THOUGH.

THE ROOSTER SAID THAT'S GREAT! HE THEN
JUMPED INTO THE WATER AND SWAM AT AN

AMAZING SPEED TO THE BELL , AND RANG IT LOUDLY ONCE AND SWAM BACK .

HE CLIMBED OUT OF THE WATER AND WALKED OVER TO MILO.

HE PUT HIS WARM WET WING OVER MILO'S SHOULDER LIKE A GOOD FRIEND WOULD.

HE SAID: THAT WAS GOOD NOW WHAT WOMAN DID YOU LOVE MORE THAN ANY OTHER? AND WHAT MADE HER DIFFERENT FROM ALL OF THE OTHERS ?
MILO THOUGHT ABOUT IT FOR AWHILE AND SAID: ANGELA WAS THE ONE HE LOVED THE MOST AND THERE WERE TWO THINGS DIFFERENT ABOUT HER FROM ALL THE OTHERS.
[1] SHE IS A GOOD CHRISTIAN. [2] SHE IS A CAPRICORN.

THE ROOSTER SAID: THAT'S GREAT! AND JUMPED INTO THE WATER AGAIN AND SWAM AROUND TO THE BELL AND RANG IT TWICE .

HE CAME BACK AGAIN AND PUT HIS WARM WET WING OVER MILO'S SHOULDER. HE SAID: MILO, NOW FOR PART THREE.

WHAT DO YOU WANT TO DO MORE THAN ANYTHING IN THE WORLD TO MAKE YOU HAPPY ?

MILO TOLD THE ROOSTER THAT THERE WASN'T ANY DOUBT ABOUT THAT ANSWER! HE WANTED TO BE WITH HIS CHILDREN AGAIN .

THE ROOSTER GOT REAL EXCITED AND SAID: PERFECT !
HE JUMPED INTO THE WATER AGAIN AND SWAM AROUND TO THE BELL.
THIS TIME HE SWAM SO FAST THAT A TWENTY FOOT ROOSTER TAIL CAME UP FROM HIS FEET AS HE SWAM.
HE GOT TO THE BELL AND THEN HE RANG IT AND THEN RETURNED TO PUT HIS WARM WET WING OVER HIS SHOULDER ONCE AGAIN .

NOW THEY FACED THE PANEL ON THE STAGE. THE PANEL HAD ALL OF THE LETTERS OF THE ALPHABET ON IT.

THE ROOSTER SAID: MILO , THIS IS THE FOURTH AND MOST IMPORTANT PART OF YOUR GAME OF LIFE. MILO'S HEART WAS POUNDING WITH ANTICIPATION OF FINALLY KNOWING THE ANSWER.
THE ROOSTER SAID: WHAT IS THE # 1 MOST IMPORTANT THING IN LIFE? MILO KNEW THAT HE SHOULD KNOW BY NOW.
HE THOUGHT AND THOUGHT, AND JUST COULDN'T COME UP WITH THE ANSWER. HIS BRAIN WASN'T COOPERATING WITH WHAT HE SHOULD ALREADY KNOW BY NOW.

THE ROOSTER SAID: MILO, YOU ARE A GOOD AND GIVING, PERSON AND YOU ALWAYS HAVE BEEN, SO I AM GOING TO GIVE YOU A HINT.
MILO, ALL YOU HAVE TO DO IS PUNCH THE LETTER "C". HE REMEMBERED FROM ALL OF THE DREAMS IN THE PAST AND STILL NEVER GOT THE RIGHT ANSWER. HIS HEART WAS POUNDING OUT OF HIS CHEST AND HE KNEW THAT HE WAS ABOUT TO FIND OUT THE ANSWER.

SO MILO PUNCHED THE LETTER "C" AND SIRENS AND THE BELLS WENT OFF! THE PANEL SPIT OUT A PIECE OF PAPER AS IT DID A HUNDRED TIMES BEFORE, WITH A PHONE NUMBER ON IT.

THE ROOSTER SAID: OK MILO, ALL YOU HAVE TO DO TO WIN THE GAME OF LIFE IS TO GO TO ONE OF THE PHONE BOOTHS OVER THERE AND CALL THIS NUMBER FOR THE ANSWER.

HE RAN TO THE PHONES AND THEN HE FELT THROUGH HIS POCKETS AND NOTICED THAT HE DIDN'T HAVE ANY MONEY, LET ALONE CHANGE FOR THE PHONE .

HE WALKED BACK OVER TO THE ROOSTER FEELING VERY DEJECTED.
HE TOLD THE ROOSTER THAT HE DIDN'T HAVE ANY MONEY FOR THE ANSWER.

THE ROOSTER SAID: MILO YOU DON'T REALLY NEED ANY MONEY FOR THE ANSWER BUT YOU CERTAINLY HAVE TO PAY BEFORE YOU PLAY.

MILO WOKE UP SWEATING. HERE HE WAS IN CATOOSA OKLAHOMA AND THE DREAM RETURNED AGAIN. THIS TIME HE WAS ABOUT TO LEARN THE ANSWER TO THE DREAM.

HE WAS GIVEN A COURT APPOINTED LAWYER. THEY WANTED TO THROW THE BOOK AT HIM. THE LAWYER SAID THAT THEY WERE GOING TO TRY AND CONVICT HIM FOR USE, POSSESSION, AND SALES OF POT.

MILO TOLD THE LAWYER THAT IT WAS HIS PERSONAL STASH AND DID THE MATH FOR HIM TO PROVE HOW MUCH THAT HE REALLY SMOKED.

HE TOLD THE LAWYER THAT HE DID NOT WANT TO BE CONVICTED OF A FELONY AND THAT HE WAS ENTRAPPED BY THE SNITCH THAT HE HAD GIVEN A THOUSAND MILE RIDE TO.
THE LAWYER TOOK THAT INFORMATION TO THE DISTRICT ATTORNEY.

HE RETURNED A COUPLE OF DAYS LATER AND TOLD HIM THAT IF HE DONATED HIS VAN TO THE SHERIFF'S OFFICE. HE COULD GET HIM OFF ON A MISDEMEANOR POSSESSION, AND 8 MONTHS IN JAIL. MILO TOLD HIM TO GO FOR IT.

THEY WENT TO TRIAL AND INSTEAD OF HAVING 3 POUNDS OF POT THERE WAS ONLY TEN OUNCES OF POT. CORRUPT COPS. GO FIGURE!

OH WELL.

"NO MATTER WHERE YOU GO"

MILO HAD FINALLY LOST EVERYTHING!

HE TURNED TO PRAYER AND FINALLY FOUND COMFORT IN THE WRITTEN WORD!

THE ANSWER WAS THERE ALL ALONG AND HE JUST REFUSED TO SEE IT.

THE LETTER "C" WAS FOR CHRIST. "JESUS CHRIST".
 AND "THERE YOU ARE".

AND THAT IS THE END OF AN ERA. WHAT WILL THE FURURE BRING?

IT HAS TO BE BETTER THAN IT WAS! WHERE ARE WE GOING NOW?

AND THERE YOU ARE